WRITTEN IN

~

Hearts and music both have one thing in common…their *beat*.

Charlie

Dancing has been my dream—and my sanctuary—since I was three years old. After spending the last year recovering from an injury, I'm at a crossroads. I have no idea what comes next…or who.

Jax

Turns out, life in the fast lane isn't all it's cracked up to be. As one of the hottest up-and-coming singers in the music scene, all my dreams are starting to come true. Until I walk into a room where an angel dances before my eyes. Now my world—and my dreams—are turning upside down….again.

WRITTEN IN THE BEAT

HEART BEATS BOOK 1

BREANNA LYNN

Dance like no one is watching!
♡ Breanna Lynn

Names, characters, businesses, places, events, locales, and incidents are either the products of the author's imagination or used in a fictitious manner. Any resemblance to actual persons, living or dead, businesses, companies, locales, or actual events is purely coincidental.

Designations used by companies to distinguish their products are often claimed as trademarks. All brand names and product names used in this book and on its cover are trade names, service marks, trademarks and registered trademarks or their respective owners. The publishers and the book are not associated with any product or vendor mentioned in this book. None of the companies referenced within the book have endorsed the book.

ISBN: 978-1-955359-00-9 (ebook)

ISBN: 978-1-955359-01-6 (paperback)

Cover Design by: Y'all That Graphic

Edited by: Jessica Snyder Edits and VB Proofreads

Printed in United States of America

https://breannalynnauthor.com

❀ Created with Vellum

For Nathan...

Thank you for believing in me, for speaking my dream into the universe before I was brave enough to. Always in All Ways.

Rest In Peace

CHAPTER 1

CHARLIE

My scuffed black Converses make loud squeaks along the concrete floor in the otherwise quiet cinderblock corridor. I've been here before—it's one of the best places to catch a concert in Denver even if the drive from Boulder is a pain in the neck with all the traffic.

But I've never been behind the scenes and never anywhere in this building when it wasn't teeming with people and music. The directions Meredith gave me take me from one look-alike hallway to another, the industrial smells of cleaning product, paint, and air conditioning irritating my nose.

Finally through the maze, I approach two hulking figures with SECURITY emblazoned across their overly-muscled chests.

I force a smile and swallow around the lump of nerves in my throat. "Hi."

"Name, miss?" Neither guard looks anything but emotionless, I'm sure accustomed to all sorts of fans who try to do or say whatever it takes to get behind the scenes without the right access. My smile falters and I clear my throat.

"Charlie—um, I mean Charlotte Walker. Meredith Pryce said that she would tell security..." My hands flail as I gesture at them. "That I was coming?"

One guard narrows his eyes as he assesses me from the top of my head to the bottoms of my battered sneakers while the other guard runs through a clipboard dwarfed by his meaty hand. The urge to fidget under the one's scrutiny is so strong that I can't help but squirm, my excitement to see Meredith dimmed by the awkwardness in dealing with two strangers.

It feels like an eternity before the one with the clipboard looks up. "You're clear."

Scurrying between the two bulky behemoths, I put them out of my mind as the sound of pounding music at the end of the hall captures my attention. Like the Pied Piper, the notes draw me closer until I pause in the doorway. The source of the music is a complicated-looking stereo system in a room full of dancers that work through a routine.

Meredith is here, her petite frame and dark curls vibrate as she calls out steps louder than the music beats through the room. Mirrors line one wall and the scents of wood polish and sweat engulf me, the smell familiar, bringing a pang of nostalgia after over a year without it.

"Turn, down, pivot, and...stop." Meredith's elfin stature is belied by her drill sergeant voice calling out the steps. She spots me in the doorway and a broad smile stretches across her face and, with a clap of her hands, she releases everyone from the rehearsal. "All right, good job, everyone. Let's call it and we'll see you back here at five for warm-ups."

Sweaty dancers file past me, swamping me with memories of being one of them, leaving a class exhausted but excited after putting my body through that physical rigor.

"Girl, you best get your scrawny butt in here!"

I step into the now vacant room, and Meredith squeals in excitement before she launches herself at me. I'm wrapped in an apple lotion-scented hug that takes me back to being an awkward fourteen-year-old girl from Boulder meeting her much cooler roommate from California for the first time at the arts magnet school we both attended in New York. It's her signature scent and never changes, a source of comfort I've missed since we've been separated.

"Too long! Missed you like crazy!" she says.

Tears burn the back of my nose and I laugh to clear the sensation. "Missed you! You've become quite the jet-setter."

After two years spent at the magnet school, we spent another four years studying contemporary dance and ballet at a private academy in New York before finishing there. Some days I still feel like a stranger in my home state, in my life here.

After the academy, Meredith signed on as a dancer on a music tour before she became the lead choreographer for this one. Jax Bryant was a rising pop artist, and, knowing Meredith, I'm sure the dancers work hard during his shows. The year since I left New York hadn't worked out for me the way I'd imagined.

"Ha! Thanks to Jax." She says with an impish look.

"Please." Pushing at her shoulder, I ignore her modest statement. "You earned it."

She shrugs. "You're better now, right? I could get you on like that."

It's been a year since my surgery for multiple stress fractures in my right foot and ankle, and despite long hours of physical therapy, I'm still not sure I'm one hundred percent. Meredith left New York and embraced her future, but is dance even an option for me after a year away?

I moved back home and have spent months as a babysitter for Bella, my baby sister, while I've rehabbed and tried to figure out a plan. Bella is a full-time job and I love her to death, but the only dancing I've done involves teaching youth classes at the local studio on a part-time basis. Techniques that I spent years honing are rusty, practiced only in the shadows of the studio when I find free time.

My face twists in a grimace. "I—I don't know if I'm ready."

The look Meredith gives me is one I know well. "Shut up. I'm sure you're ready."

"What about all the traveling you do? A new city nearly every day must be exhausting and confusing and—"

"Fun and adventurous," she interrupts with a grin and a wink. "Plus, the eye candy's not bad to look at, either."

A laugh bubbles out of me at her cheeky statement. When we'd go out in New York, she was the center of attention, flirting and dancing with whoever caught her eye. I'd always felt so awkward and tongue tied with any of the guys who approached me. It had been easier to watch from the sidelines.

"We need to jet if I'm gonna be back here in time for warm-ups. Stay put, let me go change and we'll get out of here."

We'd made plans to grab a late lunch, then I'd stay for the concert. Since tomorrow was a down day for the tour, we planned to hang out before she had to head for their next stop tomorrow night.

She snags her water bottle off the floor before heading in the direction of the other dancers. The music changes to a new song, and a rock beat fills the air. I circle the empty room, my fingers trailing across the smoothly polished barre before skimming off as I step back. I draw a deep breath as my eyelids flutter closed. The notes of the song pulse their way inside me, rushing through my blood, my body moves, absorbing the vibrations as the song takes over. I take classically trained moves and alter them to fit the harder sounds.

The music pushes everything else out. My ankle twinges, a reminder of the screw still embedded there. Pushing that sensation away, I let the music take over, and everything else fades—the doubts that I won't ever completely recover from my injury, the concern that I'll only ever be Bella's nanny, the excitement at seeing Meredith again. It all disappears.

My feet groan and echo across the floor, accompanying the song and erasing the tension knotted under my skin. Nothing exists but the flow of my body as it bends to the notes surrounding me.

CHAPTER 2

JAX

My phone rings with perfect timing. Waving to the sound engineers, I hit the green button, still smiling at the candid shot I'd grabbed of Jessie the last time I'd been home.

"Hello?"

"Jax, tell Mom that she and Dad are overreacting. All of my friends are getting jobs at the mall for the summer and I want to, too." Her words are quick, a burst of sound followed by loud breathing.

"Hi, Jessie. What? What are you talking about?"

The sigh tells me she's irritated I didn't immediately agree with her. Oh, to be sixteen again. *Not.* "Mom said she doesn't want me to get a job with my friends this summer. If everyone else is working, what in the heck am I supposed to do?"

"Okay." I take a deep breath and head backstage to lean against the concrete wall. "Did Mom say why she didn't want you to get a job with your friends?"

Logic. I can handle logic. The question is whether or not my sixteen-year-old sister can handle my questions without spiraling further down the drama coaster she's currently on.

"Because apparently she thinks I'm still sick."

Panic spikes in my chest and I halt. "Are you? What did the latest scans say?"

"Ugh!" The scream has me holding the phone several inches from my ear. "I AM NOT sick. I haven't been in years. I'm *fine*. I'm tired of being treated like an invalid."

"Jess—"

"I get it. I had cancer. *Had* being the operative word."

"Jess, is Mom there?" What the hell is going on? Mom hadn't mentioned anything when I talked to her a few days ago. Is Jessie sick again? Did the cancer come back?

Her voice cuts through my scattering thoughts. "She's downstairs. One sec." The sound of thundering feet down the stairs is followed by Jessie saying that I'm on the phone and want to speak with Mom. Little shit. She called me and now I'm about to be run over by the bus that is my mother.

"Jackson?" Mama's voice cuts through the line. "Why are you calling me on Jessie's phone? Did you try to call mine?"

Rubbing the back of my neck, I bite back a groan. "No, ma'am. I didn't call Jessie's phone. She called me about getting a job this summer?"

"Jessica Elaine. Did you call your brother while he's busy?"

Before Jessie can respond, I attempt to de-escalate the argument I can guarantee is brewing. "Mama, it's fine. I wasn't busy. What's going on?"

Her sigh reminds me of Jessie's. So that's where she gets it.

"Jessie wants to get a job at a store in the mall."

"Yes. I got that much from her. She said you and Dad don't want her to?"

"It's a lot of activity for her."

"Mama, she's sixteen." Going on thirty-five, but I know when to keep my mouth shut.

"But the cancer—" Mama's voice cracks and a corresponding lump builds in my throat.

"Jessie's cancer was gone over ten years ago." My reminder is gentle, but the sniffle of tears is still clear through the phone.

"What if it comes back?"

"Mama—"

"She has a scan soon, Jackson."

"We'll take care of it. Do you need me to send y'all some more money?" Signing my record deal had meant that I could pay off the rest of the medical bills that had plagued Mom and Dad for years. "I'll have Nick send you some."

"Jackson—" The denial is coming, so I interrupt her before she can get it out.

"Even if you don't need it for the scan, do something nice. The three of you."

"Thank you, honey."

I would give them all my money if I thought they would take it. Letting out a breath, I tackle the real reason Jessie called me. "Mama, you have to let Jessie get a job if she wants to."

I'd had one at her age. I'd worked at a fast-food place, the only need for money was to hang out with my friends and spending more money on guitars than I should have.

"But—"

"It'll be good for her. Just let her try."

"Fine." Mama sighs again, and I smile. "I'll tell Jessie she can try."

A whoop on their end of the line tells me my sister's been eavesdropping. There's a scuffle and then a breathless Jessie gets on the line. "Thank you, Jax. Love you. Talk later."

Before I can respond, the line goes dead in my ear. I pocket my phone and lean my head back against the concrete wall to study the ceiling as I think about the upcoming scan. A thought comes to mind and I grab my phone back out to tap out a text to both my parents.

JACKSON: Tell me what the scan says, please.

After I get a thumbs up from both of them, I pocket the phone again. It vibrates almost immediately, and I pull it back out to look at the screen. My jaw clenches but I know better than to let this call go to voicemail.

"Hello?"

"Are you behaving yourself?" The crisp voice cuts through the phone, no time for bullshit and straight to the point.

"Hello to you, too, Nick." Nick is my label rep with Reverb Records and a pain in my ass. He calls himself my babysitter. Every time he does, my molars lose a little more surface area.

"Well?"

Rubbing a hand along the back of my neck, I blow out a breath, ears heating at the constant reminders of why Nick has to call and ask me these questions. "Of course, I'm behaving."

"You make it sound like you're tired of that question."

"It's been a year."

"And? That was some pretty fucked up press you got. Do I need to remind you of the picture of you next to the table full of cocaine?"

"No, but—"

"Or how about the picture of you with the underage girl? Who, oh by the way, happened to be Randa's niece?" Randa Miller is the CEO of Reverb. She'd not been impressed with that story, to say the least.

"I didn't know—"

"Or my personal favorite. The video of you stumbling and slurring your words at an appearance for St. Jude."

"I'm not doing anything wrong." The attempt to defend myself is weak, and he and I both know it.

"Yes, but are you doing anything right? That's the question." He pauses. "Everything running smoothly with the tour?"

"Yeah." One-word answers usually work for him since he likes to hear himself talk, generally uninterested in anything I have to say.

"Still on for the St. Jude thing tomorrow?"

Fuck, I learned my lesson. Especially with St. Jude. Jessie didn't speak to me for weeks after that story came out. "Yes."

"You need some good publicity. Something. Anything to make everyone forget about the shitshow from the last tour." Nick's voice is bored but my throat still locks mid-swallow. "You have a lot to lose, Jax."

Ice skates down my spine. I don't need the reminder. Losing the rights to songs I'd already written is bad enough. The fact that they could rip my contract out from under me and sue me for breach of contract for not returning the advance is the kicker.

I remember the way Mom and Dad had looked when they told me my kid sister had been diagnosed with acute lymphoblastic leukemia when she was five and I was fifteen. I'd been helpless to do anything. Our lives turned around when I signed that record deal. Paying all the medical bills off was the best decision I made and I've never regretted it for a second.

But I'd also been supremely dumb and reckless with my career for a couple years, and I still deal with those consequences.

"I know."

"You're in Phoenix tonight?" He shifts gears like he didn't just remind me of the guillotine that hangs over my head.

I take a deep breath, the sound noiseless as I exhale. "No, Denver."

"For what it's worth, Jax, Randa seems happy. The publicity lately is good."

"Really?" Opening my eyes, I focus on the beams and odds and ends hanging from the rafters. Usually, I only hear about how I've pissed the label off, so this is a nice change of pace.

"Some buzz about you maybe presenting at this year's awards."

I straighten. This is new. "Are you fucking with me right now?"

"Serious as a heart attack, man. Keep it up. Don't do anything stupid. We'll see what happens." Do I detect the cracking sound of his armor breaking? A smile that comes through the phone? Nick's a little older than me, all shark, hardened by what I can only imagine is years of working for Reverb. Every once in a while, though, I catch a glimpse of the human he used to be.

"I won't." I can't afford to. The weight of expectations on me —by the label, by Nick, by myself—is heavy. I need to focus on staying in the label's good graces. I can't let myself get distracted from that end goal—by anything or anyone.

"Gotta go. Another fire that, thank fuck, isn't yours."

"Thank God."

His laughter fades as he disconnects.

Snatches of conversation circle in my brain. A new scan. Summer jobs. Tabloids.

"Fuck." Shaking my head, I turn, ready to search for Meredith to see if she wants to do something—anything—to help me clear my head and focus on something not swirling like a sick merry-go-round.

"Hey, man, you seen Meredith?" Half a dozen roadies roam the back halls. Maybe one of them has seen her.? They all shake their heads and I move on, waving off their offers to help.

Different voices call out greetings, stopping me several times in my quest. The guys in the band are all in the hallway too, their conversation more centered on the recent increase in groupies popping up at our last couple of shows. Smirking, I can't stop the roll of my eyes when I overhear their conversation.

Was it cool the first time I heard a group of girls scream my name and rush me? Fuck yes. I don't know one guy who wouldn't be all over that. But it's become like eating my favorite food over and over again, and I am ready for something different.

Unable to find her anywhere else, I bet Meredith is probably still in rehearsals. The music gets louder the closer I get to the rehearsal space, confirming my suspicions.

I stop abruptly as I turn into the doorway. Meredith isn't in the room, but someone else is. Freezing, I barely dare to breathe and hope like hell I don't interrupt her. She's stunning.

Brown hair piled on top of her head shows off the alabaster skin of her neck and shoulders, reminding me of the porcelain dolls my sister used to collect when she was younger. She runs her fingers slowly over the rail mounted in front of the mirrors, a hum working its way out of her throat. It's sensual, the way her fingers glide over the scarred wood.

Does she even realize she made that sound? What else might encourage that catchy little noise? My dick pushes insistently against my zipper, my breath hissing through my teeth at the possibilities.

She stops suddenly and her eyes fly open in surprise. Did I make a sound? Eyes the most unique color I've ever seen—the color of light filtered through whiskey—lock on mine. The phrase 'tiger's eye' has to have been coined to describe their unique color.

Her cheeks are flushed slightly, whether from her dancing or embarrassment I don't know, the soft shade of pink contrasts with that smooth creamy skin everywhere else. Her chest moves as she struggles to catch her breath, and I force my eyes back on her face.

"Sorry—didn't mean to startle you," I say.

Wide eyes take me in as I move farther into the room with my hand extended. The pink color of her cheeks darkens the closer I get. Did Meredith hire another dancer? After a few months on tour, I should know everyone, but I don't recognize her. With eyes like hers, no way would I not remember her. "I'm Jackson."

Braced for the flare of recognition, the jolt when it doesn't happen is a pleasant surprise. Her hand is cool in mine, but I can feel the strength beneath the satin as well as a zip of electricity where our hands connect.

"Charlie." She's tiny. Not as small as Meredith, but I still tower over her by almost a full foot. A spark zings up my arm and her breath catches. Did she feel it too? Reluctantly, I release her hand, and my fingers itch to snag a piece of hair that slithers out of her messy bun, brushing against her bare shoulder. Hooking my thumbs in my belt loops should help me avoid the temptation.

"Pleasure, Charlie." Hoping to put her at ease, I smile. "Interesting name. How'd that come about? Were you named after Charlie Daniels?"

"I don't know who Charlie Daniels is." She smiles, wrinkling her nose, and her cuteness factor breaks my scale. "It was my great-grandma's name. Not Charlie. Charlotte. That's my full name. I couldn't say Charlotte when I was little, so I told anyone who'd ask that my name was Charlie. It stuck."

One shoulder lifts in a shrug, setting that loose piece of hair swinging. Her teeth bite into her lower lip after her ramble, as if she feels the need to stem the words.

Charlotte. It suits her. All curves and graceful lines, smooth as I roll the name around my tongue.

"Were you looking for Meredith?" Her question interrupts my thoughts.

"Um, yeah." Shit, I'd completely forgotten about Meredith. "She around?"

Please say no, sweet Charlotte. I want a few more stolen minutes with her before continuing my search for Meredith.

"She went to get ready. We're heading to lunch."

"Oh. Did you just sign on to the tour?"

She laughs. "No. Nothing like that. Meredith and I went to

school together, so, when she told me she was heading here, we made plans to meet up."

"You went to school with Meredith in New York?"

"Yeah, in New York." She takes a small step back from me, and her expression shutters from open to nervous. Shit, I just came off as a fucking creeper.

"My family and Meredith's are good friends." I grin again to try to put her at ease and remove the guarded expression from her face. "We grew up together."

Her face brightens immediately. "Oh, you're *that* Jackson."

"That Jackson?" Is now when the recognition comes? What has Meredith told her about me?

"I heard about the Disney trip."

I can tell she's trying hard not to laugh and I swallow the groan that wants to escape. Fuck.

"In my defense, I was eleven and had just heard about a roller coaster getting stuck upside down," I say.

Our families had met at Disney World for our annual vacation and I had refused to ride any roller coaster that went upside down.

"Anything else?" Has Meredith really not told her who I am? That I'm Jax Bryant? With her denial, my body goes haywire, not sure how to react to the fact that she still doesn't know. It's refreshing when so many people show interest in me because of my name being on their ticket stub. "So...are you a choreographer too?"

Charlotte shakes her head again, setting that wayward mahogany strand of hair moving. Is it as silky as it looks? I flex my fists where they are curled around my belt loops, the desire to reach out and answer my question stronger than before. "No. Right now I teach dance classes at a studio. Toddlers."

Her pale pink tongue licks along the softness of her bottom lip, my attention drawn and fixed to the moisture left behind.

What does she taste like? Blinking to clear the lust, I focus on what she said. "You like teaching?"

She shrugs. "For the most part. Especially the age I work with. Everything they learn is new, and they just soak it up like little sponges. They're adorable."

I can think of someone else who is adorable. Her. "I think I understand. It's like learning something new on the guitar."

Charlotte laughs, her nod hesitant. "Probably?"

"And now you're here catching up with Meredith?" My stolen minutes are slipping away.

"Yeah. It's been a while since we've seen each other. Are you enjoying the tour as much as she is?" My shoulders tense with her question, but her curiosity seems genuine. She's a breath of fresh air, no pre-conceived notions about me—with the exception of whatever shit Meredith has shared. I'm not Jax Bryant, the rising star and heartthrob the label has made me into. I'm just Jackson and she's…hypnotic.

"I love it. New places, new things to see, new experiences."

Her look tells me she questions my sanity, but she nods anyway. "So, what do you do for the tour? Are you one of the dancers?"

Her question is interrupted by another deep voice that echoes down the hall.

"Yo, Jackson!" It's one of my sound engineers. I pivot my attention between the door and Charlotte.

"I guess I need to get going." I don't want to leave her. Not yet. "Are you coming back later with Meredith?"

With her nod, my mood lifts. "Meredith got me a ticket and a backstage pass."

Thank you, Meredith. Smiling, I finally give in to the impulse to snag the wayward hair that's been tempting me. Twirling the silky strand around my finger before tucking it behind her ear, I graze her jaw with a finger as I withdraw, my blood heating with her shiver. "I hope to see you later, Charlotte."

Different shades of brown swirl together with gold flecks to create her striking eye color. She smells like a mix of coconut and a flower I can't place. Taking a deep breath, I try to breathe her in as much as I can, until I see her again.

"Ok." Her voice is barely a whisper of sound, inspiring a smile to ghost my lips before I turn and head out.

CHAPTER 3

CHARLIE

"Wait, wait, wait. You met someone while you were waiting for me?" Meredith's mouth is still full of a huge bite of the sandwich she's waving around as she talks with her hands. Cringing, I wait for the whole thing to fall apart everywhere.

"Yeah." My face heats as I picture his vivid green eyes and the warm, musky scent that drifted around him, the way his smile was still visible underneath the scruff that coated his cheeks. I haven't stopped thinking about him since he walked out of the rehearsal room earlier. "He's... he's...he's freaking hot, Mer."

Her eyebrows climb her forehead with my whispered admission. "Who is he? You got his name, right?"

"His name?"

"Yeah, girl. A name. First or last. Both."

"Jackson."

Meredith sputters on the water she just drank. "Jackson?" She croaks, wiping at the drips of water that roll down her chin.

I nod. "Yeah. Why?"

"You're sure?"

My stomach cramps around the few bites of sandwich I've managed, and my nod is slow.

"What's he look like?"

"He's tall—like really tall, pretty green eyes, dimples. I didn't see what color his hair was since it was under a baseball cap."

Her eyes grow wider the more I describe.

"What? Meredith, what's going on? What's with that look?"

"Charlie, there's only one Jackson on tour—Jackson 'Jax' Bryant."

What? No. I didn't meet Jax Bryant. Did I? Nausea swirls in my stomach when the questions I asked him come back to me.

"Seriously? Jackson is Jax? *That's Jackson?*" Oh my god. Oh my god. No way am I going back to the concert tonight. He must think I'm an idiot. "I think that would have been helpful info to have, Mer. Jesus. 'Charlie, remember my friend Jackson? He's a famous singer.'"

Meredith is bent over in the booth, my stupidity the funniest thing she's heard in a while, but she still manages to nod through her laughter. "Didn't you ever google Jax? Especially since you're going to his concert tonight? He's pretty popular too. A magazine cover? Anything?"

I shrug. "I didn't really think about it. I've told you a hundred times, I know songs, not singers, and I don't know what any of them look like. As for looking in a magazine? When? The last magazine I saw was a *Highlights* magazine at Bella's dentist's office." Looking back now, I should have. Like really should have spent the thirty seconds to google him. How did I not know that Meredith's childhood friend is freaking famous? "Why didn't you tell me Jackson was Jax?"

I throw my napkin at her as images and sensations flood me. The heat of his fingers against my skin when he tucked the hair behind my ear, the slight Southern accent that added a musical cadence to his words. The way his white t-shirt had stretched across his chest that showed he was fit, but not some muscle-bound meathead. He'd been magnetic.

Meredith tosses my napkin back at me, startling me.

"I thought you knew." Her apology is at war with the smirk still on her face.

"Yuck it up. Ugh. You always called him Jackson."

"Jax, Jackson, same guy." She shrugs again. I wish a hole would magically appear for me to sink into. "Jax is his stage name, but it was a nickname he used growing up."

"I asked him what he did for the tour! He really must think I'm an idiot." Hiding my face in my hands, I don't bother to contain my groan. "I'm so embarrassed."

"Pffft. Don't be." She pops a chip in her mouth, crunching loudly, and I'm sure in her mind it's as easy as just choosing not to be embarrassed.

"I can't go tonight, Mer." Even the slight chance of running into him again is enough to make sitting in my car for the whole concert a viable option.

"What? Why?"

The heat still burns in my cheeks even after I lower my hands. "Mer."

"Charlie," she mimics the whine in my voice. "He asked if you were going to be there tonight."

I regret that I shared that detail with her now. "So?"

The grin that broadens across her face is a look I'm familiar with—and it's one that has never boded well for me. I grimace on the inside and I try to prepare for whatever idea she's going to drop on me.

"C'mon, let's finish." Picking up her sandwich again, she attacks it with gusto. I stare at mine like it's somehow to blame for the whole situation. "We need to get back."

"We do? I thought we had a few hours?"

"We do. But we're heading back early. It's makeover time."

♪♪♪♪♪

"Stop fidgeting." Meredith chastises me as she attacks me with another coat of mascara. I've spent several hours as Makeover Barbie for Meredith and Derek Montague, the tour's costume designer extraordinaire.

"Montague?" I had asked after Mer introduced us.

A perfectly sculpted eyebrow arched before he winked at me. "Yes, chère. Romeo's long-lost, better looking, perfectly living brother."

"Mer, I don't know about this." At this point, I sound like a broken record. As the sounds of the growing crowd have seeped through the concrete and cinderblock, my nerves and anxiety have increased, beating in time with the bass that now permeates the air. My stomach feels like I've just spent several hours on the worst roller coaster ever. The bag where my jeans and Converses wait for me to rescue them catches my attention. Or maybe they're waiting to rescue me.

Derek squeezes my arm. "Trust, chère."

His fake French accent comes and goes occasionally, and he has a penchant for calling me chère like he's Ray the lightning bug from *The Princess and the Frog*. People have bustled in and out of this room for the last thirty minutes to grab various odds and ends or ask Derek a question, but otherwise, I've been the sole focus of his attention as if the word "makeover" held some sort of magical powers.

Fingers stretching, I fiddle with the mid-thigh hem of the denim skirt that Derek found for me in a room full of clothes, shoes, and myriad accessories scattered through open trunks.

"Quit it." Meredith slaps my hand. It's not the first time I've tried to yank the hem down.

"Sorry." Even the thought of moving my mouth inspires fear that I'll get poked in the eye with the massive mascara wand that she wields like a battle-trained soldier. The air conditioning blows down from the vent in the ceiling, the cool breeze inciting a riot of goosebumps across my arms and chest. Even my basic tank top has been upgraded to a blue and red tank top that has ribbons for straps. The amount of skin showing would be normal if I was performing, but it's way more than I've had on display for the last year.

Meredith catches me nibbling on my lips and huffs at me.

"I swear, Charlie, don't chew off your gloss." I'd forgotten about Bossy Meredith but have been reintroduced to her today. Sighing, I can't wait for her to finish. With all the fuss she and Derek are making, I should be getting ready to take the stage for a performance rather than standing backstage. With a final flick of her wrist, she drops the mascara to the crowded table and steps back.

"Voila." Derek claps and wolf-whistles as I duck my head at his over-the-top attention. While I don't normally wear my hair down, I love the fact that I can use it to hide behind now.

"Look at you!" Meredith shakes my shoulders, forcing me to look into the mirror in front of me.

Who is that? I tilt my head one way and then the other. My hair has been pulled back for performances for most of my life. I'm not used to it being loose. It hangs in beachy waves halfway down my back, shifting back and forth as I move my head.

Spinning around, I yank Meredith into a hug and whisper a thank you to Derek, who winks at me. Roadies bustle outside the open doorway with increased frequency and I glance at the clock positioned above the door. Is it almost time for Jackson to go on? As if I conjure him, he steps into the doorway, his long stride eating up the otherwise large room.

"Derek, have you seen..." He goes still, his immediate stop nearly comical until his gaze locks on mine. Those green eyes freeze me in the same spell he's under, his stare moving down my body like a caress. My skin hums under his attention.

"Have I seen...?" Derek's amused voice, thick with restrained laughter, breaks our spell.

"Um." Jackson takes a deep breath, closes his eyes and shakes his head before turning back to Derek. "My hat?"

With his attention shifted elsewhere, my lungs begin to function semi-normally again and finally allow me to draw a full breath. Faded jeans cling to his hips and a black t-shirt has replaced the white one he'd been in earlier, caressing his shoulders and hugging his biceps. His boots are also black, but beaten down, worn in.

The scruff on his face is gone, and I'm surprised by my disappointment, even though his jawline is chiseled perfection. While I can see his hair now, I still can't make out the color, I only know it's dark, slicked back from his face, and damp.

"Jackson, I swear. If your head was not attached to your body..." Derek rummages in a trunk, his voice fading off as he locates the hat in question. With a quirk of his eyebrow, he hands it to Jackson.

Jackson dons the hat then tilts it toward Derek before locking me in his sights again. The dark hat makes his light green eyes glow under the shadowed brim. His tongue darts out to slick over his lips, his body shifting as he continues to watch me.

"You look beautiful, Charlotte." His voice is a warm rasp that I want to wrap around me like a blanket. With another tip of his hat, he's gone, swallowed by several people that clamor for his attention from the doorway. Dazed, I stand there, watching as he walks away.

Eventually, Meredith tugs me backstage to watch the end of the opening act. When they start their final number, she grabs me in a hug.

"I'll meet you back here after Jax's set, okay?"

She waits for me to nod before darting over to the rest of the dancers. Stage lights black out, and the dim lights back here are barely enough to light up the quick moving shadows of the roadies that prep for Jackson's performance. The crowd's roar—already loud as they wait for Jax Bryant—reaches deafening heights.

Staring across the stage, I see one shadow move, familiar in height and shape. The air thickens as the music starts to thump in the dark.

CHAPTER 4

JAX

The adrenaline from the concert still hums through my blood after my shower. Tonight's show was amazing. The altitude nearly killed me, but I'd felt something spark that's been missing lately.

Is Charlotte that spark? I'm nearly to the after-party, ready to seek her out, when the object of my thoughts appears. She hesitates for several deep breaths before eventually turning to walk down the hall and disappear into the rehearsal space.

I ignore the loud music from the after-party and skirt the door to follow denim-clad hips and a cascade of mahogany hair. Pausing in the door jam, I lean against it and track Charlotte as she wanders the rehearsal space, a strange sense of déjà vu freezing this moment. Her curls obscure her face as she focuses on her phone before she tucks it into the back pocket of a skirt that shows off miles of toned leg.

"Lucky phone," I say quietly.

She spins, a slight smile tipping her lips as I step into the room and close the door so the music from the after-party isn't as loud even though it still pulses through the walls.

"Enjoy the show?"

Her teeth nibble lightly on her lip even as she nods. "It was great—you were great. You must think I'm such an idiot."

"Why would I think that?" The way she fidgets is reflected in the mirror and it dawns on me. I make her nervous. Good nervous or bad nervous?

"I didn't realize who you were. Earlier, I mean."

"Don't worry about it. You're good for my ego." I shrug and offer her a grin. The answering smile grows on her face while her shoulders relax. Was she that concerned about earlier?

"Oh." Her fingers interlock with each other, and her eyes bounce around the room before they come back to land on me again. I fucking love being the center of her attention. Blood rushes to my groin and I step farther into the room, closer to where she stands. Her quick intake of breath is louder than the vibrations of music that pound outside, accompanied by her pulse fluttering in her throat. "It really was a great concert."

Performing on stage is my high, the one thing that keeps me going when I'm dealing with the label's bullshit about my image. It's my way to forget the worry that constantly eats at me with Jessie, Mom, and Dad.

All the negative falls away—the pressure to be who everyone wants me to be, the writer's block with the next album, the fact that if I fuck it all up, a lot of people that count on me are screwed.

Not only does the negative fall away, but the positive does too. Once the music starts, all that remains normally is a ride on adrenaline-filled exhilaration, interacting with the crowd, watching them react to my music—every time like the first time all over again.

Tonight was different. Standing in the dark, waiting for my cue, all I had been able to think about was Charlotte and how fucking hot she'd looked when I saw her with Derek earlier. Why do her compliments lift me higher than any of the others offered?

"Why aren't you at the after-party? Isn't it because of you?" Her question is quiet, and I have to strain to hear her.

Shit. Maybe I'm reading this wrong. "Do you want me to leave?"

"No!" It's the sharpest I've heard her speak since meeting her. Her voice drowns out the beating thumps of music as she takes a step toward me while tucking a piece of hair behind her ear.

"No?" A half smile kicks up at her quick response.

"I—I don't mind that you're here."

"You don't mind?" I walk the perimeter of the room like she had been doing when I first came in here. "If I stay?" She shakes her head, sending those waves moving. "Okay, well, since you don't mind. I'll stick around for a bit. Why aren't you at the after-party?"

"Not really my thing." Her nose wrinkles. "Crowds and I don't get along."

"No?"

"Too many people. Too much noise."

"Ah." I nod, my path bringing me closer to her. "I get it."

Regardless of who you are as an artist, those after-parties are all about the rock star image. Alcohol flows, loud music pumps through the room, and bodies crush together, the promise of sex heavy in the air. It definitely doesn't seem like Charlotte's scene.

"You do?" Surprise registers on her face. Does she think that scenario is an extension of me?

It was, moron, remember? Despite multiple warnings, that lifestyle was alluring once.

"Don't get me wrong. I don't mind crowds and making noise is what I do most of the time." I chuckle, and her giggle echoes my laugh. "It's energizing. But I like being alone with my thoughts sometimes too."

"Oh." She watches my movements as I turn the corner that leads me straight to her.

"Do you want to know why I'm here with you instead of down there in all that noise?" My voice lowers the closer I get. She nods and her breath catches audibly. "I saw you. I'd been on my way to the party, hoping to see you. Watched you walk in here."

The pulse at the base of her throat jumps, and my gaze snaps to the hammering beat. The urge to taste those vibrations, to feel them under my mouth, rockets through me.

"Y-you did?"

I'm close enough to watch her pupils dilate, turning the brown to nearly black.

"Uh-huh." Did she take a step toward me? Or is this all me, all in my head? Her body shifts, small movements, but enough that I notice it through the lust that clouds my vision. "You really are a dancer, huh?"

"What?" I've surprised her again and my smile deepens at the cute look of confusion on her face.

"You haven't stopped moving since we've been in here. You like the music?"

A blush steals up her cheeks. "I guess? I can't hear the song that well, but I can feel it."

"Would you dance with me?" My gaze is steady on her face, watching, waiting for her response, desperate for her to say yes.

"Th-there's not really any music," she reminds me.

"Is that the only reason?" I wait for her to nod before my grin turns wolfish. "I can fix that."

I plug my phone into the stereo system and pick a few songs before I press play. Turning back to her is like being caught in her orbit, and I can't help but move closer.

"So, would you? Dance with me?"

"Here?" she asks.

I nod.

"Why?"

My response is on the tip of my tongue—*because I need to feel you in my arms*—but that sounds creepy even to me. "Because you want to? Because I do?"

I don't wait for her response. When the opening strains of Norah Jones's "Come Away with Me" plays through the speakers, I hold out a hand, daring her to take it. To say yes. Elation hits me in that same electric arc when her hand slides into mine slowly, smooth and warm against my callous-roughened fingers.

The hesitancy in her body tells me more than any words could how nervous she is. I draw her into my arms and tuck her under my chin, resting our joined hands close to my heart. *Feel what you do to me*. It's an unspoken wish as my pulse speeds up at her proximity. Dropping my free hand against the small of her back, her heat warms my fingers through the thin fabric of her top.

"I wouldn't think someone like you would listen to music like this," she murmurs, relaxing into my chest.

I chuckle. "I lean more toward country music. I grew up listening to the greats—George Strait, Willie Nelson, Hank Williams. But it's not all I listen to. I have eclectic tastes in music."

"So, it's not all country?" Her voice is hazy, and I shake my head in response.

"Nope," I say with a pop. "I'll have to let you see my Spotify to prove it."

"I'd like that." It's more a sigh than a response, her breath a warm brand through my t-shirt.

My fingers trace lazy patterns along her back through her shirt as she burrows closer to me. Fuck, she feels amazing in my arms. Exactly like I knew she would, but more, she's…familiar. Taking a deep breath, I smell the subtle mix of coconut and roses. That was the smell I couldn't figure out earlier—roses. It's subtle, but the unique combination encourages me to bury my nose in her hair.

Her soft body molded to mine has an obvious reaction on my dick. It's fucking inconvenient given how I want to pull her closer, but I also don't want to scare the shit out of her, and something tells me that my hard-on might. My brain is telling me to slow down but the adrenaline from earlier has roared back.

Her breath is gasoline on the flames of adrenaline, rapidly turning the fire to lust. It's not intentional, it's not a ploy or a practiced move toward seduction. She's innately sexy, completely unaware of how goddamned alluring she is.

The languid song finishes, and she starts to step away. My grip tightens, not letting her get too far, before the heavy bass beat of Timbaland's "Scream" pounds through the speakers. The first song reminded me of her—innocence, softness, light—but this one is me. It's a reminder.

She's innocent, but like a predator that spots his prey, I can't seem to let her go. I spin her so her back is pressed against my chest, moving both our hips to the beat. Within a breath, her body moves with mine.

"Eclectic," I growl against the shell of her ear, answering her unasked question.

She turns her head to glance back at me, eyes wide with curiosity. Her mouth opens once, but she closes it in the next breath, turning back around and breaking our eye contact. My hands grip her hips before my fingers tangle with hers. Her hips continue the torturous rhythm that I set and my dick tightens further with her seductive movements.

With our bodies pressed together like this, I can't hide my erection anymore, her delectable ass pressed right against it. I slide the silky brown waves of her hair away from her neck slowly, close enough to feel a shiver work its way down her body.

A man possessed, my lips find the spot where her neck and shoulder meet, a soft kiss followed by a quick nip of my teeth. Her pulse spirals against my mouth, her moan a sexy sound that nearly brings me to my knees in a heady rush of need.

Her head tilts to the side, a sacrifice I willingly accept as I press hot, open mouthed kisses along her neck before sucking her earlobe between my lips. I ignore fabric to trace my fingers along whatever smooth skin they can find. My mouth shifts, tracking the freckles that dust her shoulder.

Slow down! Slow down! Slow down!

Ignoring my conscience, I spin her again, intent on finally tasting her mouth, the pale pink cupid's bow that has driven me crazy for the last six hours. Her eyes flutter open, the color a warm, whiskey shade darkened with her arousal. The knowledge that she's as affected as I am, that she's in this with me, is an aphrodisiac that closes the distance between us.

My mouth slides over hers. Her lips are soft, barely a glide against mine before I lick along the seam. I take the invitation when she gasps, dueling my tongue with hers and clenching fistfuls of her shirt in my hands to drag her closer. The increased weight and friction against my erection unravels me, further spurred on when she moans at the contact, the sound never leaving the fusion of our mouths.

Her fingers tentatively crawl up my arms and grip my biceps. The sharp bite of her nails registers as they dig into the muscles, the sting traveling straight to my groin. My zipper pushes painfully into the ridge of my dick.

Fuck.

My chest heaves until I break away and work oxygen back into my body, even while my lips travel along her jaw and down the column of her throat. The little sounds she makes are mere murmurs and tell me everything I need to know right now.

Charlotte's breathing is equally labored, and she tugs me closer with her nails dug deep into the backs of my arms. I capture her lips again, her taste making it impossible to think beyond *kiss, lips, need.*

The hard bass of the song fades and another one starts. The transition gives my conscience the chance to scream at me from the soundproof booth I put him in, clearing the haze of lust from my brain. Shit. Charlotte isn't another groupie. And I'm not the same guy I was on previous tours. I can't do this.

Unknotting my fingers from her shirt, I cradle her face and break the kiss gently, teasing small kisses against her lips while I attempt to get my dick under control. Those luminous eyes open on mine.

"You're so beautiful," I say. The words seem insignificant, but every other word escapes me. My voice is husky, a whisper of sound against her lips.

Her cheeks go from pink to crimson at my compliment and I press another chaste kiss against her mouth. Everything in me fights to dive back in, take the kiss further, to bury myself in her until we're both sated.

"Who sings this?" She smiles slightly once I finally find the strength to break the kiss. I smile, too, at the unique country song.

"Sam Hunt. It's called 'Take Your Time.' You like?"

She listens for several measures before she finally nods. "Yeah."

We sway in a comfortable silence for the rest of the song and I attempt to listen to the lyrics, to figure out a way to slow things down. Charlotte hasn't run out of the room, despite how fast I was moving, and I hope she's still here, still in my arms, because she feels whatever it is between us the same way I do.

I brace myself as I consider my options, and my throat constricts with the realization that my actions could scare her off. "I didn't—I didn't take things too far, did I?"

The few seconds that pass before she shakes her head are an eternity. I blow out a heavy breath and bite back the grin that threatens.

"Can I see you tomorrow?"

"Umm..." She bites her lip, drawing my attention to the swollen flesh, and another groan tries to make its way out of my throat. "Meredith and I are supposed to hang out tomorrow."

My disappointment is mirrored in her face, but I take that as a positive sign. "Tomorrow night? What about then?"

"I thought you guys were leaving tomorrow night?"

"Not until late. So, how about it? Can I see you tomorrow?"

"I'd like that."

With a sigh, I tuck her back into my chest for too short a time before I release her and grab my phone off the speaker. "Plug your number in?"

Her hands shake slightly when she takes the phone. She's barely finished before Meredith hurricanes into the room, banging the door open in the wake of her never-ending supply of energy.

"Awww, if it isn't my two favorite people!" Meredith's curls are still damp from a shower. She bounces next to me and punches me in the shoulder, making the nerves all scream at the impact. She knows the exact spot to hit to cause the most damage and I regret teaching her how to punch when we were little.

"Ow! Stop hitting me all the time."

Meredith and Charlotte both giggle at my whine while I rub and shake my numb arm.

"You better be nice to my girl," Mer threatens.

Charlotte's eyes widen and I bite back the smile that tries to break free.

"I'm being nice, right, Charlotte? So nice, that we have plans for tomorrow night."

Meredith squeals and her eyes light up like a kid on Christmas morning. I don't contain the eye roll when she looks between Charlotte and me with a big smile.

"Well, if you're finished making those plans, we have plans."

I nod, knowing that my stolen time with Charlotte is at an end, at least for tonight.

"I'm going to take my girl and we're going to bounce."

Meredith gives me a quick hug before she ushers Charlotte toward the door. "Let's go, Char."

She starts to follow Meredith but stops and turns back before she's even two steps away. My body fights to move closer, but I'm conscious as our audience watches with avid interest.

"I'll see you tomorrow, Jackson."

I grasp her wrist and bring her palm up to press a kiss to it. "Until tomorrow, Charlotte. Thanks for the dance."

With no other excuses, I make my way down to the after-party. I regret not trying to convince Meredith to hang out here for a while before they left.

The atmosphere is predictable—the same parties that have been happening after a show since I was a wide-eyed opening act on my first tour five years ago. Back then, I'd have already been in the middle of the room, several beers or shots under my belt as a groupie or two tried to attract my attention for the night.

I'd lived every twenty-one-year-old guy's dream—singing in front of thousands, partying every night, girls whenever I wanted, and sleeping all day. Older, wiser, and more cynical now, the scene I walk into holds absolutely zero appeal and is a necessary evil.

"Jax!" Bottles and glasses raise in my direction as soon as my feet cross the threshold. I'm handed a beer and lift it in response, the need to fulfill an image overriding my desire to turn in the other direction. I take a swallow of beer, the bitter flavor of the IPA removes any lingering taste of Charlotte.

The music is loud, loud enough that even I can't recognize the song, and there are people every-fucking-where. No wonder I caught Charlotte looking for something quieter.

"Jax!" A blonde staggers toward me reeking of sickly sweet alcohol and holding a lipstick-smeared glass with only remnants of amber liquid in ice. Her shirt is about three sizes too small, her tits nearly falling out of it. "Oh my *gawd*! It is you! You were so awesome tonight! I'm your biggest fan! Shit, you're so hot."

The high-pitched gushing and heavy fragrance of her perfume start a headache behind my eyes. I hope the lights are dim enough to hide my lack of enthusiasm.

"Thank you, sweetheart." *Make nice, Jax*. I smile, pose for a selfie, and sign an autograph before one of the guys in the band rescues me. Saluting him with my beer, I watch him smirk before he leads Blondie to a shadowy corner.

The nearest couch is empty. Hopefully clean too. I scrub my hands down my face. I've seen more public hook-ups at these parties than I care to admit. Physically, I'm here, signing autographs and taking pictures with the fans backstage, but in my mind I'm back down the hall, in a quiet room, holding Charlotte in my arms.

CHAPTER 5

CHARLIE

"Sooo…." Meredith takes a healthy drink of the wine we'd picked up on the way back to Boulder. Drinking in my room makes it feel like we're doing something illicit, even though we're both over the legal drinking age. "You and Jax made plans, huh?"

Her grin takes over her face. I squirm and my whole body heats as Jackson comes to mind. Meredith had been distractible in the car, answering questions about the tour and the dancers, what the next stops were, but now that I'd run out of questions, it was her turn at interrogation.

"Yeah?" I shrug in an attempt to play it cool. Yes, we'd made plans, but what if he didn't mean it? What if it was just a way to get himself out of the dance? He is a famous singer, for heaven's sake, and I am an injured dancer turned into a full-time Mary Poppins. "Well, nothing specific. He just asked me to do something tomorrow night."

"Uh-huh, a little somethin' somethin'." She wiggles her

eyebrows from her perch on my bed and my stomach sinks. She's joking, right?

"It's not like that, perv." Or is it? Of the two of us, she definitely knows him better. And we'd kissed while we danced. Doubts inch in even as I push at her knee. She falls over snorting a laugh.

Was Jackson expecting something more if we hung out? I don't deny he's the hottest guy I've ever seen. His presence makes me feel different than I have before. Like heart-pounding and breath-stopping different. I may not have a lot of dating experience, but kissing him felt like he was having the same problem breathing and I was his oxygen. The phantom touch of his calloused fingers slides down my arms, leaving goosebumps behind.

On the flip side, an alarm blares in my head. I've known him less than twenty-four hours, despite feeling like I've known him forever. Dread knots my stomach, and doubts swirl harder. Would he be interested in me if I asked him to slow down? Is he just looking for a quick hook-up while he's here?

The questions that spin through me must show on my face because her laughter fades. "In all seriousness, Char, he's a really good guy." Her words slow the doubt tornado, and her next expression makes me laugh. "He's like the older brother I never wanted. He's had a crappy few years but, if he wasn't a nice guy, brother or not, I'd steer you clear."

"Being a famous singer made for a crappy few years?" Confusion replaces my anxiety.

She shrugs. "Being who he is, everything he does is out there for public consumption—the good, the bad, and the ugly." I nod and pretend to understand even though I don't really. "But he's still the same annoying prank-playing punk he was on vacations growing up."

"Is he from LA?" His accent didn't sound like it. The memory of his slight drawl, the nearly musical cadence of his voice as he said my name, causes my body temperature to fire to inferno level. If Meredith sees the crimson heat in my cheeks, she doesn't comment.

"Nah. His family lives in Austin. That's where he grew up. Mom and Mama Danielle are friends from way back."

I take a sip of my wine and play with the frayed edge of a pillow, my curiosity bright. "How long has he been touring for?"

"Four years or so? He promised his folks that he would finish college before he tried the music thing." She polishes off her wine and sets the empty glass next to the bed. "So earlier...did I interrupt something between you two?"

The wine I just swallowed burns its way down, forcing a cough before I can answer. "Way to change the subject."

"Way to avoid the question." She sticks her tongue out at me.

"What are you, twelve?" Meredith pouts, batting puppy dog eyes at me, and I resist. It's the whiny sounds she tries with it that ultimately works. "Okay, fine. We were dancing."

"Just dancing?" I'm totally transparent, a blush cropping up as I relive the slide of Jackson's lips against mine. "Uh-huh. Did you kiss him?"

I duck my head and she has her answer. She covers her face with a pillow and uses the thick cotton to muffle her giggles since we're trying not to wake my parents. She pops back up once her laughter subsides. "Was it any good?"

I have no hope of holding back my response. "Oh my god, Mer."

"Yeah, he totally gives off that vibe. You go, girl!"

"You guys never...?"

"Ew, no, gross." She wrinkles her nose. "Brother status, remember?"

Her confession eases the tension that hides in the back of my mind. I have no idea how I would rate if a comparison launched between she and I. She's my bestie, my person, the Arya to my Sansa, but she has her choice of guys and I'm just...me.

Desperate to turn the attention away from those depressing thoughts, I turn the tables. "What about your love life?"

"Meh." She shrugs, but it's layers of reactions—hurt and anger masked by indifference—that make up the movement. "I'm keeping my options open at this point."

"Mer." Reaching out, my fingers wrap around her hand, squeezing gently.

Her smile is shaky around the edges. "It's fine."

"No one since..." I don't get her ex's name out before she interrupts.

"No." Even after a year, she won't tell me why they broke up. Maybe someday she will, but for now, I let her keep her secret.

"Gonna decorate anytime soon?" she says with a glance at the barren walls of this room that denote its guest status.

"Maybe? I don't know. It just...it doesn't feel like home, y'know? All I need is bars on the door and window to make it look like the jail cell it feels like." I can't hide the bitterness. "What other adult do you know that needs to ask Mom and Dad for permission to go out?"

"Say what now?" Her eyes widen in surprise.

"Today, in order to come, I had to ask them." It burns to admit that out loud.

"But you're twenty-two."

"Yeah."

"You lived on your own in New York before this."

"I know." What else is there to say?

"Jesus, Char." She shudders. "You're not twelve."

I can't say anything else. There's no rational reason to explain their behavior. "It has just been this way since I got back."

"Have you tried talking to them about it?"

Exhausted, I shake my head. I'm tired of doing everything they tell me. "Being here like this...it was only supposed to be temporary. Something to do while I recovered once I was able to start PT. Hey, Charlie, watch Bella for a few months while you rehab your ankle. Ha-ha. Joke was on me I guess."

"So, what happened?"

"Your guess is as good as mine. I don't know. I guess habit?"

"Charlie, you really should talk to them. Tell them what you want. Your ankle is better—it's now or never."

"They wouldn't understand."

She chews on her lip, processing my words. "Are you sure you don't want to come with me?"

For one fleeting second, the desire to run bubbles inside me and urges me to say yes. What if I did? In the next instant, I dismiss the idea. As much as I want to dance, I don't want to live like a nomad. Even the thought of it causes a cold sweat to break across my skin. I crave predictability. It's secure. A safety net when I didn't grow up with any. "I can't."

"You could," she assures me. Deep down, I know that. And, if it comes down to it, maybe it's an option. But, for now, I'll stay here and watch Bella while I try to figure out another way to dance again at my previous level. "You know I'm here if you need me, right?"

The lump of sadness in my throat reminds me that tonight is temporary. Tonight, she's here and we can pretend, at least for a little bit, like we're still in our dorm in New York.

Tomorrow, when she leaves again, I'll be back to being alone. I nod because I'm not sure how else to respond. Meredith is a constant in my life—one of the few I have—so why, even with her here, do I feel so alone?

♪♪♪♪♪♪♪

Hours later, sleep is still elusive. Talk to them. Tell them how I feel. Is it really that easy? Would they really understand if I said anything? Do I even still have a shot if I take it?

I flop onto my other side, hoping that changing my position—

again—will help me fall asleep. Meredith fell asleep around two and, while I've been trying since then, no luck. Glancing quickly at my phone, I muffle a groan with my pillow. It's the weekend so I can sleep in, but desperation to escape into sleep pounds through me. Maybe if I read for a while my eyes will get tired. I grab my phone and nearly drop it when it buzzes in my hand, lighting up the room with a text that pops up on the screen.

UNKNOWN NUMER: Hey, it's Jackson. I just got back to the room and realized we never made specific plans. Text me when you wake up.

My heart staccatos in my chest and I re-read his text. He's just now back in his room? Meredith and I left hours ago. But he texted me about our plans. I don't hide the goofy grin that crosses my lips.

CHARLOTTE: I'm up.
JACKSON: Hey, beautiful. I didn't wake you, did I?
CHARLOTTE: No, couldn't sleep. You?
JACKSON: Just got back to the hotel room. Went to the after-party for a bit after you both left.
CHARLOTTE: If you're only now getting back, isn't that longer than a bit? *wink emoji*

My response surprises me. Sparring like this, even in text, isn't like me. Neither is flirting and I'm pretty sure I'm doing that too.

JACKSON: Caught that, huh? LOL. Those things can get out of hand.

Other than the few minutes I spent at the party tonight, I have no basis for reference. If those stifling minutes in chaos were any indication, I can't even imagine what the party looked like as it was breaking up.

CHARLOTTE: I bet.
JACKSON: You're up late too.
CHARLOTTE: Not by choice. I can't sleep.
JACKSON: Why can't you sleep?
Debate wars within me. I could give him any reason I want. Why not the truth?
JACKSON: Still there?
CHARLOTTE: Yeah. Thinking.
JACKSON: You can tell me if you want. Or not.
CHARLOTTE: No, I mean, I can't sleep because I'm thinking.
JACKSON: About what?

Well, now it's the memory of Jackson's fingers gripping my hip, his lips brushing the skin of my shoulder. I toss back the covers as my whole body overheats and lay there for a minute before I type my response.

CHARLOTTE: Lots of stuff.
JACKSON: Can I call you?

Texting in the dark is one thing. But admitting out loud what's been keeping me awake? I'm not that courageous. Then again, the opportunity to hear the smooth timbre of his voice is a temptation I don't want to resist. His voice is my new favorite song.

It only takes a minute for me to make up my mind, but longer than that to ease out of bed, leaving Meredith still asleep. The house is dark and silent as I sneak downstairs and out to the front porch where no one will hear me talking before I risk sending a response. My phone rings within seconds.

"H-hello?" My voice is breathy, my heart pounds in my chest, and my palm is slick enough that I'm a little worried I might drop the phone. I'm awkward around guys, but it's never been this bad before.

"Hi." Jackson's quiet tone and the lilt of his accent make me shiver even though it's not cold outside.

"Hi."

"Thank you for saying yes."

"Oh, um, you're welcome." Thank god he can't see my face and no one else is awake to witness my epic dorkiness right now.

His light chuckle tickles my ear. "I'm glad you let me call you. I figured I'd get a text from you tomorrow, but this is much better. A good way to end the night."

"Isn't it almost time to start the day, though?" I giggle at the deep groan that works its way through the phone.

"For other people, yes. I feel like I could sleep for days."

"Is that what you're doing tomorrow? Sleeping?"

"You have no idea how bad I want to. I don't get the full day off like everyone else, though. I have a thing to do at a radio station." He sounds so normal about something so foreign to me. "What about you? Big plans with Meredith, right? That's why I only get to see you tomorrow night?"

Fire sparks through my blood with his words.

"If big plans include shopping and a pedicure, then yes."

"Um, not in my top five favorite activities," he admits.

I giggle again, hearing his laugh echo back to me.

"Can you keep a secret?" My voice drops to a whisper.

"For you? All your secrets."

How can only his voice through a phone incite the riot of goosebumps that course down my body?

"They're not in my top five either," I admit.

Meredith's enthusiasm on a normal day is intimidating. On a shopping trip, her behavior is like giving a squirrel an energy drink.

"Your secret is safe with me." He pauses. "Why can't you sleep, beautiful? You said you're thinking about 'lots of stuff,' right?"

I can picture his eyes crinkling at the corners, and even his smile is clear through the phone.

The fact that he references my text to him earlier shouldn't make me feel bubbly, but my body doesn't seem to get that memo. Taking a deep breath, I'm still not sure how much I want to share with him.

"Charlotte?" My name on his lips wraps around me like a magic spell and whispers to let go.

"I realized tonight that I don't say what I want."

"What do you mean?"

"Life just…it happens to me."

"Doesn't it for everyone?" The confusion is clear in his voice.

I smile, wrapping a strand of hair around my fingers. "I mean, probably, but that's not what I meant. I just accept what is—like with nannying for my three-year-old sister."

"You have a three-year-old sister?"

My stomach churns, bracing for the normal reaction and questions that admission gets. *Regular sister?* I usually have to hold back a snort at that. Is there any other kind of sister? Yes, there are half-sisters and stepsisters, but Bella is my full-sister.

"Yeah."

"Wow." He falls silent.

"That's it?"

"What do you mean?" He asks.

"Most people have more questions about Bella and I being eighteen years apart."

"I bet," he huffs. "I have a kid sister too. She's sixteen and my parents' surprise baby. Those questions are fucking stupid and I couldn't care less. Do you want to talk about it?"

"Not really."

"Okay, so we won't. But back to the original statement. You accept what is?" He prompts.

"My parents just assumed I'd watch her." I barely contain the frustration that bubbles up with their continued assumption.

"Bella?" He questions.

"Yeah."

"Okay?" He sounds so uncertain and I don't blame him.

"Are you sure you want to stay on the phone with me? I'm sure I sound nuts."

"I don't scare easily." His words are soft, but there's an undercurrent to them. "So, your parents assumed you'd watch your sister? What? Recently?"

"It started a year ago. It was only supposed to be for a few months while I recovered from an injury."

He whistles quietly while my fingers trace the smooth skin of one of my surgery scars.

"You were injured?"

I nod before I remember he can't see me. "Yeah, just before final performances last year."

"That fucking sucks. I'm sorry." He clears his throat. "Are you going to be able to dance again?"

"Maybe." Those doubts sit like an iceberg in my stomach. "I'm working on it."

"So, what do you want to do? Keep working on it? Not nanny anymore?"

I chew on my lip and think about his question. "I know what I don't want. I don't want to live with my parents forever."

"Understandable." His laugh is louder this time and I hug my knees to my chest, content to sit here and listen to his voice. "But not the question I asked."

Why is it so hard to say it? To own what I want? To create my life rather than have it created for me?

"To dance." My voice is a whisper.

"So why aren't you doing that?"

"I'm going to start calling you Meredith." I smile as he laughs. "Outside of the big question of if, my parents—"

"What about them? Do they know?"

"No. They wouldn't understand." This conversation sounds an awful lot like the one with Meredith.

"How do you know unless you try?"

"Maybe."

"No maybes about it." His voice is huskier, quiet in the darkness. "I'm looking forward to seeing you tomorrow—or I guess it's tonight now. What time can I see you?"

"You still want to?" How is he not running for the nearest getaway by now?

"Yeah. Do you?" There's an edge of uncertainty in his voice, a misunderstanding of my words.

"Of course. I thought maybe you were just saying that earlier."

"Saying what earlier?"

"For us to go out."

"I wasn't just saying anything earlier."

"Even after our conversation tonight?" The urge to pull my phone away and stare at it pushes at me. He can't be this perfect, right? Attractive, creative, and a good listener? There has to be a catch. There's always a catch.

"Yeah."

"Oh."

"I'm done with the radio thing by five. When can I see you?"

"Does six work? Where should I meet you?"

"I'll take six. At the venue?"

"Okay. Jackson?" My lip catches between my teeth. How will he react to what's on the tip of my tongue? But I can't take this any further with him without knowing.

"Yeah?"

"I don't—I mean I'm not—oh crap..." All the words try to leave my mouth at once.

He chuckles. "Take a deep breath, Charlotte. You sound like you're tied up in knots."

"I just—I'm not sure. What exactly are you expecting when we hang out tonight?" I'm equal parts embarrassed, nervous, and excited, and all three feelings swirl in a tornado of nausea.

"What am I expecting?" My face must be bright red based on how hot my cheek feels where it rests against my knee. "My only expectation is to take you to dinner. Get to know you."

"S-so you're not expecting..." Ugh. Why is this so hard to say? It's sex. A three-letter word. I should be able to say it without dying of embarrassment.

"I'm not expecting...?"

"A hook-up?" The word squeaks its way out of my mouth.

The silence on the phone makes me double check that the call is still connected before he clears his throat. "No, Charlotte, I'm not expecting sex. I'm not going to lie to you. Do I want you? Hell fucking yes. But I won't pressure you into anything. I don't want that. I know I moved too fast earlier. I'm worried I'm going to corrupt you. I have a feeling I'm going to tarnish your innocence."

"H-how do you know all that?" His admission has me breathless in wonder.

"I know all that the same way I hope you know I'm telling you the truth." He pauses. "It's an instinct. I just...I feel it when I'm with you. Does that make sense?"

"I think so." My smile is small. I do have that instinct with him too. His yawn echoes through the phone as the sky starts to lighten to silvery gray and pink. "I should probably let you get some sleep."

"I hope you get some sleep, too, beautiful."

"Goodnight, Jackson."

"Sweet dreams, Charlotte."

CHAPTER 6

CHARLIE

"Chawie. Chawie. Chawie." I open my eyes to bright streams of sunlight from the windows. Bella stands next to my head, finger popped in her mouth, her hazel eyes staring intently at me. Thick lashes flutter against her cheeks as she blinks.

"Morning, Baby Bella." My yawn practically unhinges my jaw. It's only been a few hours since I hung up with Jackson and while I wouldn't mind more sleep, Bella's presence next to me and my plans with Meredith mean I need to get up. I sit up and stretch, rubbing my eyes to clear the cobwebs of too little sleep.

"Moaning, Chawie. Bwekfast?" Her speech impediment adds to her cuteness factor. She's grown so much in the last year since I've been home. Soon enough, she won't sound like a baby anymore.

"Breakfast sounds great." I twist, nudging Meredith. "Mer, you want breakfast?"

"Mmph." Her head stays buried under her pillow.

"Coffee?" Caffeine has always been her weakness.

"Mmph-hmph."

"You want to shower while I get Bella some breakfast?"

Another groan causes a smile, bringing memories of other times that Meredith was equally hard to get out of bed and nearly made us late to morning classes. Tossing the covers back, I stand, Bella watching me quietly.

"Are Mom and Dad up, Bells?" She holds out a small hand for mine, our routine established after the last year. Even when they're home, she still chooses to come to me for things we normally do together.

We shuffle downstairs and I'm right. They're both up, looking like they're enjoying a quiet conversation as we walk into the kitchen. The sight of them together, not slinging obscenities, still sends a jolt through me.

This isn't normal. If love is this hypocritical, I'm going to pass. I still wait for the other shoe to drop, for the verbal bombs to start being tossed, even after they've been remarried for four years. This picturesque scene is a sham. The scars from watching them snipe at each other run deeper than the happy family image in front of me.

"Good morning, beautiful daughters." Dad smiles at Bella before turning to me, his smile turning awkward like it always does when he looks at me. It's as if eighteen years of my parents' weird history is tattooed on my face. I'm their reminder.

"Moaning, Daddy." Bella lets go of my hand and climbs into his lap. He kisses the top of her head before taking another drink of his coffee.

"Did Bella wake you?" At my nod, Mom points her finger at Bella. "Little missy."

Pain lances my chest watching their interaction. I don't recall gentle teasing growing up. Or quiet Saturday mornings at a breakfast table. Now it feels like I'm on the outside of this little family unit, like the little girl version of me living inside my soul waits for their acceptance. Blaming the sheen in my eyes on my lack of sleep, I grab Bella some cereal and set it down in front of her. Then I pour myself a cup of coffee, adding some creamer before turning around to lean against the counter. There's an open chair at the table but it might as well be on the other side of the country.

"Sorry that Bella woke you up so early."

Bella grins at the sound of her name and takes another bite of cereal, milk dribbling down her little dimpled chin.

I shrug. It's not like she hasn't done it before. "It's okay."

It is. I'm used to it. Even on the weekends. But today I'm hoping to enjoy my limited time with Meredith. And Jackson. A kaleidoscope of butterflies explodes in my stomach at his name, a combination of nerves and excitement causing them to take flight.

"Meredith heads out tonight?" Dad's voice is distracted as he fiddles with his phone and coffee cup.

"Yeah. I was…" I swallow the bitter pill of what I have to ask next. "I was hoping that I could spend some time with Meredith today. We were going to head to the mall and then maybe grab dinner later?"

I'm twenty-two years old. I lived without my parents in one of the biggest cities in the world for seven years, but I still need to ask permission to go out for the day, just in case Mom and Dad made plans and need me to watch Bella. And I refuse to tell them about Jackson, too afraid that his name will inspire them to say no.

"That's fine, Charlie. Have a good time." Mom looks at me but before I can respond, Meredith bounds into the room, diffusing the tension that sits as heavily as an elephant. She hugs both my parents, getting a giggle from Bella before grabbing her own coffee.

"I'm gonna grab a shower." I leave Meredith chatting up my family and head back upstairs. The hot water pounds on my sleep-deprived body as I tilt my head one way and then the other in an attempt to loosen the muscles along the sides of my neck.

The feel of Jackson's teeth nipping at the skin of my neck flashes through me with memories of his pale green eyes and the the sound of his honey-smooth drawl as he rasps my name. Goosebumps pop up along my skin despite the heat of the water as my hands graze my nipples. Shaking my head to clear the lust-filled fog from my brain, I finish showering and let the hot water work its magic.

♪♫♪♫♪

If the mall is a Mecca, Meredith is its number one pilgrim. The mall is, in her words, her "happy place." We barely cross the threshold before she turns to me.

"So, where'd you disappear to last night? Or should I say this morning?"

Her tone is full of the type of curiosity that tells me one thing. I won't get out of answering her question. "What do you mean?"

She shrugs. "I got up to go to the bathroom and you weren't in your room or the bathroom."

"I was on the phone."

She pauses mid-step. "I didn't hear you."

"I went outside." I'm only able to meet her eyes for a second before I feign interest in a store window.

"Why were you outside in the dark?"

I don't want her to encourage any ideas about Jackson and me. I'm having a hard enough time keeping my imagination from running amok. I also still don't quite know where she stands with him.

Meredith is bright and energetic and bold. She likes to travel. I'm shy and quiet and not sure what the rest of my life holds. I try to have faith. She said they were friends—that he's like a brother to her—but is that really all there is between them? What if he feels differently about her? How do I ask these questions without making it weird?

"Charlie?"

"Well." I tighten my fingers wrapped around my purse strap. "I got a text from Jackson."

"He texted you?" The smile on her face does not bode well for my sanity, but I nod anyway.

"Yeah."

"And?"

"Mer, you're sure there's nothing between you guys?" The awkward question wraps around my tongue like cotton.

"EW." She makes a gagging sound while smacking my arm. "I already told you there wasn't. Like ever." An ember of hope glows in my chest. "So, what did he say?"

"He wanted to set up plans for tonight. He texted and asked me to text him back when I woke up."

"But you were awake?"

I nod.

"Why?"

"Thinking. About what we were talking about last night."

"Char—"

I wave off her concern. "It's fine." It's not, especially after having to ask permission to spend time with my best friend but continuing to dwell on it just makes me want to bang my head into a wall.

She lets the subject drop. "So, you were awake?"

"Yeah."

"Outside talking to him?" Her look of confusion is funny enough that I giggle.

"We were texting, and he asked if he could call me. I didn't want to wake you up."

She smacks my arm again, harder this time. "Uh-huh. And since I once slept through the fire alarm that went off at three in the morning?" It had been a false alarm that night, thankfully, but the FDNY had not been impressed that the two of us had still been in our room, Meredith sound asleep and me trying to haul her out of bed. "You decided a phone call could wake me up now?"

"Mer—"

"Char—" She mimics my voice back to me.

"It's nothing." Or at least I'm trying really hard to convince myself it's nothing. Jackson is here for two days. He lives in his tour bus and he's from Texas. I live with my parents in Colorado. That's not the beginning of any great romance that I know of.

I don't want to make this a big deal and I know Meredith. If she's really not into him then she's next to me planning the next celebrity wedding, Jackson starring as the groom and me his blushing bride. A quick glance at her and her Cheshire-cat smile and it's obvious. That's exactly what's going on in her head.

"If it's nothing then why did you kiss him?"

"Technically he kissed me." I know better than to believe my denial will do anything but add fuel to her imagination.

"Pfft. Details. You and Jax would be cute together."

I groan to the ceiling as a response.

"You did say he was a good kisser."

"He is." I can admit that. I don't have a lot of comparisons to make but Jackson's lips were soft and warm, confident as they mastered mine.

"A-ha!"

"What?" I start and look around us for whatever caused Meredith's exclamation.

"You were just in la-la land. With Jaaa-aaax," she singsongs.

"What? No, I wasn't." I totally had been. I barely restrain myself from running a finger along my tingling lips.

"Totally were. Your eyes got all vacant." I blush, unable to deny anything she's saying. "Add in a late-night rendezvous and we have our own epic romance brewing."

"It wasn't a late-night rendezvous. Wait…our?"

"Duh, I'm living vicariously through you." She loops her arm in mine, towing me to the store set in her sights. "Plus, late-night rendezvous sounds much more romantic than a late-night phone call. That has booty call written all over it."

She's a pitbull with a bone, but she's my pitbull. "Meredith."

Her words are ripping down my doubts faster than I can wall off my excitement. Part of me wants to believe in love. That part *wants* an epic romance. Jackson is an amazing kisser. My heart tells me to jump in, but my head keeps reminding me that he leaves tonight and that epic romance doesn't exist in real-life. The war between the two causes my stomach to churn and my palms to grow clammy.

"Charlie." She forces me to stop and meet her eyes. "Just...give him a chance, okay? What's the worst that could happen?"

"He leaves tonight, Mer."

"So?"

"So?" I sigh. She doesn't see the same problems I do. "Never mind. Can we please change the subject?"

Maybe shopping will distract her.

"Of course. Let's shop 'til we drop." I'd like to say that's just an expression for her, but it's really not.

Shopping with Meredith is an athletic endeavor. If the Olympics had a shopping event, she would take gold, silver, and bronze. While she stays true to her word to change the subject from my potential relationship with Jackson, she doesn't completely change topics either, peppering me with questions while she drags me from one store to another in the large open-air mall. Both my ears and my feet throb by the time she spots her second favorite love behind shopping.

"Starbucks!" Meredith had promised me caffeine when I started to flag an hour ago.

Falling into a chair, I snag a table while she orders. I flex my feet in my sneakers, an attempt to stretch the cramped muscles after our morning marathon of walking. Meredith has convinced me to buy a new outfit for my date tonight—a pale pink tank top edged in lace, a pair of black shorts, and a pair of pink ballet-like flats that match my new top. We've also spent more time than I ever wanted to in Sephora where my cash supply dwindled further as I shelled out money for make-up I'll probably never wear again.

"What time are you meeting Jackson tonight?" Her mind is on a single track today and it's the "track-to-drive-Charlie-crazy" apparently. The incessant questioning is softened by the bribery of the Frappuccino she sets in front of me, the whipped cream glistening under ribbons of caramel and chocolate sauce. The first taste slides down my throat like manna from heaven and I swear, the caffeine and sugar give me a slight boost already.

"Mer." My whine sounds more like Bella than me at this point. I really would like to just enjoy my drink without talking about Jackson or my date with him.

"What?" She takes a noisy slurp of her own drink.

I sigh. "He said he has a radio thing until five, so we agreed to meet back at the venue at six."

She smacks her hand into her head. "I completely spaced the radio-thon."

"The what-a-thon?"

"KTWN in Denver is doing a St. Jude radio-thon. Jax agreed to man the phones. If people want to talk to him, they call in to donate and hopefully get the chance." Her fingers fly over her phone and find the live stream of the radio station. Jackson sits at a table, a forest green baseball cap turned backwards with a phone pressed to his ear.

I am a melty puddle of goo under my chair. Attractive, creative, a good listener and he volunteers for a children's cancer charity? Do I have any hope in the world of resisting him?

The live stream pans to someone else and Meredith shuts off her phone. "So, dinner tonight?"

Resting my forehead against the table, I groan.

"What? Can't I be interested in your date?"

I sit up and level her with a look I usually reserve for Bella when she's not listening. Despite my burning need to scream, I say calmly, "Yes. But the fact that you've already asked that question about six thousand times today?"

She waves me off, the straw in her mouth slurring her words slightly. "Irrelevant."

She sticks her tongue out at me when I mock her comment. Swiveling in her seat, she ignores me to people watch. My late night and the rigorous shopping today pluck at me with fingers of exhaustion despite the caffeine hit. Those hazy temptations push at the edges of my brain, encouraging me to close my eyes as my mind floats in that state of almost asleep, but not quite.

"You're not going to finish that?" Meredith's voice startles me back to full consciousness. I look up and she's standing, holding her bags in one hand and her empty cup in the other.

"Oh." My drink drips condensation on the table, forgotten. "I guess I'll take it with me."

"C'mon, break's over. Let's go." She moves her shoulder in the direction of the next store.

"Aye, aye, captain." My grin could be confused with a grimace as she hauls me away from the food court area and to the next store on her list.

We spend the entire day at the mall, shopping until Meredith spies a nail place where she treats me to the pedicure we talked about last night. My feet love me for the pause I give them in the endless beating that is part of our day at the mall. I grab a second Starbucks when we head back to the food court so I can use the bathrooms to change my clothes.

By the time I come out of the restroom, the entire contents of my Sephora bag are spread across the table and she points at a chair for me to sit down. I do as I'm told, feeling awkward as I do, the crowd still bustling around us. I don't see any of them being turned into a makeover montage.

"Don't move." Her tone is no-nonsense, reminding me of last night, which reminds me of Jackson. I try to pick up my phone to check the time, but Meredith bumps my arm out of the way with her hip. "Don't move. We have time."

Knowing better than to waste the little energy I got from my drink in arguing with her, I hold still. People more stubborn than me have tried—and failed—to change Meredith's direction when her mind is made up. It never goes well.

The scrape of the hairbrush against my scalp is soothing, her fingers quick, and before I know it, she's stepping back, dropping things back into the discarded bag.

"Done. Go look." She points me to the restroom like a toddler about to have an accident, but I still head in the direction of the mirrors. Instead of the dark, dramatic make-up from last night, she's gone softer, a light brown shadow and eyeliner that make my brown eyes look bigger. My lips are pale but shiny, and she's pulled pieces of my hair back and secured them with a few bobby pins.

Bobby pins? Where'd she get those? With one last look, I shrug, and head back to our table.

"Damn, I'm good." She whistles before bursting into giggles. I laugh, too, when she can't hold her lips right to whistle and ends up blowing a raspberry. "Jax isn't going to know what hit him."

Blushing, I don't know what to say. My stomach is already on red alert and the date hasn't even started yet. What will tonight hold? Walking to my car, I hand Meredith my keys.

"You want me to drive?" At my nod, she grabs the keys from my fingers. "Okay, just tell me where to go."

Again, I nod, afraid that if I open my mouth, I may actually be sick. Short directions work to get us back to the concert venue, but the entire drive leaves my stomach shivering. Denver weekend traffic is its chaotic norm and I find myself extra fidgety as we sit in traffic.

"Stop." She shuts the passenger visor after I've flipped it down to look in the mirror for the eighth time since we've gotten in the car. "You're gorgeous. You'll have a great time."

This time my smile is definitely a grimace. I'm not worried about me having a good time. Will Jackson? Why does he want to spend time with me? What do I have to offer? The alarm blares in my head as my pulse shifts from human sprint to hummingbird vibrate mode no matter how much logic I try to use to calm myself down.

We turn into an empty parking lot.

"No one's here?" My voice is shaky, but she keeps driving.

"Let's check behind. The buses usually park there."

We circle the building and the big tour buses come into view. They're all black, no indication of what or who they're for.

"Are they ninja RVs?"

Meredith laughs at my comparison. "Girl, they used to be plastered with Jax's name, but after too much publicity, the label had to have them repainted. You wouldn't believe what girls try to do to get on." She shakes her head, looking disgusted, and stops next to one of the buses where another car is parked.

What were they willing do? *No*, not thinking about it.

The size difference between my car and these buses up close is a metaphor—I'm just as out of my depth with Jackson. Too bad the butterflies swirling in my stomach don't seem to care.

CHAPTER 7

JAX

The day has taken forever, but finally my driver parks next to the buses and I can focus on getting ready for my date with Charlotte. Anxious to get to the shower, I nod to the guys lounging on the bus where they all play a video game on my way back to the bathroom. It's not the top end bus, but it's definitely better than the ones I rode in for my first few tours. Those were like riding in frat houses on wheels with the level of nasty and lack of privacy. At least on this one, I have a separate space and the bathroom is cleaner.

I grab a towel and turn the water as hot as it will go, humming as I wash my hair and scrub my skin.

"C'mon, man, no need for a full-fledged concert in there. Some of us need to take a piss." A pounding interrupts me as I'm drying off.

"Fuck off," I yell back. "I'll be out in five."

A grumble comes through the door, but there are no other interruptions while I finish toweling off, wrapping the towel around my waist to grab clothes out of my bedroom. Luke, the drummer, is leaning against the opposite wall just outside the bathroom and hustles in as I exit.

I ignore him and walk to my bedroom to grab khaki cargo shorts, a white t-shirt, and a light blue button down. After running some gel in my hair, I consider a shave, but Luke still hasn't emerged from the bathroom. Plus, I like the scruff. Hopefully Charlotte does too. Catcalls and wolf whistles greet me as I head to the front to wait for the girls.

"Awww, Jackie dressed up."

"Does Jackie have a date?"

I flip them all the bird. "Assholes."

The two other guys laugh hysterically. Mature enough to ignore them, I grab a seat at the small table, and pretend to mess around on my phone while I covertly watch the windows. The guys go back to their video game when they realize they're not going to get any more of a reaction from me. Luke walks by, opens his mouth to give me grief, but reconsiders when I glare at him. Thank Christ. I'm already anxious enough, no idea why, but I do know that I don't need their shit talking to make me more nervous.

My relief is short-lived. As soon as I see a car pull up outside, I'm up and out the door, their teasing starting up behind me again. Fuckers. Meredith in the driver's seat surprises me, but with a glance at Charlotte, I lose that thought. Meredith doesn't even have the chance to turn off the car before I'm right next to it.

"Hey, brat, welcome back to Oz." I lean into her window since that's closest to me.

Her response is to stick her tongue out at me, like she did when she was seven, before she opens her car door. Avoiding the sucker punch of the door handle, I glance at Charlotte with a smile, my eyes locking on hers. "Hi."

"Hey." Her fingers weave around themselves but she doesn't

make a move out of the car. I turn back to Meredith to give Charlotte a minute. Meredith's grin is mischievous as shit as she glances back when Charlotte walks toward the two of us.

"So, Charlotte, I grabbed us a car if you'd rather not drive? I probably should have checked with you first." A thirteen-year-old boy on his first date sounds more confident than me—my normal behavior has devolved to a nervous, slightly squeaky, nauseous as hell version of myself.

Charlotte smiles and nods. "I'd like that. Then I can leave my car with Meredith if she needs to use it before you guys head out?"

Meredith nods enthusiastically before crushing Charlotte in a hard hug. "See you later, girl." Meredith's voice is tight, the sheen of tears in her dark eyes. Charlotte's eyes brim with tears, a mirror image of sadness. I stand back a little, giving them time before Meredith releases Charlotte with a kiss on the cheek, then heads toward a few of the dancers outside one of the buses.

Charlotte stands there, arms locked around herself and eyes focused somewhere else. I can't take it. Within a few paces, I wrap my fingers around her cool ones. Hugging her to me, I wrap my arms around her body to offer her comfort.

"Hey." Exaggerating my drawl, I rub her back, hoping to get a smile.

"Hey." She sniffles and I look down, catching her eyes with mine.

"You look beautiful." I press a kiss to her forehead, wanting to drown in her scent and the way her soft skin heats instantly under my lips.

"Th-thank you. So do you."

I want to hold her longer. Would it freak her out if I just stood here for a few hours hugging her? Definitely. Clearing my throat, I step back slightly, still keeping her fingers wrapped in mine.

"You ready for dinner or want a few minutes?" Her stomach growls in response and I laugh. "Dinner it is then."

I draw her with me into the back of the car and tuck her into my side. Her slight weight leans against me when her legs curl up on her other side. Goosebumps tickle my palm where my hand rests automatically on the outside of her thigh. It's a heady sensation when it seems like these simple touches affect her as much as they do me.

"Cold?" She shakes her head. "So where are we heading, gorgeous?"

"Uno, Dos, Tequila." A smile hovers on my lips with her laugh and I turn toward the driver.

"Did you get that, Mark?"

"Sure did, sir. I passed that yesterday, so I know where I'm going."

As we head out, my fingers slide in absent-minded patterns along the outside of her thigh, addicted to the silky feel of her skin beneath my fingertips. Blood pools in my groin and I fidget a bit in my seat, but don't disentangle us. Instead, I start working through chord progressions in my head, fingers twitching slightly as muscle memory takes over. When I'm pretty sure my dick is going to behave himself, I stop, hoping like hell Charlotte hasn't noticed my odd behavior.

"I've never ridden in a car with a driver before," she says with her gaze pointed out one of the tinted windows.

"No?"

She shakes her head.

"Not even at prom?"

"No prom."

"No prom?" Mine was the stereotypical rite of passage, complete with the hotel room and fumbling loss of my virginity.

"We danced all the time. What did we need prom for?" She looks so adorably confused, her parted lips shiny and soft as she watches me. They beg me to lean down, to brush my mouth with hers in a light kiss. I lean back, still savoring her taste as her eyes blink open. They're hazy and her deep breath whispers between us in a soft sigh.

"Prom is more than dancing. It's the angst of whose asking who, the fear of rejection ripe in the hallways, the getting ready, the will we/won't we question at the end of the night."

"So, which one were you?"

Shit. Her question catches me off guard. I should have kept that will we/won't we piece off my description. Maybe if I play dumb, I won't have to cop to that less than stellar memory? "Which one was I what?"

"The will you/won't you?"

"Ummmm...I plead the fifth." My laugh is self-deprecating, but luckily I've learned a few things since then. "Prom's a nice memory, but I wouldn't want to relive it."

Charlotte laughs again and I squeeze her thigh as we pull up to a colorful adobe building with the words *Uno* and *Dos* lit up next to a neon margarita glass. The parking lot doesn't look crowded, but I don't want to risk being recognized, so I tug on a baseball cap as we exit the car. So far, the baseball cap has seemed to work, and people see a normal twenty-something versus Jax Bryant, famous singer. "What is this place?"

The deep red stucco of the building and the large rustic wooden doors lead us to the smell of sizzling fajitas, and my mouth waters with the scents of grilled meat and peppers. It smells like home.

She smiles over her shoulder at me and my dick kicks in my shorts. "It's one of my favorite places to eat when I come to Denver. They've won a bunch of city awards for best Mexican food and their margaritas are famous. Lethal. But famous."

"Lethal, huh?" I quirk my brow. "Define lethal."

"Two margarita limit." She nods her head as if proving her point.

"Ever had two?"

She shrugs. "More like one and a half."

"I will if you will?" I wind our fingers together and she nods as the hostess greets us. I take in the funky colored lights and the rustically painted tiles near the Cocina sign. The hostess leads us past a repurposed wood bar, sanded and smoothed to a smoky finish. Liquor bottles gleam against sparkling mirrors in spotlights, giant margarita glasses are lined up and waiting to be used.

"You weren't kidding." Nudging Charlotte, I point out the huge glasses. She giggles and shakes her head. "I'm glad we're not driving."

The booth the hostess shows us to is tucked out of the main path of the restaurant and feels cozy, like the two of us are the only ones here.

Charlotte laughs, tucking a strand of mahogany hair behind her ear. "Me too."

We order two margaritas when the server comes to our table with chips and salsa, then we're alone again. The instrumental music playing through the speakers adds to the atmosphere.

"This place is awesome." She smiles at my assessment as I grab a chip and some salsa. The pico de gallo is tart, a good blend to the salt on the chip. "Mmmmm."

She nods and takes a chip with a more normal portion of salsa than half the bowl I just shoveled into my mouth. "I love these."

"I haven't had good Mexican food since I was last in Austin."

"Hopefully this place lives up to it." She looks doubtful but she's missing a key piece of information.

Running my index finger along her hand where it lays on the table between us, I respond quietly, "This place already has Austin beat."

She catches my meaning and her smile grows bigger. Before she can say anything else, the server delivers the drinks and takes our food order.

"Yum," I say after my first taste.

Charlotte takes a sip. "I have to admit, this one is better than normal."

"Normal's pretty good then too?" I hold out my drink to hers, clinking our glasses together. "To new beginnings, normal or otherwise."

The warm slide of the tequila works its way down my throat, settling into my stomach, and I reach for another chip.

"I probably shouldn't have more than one of these." Charlotte eyes her glass warily.

"Noted," I laugh, taking another small sip and winking at her. "Me neither."

"Meredith showed me your radio-thon today." The chip I'd just taken a bite of scratches down my throat and I grab my drink to ease the pain.

"She did?" Oh good, my pre-pubescent boy voice is back.

Her eyes soften as she leans her chin on her hand. "That was so sweet of you to do."

I want to grumble that puppies and kittens are sweet, not grown men. Instead, I just smile, dipping my chin to my chest, warmth flooding through me at the way she looks at me.

"I've worked with St. Jude's since signing my contract." That explanation is simple enough and allows me to skirt my murky past with them. During the last tour I'd had a similar appearance and had been so blitzed, I remember very little of that day. Unfortunately, there's video to remind me—and Reverb—about one of my stupid mistakes.

"That's amazing. They're lucky to have you."

"The world is lucky to have them." Squirming at her praise, I blow out a breath. "They help families cover the cost of cancer treatment. Kids that can't afford it, they can get the help they need."

I'd never forget the families we met while Jessie was in treatment—the overwhelming stress on the parents, the quiet acceptance of the kids who struggled while keeping brave faces.

"My sister, Jessie, helped me learn about St. Jude. She was

diagnosed with a crazy name for leukemia when she was five and I was almost fifteen."

Her hand finds mine on the table, fingers squeezing. "Is she…okay?"

I nod, the relief when I think those words still as potent as it was the first time I heard them. "She's sixteen. Cancer free. But seeing those families, I knew someday I wanted to help. Now I can."

Charlotte nods, scooting closer to me in the booth, the heat of her leg pressed against mine. Leaning my leg against hers, I lift her fingers, playing with them as I take comfort in her touch.

"I'm glad she's okay," she says.

"Me too."

The server returns with our food, drawing me back to the present. Over dinner, Charlotte and I find similar tastes in movies, although my music taste is more mixed. She acts surprised when I tell her I read a lot on the bus. She tells me she reads a lot too, but her admission is accompanied by a blush so fierce she looks sun kissed.

I steal a bite of her enchiladas, then pounce. "Who's your favorite author?"

Her response is so quiet I don't hear her.

"Who?"

"I can't pick a favorite. I read anything Claire Hastings or Alina Lane write—can I have two?"

I shrug. "Okay. What should I read of theirs?"

"They write romance." I raise my eyebrows, still waiting for a response. "Oh. Um, for Claire—*Can't Fight This Feeling* is amazing! The best place to start."

"*Can't Fight this Feeling* like the eighties song?"

Charlotte nods. "And for Alina, *Reclaimed Love*."

The way she says it, on a sigh, has me committing the title to memory. My pinky grazes her lower lip as I feed her the last bite of my chimichanga, the moment stretching between us in the quiet restaurant.

"Dessert tonight, folks?"

The spell is broken and Charlotte shakes her head at the server.

"Just the check, please."

My hand settles on the small of Charlotte's back as we leave the restaurant. Once we're outside, I interlace our fingers as we walk back to the car.

My hands gravitate to her. There's a peacefulness that lures me to her, a calm to my chaos, and I'm dying to dive headfirst into her. The more Charlotte shares of herself, the more I want to know. The more I want to wrap myself in the serenity that surrounds her. With her, I don't have to be Jax Bryant, constantly aware of everything I say and do. I'm just myself.

My phone pings with a text and I check it as we finish our walk to the car.

MEREDITH: HURT HER AND YOU'LL BE HURTING WORSE.

She's accompanied her all-caps threat with a GIF that shows a guy being tossed in a dumpster. *Message received, Mer.* She may have been my friend first, but Meredith is definitely #team-charlotte.

Back in the car, Charlotte once more leans against me, allowing me to take a deep breath to capture her scent. Roses and coconut will forever remind me of her. I never really thought about that combination before, but it's a smell I can definitely see myself addicted to.

"I had a really great time tonight, Jackson." Her whisper floats between us.

"Me too." We're back in the parking lot before I can say much more. "It's still pretty early. You want the grand tour?"

She nods. "Okay."

Starting with the smaller buses first, there are areas to hang out in as well as one we call the food truck, a big kitchen on wheels that can feed a lot of us at once.

"They really are like RVs," she muses. She turns to take in all the buses around us. "I told Mer earlier they reminded me of RVs for ninjas."

I crack up as we walk to my bus. "You're fucking priceless, gorgeous."

Thankfully the guys are off the bus, so it's just us.

"What's back there?" She points toward the darkened back of the bus.

"A couple of bunks, a bathroom, and my bedroom." She drops down quickly on the couch closest to her. After I practically devoured her last night in a well-lit room, I don't blame her for staying up here. Sitting next to her, I motion to the TV. "All the comforts of home. Want to watch a movie?"

Her shoulders loosen on a breathy exhale before we debate movie choices, landing on the original *The Fast and the Furious* movie as we settle back into the oversized couch. I wiggle my toes once I kick off my flip flops.

"Take off your shoes, relax."

She shakes her head. "I'm fine."

"You'll be more comfortable barefoot. Then you can kick back like me."

She shakes her head again. "With so many years dancing, my feet are pretty beat up. I'll keep my shoes on."

"It can't be that bad."

Again, she shakes her head.

Her refusal increases my curiosity, and I stare down at the part of her foot I can see. It looks like a normal foot, light blue veins visible against her pale skin. Leaning down, I bring it up to my mouth, grazing my lips along a deeper blue mark that mars the skin by her ankle.

"It can't be that bad." I repeat with another kiss to her foot. Using her distracted state of mind, I pull off the pale pink shoe. I can't tell anything's different. Her nails are short but they're also a pretty pink color. "Am I missing something?" I move her foot around to look at it from all angles. What am I missing?

She points to the callouses and bunions on her foot. "The polish hides that a few of my toenails are still purple—bruised. And this." Her fingers trail along a line of silvery skin. "It's awful."

"What? Why? What is that?"

She looks at me and I can see the disappointment, frustration, and sadness fill her eyes. "It's a surgical scar. Just before final performances last year, I was in so much pain, my instructor wouldn't let me dance. Instead, they sent me to get checked out by a doctor."

"And obviously there was something wrong." My fingers tangle with hers, brushing against the mark.

She nods, swallowing. "I had three stress fractures, two of which were in my ankle. There's still a screw in there."

"Does it hurt?"

She shrugs. "Sometimes. I've been rehabbing for the last year, so it feels more tight than anything."

"How did the fractures happen?"

"It can be common in dancers. The repetitive motions, the impact we put our feet through. It all creates risks."

"But you were dancing anyway?" When she nods, I whistle. "Didn't it hurt?"

"It didn't feel different until it did. Practicing for final performances was...intense. It wasn't unusual if I was dancing for hours."

"Wow." She's a fucking rock star. "Beautiful. Strong."

A shadow of sadness passes over her face, her eyes distant as her teeth nibble at her lip.

"There's something more." It's a statement, not a question, since her sadness is now palpable between us.

She shrugs, shaking her head. "It's…"

Her voice trails off and I run a finger up the arch of her foot, prompting a small smile to curve her lips even as I try to get her to continue.

"It's?"

Her eyes lock with mine. The emotion in them has grief rising for her. "This type of injury. It…it can be career ending. I don't even know if I'll be able to dance at the level I did before."

The scar seems so small, so innocuous, to have the amount of power it does.

"Fuck." Her strength amazes me. If I wasn't sure I could ever play the guitar again, I'd be a mess.

She nods. "Pretty much."

"How will you know if you'll be able to keep dancing? At that level?"

"It's the likelihood of my getting a professional dance job." Her smile turns rueful and I'm reminded of our conversation last night. How badly she wants to try. "It's not like a ton of dance opportunities exist here. So, I don't know."

"That fucking sucks. I'm so sorry." She shrugs and silence lapses between us.

I gently massage the bottom of her foot until her head falls back against the pillows with a groan. Applying a little more pressure, I smile when I'm rewarded with another groan.

"If you stop now, I'll have to kill you."

Laughing at her growled warning, I can't do anything to stop my body's response to the husky quality of her voice. Stopping is the last thing on my mind. Working her foot more, I move up to her slim ankle and calf. She giggles when I find the ticklish spot behind her knee. Keeping my touch light, I snag her other foot, knocking off that shoe so I can show equal attention to the other leg.

If someone had asked me a month ago if I was a leg man, I'd have looked at them like they were crazy. But Charlotte's legs are driving me out of my mind. Her moans of pleasure have my dick rock hard against the seam of my shorts. Shifting, I try to adjust myself to a more comfortable position. When I'm finished with both legs, I crawl back up on the couch, reclining next to her, snuggling her against me to keep watching the movie.

"That was amazing, thank you." Her lips are barely on my cheek before she lays her head back down in the crook of my arm. "No one has ever rubbed my feet before."

She hasn't admitted it, but I get the impression that she's more innocent than I initially thought based on some of her reactions. Squeezing her to me, I vow not to corrupt her. "My pleasure, gorgeous."

CHAPTER 8

CHARLIE

Jackson has magical powers. That's the only way his hands could find every sore spot on my feet and legs and melt me like butter. Burrowing closer, I'm amazed by how comfortable I am with him. I haven't shared all that with anyone. Meredith understands only because she was there when it happened.

But he *gets* it. He *gets* me. That same passion he has for music beats through my blood too. His citrusy scent engulfs me, and I can't resist burying my nose in his shirt, breathing deeply, hoping to keep the way he's making me feel with me even after the buses are gone.

"What time do the buses need to leave?" What time do I need to let him go? How long can I live the fantasy that we could be at the start of something instead of at the end? Lifting my head slightly, I meet his eyes, glittering emerald in the light from the TV screen in front of us.

He's tracing light patterns on my back but his fingers still as I lift my head. My body misses those patterns as soon as they stop and I barely restrain myself from rubbing against him like a cat, aching to feel those callouses through my shirt again.

"We usually leave between one and two. Everyone needs these down days, even more so with how hectic it's been lately." The question must register on my face since he continues. "At the beginning of the tour, there was a lot of bad publicity to overcome."

His discomfort makes me curious. Leaning my chin more fully into his chest, I keep my eyes on his face. "You did?"

He nods, fingers playing with the ends of my hair. His eyes have a faraway look, like he's sorting through memories—he's here, but not completely. "This is my fourth tour. After my second one, I had a couple of songs gain some popularity, so Reverb started paying more attention to me, making big plans. Suddenly, I wasn't the opening act, I was a headliner. Crowds, after-parties…" He trails off, clearing his throat before continuing. "But the attention can be bad too. Pictures showed up."

"What kind of pictures?" Unease settles in my stomach, asking me if I really want to know the answer to this question.

"Pictures of me with drugs, one with an underage girl." I stiffen and his arms tighten around me. "I always seemed to be in the wrong place at the wrong time for those."

"For those?"

His eyes close, a deep breath escaping before he opens them again, and his hands tense in my hair. "The pictures weren't everything. If they were, Reverb would have probably just ignored them. Well, most of them. I partied, I drank, but I never did drugs. And the girls…"

"Meredith said you're not a player."

He smirks. "This lifestyle. When you're not used to it, you don't make the best decisions, decisions that are normally you. I didn't."

"What happened?"

"I fucked up. Big time. Parties screwed with the tour schedule. We had a few close calls since I didn't show up to the busses on time. I ended up missing a show during the last tour because I was passed out from a party the night before." He sighs. "I told you earlier I started working with St. Jude when I signed my record deal."

I nod. "Yeah."

"During the last tour, I had an appearance set up for them. Kind of like today. I showed up drunk. Stumbling, slurring, mostly black-out drunk. And that was the last straw. Reverb gave me an ultimatum—either get my act together or I could hit the road. Without my songs. And owing the label every dime they had already advanced me and any money they lost due to cancelled shows."

"Obviously you did what they wanted?"

He nods. "I've been their beck and call boy since. They say jump and I don't even ask how high before I'm jumping. Their priorities are mine. It doesn't matter what I want, how I feel." His eyes stop filtering through memories and catch mine again. "Music is…it's what I've wanted since I picked up my first guitar. Touring is a necessary evil. But it's also my Oz."

"Oz?" It's the second time tonight I've heard him say that and I'm curious what he means.

"You've seen the *Wizard of Oz*, yeah? Touring reminds me of that. Is it a trippy dream where you meet all kinds of characters on your way to finding home? Or is it reality? You never really know, but you know you're a better person for having traveled the road." He groans, closing his eyes, even as his arms cinch tighter around me. "Fuck, that was a lot of shit I just laid out."

I chew on my lip, mulling over Jackson's poetic words. "I get it."

"You do?" The hope in his voice creates a prick of pain in my stomach.

"Yeah. Touring for you is like what New York was for me.

And what music is for you is what dancing is for me, primarily. It's not that I have to do it, but I want to, I need to."

"Primarily?" Jackson's fingers sink into the small of my back.

Sighing, I voice the thought that has coalesced over the last year. "Dancing offered me stability. It was structured, safe. A place to belong. Independence."

He nods but confusion furrows his brow. How much could he possibly understand unless I give him more?

"My parents divorced when I was little." My voice is quiet, muffled into his chest. "So, I don't remember them ever being together when I was a kid. They hated each other. Like seriously despised one another. And I was a tool they used to inflict damage. Moving to New York, it wasn't as easy for them to use me in their war, and I found something I never had growing up here—I got to make choices for myself. I got to make decisions that made me happy. I didn't have to ask permission to go out with Meredith. I didn't have to subject myself to 'love' being used to destroy." I don't bother to hide the cynicism in my voice.

"It sounds like you don't believe in love there, gorgeous."

Shaking my head, I respond. "Not really, no. The epic kind of love? That's fairytales. It's make-believe. Happily ever afters exist in romance novels, not real life. I've seen 'love' cause more pain than happiness, so how is that love?"

"It exists, I promise. My parents are an example. And Meredith's parents."

"So, it's the exception and not the rule."

His green eyes warm with sympathy. "I'm sorry, Charlotte. I wish I could change that for you. That it would be your rule."

He tugs me against him in a strong hug, his heartbeat pounding solidly under my ear. I take a deep breath before letting it out on a sigh. The sound is relaxing, as is the pattern his fingers create on my back. Small strands of embarrassment wrap around me for everything I've shared—hello, train wreck—but I'm less embarrassed than I would normally be, comfortable with Jackson in a way I've never been with anyone else. What is it about him that has me sharing everything?

My eyes stray to the TV, to the movie neither of us has been paying attention to. Jackson doesn't say any more but keeps up the slow slide of his fingers against my back, both of us watching the movie in silence until the credits start. When I try to sit up, his hold on me stiffens, keeping me next to him.

"I don't want you to go." His arms make me feel warm, safe, cared for. "Stay."

"You've convinced me." Smiling, I lie back against him, content and wishing I could stay here longer. The laugh rumbles up his chest, vibrating under my cheek.

"I wish you could come with us." His words are so quiet I barely catch them. What would it be like to travel with Jackson? As enticing as he is, my brain shuts down the anxiety ridden thought of living like a gypsy. "I wish we weren't leaving tonight."

His next admission is even quieter, like he's worried that someone might hear us. His bright green eyes are serious as they look at me.

"Me too." We're in a bubble, he and I, the connection tangible between us, taut in the silence. His gaze flicks from my eyes to my lips, watching my tongue drag along the parched skin. The Sahara has nothing on how dry my lips feel under his intense gaze. The moment stretches between us. As if in slow motion, he lifts his head, angling down until his lips can press against mine.

The kiss starts as a chaste brush of his lips, but as we connect, the spark that happens whenever we touch fires. It's like I'm awake after years of living in a sleepwalking state—because of him. His hands tug me farther up his body as he deepens the kiss, licking along the seam of my lips in a request for entry, coaxing my tongue with his, groaning as my breasts crush against his chest. His fingers curl into my hair and his callouses scrape deliciously against my scalp while the vibrations under my hands accelerate to match my own ragged pulse. Breaking the kiss, he pulls back. His eyes are an emerald fire as they meet mine.

"I've wanted to do that all day." My lips tilt when he presses a kiss to the tip of my nose.

This moment feels bittersweet. I'm not ready for my time with Jackson to end. I've wanted him to kiss me all day, to kiss him in return. Leaning forward, I take the initiative, opening my lips against his. He tastes like a combination of cilantro and tequila but still uniquely like Jackson, the flavor I've associated with him since he first kissed me last night.

His lips are like my favorite candy and I've been offered as much as I can consume in a twenty-four-hour window. His deep groan vibrates between us. His lips slant under mine, never breaking the connection as his hands move to my hips, his fingers gripping to lift me to straddle him. My core throbs as his fingers press me closer to his erection, and this time I groan. Fireworks ignite at the friction where I crave it the most when he flexes his hips slightly.

"Charlotte—beautiful." We're both breathing hard when he rips his head away. My eyes blink open slowly and my mouth tingles, swollen from his kisses. His fingers still flex against my hips, burrowing hard enough to bruise, but also adding gasoline to the fire he's lit inside me. "We should slow down."

No. I shake my head. He's leaving soon. Leaving and taking this feeling away. My fingers fist into the soft material of his t-shirt before moving to tangle in his soft hair. Leaning back toward his mouth, my lips brush his when I speak. "Please. Kiss me."

A small piece of me knows we should slow down. But the other part, the bigger part, loves the way he makes me feel when he looks at me, when he touches me, when he kisses me and doesn't want to stop. I push rational thought to the back of my mind, intent on just feeling for as long as I can as he kisses me back, granting my request.

He stands suddenly and I squeal, wrapping my arms and legs around him. His hands lock under me as he moves to the back of the bus. When he presses me against the wall outside a closed door, his erection rubs my center, fanning the flames that consume me.

"Privacy." Groaning, he teases kisses along my jawline, blindly navigating us to a dark room before lowering me to the bed. My legs disengage from his hips, my core immediately missing his heat as he lifts himself up, and my arms fall to my sides as he stands tall and looks at me.

His eyes hold mine, searching, waiting. His smile is equal parts wolfish and impish as his eyes move, tracing down my body in a heated sweep. He must find what he's looking for because he nods once before he leans over and drags my lips back into a searing kiss while his hands play with the lace hem of my shirt. Roughened fingers graze my skin, and I shiver before he breaks the kiss long enough to tug the shirt over my head.

His chest heaves and the heat of his gaze burns as it caresses my neck and collarbone. My pale pink bra doesn't hide or enhance much but seems to mesmerize him. His fingers reach for me but he stops, eyes locking on mine.

"Can I?" His voice is hoarse, husky in the stillness that surrounds us. He motions to my bra and I nod. "Words, gorgeous. Give me words, please."

"Y-yes." Nerves encroach on the lust coursing through my body as I watch him bend, his strong hands flicking the front clasp as soon as the word leaves my mouth. His eyes glow in the darkened room, two emerald embers that light my body on fire wherever he looks.

His head lowers and his tongue swirls around one stiff nipple while his fingers toy with the other before he switches. Arching my back, I gasp at the electric pulses that arc from my breasts to my center. The slide of his tongue around my nipple is soft compared to the quick tugs on the other. If I'm being burned alive, I'll gladly go out this way.

"Jackson." My groan is mindless, body focused on keeping these sensations as I weave my fingers into his hair, tugging his mouth closer. His weight shifts until he's cradled between my thighs, forearms flexed as he holds himself up, his mouth sucking and tugging.

My hips lift, grinding into his, and my hands shift, roving under his shirt to splay against the warm skin in my reach. He shrugs out of his button down, and his hands rush to reach for the back of his t-shirt to rip it over his head.

Doubts try to push through with a last feeble attempt to breech the edges of pleasure that surround me. The sight of his sculpted chest scatters those gathering questions like leaves in a fall breeze.

A sprinkle of chest hair narrows to defined abs. How much does he have to work out to get those v-lines? He burrows an arm behind my back to haul me closer and my gasp turns to a whimper when my sensitive nipples rub against the light dusting of hair. Jackson drops a kiss against my mouth before blazing a trail of open-mouthed kisses down my neck to my collarbone, learning every line from shoulder to shoulder, hovering on the pulse vibrating at the base of my throat.

His mouth gets reacquainted with my breasts, but he doesn't stop there, shifting lower to press feather-light kisses on my stomach above the waistline of my shorts. Clamoring nerves temper the lust, awareness of how far we've come in such a short time creeping in, and my body stiffens with hesitation.

"Gorgeous." His breath tickles across my skin before he looks up, eyes wide and searching as they meet mine. "We can stop." He shifts to crawl back up my body.

"N-no." My voice wavers and I clear my throat. I don't want him to leave here tonight without knowing what this is between us. "No. I want this. I want you."

The sight of his lips so close to my stomach, those deep green eyes meeting mine through the valley between my breasts, sends another wave of lust licking through me.

"Are you sure?"

His hair is a mess around his head as a result of my fingers, his mouth swollen from our kisses. But his eyes don't waver when they search mine with earnest intensity.

"I'm sure."

His body lifts, his exhale brushing cool air against my belly and my stomach muscles contract at the sensation. He presses another warm kiss against my skin.

"Tell me." Soft lips brush that sensitive spot again before he looks up. "Tell me if you want to stop."

His tongue plunges into my navel and the button and zipper on my shorts release under the attention of his fingers. His head follows the drag of the zipper down, pressing kisses millimeters above my panty line. I squirm, my eyes closing to handle the sensations that rush through my body all at once in an attempt to catalog every nerve as it catches fire.

My hands graze his hair before they drift aimlessly to the bed, twisting the smooth fabric to ground myself even though my body wants to launch into orbit. Jackson tugs at one of my hands tangled in the material, planting kisses along every finger, against my palm and wrist, before he pushes my hand against his naked chest.

"You can touch me too." Both hands lift as I move them slowly along his warm skin, the short, springy hair tickling my palms. He's absolutely still, a living statue under my explorations even as his eyes shift to molten green. When one of my hands grazes the waistband of his shorts, he hisses. His voice is thick and gruff. "Are you okay with this?"

I nod before I remember his request. *Words, gorgeous.* "Yes, Jackson."

My hips lift involuntarily as I speak, seeking the friction from earlier, encouraging him to move again. He slides my shorts and panties down my legs in one fluid motion before he stands to toss them behind him, nostrils flaring as he takes in my body. I keep still even as a different heat travels from my breasts to my cheeks.

"Baby." His shorts are perched on his hips, stretched where his erection pushes against the front. His breath comes in shallow pants as he reaches behind him without looking to close his door. A window back here lets in enough light from the parking lot that I can still see him, even though he's cast in shadow.

Shucking his shorts and boxers, he stays bent, leaning over to kiss my knee, the heat of his mouth causing my stomach to quiver as my eyes slide shut. He kisses a trail north along my thighs, delicious heat spirals higher until he spreads my legs, kneeling between them.

"Charlotte." My eyes blink open at the sound of his voice. "I have to taste you."

I've barely processed his words before new sensations buffet my body with the brush of his mouth against me, the lick of his tongue from back to front before he swirls it around my clit. Every nerve ending in my body is focused on the weight of him between my thighs. I moan and my body arches into him, every muscle tensing to the point of near pain with each sure stroke of his tongue.

"Jackson—I—I…" My hips rise and fall, moving faster. My words turn into a garbled sound, unable to complete my thought. His groan vibrates through my core, teeth now nibbling around my clit. His fingers brush against me before one finger presses inside. Another finger quickly follows and my core spasms. My body still aches for "more, please, more."

Is that my voice? My heart pounds, my body's demands drowning out the wordless sounds coming from my mouth.

"So fucking tight." I feel his growl where his mouth devours me.

"Oh my god, oh my god, Jackson." My entire body locks before it flies apart, a kaleidoscope of lights and colors dance behind my eyes even as my fingers flex mindlessly in his hair. I'm flying. I've died and gone to heaven. The wave of pleasure continues, rolling through me before the orgasm releases me with a shudder to drift slowly back to reality.

Jackson crawls back up my body in a trail of hot open-mouthed kisses against my flushed skin. A drawer opens, accompanied by the crinkle of foil.

Jackson's eyes find mine, still hazy with aftershocks. "Are you sure?"

I blink, bringing him back into focus. His erection juts proudly in front of him. How is he supposed to fit?

Taking in my widening eyes, a small smile plays on his lips. "Eyes up here, gorgeous." A smirk curves his mouth when my eyes meet his. "I don't want to do anything you're not ready for."

His willingness to stop has the opposite effect on me, despite the nerves that jangle along my skin.

"Jackson, I'm a—" My face is on fire. I never pictured myself here, ready to have sex with a man, before I told him. How will he react? Will he laugh at me? Will he not want to? "I'm a...virgin."

His eyes widen before they slam shut, and a deep groan echoes through the room. "Fuuuuuck. I figured you were inexperienced. A virgin? We should stop, Charlotte."

I'm suddenly hyperaware of my nakedness, his rejection driving out the remnants of pleasure. He doesn't want me. "I understand."

Two fingers quickly tilt my chin back up. "What do you think you understand?"

I want to slink back to my car, forget this night ever happened. "That me...that I...ugh. That my being a virgin means you don't want me anymore."

The words are barely out of my mouth before he's pulling me

back against him, his erection pressing against my stomach as he leans his forehead against mine. "I want you, Charlotte. Fuck. Hearing you say you're a virgin? It doesn't turn me off—it makes me hotter for you."

Did I hear him right? The serious look as his eyes burn into mine tells me I did. "It does?"

"You are temptation incarnate." He brushes a chaste kiss to my lips. "I shouldn't take your virginity from you, Charlotte. We should stop."

"No. I don't want to." I shake my head. "How can you take something from me that I'm trying to give to you?" The words fly out of my mouth quicker than I can think them.

His eyes flare as what I say sinks in.

"Charlotte." My name is a groan on his lips, sexy, and my core pulses at the sound. I sit up, pressing my lips to his shoulder, feeling the muscles jump under my kiss.

"I've never felt this way before." My admission releases in a breath across his bare torso and I watch in fascination as goosebumps travel across his skin

"Me neither." His response calms the butterflies in my stomach caused by my confession.

"I want to, Jackson." Feeling the truth of my words with every cell in me, I continue. "Kiss me. Please."

Another groan tears from his mouth as he answers my request, leaning back over me until we're back where we started. Hearing the foil packet rip, my brain pings with questions about what it will feel like before Jackson captures my mouth in another hot kiss, scrambling those errant thoughts. His fingers find one of my nipples, tugging, making me cry out as pleasure ricochets through my body. Lifting my knees up and back, his tip is poised at my entrance before he stops, resting his forehead against my shoulder. "Fuck. I shouldn't do this."

"Please." Begging, I lift my hips, his tip sliding in slightly.

"Still, gorgeous. You need to be still. I don't want to hurt you." His hips cant farther. Closing my eyes, I'm ready.

"Jax?" A knock at the door inspires a high-pitched squeak from me. I try to burrow under him to hide, so glad that he closed the door earlier.

"It's okay." His assurance is quiet, meant only for my ears. As is the groan that comes next. His voice then raises to answer. "Yeah?"

"Everyone's back—did you want to pull out a little earlier?"

A grin spreads across his face at the innuendo. The smile shifts to a grimace when he glances down between us.

"Twenty minutes?" I can't stop the flinch at the reminder that our time is almost done.

"Sure thing." Another knock and the room is quiet.

Like a bucket of ice water, reality intrudes with every thought I'd managed to push away while we hid in here. I almost slept with someone I've known less than twenty-four hours. I'd been willing to give him my virginity. A tell-tale heat blooms on my chest, traveling to my cheeks. I want to push away, grab my clothes, and run. But if I move, I'm naked in plain sight. I stiffen at that fun thought and Jackson must feel it because he lifts himself off me. My eyes shut, refusing to open. If I can't see him, he can't see me, right?

"Hey." Soft fingers skim my cheek. "Open those pretty eyes, gorgeous."

His whisper makes my eyes flutter open. He's wearing his shorts again, my clothes bundled in his arms.

"I'm sorry." He sighs, continuing when I remain silent. "Not about what almost happened. The timing. It fucking sucks."

I shrug, sitting up and getting dressed as fast as I can with fumbling fingers while trying not to show too much. Why am I bothering since he's had his hands and lips on most of my body tonight?

The warmth that surges into my stomach isn't embarrassment. It's a shot of lust that hits my core, my thighs clenching even as I try to think of something to say to him. By the time I'm dressed he has shrugged into his t-shirt again and I clear my throat to let him know I'm done since he had turned around. He faces me, immediately drawing me into his arms where I go willingly.

"Did I ruin my chances with you?"

CHAPTER 9

JAX

She shakes her head and I release a sigh, my body relaxing around hers. "Thank fuck."

"I-I don't know what I'm doing, Jackson." It's a whisper against the soft cotton of my shirt.

"I don't either."

She looks up, amber colored eyes wide with surprise and I can't help but press a kiss against her forehead.

"I've never done this before," I say.

"I somehow doubt that."

I don't fight the grin at her snappy comeback. It's a reminder of her taste and wakes my dick back up. I want nothing more than to dive in for another bite, to savor the smile on her lips with my tongue.

"I meant what this feeling is. Between us." I lean into her, letting her smell travel my senses as I think of how to say it. "It's new for me. I've never felt like someone I just met is someone I've known forever."

She nods. "Now you're leaving."

"To Phoenix." It might as well be Mars. She buries her head under my chin, taking several breaths.

"I should probably let you guys get going then."

"Meredith still has your keys." I intertwine our fingers, opening the door on reality. The lights at the front of the bus are bright compared to the darkness of my room. I grab Charlotte's shoes and slide my flip flops back on, glaring at the guys hanging out on the couches now, daring them with my eyes to say one word as Charlotte cowers behind me. Squeezing her hand in reassurance, I pull her with me into the night.

Watching Charlotte say goodbye to Meredith creates a sharp pain in my ribs. I can tell saying goodbye is painful for her, despite Meredith's attempt at levity. And now, I'll have to say goodbye. How many goodbyes would I force on her if I kept this up? I'm a selfish bastard for starting anything to begin with. I chose this life—the travel, the public scrutiny, the expectations—she didn't.

My arm squeezes around her shoulders as I walk her to her car, tears still glimmering in her eyes from her goodbye with Meredith. I need to let her go. I already have too many balls to juggle as it is. My family, Nick's demands. For once, I want to make a choice for me. To add Charlotte, to keep her in my life.

The quiet of the parking lot is interrupted as buses fire up, the drivers gathering near one bus to discuss the route to Arizona for the night. It's familiar to me, these steps, we've been doing them since the tour started. But for the first time, I'm reluctant. I don't want to let go of the beauty at the tip of my fingers.

It's slow going to Charlotte's car, as if she's just as unenthusiastic about this goodbye as I am, our slower pace gives us a few more seconds of stolen time. She turns when we reach her car, leaning against the door. Headlights from the buses provide enough light to see her eyes but not enough to put them on display, to give me a look of the warm cognac color before we leave.

I brush a wayward piece of hair behind her ear and my fingers trace along her smooth jawline, a way to soak in every touch that I can before I say goodbye. She breathes out a sigh, closing her eyes, and leans into my touch, causing the ache in my chest to ping.

Shivering, she looks up, and her eyes search my face before they blink. When she opens them, her shoulders square.

"Jackson, I—" She pauses, chewing on her lip, considering her words. "I am beyond happy to have met you."

Her eyes glisten obsidian in the semi-darkness that surrounds us. The waver in her voice tells me more than her words. She's trying to say goodbye. Permanently.

"Me too." I step closer, unable to stop myself from aligning our bodies, mine pressing us against her car. Her sharp intake of breath tells me that she feels this connection just like I do. It's that thought that tells me I'm not ready to say goodbye.

"Can I call you?" I lean in, my mouth a breath away from hers, my eyes tracking a swallow that works its way down her throat before she nods.

"O-okay," she whispers so quietly I barely hear her.

"And FaceTime?" My lips brush hers as I speak. Her nod is almost imperceptible against my lips. Closing the distance, I capture her lips with mine. They're still swollen from my kisses earlier, but she tastes decidedly like her as I nibble along the bottom one, sweeping my tongue inside as her mouth opens, deepening the kiss and yanking her tightly against me.

My dick is screaming at me, begging me to carry her back to the bus as my tongue tangles with hers. I groan, breaking the kiss to rest my forehead against hers, rubbing my hands up and down her arms while we both catch our breath.

"I'm getting carried away again." My lungs fight for oxygen

even while my dick threatens blue balls and demands that I dive back into that kiss.

A small smile lights Charlotte's face. "Me too."

My arms wrap around her, my nose finding her neck when I lift her off her toes and breathe in her unique scent. With enough deep breaths, I can take her to Arizona with me, right? "Let me know when you get home, okay?" My whisper tickles her neck and causes her to shiver.

Her voice is thick when she agrees, "Yeah."

Putting her back down on her feet, my body physically rebels as I release her. I open her door, then watch as she sits down and buckles her seat belt. Leaning down, I let myself take one more kiss before I back up. Her sad smile mirrors my own through the window and, with a little wave, she puts the car in gear, heading for the exit.

When her taillights disappear around the building, I scrub a hand down my face. Saying goodbye to someone I just met shouldn't fucking hurt this much.

The right thing to do would have been to let her go. Instead, I surprised the hell out of myself asking to stay in contact with her. But she's more than another girl at a concert. I rub at the mix of hollowness and excitement in my chest—it's a new experience. Looking around, everyone is on a bus, waiting for me, relying on me. And I can't let anyone down.

♫♪♫♪♫

CHARLOTTE: Home safe.
JACKSON: *smile emoji*
CHARLOTTE: You guys on the road?
JACKSON: Yeah. We left shortly after you.
CHARLOTTE: What time will you get to Arizona?
JACKSON: Depending on fuel-ups and stops, mid-day tomorrow, maybe?

CHARLOTTE: Don't you have a concert tomorrow night?
JACKSON: Yeah.
CHARLOTTE: When do you get to relax?
JACKSON: No rest for the wicked, gorgeous. *wink emoji*

The road hums under the bus as I lay in bed, texting Charlotte. There's no relaxation on a tour. I'll relax once it's done and I'm not under pressure from Reverb and from Nick to be on my best behavior. Sound checks, radio promos, PR opportunities, all of that takes time when I'm not performing. Then after the concert is the after-party while the stage gets torn down and packed up. We load up and do it again, my own personal Groundhog Day.

Exhaustion creeps up the more I think about my hectic schedule, but I don't want to get bogged down in that tonight.

The sound of the guys yelling about Call of Duty echoes through my door, but I'm not thinking about that either. Or the smirks and knowing looks I'd gotten when I'd climbed the bus steps. My guitar is next to me and my door is closed to keep the roses and coconut scent lingering the air as long as possible.

JACKSON: I wish you were still here.
CHARLOTTE: Not all of us can be famous singers. Some of us have to work tomorrow. *wink emoji*
CHARLOTTE: I wish I was too.

Staring at her latest message, the phone creaks as my fingers clench. How is it that someone I just met can get under my skin so quickly? Before I can respond, another text comes through.

CHARLOTTE: What will you do to pass the time to Arizona?
JACKSON: I can play video games if I want or watch a movie. I'll probably try to sleep some. Right now, I'm hanging out in my room with my guitar.

The blankets on the bed had still been bunched up when I'd come back in here once we were on the road, and like some fucking lovestruck teenage girl, I'd picked up the pillow where Charlotte had been and buried my nose in it to inhale her subtle scent.

I'd stripped off my shirt and propped myself against that pillow before tuning my guitar. My laptop sits open to record and a pad and pencil are within arm's reach in case anything worth writing down comes to me. Waiting for her response from the three dots on my screen, I stretch my arms overhead.

CHARLOTTE: What's your favorite song to play?
CHARLOTTE: Not one of yours either. *wink emoji*
JACKSON: That's hard—it's like you picking your favorite author.
CHARLOTTE: LOL Touché
JACKSON: I like John Mayer.
CHARLOTTE: Does he sound like you?
JACKSON: Remember what I said, gorgeous?
JACKSON: Eclectic.

Memories of the last time I said that to her, images of us in the rehearsal space last night, hit me like a freight train. My dick swells with the memory of her hips gyrating against me. The fantasy shifts and this time we're skin to skin. She and I and pounding music. My cock is pissed as fuck at me for the interruption earlier and I unbutton my shorts, hoping for a little relief.

CHARLOTTE: Is he any good?
JACKSON: You've never heard of John Mayer?
CHARLOTTE: Maybe? If they play him on the radio?
CHARLOTTE: I'm more a songs than singer person.

JACKSON: Baby, I need to educate you about music. *wink emoji*
CHARLOTTE: Whatever. I do know SOME music.
CHARLOTTE: What's the last song you listened to?
JACKSON: Somewhere with You

Switching apps, I find the song by Kenny Chesney to send it to her and listen to it myself so I can text her when it's done.

JACKSON: So, what'd you think?
CHARLOTTE: I liked it.
JACKSON: Good.
CHARLOTTE: You like country music, huh?
JACKSON: It's honestly what I like to sing more. Reverb wanted me to be pop, so that's what they did. Somewhere with You is probably one of my favorite songs.
JACKSON: Since you asked me, I'll ask you. What's YOUR favorite country song?
CHARLOTTE: I don't have much experience in that category.
JACKSON: Okay. I suppose that's acceptable. So not country then. Favorite song any genre?
CHARLOTTE: You won't know it.
JACKSON: Try me.
CHARLOTTE: Have you heard of Christina Novelli? Concrete Angel?

Both the artist and the song are unfamiliar, which is a surprise given how much music I listen to. I find the song and am blown away. It's haunting. My throat constricts with emotions that rise to the surface the longer I listen. Images of Charlotte that invade my imagination, her body moving to this song, are so realistic that her smell wraps around me.

JACKSON: Wow.

CHARLOTTE: It's great, right?
JACKSON: It's fucking beautiful.
JACKSON: Just like you.

The best- and worst-case scenarios rack my brain when she doesn't respond right away. Best case scenario is she fell asleep, worst case is that I've scared her off.

JACKSON: Did you fall asleep on me?
CHARLOTTE: No.
JACKSON: Did I freak you out?
CHARLOTTE: Not exactly.
JACKSON: *smile emoji* I just wanted you to know that.
CHARLOTTE: You hardly know me.
JACKSON: I know enough.
JACKSON: Inside and out.
JACKSON: You're beautiful.

CHAPTER 10

CHARLIE

"Hey, gorgeous." Jackson is breathless, and the faint southern drawl still sends shivers through my body.

"Hey. How was your show?" I'm snuggled in bed, the house silent around me.

"I think my Denver show was better."

His words have me sitting up. Worry that something has happened settles in my stomach like a lump of clay. "What? Why? Did something happen?"

"No." The smile in Jackson's voice is clear and allows my body to relax, but I'm still confused.

"No?"

"The show was fine."

"But I thought you said your Denver show was better?" What am I missing?

"It was." His reply doesn't explain anything.

"Is it a better venue?" I've never been to Phoenix so can't picture where they were tonight.

His laugh vibrates through the phone. "Fuck, I miss you. I liked my show in Denver better because you were there."

"Oh." Warmth builds in my chest as his words rasp through the phone. He laughs again and I smile, a noisy yawn overtaking me.

"You sound tired." Jackson's voice is lower, similar to the way it sounded beneath my cheek on the bus. His husky whisper has goosebumps brushing across my shoulders.

"Little bit."

"I just wanted to talk to you for a minute. Get some sleep, gorgeous. Goodnight."

"Night, Jackson."

♪♪♪♪♪♪

It's been weeks since Jackson and Meredith were here, but my phone calls with both of them continue. While Meredith and I talk every few days, my calls with Jackson have become nightly.

"Hey." Smiling, I lean against my pillows. He's the best part of my day.

"Hey there, gorgeous."

"How was your down day today?" He'd been so excited to have most of the day off.

"Good. Mer and I hit the beach and then we had dinner with her parents. Guess what?"

"What?"

"I got something." A kid at Christmas doesn't sound as excited as he does right now.

"A new guitar?" I laugh when he gasps.

"You better be glad Berniece didn't hear you."

"Berniece?"

"My guitar."

"Your guitar has a name?" I can't tell if he's joking or not.

He chuckles. "It does. Although I have to admit I didn't name her Berniece. But no, no new guitar."

"What'd you get?" I sit up, curious about why he's so excited.

"Did you know that Meredith's parents have copies of all the recitals you both were in?"

"What?" My voice is strangled. What videos? Which recitals? He's a famous singer and while I'm professionally trained, I don't think my recitals are the same as his concerts. I've seen him in his element, but the thought of having him see those videos creates a swirl of uncertainty in my stomach. Meredith's mom, Val, always recorded the recitals, but I never realized she was filming me too.

"Val let me borrow them so now I can see you dance."

I don't mirror his excitement. "Ugh." Hiding my face with one hand, I close my eyes and fall back into the pillow.

"What? What's the matter?"

"It's embarrassing," I mumble into my hand.

"What? No. Don't be embarrassed. You've seen me in action. I want to see you."

"What you do is on a different level, though, Jackson. Those videos are school recitals."

"Do you really not want me to watch them?" His disappointment travels through the phone, and guilt creeps in since my reaction has dimmed his excitement.

"You won't watch them if I ask you not to?"

"No," he sighs. "I won't."

"You really want to, though, don't you?"

"Yes." The smile normally present in his voice when I talk to him is gone and the guilt intensifies.

"Seriously? I'm not even sure which ones you got copies of." Why do I feel like I'm losing this battle?

"Please?" Picturing the pout on his face, I try to hold strong. "Pretty please?"

Sighing, I laugh at his antics. "Ugh. Okay fine. Just don't say I didn't warn you."

"Thank you, gorgeous. I can't wait to watch these. I miss you."

♪♩♪♩♪♩♪♩

I miss you. I catch the blush staining my cheeks in the mirror.

"Bye, Miss Charlie." The little girl twists, her hand still in her mom's, as she turns and waves at me.

"Bye, Peyton."

The studio is empty, Peyton the last student to leave and no other classes are scheduled.

Moving my leg up to the barre, I fold forward and stretch first one leg and then the other, mulling over Jackson's words. They've come back to me over and over again, no matter what I'm doing.

When I should be focusing—either on Bella or my students here—his words crash into me with the impact of a lightning bolt. Grimacing, I push through the stretch with my right leg until the twinge disappears. Will it always be there?

I push that thought away and step back from the barre, my legs warmed up, and I move to the music still playing through the speakers. It's less advanced than I'm used to, but I'm still hesitant to push my ankle, terrified of not being ready. *You should be by now,* the little voice of doubt reminds me. *It's been a year.*

Meredith tells me to try. Jackson tells me he believes in me. He's also shared with me that when the tour gets to be too much, he'll picture me and I'm his oasis in the chaos. If I'm his, then he's mine. It's difficult balancing Bella in the early mornings and Jackson late at night, but he's worth it.

"Belle, ma chérie." Madame's jasmine perfume makes it to me before she does, the smell bringing back memories of hours spent dancing, watching, learning from her softly spoken instructions. Her voice brings my attention back to the small studio.

"Merci, Madame." I stop in the middle of the room, chest rising and falling.

"Done for the day?" At my nod, she walks to the stereo, flipping it off. "Could you come with me?"

I follow her out of the studio to her small office in the back. Have I done something wrong?

"Madame, is everything okay?"

"What?" Her eyebrows arch with her question. "Oui bien sûr. I'm so sorry if you thought otherwise. I just wanted to talk to you about a telephone call from an old friend."

Having been around her since I was three, I'm able to translate the mix of English and French but it takes me a minute to process her words.

"A phone call?"

She nods. "Oui. A good friend of mine, Meric Toussaint, just phoned me. Meric owns a casting company in Los Angeles. He has an opportunity, a casting call. He asked me if I knew of anyone who I thought could audition."

"Auditions?" My heart races and sinks at the same time. "Auditions for what?"

The last time I auditioned was after she told me about the arts magnet school in New York. She had helped me prepare and wished me luck before I moved.

"He is looking for a dancer for a music video. The artist has une idée précise and has asked Meric for help."

Whoever the artist is must be pretty big if his specific idea is driving the auditions.

"Oh?"

She nods. "I've told Meric to expect you at the audition in Los Angeles at the end of the month."

She tilts her head to study me when I freeze. "Audition?"

"Oui."

"Madame, I don't think I'm ready." Or if I'll ever be. Swallowing those words down, I grimace as they pierce my heart.

She holds up a hand. "This I know. But you are close. La fogue lives in there." She points at my chest. *Passion lives in my heart.* "I am not saying you will not work hard, ma chérie. But I will help you."

Opening a drawer, she pulls out a set of keys, placing them in my hand and wrapping my fingers around them.

"What are these?"

"Spare keys to the studio. It is yours to practice in as much as you want." Madame smiles, her belief in me sparking my own. I can do this. "Mon Dieu! You must need to get home."

I glance at the clock and see that she's right. Mom and Dad will be expecting me soon. Madame kisses both of my cheeks before she walks me to the door, locking up behind me as she closes down for the night. The keys in my hands jangle and I zip them into a side pocket on my bag. Excitement starts to zing through me. Maybe this is my chance?

♪♪ ♪♪♪

By the time Jackson FaceTimes me, I'm determined. I'm going to audition. Any spare time I'm not watching Bella will be spent in the studio—if I can get my parents to agree.

"Hey." My smile is huge as I answer.

"Hey, gorgeous, you look excited."

"I am. You'll never believe what happened today." I share what Madame told me, finishing with my decision to try as hard as I can to prepare and audition.

"Baby, that's great. Whatever I can do to help, you tell me, okay?" I nod but there's something off about his voice. I study the phone and notice the dark circles under his eyes and the tension that tugs his mouth down.

"Are you okay, Jackson? You look tired. Not like yourself."

He tries to smile, but it's half-hearted at best. "I'm sorry."

"Why are you sorry?"

"I'm bringing you down from your news."

"You have me a little worried," I confess. "Usually when I talk to you, I hear your smile. But it's missing tonight."

His chest rises and falls with a sigh. "I've just been getting lots of calls lately from Nick, my label rep. Every call is the same. He reminds me that I have a lot to lose if I screw up. Almost like they're expecting me to screw up again."

"Jackson—"

"It's just I have to wonder if anything I do will ever be good enough for them, y'know?" I don't really know the intricacies of what he's talking about or what he might lose, but I get not feeling understood.

"I'm sorry."

"Fuck, I wish you were here. I miss you." He groans, eyes closed as if in pain.

"Me too," I echo his wish. "Are you sure that's it? That's all that's bothering you?"

Shut up, Charlie.

"What do you mean?" He's more alert, eyes focused through the screen, the confusion clear in his tone.

"I thought...I thought maybe you were calling me..." My voice fades, fear locking my tongue around the next words.

"Calling you...?"

I close my eyes, spilling the words on an exhale. "I thought you might be calling to tell me you didn't want to call me anymore."

Saying it out loud sounds so much crazier than in my head.

"What? Why?"

"I just...I know you're under a lot of pressure from them. Your label, I mean. And I don't want to be a distraction...and I'm me. Nobody famous. Why me?"

My google searches show me that the people he's normally photographed with are glamorous. When I googled how many famous people date non-famous people, the articles were scary with how often things *didn't* work out. There's silence after my rushed words, my pulse skittering as I wait for a response. It's stupid. If he wasn't going to call me anymore, wouldn't he just stop calling?

"Charlotte." I peek one eye open at my name, opening both eyes to see him staring at me.

"Yeah?"

"You're the best thing about my day." His words wrap around my heart.

"I am?"

"You are," he repeats. "I don't want to stop."

"Oh." There's a soft smile on his lips and my own curve in response.

"Do you?"

"What?" I shake my head. "No, of course not."

"Good," he pauses, his attention elsewhere before he looks back at the screen. "Gorgeous, you need to get some sleep and I need to go answer a question. Talk tomorrow?"

"K. Goodnight, Jackson."

"Sweet dreams, Charlotte."

♫♪♫♪♫♪

"Okay, Bells, put your plate in the trash, okay?" I point to the trash can for Bella as I wipe crumbs off the table from our lunch the next day.

"Okay, Chawie." She does what I ask before turning back to me, hazel eyes big and pleading. "Dance, Chawie?"

"Sure, Bells, we can dance. Grab your tutu." She scampers off as fast as her three-year-old legs can take her, coming back with a fluffy tutu I found on Etsy for her last birthday. I help her into it before the video starts for the Barbie dancers she's obsessed with right now. No sooner do I put the remote down when my phone chimes with an incoming text.

JACKSON: Ding dong.
CHARLOTTE: Knock-knock jokes are supposed to start with "Knock Knock."
JACKSON: Ha-ha, funny girl. Special delivery.
CHARLOTTE: ?
JACKSON: Did your doorbell ring yet?

The doorbell echoes through the house, and I jump. I make my way slowly to the door, not sure what to expect. Excitement surges through my veins. Is Jackson here? My heart sinks when I look through the peephole, disappointed that it's someone in a delivery uniform.

"Hello?" I smile at the person waiting on the front porch once I open the door.

"Charlotte Walker?"

"Yeah?"

"Delivery. Could you sign here, please?" I scrawl my name on the device he hands me before he trades me, taking back the device and handing me a sealed envelope with my name but no address scratched into the front. Distracted by the envelope in my hands, I close the door and grab my phone.

CHARLOTTE: Why do I have an envelope with just my name on it? What's going on?
JACKSON: Your doorbell rang?
CHARLOTTE: Yeah...
JACKSON: Open it.
JACKSON: The envelope.

A glance at Bella shows she's still happily dancing along to her video. I rip the envelope open and pull out a laminated pass and ticket.

CHARLOTTE: A backstage pass and a ticket?

JACKSON: Yep. *smile emoji*
CHARLOTTE: For Vegas?
JACKSON: Our next stop. We're almost there now.

Excitement builds, quickly fizzling when I register the date on the ticket.

CHARLOTTE: The ticket's for tomorrow night. I can't drive to Vegas that fast and my parents aren't home yet.

The garage door opens as soon as I send the text.

"Mom? What are you doing home?"

Mom walks in and Bella tears down the hallway to greet her.

She smiles at me as she lifts Bella onto her hip. "Meredith called and asked if we could let you do a girl's weekend with her."

"Meredith?" Not Jackson. I don't say that out loud since Mom and Dad still don't know about him yet.

"Yeah." Mom looks confused at my question. "Thankfully I had some PTO so I could come home."

I really want to roll my eyes. Of course, the only reason I can go is because Mom has time off to take. If not, I'd be here watching Bella, no ability to go to Vegas to see Jackson or Meredith. Why? With everything else changing—meeting Jackson, the upcoming auditions—why does this have to stay the same? Mom and Dad can afford daycare, I know it. So why can't this change too?

My phone chimes with another text, interrupting my spiraling thoughts.

JACKSON: Better hurry. Your next surprise gets there in an hour and you need to pack. *wink emoji*

Smiling at the text, I rush upstairs and throw a few things into my small suitcase. When the doorbell rings again, I glance at the time on my phone. Has it already been an hour? My phone chimes again as I bump downstairs with my bag.

JACKSON: Your next surprise is ready. Are you?
CHARLOTTE: Jackson, what did you do?

He doesn't respond right away. Tucking my phone into the back pocket of my jeans, I open the door, this time to another man in uniform. Instead of a courier's uniform, he wears a smart black suit, and a dark sedan sits at the curb behind him.

"Ms. Walker?"

"Yes?" He reminds me of someone in the mafia or FBI. Either way, I use the door as a buffer.

"My name is Jake. I've been hired to take you to the airport." Airport? Driver? As expensive as it would have been, I could have taken an Uber or Lyft to the airport, a fact I'm still stuck on when he motions to my suitcase, forgotten where it's clutched in my hand. "May I?"

I hand it over in a daze, watching as he heads toward the car.

"Who's that?" Mom and Bella come up behind me.

"I, uh, I guess he's here to take me to the airport?"

Mom's eyebrows raise, curiosity evident on her face, but she doesn't say anything. After a quick goodbye to Mom and Bella, I head for the car.

The car ride is smooth, uneventful despite Denver traffic. As we approach the airport, I watch the exit I usually take for departures zoom behind us. My heart jackhammers in my chest, breath stalling in my lungs. Shouldn't we have used that exit to go to the airport? My hands shake as I wrap them around my phone, texting Jackson.

CHARLOTTE: Um, in case I'm being kidnapped I wanted you to know.
JACKSON: LOL. What?

CHARLOTTE: We didn't go to the normal departure area.
JACKSON: You'll see. *wink emoji* Don't worry.

A sign pops up on the side of the road advertising the entrance for a chartered flight company and my eyes round in surprise.

"Oh." I'm grateful that my voice betrays none of the nerves currently coursing a conga through my body. Instead, they reveal themselves in the way I squeeze my fingers around the strap on my backpack I use for a carry-on. The times I've flown in the past —mostly from Colorado to New York and back again—were always on overcrowded commercial flights in coach. When the car parks next to a small, gleaming white and chrome jet, swallowing around the thick ball of nerves that has moved from my stomach to my throat becomes a full effort.

Jake opens my door and I take a tentative step away from the car—ironically, now my sanctuary—and toward the plane. "I'll bring your bags directly, Ms. Walker."

I shift my eyes from the plane to the driver. Do I head for the plane then? I can't stand here forever. Jake makes up my mind for me by grabbing my suitcase and motioning me toward the stairs leading up to the plane. The utilitarian steps lead to a plush cabin with sumptuous leather seats and a citrusy, wood smell that permeates the cool air.

"Ms. Walker, welcome aboard. Please choose whatever seat you'd like, and I'll let our captain know we can depart." The woman who greets me is around my age, dressed in a navy button down shirt and slacks. Her smile is warm as she gestures to the seats I can choose from.

Sitting—or rather falling—into the bench seat, I clutch my bag in front of me, trying not to show how completely awestruck I am by my surroundings when, in reality, my eyes want to bug out of my head and explore the luxurious cabin. My phone chimes again and I grab it from my pocket.

JACKSON: Airborne yet?
CHARLOTTE: How much did this cost? *wow emoji*
JACKSON: Don't worry about that.
CHARLOTTE: Jackson.
JACKSON: Charlotte.
JACKSON: Don't worry about it. It's not as expensive as it looks.
CHARLOTTE: What it looks like is a REALLY nice plane that I get to enjoy.
CHARLOTTE: I could have flown on a regular flight.
JACKSON: The next flight from Denver to Vegas doesn't leave until 10 tonight.

My watch tells me it's barely three in the afternoon and I have to admit he makes a good point.

CHARLOTTE: You know you're crazy, right?
JACKSON: Crazy about you, beautiful. *smile emoji*
CHARLOTTE: *eyeroll emoji* You're a lunatic.
JACKSON: LOL
CHARLOTTE: The attendant is saying I need to turn off my phone.
JACKSON: Safe flight. See you soon.

Turning my phone to airplane mode, I open my Kindle app, glad to see I've already got my next book queued up and ready to take me back to the Virgin Islands.

"Would you like anything to drink, Ms. Walker?"

Glancing up, I smile. "No thank you."

"Just let me know." She smiles again then walks back to her seat for takeoff. I buckle up as the plane taxis down the runway and we're airborne in minutes. I let my book distract me from the fidgety sensations twitching my feet. Time to get lost in Leona and Cullen's love story.

CHAPTER 11

JAX

Not telling Charlotte everything last night dampens the excitement of meeting her plane soon. The surprise trip had already been planned, all the last-minute details ironed out and ready to move forward.

The words had been on the tip of my tongue, both for the trip and the latest demand from Nick. To tell her about the picture that had popped up last week. I'd forgotten how ruthless the paparazzi are, how quiet, how greedy they can be in the pursuit of a story to sell. The picture of Charlotte and I locked together next to her car has been picked up by reputable media outlets, everyone wanting to know who she is and what she means to me. Nick was practically animated when he called me about it.

"Hello?"

"Jackson."

"Nick."

"Do you know why I'm calling you?" He sounds way too

happy to be talking to me. If it hadn't been for him saying my name, I'd question if he called the right person.

"To remind me that I have a lot to lose?" Pinching the bridge of my nose, I lean my head back against the cement wall just outside Derek's wardrobe room at the venue. As the make-up and wardrobe person, he always seems to know where everything is despite having twenty trunks that all look the same and he'd just found my hat—again—when Nick called.

He laughs and the hairs on the back of my arm stand up. What the fuck is going on? "Funny, kid."

Kid. Like he's so much older than me. I grind my molars to avoid saying something I can't take back and wait for him to continue.

"Have you seen *US Weekly's* website today?"

"No, why?" Panic fills me. What shot did the paparazzi get now? My phone vibrates in my hand.

"Click on the link." I bite back the frustration at his non-answer and open my texts and click on the link he sent. The picture it loads takes me back to that night. The light above Charlotte's car provides the perfect light to see us, Charlotte backed up against the car, my body wrapped around hers as our mouths connected. Fuck. Fuck. Fuck. I brace myself and hold the phone back up to my ear.

I don't get anything out after clearing my throat.

"Denver Delight. Who is Jax's new girl..."

"I know how this looks—"

"This looks like gold, Jax. PR gold." His words scatter every thought in my brain.

"Huh?"

"Randa and the other execs are salivating over the fact that you are one of the top stories on that media outlet and several others. Everyone wants to know who she is. Everyone wants to watch a love story unfold." The fog in my brain refuses to process anything Nick says.

"Randa and other execs? Hold on… Love story?"

"Keep up, kid. Who is she?"

I don't know if Charlotte wants me to say anything. "Um, I met her in Denver."

"You're attracted to her." I scoff at his statement. Just looking at the picture has my dick pressing against the seam of my jeans. "We want to use this."

Just like that, ice fills my veins, my hard-on dying a quick death. "Use what?"

"We like the idea of you in a relationship, a love story. Spin you into a happily ever after."

What. the. fuck?

"Would she be into it?"

"Into what?" I scrub a hand down my face. Nick needs to spell out what he's dancing around.

"Being in a public relationship with you. We want you to date her, grab the good PR and run with it."

"Um…"

"Don't tell me right now. Talk to her. Let me know." The line clicks in my ear and I stare at the phone, anger burning to rage. What I've done isn't good enough. Now they want to involve Charlotte too. Hell. Fucking. No.

Every time I've called her since, I had every intention of telling her about that conversation, but the thought of telling her that the label wants to use her leaves a sour taste in my mouth. Last night after another particularly brutal call from Nick badgering me, I was vague, just telling her part of the truth. I'd confided in Meredith, both of us trying to figure it out before Nick stops being patient. We're both looking forward to seeing Charlotte again.

My phone chimes with a text.

MEREDITH: I'm so excited! *big smile emoji*

The hot Vegas sun beats down on me where I stand. I tug down the baseball hat, shielding my eyes from the bright desert sun. I'm just as excited as Meredith. Maybe more so. For two weeks, Charlotte and I have texted and called whenever we can, but, being on opposite schedules, it's more stolen time than anything else.

Every new thing I learn about her tangles me further in her web. It's gotten so that I can't fall asleep until I've heard her voice for a few minutes. She reminds me that my life isn't all demands from Reverb and Nick or worry about Jessie and my parents.

The old me would have given me shit for how pathetic I've become in such a short time. The new me has no fucking clue how to handle any of this. I just know that I need to see her again, to touch her, inhale her scent.

Meredith's text takes my heart from "nice jog around the track" rate to "100-yard dash against Usain Bolt" level. If the sun didn't make me feel like I'd stepped into an oven set to broil, I'd be pacing next to the car instead of just standing here, waiting. The last two weeks swirl in a mix of conversations with Charlotte and with Nick.

Pushing Nick out, my thoughts center on Charlotte. Her beautiful caramel colored eyes, the sweet sound of her laugh, her scent, her taste, the little sounds she'd made as I'd kissed her senseless on the bus. I'm amazed that my dick isn't raw from how many times I've jacked off, reliving that night with her. The taste of her skin, the feel of her hard nipples rubbing against my chest, the taste of her sweet pussy and the sounds she'd whimpered as I'd devoured her all get me to come in record time.

My dick hardens in my shorts but I need to chill the fuck out. The plane's going to be arriving any minute and I don't want to greet Charlotte with a noticeable hard-on.

The only peace I've found outside of my hand has been planning with Meredith to get Charlotte to another show. From LA forward, the plan solidified. Charlotte would meet us in Vegas after we surprised her. Meredith had gotten in touch with Charlotte's mom, telling her that she wanted to surprise Charlotte with a girls' weekend in Vegas and asking for permission for Charlotte to come. Rolling my eyes, I still can't believe that had to be a step in our plan. I get Charlotte's frustration with that shit.

The sun glints off a plane in the distance and, squinting my eyes, I focus on its approach. Is this her plane? When I'd chartered it out of McCarran, I'd gotten directions on where passengers could be picked up but, in my excitement, I'd gotten here way too early and spent the last thirty minutes in my own head. The plane swoops and descends, touching down on the runway, slowing down and making several turns until it's headed in my direction.

My pulse picks up, a grin spreading across my face even as I wipe my sweaty hands on the back of my shorts. The best part about chartering the flight—besides the awesome deal Meredith's dad helped me get and getting Charlotte here several hours sooner—is that I get to meet her here, as soon as her feet touch down on the tarmac. And I get to greet her without an audience so long as I constantly double check that there aren't any cameras at the ready this time.

The engines on the plane hum to a stop as I wait impatiently for the door to lower. I swear I stop breathing while I wait the few minutes it takes before Charlotte is framed in the doorway then makes her way gingerly down the steep steps.

She hasn't noticed me yet, so I take my time and drink her in. Faded blue jeans and her beat up Chucks on her feet. A long, lacy blue tank top accentuates her curves, making my mouth water for a taste of her. Her hair is a riot of brown waves, whipping everywhere in the desert wind.

A half smile kicks up one side of my mouth as she tries and fails to yank the wayward strands out of her face. Her eyes round in surprise as she glances up and notices me waiting for her. A smile lights up her face, matching mine as I start walking toward her. Her steps quicken, racing across the small space separating us. I hug her to me, lifting her off the ground. She wraps around me, squealing when I spin us both.

"Jackson!"

My nose buries itself in her neck, desperate for her smell, inhaling deeply even as my lips seek hers. Thoughts of a brief kiss shatter, the first taste drawing a soft sigh from her that ignites the need that simmers behind my wall of control. With a slant of my mouth, I deepen the kiss, dipping my tongue to tangle with hers. Boosting her slightly, I'm rewarded as her legs wrap around my waist without hesitation while her arms tighten around my neck. Her fingers play with the long edges of hair under my cap and create a fire that pulses through my blood.

My control is barely hanging on while images of me lowering us to the runway—or ravaging her in the nearby car—play in my brain like an erotic slide show. Forcing myself back slowly, I plant several more chaste kisses along her lips.

"Hey," it's a whisper, our lips so close that mine brush hers.

"Hi." Pink spreads across her cheeks, her chest rising and falling as she tries to catch her breath. The loss of her slight weight as she untangles her legs from around my waist and slides down my body is both heaven and hell. Biting back a groan, I keep an arm wrapped around her, heading for the car.

"Good flight?" There's no space between us as we slide into the backseat.

She nods. "Faster too."

I fucking love that she fits so perfectly against me, snuggling into my side like she did that first night on our date. "I know. I wanted to spend as much time with you as possible."

My lips brush her temple and I can't fight the smile at the feel of her in my arms. Driving back to Vegas, I'm mesmerized watching Charlotte peer out the window at the desert landscape whirring by us.

"Have you ever been?" My voice is low, gravelly, and a smirk settles on my lips when goosebumps shiver down her arms.

"To Vegas?"

"Mm-hm."

She shakes her head, still looking out the window while pressed against me. "You?"

"A few times. Some buddies and I came here for my twenty-first birthday." She turns her head, eyes meeting mine, a smile playing on her lips. I give her a crooked grin, remembering the pieces that I can of that weekend.

"What?" Charlotte's eyes are curious.

"Well." Rubbing the back of my neck, I'm embarrassed to tell her my story. What is it about us, car rides, and my embarrassing escapades? "I remember getting here—on a regular flight—and I sort of remember leaving. The rest is…fuzzy."

She giggles, leaning into me before falling silent. It's comfortable, this quiet between us. I'm relaxed for the first time since our date, my thumb drawing lazy patterns where it rests on her hand.

"Anything you want to see in Vegas?"

"Besides Meredith?" Charlotte's response draws a laugh from me. "Can we see the Bellagio Fountains?"

"The Bellagio Fountains?"

"Yeah."

"It's a plan, gorgeous." My voice is a whisper, our bodies clinging together like two magnets that can't seem to stay apart.

We pull up to the curb of the casino that houses the concert venue as well as our hotel rooms to find Meredith bouncing on the curb when she spots the car. Charlotte lets out a little squeal, nearly opening the door while the car is still moving.

"Easy there, speedy." I smile, watching Charlotte's excitement mirror Meredith's. Fuck, she's cute. "I know I didn't give you much time to pack. Meredith has instructions from me to take you shopping. Something for a club she wants to go to tonight. She has my credit card." Heaven help me. "I'll get your bag checked in and taken to your room. I'll text you the number and there's an app you use to unlock your door."

"My room?" Charlotte's confusion does not help my dick calm down.

"I didn't want to make any assumptions."

Her eyes turn liquid at my response.

"Although I'm more than happy to share my room with you if you want." My growl vibrates against her ear before my lips press a kiss below her earlobe. Her body tightens at my words and I want to know, more than anything, if she's remembering our few days in Denver before the tour left for Arizona. I'm barely able to say goodbye before Meredith is carting Charlotte away. She glances over her shoulder, eyes watching me as I blow her a kiss with a wink.

With hours to kill before I'm supposed to pick her up for our next date, I change into basketball shorts and a t-shirt, then head to the hotel gym before spending another hour signing autographs and posing for selfies once someone recognizes me. Finally, free of the crowd, I head back to my room to shower and get ready, grabbing my phone to see how Charlotte is doing.

JACKSON: Having fun?
CHARLOTTE: Does it make me less of a girl if I say no?

Nothing she could do would diminish how attractive I find her.

JACKSON: No
JACKSON: fucking
JACKSON: way
CHARLOTTE: LOL
CHARLOTTE: Do we have to go to the club tonight?
JACKSON: I feel like I have to say yes.
JACKSON: Meredith planned it.

CHARLOTTE: She just told me I have to go tonight.
JACKSON: LOL
CHARLOTTE: Can I ask you something?
JACKSON: Anything.
CHARLOTTE: Why don't you use my nickname? Why do you always say my full name?

Meredith had asked me the same thing, several times, over the last few weeks. She thinks it's hysterical to give me shit about how much I talk about Charlotte. I hadn't answered—it's none of her fucking business—but had instead resorted calling Meredith her childhood nickname, Mery. A name her dad is the only one allowed to still use. Finally, she'd stopped her teasing. But now that Charlotte has asked me, I don't hesitate to share my reason with her.

JACKSON: I like the way your name tastes in my mouth.

I don't hear back from her, imagining that, yet again, I've come on too strong.

JACKSON: See you later, gorgeous.

CHAPTER 12

CHARLIE

Famous last words. As Meredith had yanked me away from Jackson, she'd uttered them with confidence. *Trust me.* Our trip through the casino to the shops was a blur of cheap air freshener, plinking sounds, bright lights of the games, and cool air conditioning.

Now I find myself in a dressing room, my fingers fidgeting with the hem of an extremely short dress that she declares is "the one" I need to go dancing tonight. I really should question my sanity whenever she uses the words "trust me."

"Char, I want to see." She waits impatiently on the other side of the dressing room door.

With a sigh, I open the door to let her scurry in.

"Holy shit, Charlie. You look hot AF, girl."

"Mer, this dress is really short. Are you sure it's not a shirt?" The dress hits me mid-thigh—if I'm measuring generously—but other than the short length, I love it. It's black lace over black, the deep V-neck softened by scalloped edges. I finger the soft lace even while my other hand tries once more to yank the dress down.

"Stop. Of course it's a dress." Meredith slaps my hand away. I don't have to get it. I can find something else. I can say no. "Jax is gonna lose his mind seeing you in that."

Her words stop all thought in my head as I imagine his reaction. I *want* to see his reaction to me in this dress. "Okay."

She squeals, throwing her arms around me in a hug.

"What'd you find?" I ask. Meredith had still been searching when she'd shoved the dress at me with instructions to try it on.

She holds up a red sequined top and black miniskirt. After changing back into my regular clothes, I sit on the bench watching her try on the outfit.

"I'm so excited you're here," Meredith gushes, her voice muffled as she switches out her shirt for the red one. With her beautifully tan skin, the color looks amazing on her. She turns, checking out the back of it.

"Me too. I can't believe I'm here."

"I can't believe your mom said yes." Meredith nods, trying the skirt on next. I roll my eyes, not wanting to open that Pandora's box of thought. "Hopefully you can cheer Jax up."

Releasing her mass of curls out of the messy bun on her head, she turns again, this time with her hair down.

"What do you mean? I know he seemed pretty down last night when I talked to him. He said the label's been on his case."

Meredith lights up. "Good, he finally told you."

I frown. "Told me what?"

"Shit," Meredith sighs. "I thought that meant he told you."

"Told me what?" I repeat. Grabbing her phone out of my bag, she keys something in and hands it to me. It's a picture of Jackson and me saying goodbye in Denver. I can't see my face, just my profile, but my eyes widen at the *US Weekly* logo on the corner of the website. "Holy crap."

Meredith smiles. "That picture is three alarm hot by the way.

Anyways, Jax told me the label called him when the picture first came out. They want him to use a relationship with you for good PR."

The word *use* sticks in my mind. "Is that what this trip is about?" Am I only here as a PR tool for Jackson?

"What?" Meredith glances up sharply from where she'd been buckling her sandal. "No. Char, Jax has been planning this trip with me since LA. That was a few days before this picture came out."

Meeting her eyes, I watch for signs that she's not being truthful. "You're sure?"

"I'm sure, Charlie. I'd never lie to you. Ride or die, right?"

I sigh heavily, staring down at the picture again. I can still feel the crush of his lips against mine, the way his heat wrapped around me, firing every single nerve ending wherever he touched. But the word *use* sticks in my mind too, and now I'm not sure I'm here for the right reasons.

"C'mon, let's go check out."

Grabbing our stuff—I'm still second guessing the dress—she heads out to the cash register, plunking everything down and handing the clerk a black Amex card. Before I can blink, she's hauled me into the shoe store next door. This time when she tries to pay for the three-inch, red-soled shoes, I hesitate.

"Mer, these are really tall." It's not the height that bothers me, but the stability of my ankle.

"Pfft, you've stood en pointe for years, these are nothing." Meredith is already boxing them back up, ready to take them to the register.

"My ankle—"

"It'll be fine, Char. It's for a few hours and I'm sure you've been rehabbing the shit out of your ankle. You'll be fine," she repeats.

Grimacing, I acknowledge her comment. I have been working hard on my rehab. I try a different tactic.

"Mer, there are cheaper shoes," I say it quietly, hoping the clerk doesn't overhear us.

She shrugs. "Not as hot as these are."

"Mer—" I try again.

She holds up the card. "Jax's treat."

"I don't know." Chewing on my lip, I'm not sure how I should feel about Jackson spending as much money on me today as the dress and the shoes are going to cost. But he is getting Meredith's too, so maybe I'm overthinking things. Meredith holds a bag in front of my face, waking me from my thoughts. How did she do that so fast?

My phone chimes and I grab it from my pocket. Reading the text from Jackson, heat flares at the words he sends me. I don't want to go to the club, I'd rather just spend time with him.

"Yes, you have to go tonight."

I jump, not aware that she was reading the texts over my shoulder.

"Jesus, Mer."

She laughs and I hide my phone a little better to keep texting him without her input.

A question niggles in the back of my brain. I've chickened out asking it several times, but the longer I put it off the more I want to know.

CHARLOTTE: Can I ask you something?
JACKSON: Anything.
CHARLOTTE: Why don't you use my nickname? Why do you always say my full name?
JACKSON: I like the way your name tastes in my mouth.

If I thought my body was on fire before, it's nothing compared to the inferno that response creates.

♪♪♪♪♪♪

Nerves get the better of me as I fidget with the short hem on the dress, the second guessing from earlier turning into serious doubts. I'm waiting on the couch in my room while Meredith finishes getting ready in my bathroom. Jackson will be here any minute to take us to the club on the roof that we're going to tonight. My heart rate rivals a hummingbird's when there's a knock at the door.

"I got it." She rushes out of the bathroom, heading for the door while I stand, swallowing the nerves rioting through me. She opens the door and I forget to breathe. "Hey, Jax."

"Mer, you look nice." My vantage point allows me to see him, but the way she has the door only partially open means he can't see me. He leans forward, squeezing her upper arms. Dressed in black jeans and a black button down shirt, for once he's not wearing any kind of hat. His hair is styled while a five o'clock shadow has my skin itching to know what it feels like when he kisses me.

"What'd you do?" His voice is curious, directed at Meredith, who widens the door so he can see me. I hear her ask me if I'm ready, but my focus is on Jackson, the way his eyes heat as they travel up and down my body. He takes several steps toward me and I'm aware of the door closing, but still can't break the connection from the man walking my way.

"Wow, Charlotte—" His struggle to find the right words plays across his face as he moves closer. "You are fucking stunning."

He's close enough that the heat of his body radiates, wrapping around me. Close enough that I can see the brown flecks in his peridot-colored eyes. Reaching a finger out, he traces it down my arm, gooseflesh rippling and shivering in its wake.

"If—" His voice cracks and he clears his throat. "If I kiss you right now, we won't be leaving this room. And I very much want to dance with you again."

His admission has my breath ratcheting up and fire licking along my body. "So, we should probably go?"

My own voice is so husky it's hardly recognizable. He nods, eyes still locked on me, not moving for the door.

"Jackson?" Stepping closer, I reach out a hand.

He retreats, grabbing my hand, interlacing our fingers. His lips sear a white-hot brand against the back of my hand when he presses a kiss there.

"We better go, gorgeous."

♫♪♫♪♫

After hours of dancing, I want nothing more than to kick these shoes off and hide them, so I never have to wear them again. Even the amount of alcohol Meredith encouraged isn't enough to fully block the throbbing in my feet that seems to have translated from the bass of the club. Meredith is singing along with the Muzak in the elevator as we head up to our rooms. Derek is carrying her shoes while he wraps an arm around her to keep her from listing over.

"Ohmygod, Char, I love you." She leans backwards, nearly falling over and taking Derek with her. "You need to come on tour. We can do this every night."

My feet scream in protest, but I giggle anyway. "What about the nights of the shows?"

"Girl," she slurs the word to several syllables. "One word. After-party."

"That's two words, Mer." Jackson's arms flex around me as he nuzzles my neck. His response in my room earlier tonight still causes goosebumps to riot along my arms.

The elevator dings and we stop on Meredith and Derek's floor, the sound startling me from my thoughts, my breathing embarrassingly loud in the small space.

"I'll take care of party girl here. Goodnight, you two." Derek walks after Meredith, disappearing as the elevator doors close.

Jackson's heat surrounds me and my nerves disappear, remembering the intense way his eyes had taken me in earlier.

Licking my lips, I turn in his arms. "Do you want to come hang out in my room?"

His eyes widen before he nods. "Yeah, sure. Let me just grab my guitar from my room. I want to play something for you."

My stomach swirls with a mix of excitement and leftover nerves, but I nod. "Okay."

The elevator ding signals my floor, and he leans forward to brush a soft kiss against my lips. "See you soon."

My fingers shake when I touch my lips, but I manage to get the door to my room open and flip on a lamp by the couch before I grab a bottle of water. I don't have time to do much else before there's a quiet knock on my door. With a deep breath, I cross the room again and open the door.

"Hi." A small smile winks through the five o'clock shadow that covers his cheeks.

"Hi." I let him in, making sure the door latches completely. Jackson turns around in the living area of the room, taking it all in before he sits on the couch, guitar case still clutched in his hand. "Do you want something to drink?"

He nods to the bottle of water still in my hands. "Water?"

His citrusy cologne tickles my nose as I grab another bottle. Fireworks arc as his fingers brush against mine when he takes the bottle. Uncapping his water, he swallows a large portion in one drink before he sets it down next to him, hands moving along his guitar that he's pulled from the case. "Thanks."

"Sure. You're really going to play something for me?" I try to tuck my legs up, but the length of this dress makes that not a good idea. Instead, I shift in my seat, watching him.

He nods and strums the strings, and I recognize one of the John Mayer songs he sent me last week—*A Face to Call Home*. It makes me smile.

I've started to learn artists along with the songs, and the lyrics of this particular one remind me of us. We've known each other such a short time and already Jackson sees me—normally invisible, blend into the background, quiet me. But he sees the me that no one else does, the one I don't share with anyone, ever.

His eyes lock on mine after a few beats and don't move as his fingers lure the melody expertly from the strings. He doesn't sing, it's just the sound weeping from his guitar and those steady eyes on mine. Two weeks. I've known him two weeks, and while he plays this song for me, strings wrap around my heart, telling me I'm doing the right thing. Telling me that this could be our beginning. Making me want to believe that love isn't as far-fetched as I think.

A half smile quirks his lips as he plays. Maybe he can read everything I'm feeling on my face, in the way my choppy breath becomes a duet with the guitar. Emotions move through me with the music as I sing the lyrics in my mind. Is Jackson inking my heart day by day?

The song fades but he doesn't put the guitar down right away, plucking at strings, creating light notes in the silence around us.

"I love that song." My whisper makes him smile.

"Me too."

"Thank you for playing that for me." He nods again, ducking his head as if my gratitude embarrasses him. It's cute, how similar we are. "I talked to Meredith earlier."

He looks up at me, a smirk on his lips. "Didn't we all?"

I giggle and he laughs. "No, I meant earlier. When we were shopping."

"What'd you talk about?" There's a hesitancy in his voice, like he's afraid of what my answer might be.

"She showed me the picture." His breath hisses in on a quick intake and I watch his shoulders tense.

"Anything else?"

"She told me what the label wants you to do. That they want you to use me for publicity." His fingers rest on the strings before he puts his guitar down, leaning his head back against the couch and covering his face with his hands. After a minute, he sits back up, looking at me.

"I don't want them dictating this piece of my life."

"So you don't want to be with me?" Panic flares in my chest and I reconsider my plan.

"Fuck. Yes. I mean...no. Shit...I mean I want to be with you." Reaching forward, he pulls my hand into his, locking our fingers together. "I want to be with you. Just us. Nobody else."

Uncertainty swirls in my stomach. "But what about the picture?"

"What about it?"

"I-is that why I'm here?"

"What? No." He shakes his head, grabbing my hand again, the sparks just as strong as ever. "I missed you. I wanted to see you again. Me. Not the label. Not because they're telling me. Because I can't stop thinking about you."

His words melt the frost that had been building since Meredith showed me the picture.

"Dance with me?"

He shakes his head in confusion. "What?"

"Dance with me."

"There's no music."

I nearly laugh at the look on his face, swallowing it before it escapes. The song he just played is in my favorites, so I grab my phone and hit play before standing up, pulling him with me. He wraps his arms around me, and I rest my head against his chest, listening to his heartbeat vibrate under my cheek for several measures before looking up, meeting his eyes.

"I want to be with you too, Jackson. Label or not. Forget about them. Let's be us and they can do whatever they want."

His eyes search mine. Holding his gaze, I try to show him what he needs to see.

"You're serious." He says it as a statement, not a question, but I nod anyway.

The music keeps playing and I lean my head against his chest, letting him move us through the music. My heart rate slows in the silence, soothed by the quiet.

Eventually, the hush is interrupted by his near whisper. "If I haven't told you yet, thanks for coming."

"I don't think I told you yet, thanks for my surprise." Squeezing my arms around him, I breathe in and out, my breath washing through the cotton of the button down he wore to the club tonight.

Tilting my chin, I wait until his eyes open and fasten on mine.

"Kiss me," I say.

His fingers flex where they grip my waist. "What?"

I've surprised him. My lips curve and I wrap my hands around his neck, tugging until his lips are closer to mine.

"Kiss me."

I don't wait, closing the distance, my mouth brushing against his. The kiss starts softly, a slow graze morphing as it deepens, the mood shifting from soft and dreamy to a lust-filled craze that ignites us both as his tongue takes control. I spear my hands in his hair, holding him to me. His fingers shift to the small of my back, bending me until I'm curved and pressed into him. My slight moan is loud to my own ears when he breaks the kiss to nip at my jawline before dancing kisses to my ear.

"Jackson." His face pops back into view as I flutter my eyes open. "I want you."

He freezes, brows drawn. "You do?"

"Yes." My whisper morphs into another moan when the scruff on his jaw scrapes along my neck with the kisses he traces along the column of my throat before moving to my collarbone and ending against the pulse fluttering in my neck.

"Charlotte." Moving away, he waits until my eyes open again. Those bright orbs steadily watch me, searching. "You're sure?"

I nod, bringing my mouth back against his as his hands run down my arms, luring me closer. His lips are cool on mine, but I still taste the beers he had earlier as he deepens the kiss while his hands tease the short hemline of my dress.

"Fuck, this dress has been torturing me all night." His voice is a groan as he fists his hands in the back of said torture device.

"I-it has?"

"My lips were fucking dying for a taste of all this skin."

My core throbs at the possessive tone of his admission. Reaching behind me, I grasp the zipper, pulling it down, feeling his hands relish the skin being revealed inch by agonizing inch. His mouth finds the tendon where my neck and shoulder meet and he sinks his teeth roughly into the spot before laving the mark with his tongue.

With a cry, I forget the zipper, burying my hands in his hair as his head moves down, dropping kisses along my collarbone. His fingers finish the job I neglect, his lips move to tongue the lace between the valley of my breasts. As the zipper lowers, the fabric against my chest loosens and he noses it further aside to capture a nipple between his lips.

"Oh." I arch my back, pushing myself toward him, trying to get more of the bursts of light that spark behind my eyes. Jackson's hands move to push the shoulders of the dress down my arms, pooling the material around my waist. The dress hangs there for a beat before he keeps going, over my hips, until it flutters to puddle at my feet.

I reach for him as he steps back to rake his gaze from my head to my feet. I'm still in the high, thin heels from earlier and a pair of black lacy thong underwear. Warmth rises up my chest and neck, settling in my cheeks as he bites his lower lip, teeth sinking into the swollen flesh while his eyes glitter in the semi-darkness.

"Fucking beautiful." His fingers trail along my flushed skin and my eyes drift shut at the intense look on his face. I sway slightly on my feet, unable to hold still as the lightning strikes where his fingers trace to arc to my core. The persistent ache causes my thighs to clench. With a drop of his head, he tugs a nipple back into his mouth while his hands palm my ass to pull me against his erection. I whimper, my hands clutching his shoulders as I fist the smooth material of his shirt.

He releases the nipple with a pop and straightens. My eyes open slowly as cool air rushes against the tight peak.

"Undress me, gorgeous."

My fingers start clumsily at the top button, my breasts quivering as they ache for his touch. My confidence grows as I work down the placket of buttons to tug his shirt from his jeans. His chest is warm and the hair rubs against my palms as I smooth my hands back up, catching the shoulders of his shirt to push it off, letting it bunch at his wrists before I set each hand free to watch his shirt join my dress on the floor. The ache between my thighs pulses and I press myself against him, kissing the scruff at his jawline, while I bring my hands to his belt. The sound he makes urges me on as I unfasten the belt and fly on his jeans with quick fingers. Jackson helps with his zipper, toeing off his boots before he strips himself of jeans and boxers at the same time.

His erection, freed from the confines of denim and cotton, stretches toward me. I'm drawn to it, a mix of excitement and concern about how everything is going to work battling it out to dominate my mind. My hand wraps around him and I marvel at the smoothness of his skin, the heat that feels like it could singe my palm. Jackson hisses and I let go, worried I've done something wrong. Grabbing my hand before I can get too far, he wraps his fingers around mine, keeping me in place.

"Fucking hell." His voice is nothing but gravel, the muscle in his jaw working while every muscle tenses with his fight for control. He thrusts his hips into my hand and I squeeze gently. On a groan his lips find mine and my nipples bead where they brush against his chest.

With our mouths fused together in a kiss, he walks us to the bed and falls back onto it, holding me close so I bounce slightly against him as he lands. The friction of my breasts rubbing against the hard planes of his chest starts a moan I can't stop, and I flex the hand holding him.

Another deep groan rips from his throat, his fingers disentangling mine. "No more."

Between one breath and the next he rolls us, the cool sheets on my back a counterpoint to the trail of heat created as his mouth moves down my chest, spending time with each breast as he tongues one hardened point and then the other. My body rubs against the bed, seeking relief, his kisses trailing down my stomach.

"I don't think you'll need these." He draws the small lace scrap of underwear down my legs. "But these can stay." He taps a heel, fire burning up my body at the image his words conjure. His chuckle is dark as he makes his way back up my body, kissing one thigh and then the other before nuzzling their apex.

His growl vibrates against my center before he swirls his tongue in my belly button then comes back up to my breasts.

"And your fucking tits." Electric current travels through my body at the deliciously dirty things he says. Closing his mouth around my nipple, he alternates swirls of his tongue with light nibbles. My fingers wind their way into his soft hair, holding him closer while my thighs part, allowing him to settle between them. One calloused hand trails lightly down my side before he brushes against me, his fingers skimming my folds. With a whimper, my thighs tighten around his, pleasure building higher. "So wet for me."

Dragging his fingers through my slickness, he slides them to the bundle of nerves tight with need. One finger traces a lazy circle, once, twice, and my hips shift restlessly with the orgasm that builds. His hands torture me, keeping the grand finale of fireworks barely out of reach until I feel like I'm going to explode right along with them.

"Jackson."

His mouth nibbles at my distended nipple and I groan, eyes squeezing shut as the bliss centers to a point of white-hot pleasure. "I need..."

"You need?" His fingers take another turn around my clit before one finger presses knuckle deep inside me. It's not enough, only heightening the need to frantic levels.

"Please." I lift my hips, attempting to ride his finger. He adds a second and my focus narrows to the feel of his thumb as it brushes against my clit until I can't focus at all. Wave after wave of bright ecstasy breaks over me in a sparkling explosion. My lips scream Jackson's name as my back bows off the bed. His fingers still work, stretching the pleasure until it ebbs. My eyes flutter open as the climax recedes, I watch as he brings his fingers to his mouth, licking them, groaning at my taste.

"Stay put." His voice is almost unrecognizable as he stands quickly, scrambling for his jeans, coming back into the room with a gold packet clutched triumphantly between two fingers. His eyes heat as they roam my naked body, still tingling with the aftermath. In one breath, he sobers, looking at me from where he stands.

"Are you sure? We can stop now. Say the word."

"Jackson, I want you." My arms open with my response, my smile widening at how quickly he rejoins me on the bed. His hands shift my legs further apart before he glances down, groaning, dropping his forehead to meet mine and claiming my lips in a swift kiss.

"I need you to tell me, gorgeous." His words are a desperate whisper against my lips. "I need to know if I'm going too fast."

Nerves flutter in my stomach. I'm going to have to talk through this?

"Promise me." His eyes are serious on mine, waiting for my response.

"I promise."

Jackson groans, ripping open the packet and rolling the condom on. My muscles tense, unsure of what to expect, my core clenching as he positions himself at my entrance. "Relax, baby."

I nod, attempting to do as he says as I feel him nudge forward. The friction of his cock rubbing against my already sensitive clit sends more aftershocks shooting to my core. Closing my eyes, I moan, lifting my hips slightly against him, but then pause when a tight sensation starts to creep in on the pleasure. Jackson pushes a little further, and the pain overwhelms the pleasure, radiating from where he continues to move slowly, inch by inch. I whimper again and he freezes. Sweat gathers at his temples, visible when he leans down, pressing a kiss to my forehead.

"I'm sorry," he says.

He thrusts all the way in and holds still, allowing my body to adjust as though he can feel the pain zipping through me in a blinding white flash. It steals my breath as tears gather in my eyes. His voice whispers to me but I can't make out his words until the pain starts to recede. My eyes open to see his face lined with worry.

"Charlotte?"

I give him a shaky smile. "I'm okay." Saying it just as much for myself as for him, the pain is less intense now. He moves slowly, his gaze never leaving mine.

"How's that?" Jackson pulls almost all the way out before pushing back in at the same molasses-like pace until he's buried inside me completely again.

"Better."

Another slow withdrawal and push forward. "Still okay?" His voice is strained and sweat runs down his neck at the effort he's using to maintain control. Nodding, I lick my lips, moaning as he bottoms out again. My muscles pulse around him, my next groan the signal he's been waiting for. His pace speeds up and my body tightens in a race to another orgasm as Jackson increases his tempo. Emboldened as the pleasure overrides the pain, I meet his thrust with one of my own.

"Oh fuck…Charlotte." He falters, recovering to an even faster pace. I run my hands over his back to dig my nails into his shoulders.

"Ja-Jackson." My body is right on the edge and he shifts us slightly, bringing a finger to my clit. With one touch, I tumble over the cliff, taking him with me.

CHAPTER 13

JAX

Holy fuck. Does my brain still reside in my body? My lungs are working overtime as they try to gulp and replenish oxygen, so I guess so. I roll to the side, tugging Charlotte with me. A wince mars her face as I slide out, a reminder that this was her first time.

"I'm sorry." I graze my lips against her forehead. "I didn't want to hurt you."

She meets my eyes, her voice quiet but strong. "I'm okay."

The brown depths of her eyes remind me of firelight through whiskey, flecks of gold sparking in the deep brown.

"You're sure?" I ask. Relief floods me when she nods. "Be right back."

To climb out of bed with her still naked in it is one of the hardest things I've ever done. Enough light filters into the dark bathroom that I can see to dispose of the condom and use a washcloth to clean myself up before I grab another and rinse the stiff cotton in warm water.

Charlotte is under the sheet when I return, the white linen wrapped up to her neck. Forcing down the smile that threatens at the picture she makes, I focus on her silky hair spread out against the pillow, the mahogany strands contrasting with the white sheets, her pale skin glowing. Her eyes travel down my chest, growing wide when she takes in my dick before quickly coming back to my face. The smirk on my lips is impossible to hide, but I soften it to a smile when I sit next to her on the bed.

"Here." Grabbing a hold of the sheet that's clutched in her hands, I try to tug it down. She squeaks and holds it tighter while a red hue creeps up her chest and neck. "No reason to be embarrassed, baby."

My lips cover hers in a featherlight kiss, a languid meeting of tongues and with a broken sigh, her fingers release the sheet to tangle in my hair. Her nails prick my scalp, bringing my mind back to the task at hand and I move the sheet down. My fingers slowly skim her velvet skin, dragging goosebumps down her body. She stiffens when my hand brushes the apex to her thighs, and I gentle my touch further.

Another tangle of tongues leaves her legs parting on a light whimper, her responsiveness to my kisses having a predictable response on my dick—it's fucking hot how quickly her passion meets my own. Tossing the used cloth in the corner, I crawl back next to her in the bed, tunneling an arm underneath her and drawing her to me so that her head rests on my chest. I can hear the wheels turning. "What's on your mind, gorgeous?"

"My mind?" Her lashes flutter and tickle against my chest.

"A million miles away right now, aren't you?" My fingers trace random patterns along her shoulder.

"A little."

"What were you thinking about?"

"It's stupid." Her voice is muffled as she turns into my chest, and my laugh vibrates against her forehead.

"I doubt that." Keeping her from burrowing further into me, I remind her. "You can tell me anything."

Worry edges in when she remains silent. What does she not want to tell me? Did I hurt her more than she's letting on? Does she want me to leave?

Her deep sigh keeps me mostly patient, despite the questions running through my mind with every second that ticks by. So far, whenever I wait, she tells me—anything from what she wants to how she's feeling. All kinds of scenarios skip through my mind in the silence, and sweat beads on my forehead. Another breath blows across my chest.

"I was thinking—" She stops, and I can't tell for sure, but I'd bet money that she's chewing on her lip again.

"You were thinking?" I prompt. "What were you thinking about?"

"About…what…wejustdid." The words tumble out in a mess.

"Okay?" I'm not sure why this sudden case of nerves has her closing off. It'd be fucking adorable if it wasn't scaring the shit out of me thinking she regretted what just happened.

"Well, I…you know."

"I know what?" This conversation is not clearing up my confusion.

Her hand creeps up, covering the little bit of face not hidden in my chest. "Orgasmed."

Did I hear her right? Her whisper is so quiet I can't be sure. "You what?"

"Orgasmed." Still a mumble, but at least loud enough to confirm what I thought I heard.

A shit eating grin splits my face. "You did." I don't even have to question that, remembering the feel of her muscles flexing around my cock.

"So…you probably know…I li-liked it." Her adorableness is killing me.

"I hope so," I tell her.

Her nod brushes against my chest. "Did you?"

These words are the quietest yet, but I don't ask her to repeat them. Stifling the laugh that threatens to bubble up that would send the wrong message, I finally understand that her distraction is not in regretting having sex, but concern that I didn't enjoy myself, and every muscle in my body relaxes.

"Did I…enjoy having sex with you?"

She groans into my chest, her head stuck like superglue when I attempt to get her to look at me.

"Charlotte. Gorgeous. Look at me." I succeed in prying her head up and our eyes meet. "What we just did? That was fucking incredible."

Sex with her is a new experience. It's skydiving and fireside cuddling all at once. My cock stands at attention, ready to show her how much I enjoyed it with round two. Charlotte gasps, finally noticing. Kissing the tip of her nose, I reassure her. "Not tonight, gorgeous. He'll behave."

Grinning, she lowers her head back to my chest.

"I have to ask you something," I say. Her head props up on her hand to look at me, and it's my turn to be nervous. "What, um, what inspired all of this tonight?" I ask. I never would have pictured her initiating our first time.

Her face pinkens but her eyes don't leave mine. "You."

"Me?"

"Around you I feel like I've never felt before. Brave. Confident. Special. I'm not afraid to go after what I want when I'm with you," she admits.

Lifting my head, I brush my lips against hers. A lopsided grin kicks up one side of my mouth. "I just thought you wanted to watch a movie again."

We both laugh quietly for a moment.

"Sing to me?" she asks, all soft and drowsy.

"You really want me to sing to you?"

Her hair moves like silk along my chest with her nod. Hands

roaming her back, I start to sing quietly, a whisper of sound in the room. Her body melts against mine during the first song, and by the end of the second, she's asleep. Her rhythmic breathing is my lullaby as I fall asleep to the feel of her chest rising and falling against mine.

♪♪♪ ♪♪♪♪♪

The closed curtains dim the sun's glow when I wake up. Charlotte is snuggled against me, her back to my front, and my dick pushes insistently against her ass, still ready for the round two I denied him last night. My nose is buried in her hair, the faint smell of coconut teasing me on every inhale. Her hip is warm and smooth under the possessive grip of my fingers, holding on as though I was drawing her to me even in my sleep. With every breath she takes, her shoulder dips and I find myself drawn to the freckles that dust along the top it. Do they continue to the other one? Her leg tenses under my hand, a sign that she's waking up.

"Morning, beautiful." Her shoulder is warm and smooth under my lips, her eyes fuzzy with sleep when she turns her head to look at me.

"Morning." Her lips are a deeper pink against her pale skin, drawing mine like a magnet. We connect in a sleepy kiss, my lips moving slowly, nibbling at hers before breaking away.

"How'd you sleep?" I ask.

"Good." Her arms stretch in front of her, and the movement presses her ass against me, and I bite back a groan. "You?"

The question ends on a gasp as she feels me rock-hard behind her.

"Ignore him." Teasing another kiss against her shoulder, I refrain from flexing my hips against her the way my body begs me to. "I slept like a baby. Are you hungry?"

She nods. "Starving."

"You wanna go grab some breakfast?" The sheet pools at my

waist as I sit up. She rolls over with the sheet tucked around her chest, denying me a look at the rest of her. My pout morphs into a smile as her eyes dart down my chest, light pink tongue dragging across her lips. My cock jumps under the sheet, but I don't think she notices. "Charlotte?"

She blinks, eyes refocusing on my face. My smile grows at how amused I am by her distraction with my naked chest.

"Hmm?"

"Breakfast? Do you want to go grab breakfast?"

"Yeah."

I stand and head for my jeans, my skin heating under her gaze. I'm comfortable with my nakedness—she can look however much she wants—and I doubt she even knows she's doing it. It's another unknown response that turns me on to the point where jumping back in bed with her for the day sounds better and better.

I whistle when I notice the time on my phone. "I guess lunch would be a better idea."

"Really?" Her eyes widen before pinging around my body.

"See anything you like?" I can't help the laugh that escapes at her expression, embarrassment at being caught mixed with lust. I tug at the sheet still clutched around her, teasing her. "We should shower."

I move for the bathroom, the heat of her gaze singeing my shoulder blades. Almost to the bathroom, I turn and catch her ogling my backside. "Coming?"

"Don't you need clothes?"

I shrug. "I can wear mine from last night back to my room when we're ready. Change before we grab food."

Charlotte's feet touch the floor and she stands, wrapping the sheet around her. Her hair cascades down her back, a waterfall of russet silk against the white. A Greek goddess in the flesh. I lead the way to the bathroom and flip the water on while Charlotte stands in the door, her tawny eyes wide and watchful. My eyes meet hers, nostrils flaring as she releases the sheet. Fuck. How am I supposed to keep my hands to myself when she does that?

The smile on her face tells me she knows what she just did. She brushes past me to step into the shower and the water turns her hair nearly black. Joining her, my eyes follow the water sluicing down her neck, across her breasts before making its way down her stomach and thighs. I memorize the path, my cock hardening painfully while I growl at the torture in front of me.

Desperation claws at my stomach even as my head reminds me that she needs time to recover. The reminder doesn't stop images as they filter in of me lifting her against the wall, pounding into her until she screams my name. They grow stronger the longer we stand here. Charlotte's eyes open at my growl.

"Everything okay?" She has no idea the war that wages in my head, the effect she has on me.

"You are so goddamned beautiful." My lips bruise hers in a kiss, all tongue as I back her against the tile wall. One small lift could have her poised above me. Fuck.

I gentle the kiss and watch those mesmerizing eyes of hers open, flecks of gold shining in the bathroom light. My cock jumps between us with the flat-out fucking need I have to be inside her again. Instead, I grab the shampoo, filling my hands with it and washing her hair instead of worshiping her body the way I want to.

The warm water and steam have turned her entire body a light pink. Taking my time, I wash and rinse her hair, then use the body wash to slide my hands against her slick skin. My dick weeps at my slow, unhurried pace, but I ignore it. When I finish rinsing soap from her body, I grab the shampoo again and wash my hair while she watches me.

"Does that hurt?"

I open one eye as shampoo rinses down my neck. "What?"

Her hand gestures to my dick, not even close to deflating. “That.”

“My dick?” I choke back the laugh that threatens. “Not like you’d think. I fucking ache to be inside you again, but he can wait.”

Shutting off the water, I wrap towels around both of us and tug her into my arms.

“I meant what I said last night,” she says softly. Her dark hair is slicked back from her face when she looks up at me.

“What?”

“I want to be with you.” Her voice strengthens with her words. I lift her off her feet, pressing a kiss against her lips. “Fuck the label.”

Having never heard Charlotte cuss, I nearly drop her. Her cheeks pinken with her statement. I repeat it, raising my eyebrow. “Fuck the label?”

“I mean. Who cares what they’re going to do? Let them. We’ll just be us.”

My lips slant against hers, tongue plunging into her mouth as desire surges through me. I nod my agreement. “Us.”

CHAPTER 14

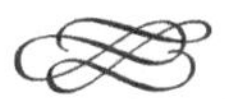

JAX

It's Charlotte. My shows are definitely better when she's here. The spark reignited tonight, reminding me why I wanted to do this in the first place. With her, all the other thoughts clamoring for attention fade. Leaving the stage, I head straight for her, sweeping her up in my sweaty embrace.

"That was incredible!" Her squeal is cut off as my lips capture hers, and the kiss escalates until my dick is pressing against my jeans and I have to come up for air or suffocate. Even then, it's a tough choice.

"Thank you, baby. I love that you're here and I can do this right now." My arms squeeze around her while she giggles.

"After-party, bitches!" Meredith interrupts, hugging both of us to her before disappearing into a crowd that feels larger than normal surging around us. Charlotte stays securely wrapped under my arm as we head to the door of the rehearsal space.

"Wait here for me?" She nods, ducking into the empty room and closing the door for good measure. People call my name and

I wave, my long stride eating up the path to my dressing room to avoid stopping. My phone pings with a message and a quick glance shows a new text from Nick.

NICK: Numbers are up. Don't fuck this up. Good things on the horizon. Talk later.

I don't bother responding before I step into the shower for the quickest one I can manage. If anyone saw me trying to be stealthy on my way back to the rehearsal space, I'd have some explaining to do. Fortunately, no one is still lurking in the hallways, either busy tearing down the set or partying in the hospitality suite. The door opens soundlessly to the rehearsal space where I left Charlotte. It's our first meeting all over again, her walking the perimeter of the room without realizing I'm watching.

"Hey." I close the door, the lock snick quiet accompaniment behind me.

"Hey." She watches me lean against the door, frozen where she stands across the room, her denim skirt and tank top reminding me of the first concert she saw and our time after it. She'd been so incredibly sexy that night, dressed much like the way she is now. My mouth waters for a taste of her even as my dick punches at my zipper.

Moving closer, her chest rises and falls with each breath. My connection to her is a living thing, pulsing between us in the room that I suddenly don't want to leave, but it's not just up to me.

"Want to go to the after-party?"

"Not really?" Her grimace gives me more of an answer. With so many people, our absence shouldn't be noticed. I'd rather be here with her, alone. Or back in our hotel room. "Can we stay here a bit longer?"

Is she thinking about our dance after the Denver concert? Does she want me half as much as I want her right now?

"Gorgeous, we can stay here the whole time." I let Meredith know we won't be there with a quick text.

Charlotte fiddles at the sound system for a moment before music beats quietly from the speakers. She crosses to me, so close that every time she breathes her breasts brush my chest. "Dance with me?"

One side of my mouth curves in a half smile as I spin her so her back bumps up to my chest. The beat of the song moves her body against mine while her hips sway to the music. I grip them lightly, shifting her against me as Tove Lo sings about talking bodies.

My dick strains against my zipper and I do what I did that first night, trailing hot, open-mouthed kisses to her neck, sucking her earlobe into my mouth before nibbling lightly. It's as if the whole day has been building to this minute and Charlotte is right there with me. My lips have a mind of their own, moving to trace the freckles that dust her shoulders. She moans, pressing her ass against me even more.

"Fuck, baby, you feel so good."

My hands reach up to cup her breasts and my fingers pluck at her nipples through the thin fabric of her shirt. Her fingers reach up to clasp around my neck, pushing her breasts even more into my hands while a wolfish grin quirks my lips against the column of her throat.

"Jackson." The siren's call of my name on her lips renders me powerless against her. "What are you doing to me?"

"The same thing you're doing to me." My response is a muffled growl against her shoulder. I spin her again to devour her lips before my tongue dips to taste her. Memories of that first night hit me, past and present blurring together as one of my legs moves between hers, and my hips move us to the music. Long lashes flutter, revealing whiskey-colored eyes full of desire. Her mouth is slick, swollen with our kisses, and begs me to kiss her again.

Mine. Possessiveness spreads through my body and I deepen the kiss while need beats ferociously through my blood. My hands move under her denim skirt, the smooth skin of her ass telling me that she's worn another thong. My fingers flex and she moans, the sound muffled by the fusion of mouths.

Her hands trail up my chest and unravel the small threads of my control when her fingers spear into my hair.

"Charlotte." Her name is a groan as I kiss down her neck, nosing the strap of her tank top down her arm before it snags on her shoulder. My fingers release her ass to dip further and trace the outside of her panties. I nibble at the strap of her top, gripping it in my teeth to tug it apart before nuzzling the loosened strap off her shoulder completely. "Fuck, baby, you're so wet."

My mouth moves to the other strap to repeat the steps while my fingers continue to stroke her through the damp fabric. Her shirt falls to her waist as the second tie loosens, leaving her bare to my gaze. Lust clouds my vision and I dip my head to capture a beaded nipple into my mouth. Her fingers tense in my hair, the slight tug of pain registering enough that I bite down gently. Her voice breaks as she cries out. Her panties are soaked, the smell of her arousal heavy in the air. Sliding under the edge of lace, I trace her swollen lips.

"Oh god." Charlotte's voice is a breathy gasp in the quiet room, the only backdrop the music that plays around us. My fingers trace circles around her clit, additional moisture coating my fingers.

"Are you sore, baby?" My voice is a raspy whisper against her ear.

"Ah...no?"

"No?" My mouth finds her other nipple, hands gripping her hips as she pushes closer. I release her nipple with a pop. "That sounds like a question."

She shakes her head, hands still tangled in my hair as I nip along her jawline. "No. Not sore. Jackson. Please." Her words break off in a moan as my tongue traces the shell of her ear.

Boosting her in my arms, she wraps her legs around my waist while I move until her back presses against the mirrored wall. The sight of Charlotte's body pressed to mine, her breasts rosy and nipples puckered from my attention, is so fucking erotic I have to close my eyes again. My knuckles graze her clit as I fist her panties and, with a rip, they flutter to the floor below us.

I pin her upright with my hips while my hand works frantically at the fly of my jeans, loosening them. I'd rather touch her. I grab the condom that's tucked into the front pocket, then rip the foil with my teeth and free my cock. Condom rolled on, my cock nudges her entrance. In one swift motion, I push inside her, groaning as her tight walls spasm around me.

"*Fuck*. Gorgeous."

Her pussy clenches around me. She's close. My lips trace her jawline, hips moving in and out of her while her head leans back against the mirrors. I take the invitation, dropping my head to suck a nipple back into my mouth. Christ, she tastes amazing. My orgasm speeds toward me and I need her to come.

I bite down, sharper than before, tugging and plucking until she shatters around me. My hips lose their rhythm, pistoning in and out as the orgasm surges from my spine into my balls and I still inside her. My chest heaves as I regain coherent thought, and I lean my forehead against hers, our breaths mingling between us. Charlotte's legs disengage from around my waist as she slides down my body, boneless against me. How the fuck am I supposed to let her go after this?

♪♪♪♪♪

My stomach churns as the car stops and she lifts her head from my shoulder. The plane glimmers in front of us, a real reminder that our weekend is nearly done. Squeezing her hand, I unfold myself from the backseat, tugging her with me.

"I feel like Cinderella at midnight." The words are a mumble against my chest as she snuggles into me. "Can't we just stay here?"

Her question makes me chuckle—I'd been thinking the same thing—and I breathe deeply. She doesn't smell like her, but instead the smell of my body wash fills my nose. "I'm sure there's an FAA regulation against that, gorgeous."

Her laughter fades as her eyes meet mine. Lifting on her toes, her lips graze the scruff on my chin while mine brush the tip of her nose.

"I'm going to fucking miss you." It's embarrassing to admit, but I don't want her to leave without telling her.

"I'm going to miss you too." Her arms cling to me as we watch the door descend from the plane. When she pulls back, I track a finger along her jawline, smiling as a shiver works down her body. Leaning down, my lips touch hers. Her grip tightens along the back of my biceps as she returns the kiss.

Once we both need to come up for oxygen, my lips brush her forehead. "It's not goodbye." Whiskey colored eyes turn watery because it *is* a goodbye. "Another month for the tour. That's it and we'll FaceTime and text and call the whole time."

She nods, tears still trailing her cheeks. I gently cup her face and thumb away the wetness.

"I have to go," she whispers.

"I know." I snag her backpack sitting next to her feet, sliding the strap up her arm before settling it on her shoulder.

"I'll text you when I land."

"No." Shaking my head, my eyes lock on hers. "Call me. I want to hear your voice tonight."

She nods before turning toward the plane.

"Hey, gorgeous?" A light smile plays on her lips when she turns around. "Safe flight, okay?"

She nods again before turning back around, walking to the plane and disappearing through the door.

I stand motionless as the plane taxis away for takeoff. My phone rings as soon as I shut the car door, still searching for a plane I'm sure I can't see anymore.

"Hello?"

"Did you talk to her yet?" I'm surprised this is the first time I've heard from Nick all weekend since he's been calling or texting me daily to get my answer.

"Jesus, do you ever hound anyone else the way you do me?" I rub the back of my neck while a scream sits right at the tip of my tongue. Frustration and sadness mix to result in no filter.

"Well, if you did as you were told the first time, I wouldn't have to keep calling."

"I talked to her." Grinding my teeth, I bite back what I really want to say. *Fuck you* doesn't seem like a smart thing to say to Nick.

"Okay? Do I get a name here, Jax?"

"Charlotte. Charlie," I quickly correct.

"Is Charlie on board?"

"We're seeing each other."

"Is she ready to be part of your image?"

"Fuck, I don't know. I don't care." I just want him off my ass and off the phone. "We're seeing each other. Tell Randa. Do what you need to do. Just keep us out of it."

"Jackson, I—" Nick's voice is softer, less harsh than normal. The human coming out to play. "I'm only trying to help keep you out of trouble. To help you keep your dream."

"Your job." The anger deflates, and I'm left with the melancholy feeling from my goodbye.

He clears his throat and the human side disappears again, vanishing as quickly as it appeared. "You remember the text I sent you last night after the show?"

"Yeah?"

"The producers of the Annual Music Awards want you to present at this year's show."

My mind blanks while his words sink in. "Seriously?"

"As a heart attack, Jax. The chick I talked to kept asking about 'Denver Delight.'" He laughs.

"Does this mean you're finally happy?"

"Dude, Randa's over the goddamned moon with this latest information. Almost enough to forget about your antics from the last tour." Damnit. Scrubbing a hand down my face, I'm at a loss. Will anything ever make them forget that shit? Or will it always be used to manipulate me? "Maybe Charlotte will get them the rest of the way there."

"Charlie."

"What?"

"Charlie. Call her that." Not Charlotte. That's mine.

"Okay." Nick draws out the word, I'm sure questioning my sanity. "The producers for the awards want your confirmation."

"When's the show this year?"

"End of your tour. You have time."

"Okay, yeah, let's do it."

"Fuck yes. I'll get details to you ASAP. Have a good show in Wyoming. And seriously, don't fuck this up."

"Jesus Christ, Nick. I'm trying. I've been on my best behavior for over a goddamned year."

"So, keep being on your best behavior and the label will stay off your ass."

"Will you?" My smart-ass comeback goes unanswered since Nick already hung up. I've done everything the label's asked me to do—what more can they possibly want?

CHAPTER 15

CHARLIE

"Chawie, coo-keys?" Bella points a chubby finger to a package of chocolate chip cookies on the shelf I've been staring vacantly at while memories of my weekend with Jackson play on repeat in my head. Wide, pleading eyes capture mine.

"I dunno, Bells, it's not on our list." All I want to do is say yes, wanting to share the bubbles of happiness that dance in me like champagne. I'm drunk on this feeling, drunk on my weekend with Jackson and the confidence he's inspiring in me.

"Pwease, Chawie?" The lower lip that protrudes in a pout tips the scales in her favor.

"Okay, you little con artist." I'll deal with the fallout at home since Mom and Dad don't like to encourage junk food in the house. Ruffling Bella's downy hair, I grab the package and toss it in the cart. Bella chats happily with the stuffed animal tucked in the cart with her while we cruise the aisles.

This morning before we'd left, a big bouquet of pale pink

roses showed up with a card. *Wish I could give these to you in person. Xoxo, J.* When I'd texted to thank him, he'd told me that the pale pink had reminded him of my blushes from the weekend. I'd taken a selfie and sent it to him, proving him right.

Picking the shortest grocery line, I wait for my turn to check out, eyeing the time carefully. Bella's nap time is getting closer and my goal is to get her out of the store without a meltdown. My attention drifts to the magazines lining the checkout counter, and a picture on one captures my attention. Jackson and I are leaving the club my first night in Vegas, fingers intertwined.

Jax spotted with Denver Delight in Vegas. The headline teases that the magazine has additional information inside. On autopilot, I add the magazine to the belt, looking around for someone to pop up with a camera. It's not until after we're home, groceries are put away and I'm able to get Bella settled for a nap that I dare to scan the article.

> *Jax Bryant is BACK. This sinfully sexy singer seems to have finally polished his reputation after some disastrous events during his last tour. Bryant's DREAMS tour stopped in Vegas over the weekend where he checked out the nightlife with a brunette beauty. According to a rep with Reverb Records, Bryant's beauty is Charlie Walker, a young dancer who calls Colorado home. Readers will remember that the two were recently caught canoodling after his concert in Denver. Now the lovebirds have been spotted in Vegas. According to sources close to Bryant, the two recently started dating and are happy to be able to spend time together. Break out the tissues, ladies, it looks like Jax is officially off the market.*

Taking a deep breath, I read through the brief blurb a second time. They know my name. They know where I live. Overall, the article is positive, and I know it's exactly what the label wanted. But I hadn't expected that seeing my name and face would create the panicked edge I'm feeling. Finished with the article, I text Jackson.

CHARLOTTE: Jackson, can you call me when you're free?

The phone rings almost immediately.

"Charlotte? Everything okay?"

"There's a picture. Of you and me. They know my name. They know where I live."

"Already? Jesus, Nick got that info out fast." His voice is muffled, like he's not actually talking to me.

"What? What happened?" I'd told him I didn't care what the label did, but a little advanced warning would have been nice.

"I'm sorry, gorgeous. I hadn't had a chance to call you yet. Nick told me last night that they'd gotten some questions and pictures from Vegas." His voice lowers until he's whispering into the phone. "This doesn't change anything, Charlotte. You're still my girl." The tone of his voice sinks in. Is he worried that I changed my mind?

"It's us," I reassure him. I'm not changing my mind.

"Us," He repeats. "Fuck the label."

I laugh slightly as he repeats what I said to him.

"I gotta go, baby. Call you after the show?"

"Okay." I have no idea what I interrupted in his day and I know how busy his schedule usually is. The fact that he called me so quickly tells me he's still listening to me, even miles away.

♪♪♪ ♪♪♪♪♪

Mom and Dad being surprised by some random news article would make the situation at home worse than it already is, so I approach both of them that evening.

"You remember how I went to the concert in Denver to see Meredith?" I wring the magazine in my hands while they nod. "I met someone there."

"What do you mean, Charlie? Who did you meet?" Mom's

eyes move from the magazine to the flowers sitting on the table. "Did you get flowers?"

"Yes, they're from Jackson. The guy I met." Neither of them shows any recognition of his name. "Jackson as in Jax Bryant." Mom's eyes widen and I hand them the magazine. "When I went to Vegas this weekend, I spent time with Meredith, but I also spent more time with Jackson. We're...together."

Two sets of eyes fall to the magazine. Mom flips through until she reads the same article I did, gasping when she gets to the part that lists my name and where I'm from.

"Charlie, I don't know how I feel about this."

"I know exactly how I feel about this." Dad crosses his arms across his chest. "I don't want our name dragged through trash like that." He indicates the magazine with a tilt of his head. I don't bother to tell him that this isn't a tabloid. "Nor do I think now is the best time to be getting involved with anyone."

"What? Why?"

"Your mother and I just got news at work. Our schedules are going to be changing and we're going to need you to shift your schedule to watch Bella more. And I don't want her at-risk from tacky reporters looking for a story." Mom and Dad working together for the same tech company in Broomfield has already caused problems with scheduling my classes at the studio.

"What do you mean my schedule has to change?" Dread crawls through me.

"Charlie, your dad and I were talking. With the schedule change and everything, you'll need to tell Madame Laurent that you can't teach there as much—"

"So obviously, since you two have talked about it, you've known for a while." Shaking my head, I can't believe what I'm hearing. "Teach there as much? I teach two classes a week."

"We're going to need you to stop teaching, at least for now, there's a special project—"

"No. This—" I sputter, gesturing to the kitchen and house.

"This was supposed to be temporary, remember? A few months while I recovered from surgery. It's been a year. I'm still watching Bella. What about my life? My dreams? I have an audition to prep for. It's in LA at the end of the month. Madame Laurent told me about it, a friend of hers with a casting company."

"Charlie, what do you expect to happen with this audition?"

"If I dance well, I'll get the job."

"And then what?"

"What do you mean?" Red flags tell me I already know the answer, but despite the rock in my stomach, I ask.

"The doctors said they weren't sure you'd recover completely."

"How would you know? Were either of you there? Did either of you bother showing up when I had surgery? I'll tell you the answer, no. *My* doctor, my instructors, even Madame have all told me that I am capable of doing what I did before."

"What if you are and you still don't find a job? What's your future then?"

Speechless, I can only stare as my dad looks at me, a mix of pity and resignation on his face. My mouth hangs open as my brain tries to process what he's just said. Mom squeezes his arm, a silent show of support.

"You don't think I can do it?" Tears burn the backs of my eyes, disappointment and frustration combined.

"It's not realistic." He tosses the magazine into the trash can. "And neither is this boy."

Something snaps. From somewhere inside, fire sparks reminders of conversations I've had with Meredith, with Jackson. To speak up. Tears disappear in the wake of fire, burning over the fear and awkwardness that normally keep me quiet.

"No."

"No?" Dad shakes his head, like he didn't hear me correctly.

"I'm not always going to be here to watch Bella. You need to figure something else out. I am auditioning in LA at the end of the month. It's going to require extra work which means I won't be here as much." I turn to leave, having said everything on the tip of my tongue, but turn around. "This is my life, my choice. I am going to keep seeing Jackson. I care about him and he cares about me."

Reaching the stairs, I turn once more. "I will help with Bella when I can. She's my sister and I love her. But I need to find my path. I'd like your support in that, but I'll do it on my own if I have to. I'm sorry I'm your reminder."

"Reminder?" Mom and Dad look at each other before looking at me.

"From before. The way it used to be."

"When Dad and I weren't together?" Mom's voice wavers, making me feel worse.

I nod. "I get that it's awkward. Me being here. But treating me like a little kid isn't going to work. I'm an adult. I just want you to respect that."

Mom nods. "Of course we respect that, Charlie."

Dad doesn't say anything. Emotions play across his face—sadness, disappointment, resignation—before he turns, leaving the room. Mom watches him before turning back to me.

"Give us some time to talk, Charlie."

I nod and head for my room. Closing the door, I lean against it. Holy crap. The weight falls off my shoulders after finally saying everything that has been burning in my stomach for the last year. My heart jackhammers in my chest as what I've just done hits me.

Yes, I stood up for myself, but what does that mean? Uneasiness and exhaustion settle over me like a weighted blanket, the adrenaline from my confrontation fading. Mom and Dad will have more to say, I'm sure.

But something changed tonight. I'm not letting my life happen to me anymore. I have to go for what I want. I'll have to tell Jackson he was right. I do feel better having told my parents the truth.

The only question is, now what?

♪♪♪♪♪♪♪

My phone ringing with an incoming FaceTime call wakes me several hours later. Sitting up, I press the green button and Jackson's bare chest and face fill the screen.

"Hey." My voice is raspy with sleep.

"Hey, gorgeous, did I wake you?" His smile is small as his eyes move over me and drink me in.

"Mmmmmm." I stretch, trying to wake up. "I must have fallen asleep. What time is it?"

"It's late. I'm sorry. Close to two here. I just wanted to see your face before I went to bed." His words create a warmth in my body that's been missing since I first smelled the roses he sent me this morning.

"I'm glad you called. Today sucked."

"It did. What's the matter, gorgeous? You seem more upset than earlier."

"My parents." I'm still not exactly sure what I've done by standing up for myself with them. Mom seems more on board than Dad.

"Are they upset about us?" His eyes flare when I nod.

"They don't want me to be with you. They also want me to quit the studio."

"What?"

"They have some schedule changes at work, and they need me to watch Bella more."

"So, you're gonna quit?"

"No." Determination sparks in my blood, my voice getting louder. "I told them that I wasn't going to quit. That I'd be spending more time at the studio to get ready for that audition I told you about."

I'd shared my plans with him as we walked to the Bellagio Fountains over the weekend.

"You stood up for yourself."

"I did." Nodding, I smile at the look of pride on his face. "And I told them they didn't get to make my choices for me. You're my choice."

"Baby, I'm so fucking proud of you." Ducking my head at his words, I hide behind my hair. "God, I miss you."

Pushing a hand through my tangle of hair, I can tell by the screen that I look like I've been sleeping. "I probably have drool on my face."

He laughs. "No, no drool. Just those beautiful brown eyes of yours."

"Jackson." I'm so awkward when accepting compliments, I have no idea what to say. He chuckles at my reaction.

"I need you to see yourself through my eyes. If I were there right now, I'd make sure you did. Kiss you until you didn't remember ever thinking differently. Start at the top and work my way down." His eyes blaze as they stare at me, dilating until they're nearly black.

My breathing speeds up at his words, at the memory of the way he'd tasted every square inch of my skin. My core pulses in demand, wishing he was here. He shifts on the screen, drawing my attention to the muscles bunching in his chest. My tongue darts out to slick along my lips and he groans. "Damn, I wish you were here with me right now."

"Me too."

"Will you try something with me?" His voice is gritty, the growly sound working goosebumps along my spine. Squirming at the sensation, I nod. "I want to see you, gorgeous. I want to see that amazing body of yours."

Heat climbs through me as his words register. "I want to, too."

"Undress for me." Disentangling from my bed, I look around for something to prop my phone on.

"On your pillows."

I use his suggestion and step back until my full body shows in my screen. Catching my lower lip between my teeth, I grab the hem of my tank top, tugging it up and over my head, dropping it to the floor next to me. My fingers brush the button of my shorts and I pause, teasing him.

"Keep going," he says.

I can't help the smile at his groan. I unsnap my shorts before shimmying them down my legs. Jackson's tongue moves across his mouth as I stand there in my bra and panties, the light in my room dim but still enough for him to see me. My hands reach behind me, unhooking my bra before I let the scrap of material fall to the floor, my panties soon following.

"Fuck me." His gaze lingers on my breasts before following the curve of my hip. "You're so goddamned beautiful."

Walking back to my phone, I pick it up.

"What about you?"

His view shifts, showing me he's already undressed too. My thighs clench at the sight of him, hard, ready for me. The camera changes again and his face is visible, eyes an emerald fire as they burn into mine.

"Touch yourself, gorgeous." His command is a plea, uttered on an exhale. I hesitate, having never done this with an audience. "Baby?"

I nod and lay on my bed, setting up my phone so I can still see him. I close my eyes and focus on the sound of his ragged breathing. Reaching up, my hands cup my breasts and my fingers curl to pinch my nipples where they bead against my palms. A moan comes from my throat, and I imagine it's his hands, his fingers, instead of mine.

"That's it."

"Jackson." My head falls back as I continue to pinch and twist, my hips growing restless as his breathing gets heavier.

"I can practically taste you in my mouth, gorgeous. Fuck, I'm so close."

"Me too." I drag a hand down my stomach, the awkwardness gone with my orgasm on the horizon.

"Touch that sweet pussy for me. Fuck, I bet you're soaking, ready for me, aren't you? Ready for this?"

Opening my eyes, I see his phone angle shift, one of his strong hands working himself. I lick my lips at the sight and my hand dips to move through my folds to my clit.

"Tell me, gorgeous. Tell me how wet you are for me." I moan his name and move the phone so he can see for himself. His growl echoes through the room. "Fuck, I want to taste you so bad right now."

My fingers lose their rhythm at his words, heat spikes through me as the orgasm starts to take over. "Jackson, I'm coming."

Lights flash behind my eyes as the orgasm rips through me in a flash fire of pleasure, my fingers pressing against my clit as waves pulse. He growls his own release, and I open my eyes in time to see it cover his chest and stomach.

The only sound for several minutes is our breathing as we both recover.

"Holy shit, that was hot." Jackson snags a t-shirt off the floor and wipes it across his abs.

Nodding, my eyes grow heavy after the full day. I'm so close to falling asleep that I know he's going to say something about hanging up.

"Don't hang up yet," I slur.

"I won't."

"Sing to me?" Will I ever be able to fall asleep again without that? He starts to sing but my eyes are too tired to stay open.

"Goodnight, gorgeous."

CHAPTER 16

CHARLIE

In the two weeks since my confrontation with Mom and Dad, I've stepped back at home, focused on preparing for the audition that's just a week away. Mom and Dad are making it work, either watching Bella themselves while I'm at rehearsal or finding a sitter. They haven't brought up Jackson again, and we're all avoiding that topic.

He and I haven't had the chance to FaceTime again since his tour has ramped back up, but hearing his voice is almost as good. Heat overwhelms me at the thought of doing another FaceTime, but, for now, it's lunch time in the Walker house and Bella's ready to eat when my phone chimes with a text.

JACKSON: Gorgeous *kiss emoji*
CHARLOTTE: Hey, handsome. *wink emoji*
JACKSON: YOU'LL NEVER BELIEVE WHAT'S HAPPENED!
CHARLOTTE: LOL, what?

A link pops up from him next, sending me to a Top 100 Chart. I'm not sure what I'm looking for, about to ask Jackson, when I see it. #82—Jax Bryant "Dreamer."

CHARLOTTE: OMG, Jackson, that's amazing. *heart-eye emoji*
JACKSON: I literally can't stop smiling, I'm so pumped

He sends a selfie, big smile plastered on his face, while Meredith photobombs in the background, a huge grin on her face and her fist in the air.

CHARLOTTE: I'm so happy for you!
JACKSON: We're celebrating tonight. Wish you were here to help us

"Chawie, I hungwy." Bella's tug on my shirt reminds me that her sandwich is still on the counter.

CHARLOTTE: Me too. *sad emoji* I hate to do this, but I need to go. Bella wants lunch.
JACKSON: Okay, gorgeous, I'll call you later, okay? You'll be back from rehearsal at 8?
CHARLOTTE: Yeah. Can't wait to talk to you.
JACKSON: Me too. *wink emoji*

In a distracted daze, I give Bella her lunch. I really do wish I was there to help Jackson celebrate. Or even just to see him again, have his arms wrap around me, tell me that I'll do great with the audition, that everything with Mom and Dad and their schedule will work out.

Between watching Bella, practicing, and staying up late to talk to Jackson after his shows, my body begs me for sleep. I'm still not one hundred percent—my muscles and ankle constantly ache as I try to pull everything together before the audition. He's told me on the phone that he's rooting for me, asked me what he can do to help, but being so far away, there's not much he can do.

He sends me pictures of different stages being prepped or weird attractions along the different highways as they travel. They're images of his life on the road and I find myself less and less anxious about the nomadic lifestyle he loves.

Yawning, I clean up after Bella eats, swallowing a few ibuprofen with a cup of coffee, hoping for the caffeine boost. Mom should be home while Bella naps and I'll head to the studio to practice, but I'm also strongly considering a nap too.

My phone chimes again as I finish my coffee.

MEREDITH: Hey, bestie
CHARLIE: Hey, are you guys celebrating like crazy right now?
MEREDITH: OMG, Char, Jax is on CLOUD 9 right now. No concert tonight so we're going out to CELEBRATE. *party emoji*

I snort laugh at Meredith's GIF of a little girl shaking with excitement before it hits me. My Google feed is filled with "news" articles speculating about Jackson and me. We haven't been seen together since Vegas and other stories have cropped up that link him to different celebrities. Every time something like that comes up, doubt cramps my stomach. I haven't mentioned anything to Jackson or even Meredith because it's a stupid reaction and I don't want to bother them with gossip. Breathing deeply, I wait for the current doubt pricking me to disappear.

CHARLIE: Try to behave at least a little bit tonight.
MEREDITH: Yeah, yeah, Mom. You got it. *angel emoji*
CHARLIE: Have fun and be safe!
MEREDITH: <3 U, girl!
CHARLIE: Love you too!

Once Bella's asleep, I grab my bag. Mom should be home any minute, and I'm meeting Madame to have her help me with my audition piece.

♪♪♪♪♪♪

Hours later, I've texted Madame and told her that I'm not able to come. I've texted Mom a dozen times and Dad half that. I've tried calling both of them. Panic and frustration war inside. Did something happen? Are they okay? Mom knew I had this practice tonight. Why would she blow me off? She promised.

Relief sets in when I hear the garage door, but in the absence of panic, anger and frustration build with the burn of tears behind my eyes.

"I'm home." Mom comes into the living room where I've been sitting on the couch, my bag at my feet. Her eyes widen as her gaze lands on it. "Oh, Charlie, your practice. I forgot. I'm so sorry."

I stand, shouldering my bag.

"What about all my calls, my texts?"

Mom shrugs, still looking contrite. "I turned my phone off to focus on a report I needed to do at work."

"I've gotta go." My hand is on the doorknob, knuckles white, when she speaks up again.

"You're still going?"

"Yes." I don't trust myself to say anything else right now.

"What about dinner?" I don't know if she's asking if I want dinner or why I didn't make any. I choose to hope it's the former.

"Not hungry," I call over my shoulder.

♪♪♪♪♪♪

The studio is dark when I turn into the vacant lot. Madame went home hours ago. My key slides effortlessly into the lock.

The smells of lemon scented wood polish and Madame's jasmine perfume swirl in the shadows, welcoming me like an old friend as I push the door open. It closes soundlessly behind me and I lock it before walking to the changing rooms in back.

After I change, I head to the smaller of the two studios. I'll never look at a mirror the same way after Vegas. I attempt to push out those memories and warm up, my ankle screaming with my stretch. Pushing through the pain, I finish the basic exercises and move to the stereo system in the corner. Phone plugged in, I start the music, using the fire in my body, the emotions, blending it all together as I bend and flow with the music. I spin and twist to elongate the shape of my body with my arms and legs, driving it to its physical limit. I ignore the tears that drip down my cheeks and stay lost in melodies, in memories.

Songs blend from one to the other until the last song fades to deafening silence, fractured only by my deep breaths. My feet throb in protest as I hobble to the stereo cabinet where my phone sits. Sinking to the floor, I lean my head back against the mirror and cue up Jackson's music, listening to his voice for several minutes in an attempt to soothe my aching body.

"Jackson." His name is a whispered invocation in the quiet, a wish for him to be here so I could curl into him. My heart races when my phone lights up and sinks when I see it's only an email notification.

Rising, I groan at the ache in my legs as I stand. I've been dancing for hours—everyone at home will be asleep by now. I limp to the front door and lock back up, stopping to look up at the dark sky. There are no stars, only a lonely moon, disappearing and reappearing behind clouds like a magician's trick. I shiver, the clouds giving me an odd sense of foreboding.

By the time I get home, it's getting closer to the time that Jackson normally calls me. Maybe we can FaceTime again. I need his smile tonight. Flipping on the shower, I send him a quick text, hoping he'll see it before he calls.

CHARLOTTE: FaceTime tonight?

♪♪♪♪♪♪

My bedroom light is still on and sunlight filters through the curtains when I blink awake. As sleep recedes from my mind, I search frantically for my phone, afraid I've missed Jackson's call since I fell asleep after my shower. I find it shoved under my pillow, but it doesn't show any missed calls or texts.

Did I answer in my sleep and not remember? Unlocking the screen, I don't see any recent calls. I switch to my texts and see the most recent one is delivered but unread. My pulse jumps, racing. Has something happened to him? Jackson always reads my messages, usually responding back immediately unless he's on stage. Inhaling a deep breath, I release it, trying to calm the shaking in my hands to type out another text.

CHARLOTTE: Hey, is everything okay? I didn't hear from you last night...
CHARLOTTE: I'm worried about you. Text me and let me know you're OK.

I follow my texts to Jackson with one to Meredith.

CHARLIE: Hey, you guys okay? Haven't heard from either of you since yesterday afternoon...text me back.

Screwing up my courage, I google Jackson's name, squeezing my eyes shut to stave off the fear that he's been in some crazy accident. Like watching a scary movie, I peek my eyes open, letting out the breath I've been holding when no accidents show up. But just like that scary movie when the music has paused and everyone is safe, the music crescendos and the boogeyman attacks. The headlines I do find still make my stomach somersault with nausea.

Jax Parties in the Windy City Alone...Where is Charlie?

Jax Flying Solo in the Windy City

Bryant's Babe-Filled Night

If the headlines aren't bad enough, the pictures are so much worse. Pictures of Jackson at a club, no Meredith in sight. Had they been in Chicago yesterday? In one image, he is on a couch, a huge smile on his face and his arm around some girl who looks like a supermodel. Her hand is high on his leg, fingers resting close to the crease where his thigh and body meet, her head leaning against his chest.

"Oh god." Tears blur the pictures. He hadn't called me last night, hadn't texted, and now I know why. This. As quickly as the tears form, they burn away. This is *exactly* why I don't believe in relationships, why love is for fairytales. It's not real, just an image, easy to fake. Screenshotting the last picture, I send it along with another text.

CHARLOTTE: Apparently being together means something different to you. This doesn't look like Meredith to me.

Turning off my phone, I toss back the covers and dress for the studio, moving slowly on aching legs. I don't need Jackson to dance. I don't need anyone. I can do it on my own.

CHAPTER 17

JAX

Construction workers inside my skull are destroying whatever is left of my brain cells after last night. My mouth is a mix of Death Valley and cotton. Taking stock inch by painful inch, I contemplate getting up to grab some water while pins and needles run through my arm, asleep since someone's laying—

"Holy shit!" I jump out of bed and immediately regret the sudden movement, grabbing my head before it can fall off my body.

"Ugh." My knees buckle with the familiar groan that comes from the covers. "Shut up, Jax."

Given that it's Meredith in bed with me and the fact that I'm still completely dressed—shoes included—means I didn't do something royally fucked up. I pat my pockets for my phone.

"Mer." She swats my hand away when I attempt to shake her awake. "Mer, have you seen my phone?"

"If you keep doing that, I'm gonna puke," she mumbles into her pillow.

"What about your phone?" Leaving her grumbling, I head for the main room of the Chicago hotel suite I'm staying in for the weekend.

Any chance in hell I have of finding my phone is going to require both water and aspirin to reset my brain. I barely get two tablets swallowed when a knock on the door reverberates through my skull. Wincing, I check the peephole before throwing the door open to a dark sunglass-bespectacled Derek.

"I hate you." He shoves past me into the room.

"I hate me too."

"What the hell happened last night?"

My overwrought brain stumbles through flashes of a multi-colored dance floor. Derek, Meredith, and I dancing when a remixed version of "Dreamer" hit the speakers. Other club-goers moving to my music. The next image flashes, me hauling Meredith and Derek to the bar for shots of… "Oh, fuck, Patron."

"Tequila's a bitch." Derek's reply is tossed over his shoulder as he stumbles to the bedroom. I nod, or attempt to, even though he doesn't see me, and my head throbs.

"I lost my phone." Christ, if someone gets their hands on it. My heart races, pounding in sync with my brain as panic sets in.

"No, you didn't." Derek reaches into his pocket, handing me my phone and my sanity. "Not sure how I ended up with it, but here it is. Dead though."

Moving as fast as my hangover will allow, I head for my charger. Meredith groans again as Derek kicks off his shoes, both of them thumping to the floor where his feet hang off the bed.

"I'm never drinking again." Meredith's still talking into the pillow.

"Preachin' to the choir, baby girl." Ignoring them, I stare at my phone, fingers tapping anxiously against it, waiting for it to power on.

"Fucking finally," I mutter and key in my passcode. "Oh fuck."

Meredith and Derek both shush me.

Thirty. I have thirty voicemails since last night. Scrubbing a hand down my face, I see I have nearly that many texts from Nick that hyperlink to different stories. Shit, shit, shit. The blue dot appears next to Charlotte's name and I smile, clicking on her message. My smile transforms into a grimace as I read her texts.

CHARLOTTE: FaceTime tonight?

That one was sent late last night, usually about the time I would have called her. My dick perks up at the thought of another FaceTime call. The other texts are all from this morning.

CHARLOTTE: Hey, is everything okay? I didn't hear from you last night...
CHARLOTTE: I'm worried about you. Text me and let me know you're OK.

Following that text is a screenshot of a picture, and the next text sends terror through my limbs.

CHARLOTTE: Apparently being together means something different to you. This doesn't look like Meredith to me.

"FUCK!" My fingers trip over themselves in an attempt to get to the phone app. Clicking on her image, I wait as the phone rings twice before immediately going to voicemail. Shit. "Hey, baby, it's me. Sorry I didn't call last night. Call me, okay? I want to talk about the picture you sent me...please? It...just call me, okay?"

I disconnect and switch back to my texts with her, attempting to type on the small ass screen keyboard. Why is this damn thing so tiny?

JACKSON: Gorgeous, I'm so sorry. It's not what you think. Nothing happened. Please believe me. Call me, please?

My text sits there, not switching to read, nor do the three dots pop up that tell me she's texting me back. Fuck, it doesn't even show delivered. Pacing, I click on the text string from Nick, hoping his links will shed some more light on things. All caps messages are interspersed with links. My queasy stomach nose-dives toward projectile vomit mode the more stories I click on, the more headlines I read, the more pictures I see. Putting it off as long as I can, I dial Nick's number.

"Well, well, well, Prince Charming, or should I refer to you as and I quote the Windy City golden boy? Have fun last night, asshole?" Nick has one volume—on. I rub at the headache taking up an extended stay residence in my temples.

"Hello to you too, Nick." The hangover from hell that rides shotgun this morning makes it harder than normal to deal with Nick's abrasive personality.

"Do you have any idea what you've done? How pissed Randa is since we just put the story out about you and Charlie dating? How many calls I've fielded this morning asking for a comment on if you two broke up? Or should I say calls I started getting last night?"

Groaning, I try to apologize. "I'm sorry—"

"Capital P in fucking pissed, Jax. A year! A whole goddamn year of good behavior, the light at the end of the tunnel thanks to the media falling in love with your love story and you do this shit? Now? Fuck. Randa even threatened to jerk you from the awards show presentation. You don't even want to know how close you came to losing that opportunity."

My stomach nosedives. "Shit, I did?"

"No, dickhead, you didn't, thanks to my skills in groveling." I know better than to attempt commentary while Nick steamrolls through a well-deserved lecture. Thirty minutes later, his terse command to straighten my shit out is followed by a directive that sends ice through my veins. "Get with Charlie and get something good out there. Now." With a click, he's gone.

And the phone lights up with an incoming call from Jessie.

"Hey, Jess, now's not a good time—"

"Are you trying to ruin my life?" Are my ears bleeding? If I thought Nick's volume was bad, Jessie's is deafening.

"What?"

"All of my friends know I'm your sister, dumb-dumb."

"Jess, what are you talking about?"

"Can you try to stay out of the tabloids for just a little while? Maybe then my friends will stop giving me their opinion on your love life. Because ew."

Part of me wants to smile, but the other part is too hungover. "Jess—"

"This is worse than last time, Jax."

"I doubt that."

"Whatever," she sneers. "Last time they didn't talk to me because they thought you were an addict. They weren't shy this time when they called you a douchebag for cheating on your girlfriend. And why didn't you call me and tell me you had a girlfriend? I had to learn about it—"

"Whoa, whoa, whoa." Taking a deep breath, I count to five to calm the temper threatening. "First, it's none of their business. Second, I did not cheat on Charlotte."

"That's not what it looks like." Her comeback is the final snap in my temper.

"Jesus Christ. Just because something looks one way doesn't mean it is. Fuck what it looks like and fuck all your little friends who think they get to pass judgement on my goddamn life."

The phone beeps in my ear. She hung up on me. Par for the course this morning. Scrubbing a hand down my face, I dial her number and am not surprised when it immediately goes to voicemail.

JESSIE: Don't call me, asshole. Go screw yourself. *middle finger emoji*

Did I die? Am I in hell? I've pissed off Charlotte, Nick, my label, and apparently now my sister. Great. Just great. Hungover, feeling like shit, my brain is still attempting to play catch-up. This has to be some nightmare instead of painful reality. My text to Charlotte still has no response.

Fuck. I debate between coffee or a hot shower first. Caffeine, please. Picking up the in-room phone, I order coffee and a few things that should help all of us recover from our hangovers.

Meredith is still practically comatose under several pillows, but Derek is coherent enough to hear my request to listen for room service. I grab a spare set of sweats and a t-shirt and head for salvation in the form of a shower. The bright lights of the bathroom assault my bloodshot eyes and my head plays the 1812 Overture with gusto. I stare at the light switch, ultimately deciding that showering in the dark, while better for my head, would probably result in me slipping in the shower and killing myself.

Squinting at my reflection as the water warms up, I look like shit. My hair is mashed down on one side, sticking out on the other, and dark circles ring my eyes like a human raccoon. My stubble reminds me more of Grizzly Adams than scruffy sexy. Too disgusted to keep looking at myself, I check my phone again. No response. The pictures she saw make me seem like I'm some cheating asshole, and since the public loves a scandal more than they love a love story, I'm sure there are comments already that claim that. Fucking paps and their cameras.

"I'm never drinking again," I whisper-groan to no one in particular, the hot shower beating down on my ravaged body. Tilting my head back, I hope the water washes away the foggy brain I'm dealing with so I can fix the mess I've landed myself in. The last time I fucked up this bad the label had sent Nick in person with an ultimatum. And I know they don't believe in second chances.

The shower makes enough marginal improvement in my hangover that I can dress and brush the furry feeling from my teeth without any percussion accompaniments in my head. When I open the bathroom door, Meredith is sitting up against the pillows, slightly green, while she slowly sips on coffee. Derek stares at the food in equal parts horror and contemplation.

"How bad is it?" Meredith's voice is quiet. I pour myself some coffee and look up to see her eyes closed. I sigh before taking a drink of the life-revitalizing nectar.

"You remember when Nick delivered my ultimatum?" She and Derek both nod. "Amplify that. Add in Nick, who has already reamed my ass, a pissed off label, national headlines with pictures to remember the fun event by, and a girlfriend who texted me a screenshot of one of those pictures."

Her eyes widen as I show her Charlotte's latest message. "Oh shit."

"Yeah." We're silent for a few minutes and I try to digest this current shit storm. "That also doesn't include pissing off my sister by jumping all over her case when she called to bitch me out this morning."

She's sixteen. She's allowed to be dramatic. Taking my frustration out on her was stupid as hell and I'm sure I'm going to hear from either Mama or Dad about it.

"Any idea where my phone is?" Meredith's normally vivacious eyes are dulled by a hangover that I commiserate with. I shrug.

"Derek had mine." We both look at Derek who shares my shrug.

"I had Jax's. No idea where yours is, baby girl."

Swiping Derek's from the bed, she punches in her number, and all three of us turn to the couch when we hear a muffled vibration. I fish into the cushions to find her cell and toss it to her.

"Asshole," she mutters. "My phone's almost dead. I got a text from Charlie."

She holds it up and I see a similar message to one of the first I got this morning.

CHARLIE: Hey, you guys okay? Haven't heard from either of you since yesterday afternoon...text me back.

"I tried texting her when mine powered on. She hasn't texted me back." I'm wondering if she even will after the pictures.

"Let me try." Meredith's fingers move over hers before she puts it down, closing her eyes as she leans against the wall.

My phone chimes, but my stomach churns when I realize it's still not a response from Charlotte. I'm pissed at myself and my own stupid choices.

What the fuck had I been thinking? Short answer, I hadn't.

"Not Charlie?" Meredith hazards a guess.

"No, Russ reminding me about sound check."

Meredith's eyes watch me, full of concern. I'm sure they mirror my own as I think about how my dumb ass drunken actions will impact my relationship with Charlotte. After last night, do we even still have one?

CHAPTER 18

CHARLIE

The music from my playlist starts again and I take my starting position, forcing my legs where I need them to be. I've spent hours in the studio, repeating steps over and over again. Practicing the dance, every move, ignoring the way my eyes skitter to the pocket on my bag where my phone is any time my brain starts to let reality intrude.

I'm halfway through my audition piece when the music stops. I look up, a protest on my tongue.

"Charlotte, ma chérie. Ça suffit!" *Enough.* "You dance as if the devil is chasing you."

"I have to get it right. There's not much time left." Time is running out. I have to be ready.

She steps closer and I feel my walls start to crumble with the way her floral smell wraps around me. Tears burn my throat as I try to swallow them, and her cool hands surround my flushed cheeks. "You will be ready. But I do not want you to injure yourself permanently. You have been dancing all day. No breaks."

The sun slants through the windows. She's right. I haven't stopped all day, afraid to stop. To face demons who look like supermodels.

A tear rolls down my face, and her soft thumb wipes it away before it gets too far. "I know this means much to you. But go home. Come back day after tomorrow." Her face is full of concern.

"But I can come tomorrow—"

"Tomorrow, ma chérie, you are not allowed. Rest your body. Then go for a walk. Rest your mind and come back the next day."

"But, Madame—"

"Non, Charlotte." Her words, though quiet, are final.

Leaving me in the middle of the room, she walks to the stereo, untethering my phone and bringing it back to me. "Home."

Panic wells. Is she sending me home because, despite how hard I've worked, I can't do this? Were my parents right to question me? Maybe I should give up. Stop trying. Just accept what I have.

Not bothering to change, I limp to my car. The studio and shopping center around it are deserted for the evening. Exhaustion weighs heavily on me as I start the car, forcing my feet to move from brake to gas until I stop in front of the house.

"Charlie, are you okay?"

I've taken the first hobbling step to the stairs when Mom comes around the corner, eyes lined with concern.

"I'm fine." I focus on moving my throbbing feet.

"You're limping."

"I overdid it." Biting back a groan, I lift one leg and then the other, taking more weight on my left leg than my right. The thought of climbing these stairs feels like a Mt. Everest expedition.

"Are you hungry? Dinner's almost ready."

I haven't eaten all day, the thought of food not occurring to me until now. Even still, I don't feel hungry. "Maybe later." Another stair and my bag thumps painfully against my hip.

"Why don't you take an Epsom bath? Those always work wonders." Mom smiles and I nod my agreement.

"I'll try it. Thanks."

Leaving my bag in my room, I step into the bathroom. My eyes are flat and dark as I stare at myself in the mirror. My skin is paler than normal, nearly translucent, while my hair pulls tightly against my scalp. I groan with the effort it takes to shed my clothes and turn on the water. The light smell of the Epsom salts fills the room and I take a deep breath. I wait for the tub to fill before I step in, hissing at the heat as I lower myself to the water. Closing my eyes, I drift, the pictures from earlier fading in and out. The first sob rips out of me before I bite my fist to muffle the ones that come after.

♪♪♪♪♪♪

"Charlie? Everything okay?" A knock precedes Mom's question through the door.

Okay? No. "I'm fine."

"Okay." There's hesitation in her voice, her shadow under the door holding still for a second. "I brought you up a sandwich, so you didn't have to mess with the stairs."

"Thanks, Mom."

"I'll put it in your room."

I don't say anything else and eventually she retreats. The water has cooled by the time I lift myself out of it to stand on rubbery legs and dry off. I wrap the towel around myself and head for my room. The sandwich is on the nightstand along with a bottle of water.

Closing my door, I turn off the overhead light, keeping the side lamp on next to the bed. I don't bother with pajamas before I ease onto my bed in my towel to grab the sandwich, forcing bites down until it's gone. The water is next, but that goes down easier. Only when the bottle is empty do I allow myself to turn out the light, pulling the covers over my head, hiding from the rest of the world. Is this it? The heartbreak I always knew was coming?

Sometime later, I jerk awake, suffocated by the humidity under the blankets. Pushing them off, I yank the twisted towel out from under me then stare at the ceiling. A cramp locks my leg and I groan, rubbing at it until it fades. I get up to grab some ibuprofen from my studio bag, and my fingers brush against my powered off cell phone before wrapping around the bottle.

Mom and Dad won't need to call me since it's the weekend, so I leave the phone where it is and take two pills. Then I lay back down, ready to forget yesterday again.

♪♪♪♪♪

Deja vu hits me when I open my eyes again several hours later to sunlight streaming through my curtains. The only exception is that my light isn't on. I don't panic and search for my phone. Blinking my eyes open, I stare at the wall, hearing Bella laughing about something downstairs.

I let sleep reclaim me, escaping once more.

"Charlie?" Dad's voice calls through the door, but he doesn't knock, doesn't open the door.

"I'm up." How convincing does it sound when my voice is still slurred with sleep?

"Are you okay?" Why does everyone ask that question?

"I'm fine, Dad."

"Your Mom and I are going to take Bella to the park. Did you want to come?"

"Um, no thanks. I'm heading to the studio later." What's the harm in a white lie? I wish I was able to. It's Sunday, so the studio is closed for classes and it would be the perfect time to rehearse more. But knowing Madame, she'll make me stay home another day.

Another pause before he knocks on the door once. "You got it, kid. See you when you get back. Oh, Charlie?" His voice comes stronger through the door.

"Yeah?"

"Meredith called. She said your cell phone must be dead."

"Thanks, Dad. I'll call her in a bit."

I hear the garage door open and close. The silence a welcome reprieve. But I've slept too much, and my body isn't tired anymore. Moving slowly, I dress in pajama shorts and a tank top and shuffle downstairs for a yogurt before climbing Mt. Everest again.

The headlines and pictures from yesterday still spin in my mind like a frenetic merry-go-round. Sitting back on the bed, I fold my legs up under me, staring at the bag that hides my phone in a pocket. It lays there like a tempting neon light while I force myself to eat the entire yogurt and throw the container in my trash. Finally, I step cautiously toward the bag and lean over with a groan to fish in the side pocket.

The device is dark, its silence taunting me. A massive lump fills my throat and I swallow, pressing the power button and keying in my passcode. The phone goes crazy, vibrating repeatedly until it slows and finally stops.

Several voicemails from Meredith range from apologies, to asking me to call her back, to demands to call, to the threat to call my parents and her texts all repeat the same thing. A sharp breath hisses through my teeth as I look at the blue dot next to Jackson's name. Closing my eyes, I push my thumb down and open our text thread. The first message came a few hours after I sent the screenshot to him. It isn't what I think? Scoffing, I keep reading.

JACKSON: Gorgeous?

Another text several hours later.

JACKSON: Baby, I'm worried. If you don't want to talk to me, text Meredith please.
JACKSON: Charlotte, I haven't heard from you all day. Please. Text me. Even if you tell me to fuck off. Please.
JACKSON: Please. Tell me I didn't ruin us.
JACKSON: Charlotte?

With a sigh, I re-read all of Jackson's texts. Believe me. His words swirl around me in some crazy dance with the headlines and the pictures, a tornado of emotion making me feel like the yogurt is about to make a reappearance. My hand presses against my stomach, hoping to keep it down while I stare at the words on the screen.

The phone vibrates in my hand with another text as I stare at the jumble of words.

JACKSON: Charlotte?

The screen goes black for an instant, lighting back up with a picture Jackson and I took in front of the Bellagio Fountains in Vegas. He's leaning against the rail, one arm wrapped around my shoulders while the other holds the phone for a selfie. It's the picture I set as his contact. The phone continues to buzz in my hand before finally stopping and I let out the breath I was holding.

JACKSON: I can see you read my latest text. Can I talk to you?

Blinking tears away, I click on the response window before deleting everything I type.

JACKSON: Charlotte?

I don't respond, and my heart cracks when the phone rings again. And again. And again, before another text chimes through.

MEREDITH: I just smacked Jax upside his head and told him to calm the fuck down. He won't call you until you text him. Call me?

I shake my head and key in a response.

CHARLIE: I'll call you later.

♫♪♫♫♪

Every day for the last five days, Meredith has called me. Every day for the last five days, Jackson has texted me. I respond to Meredith every time, telling her I'll call her back later. I don't respond to Jackson, but he can still tell that I read his text messages. My five days have revolved around watching Bella, prepping for the audition, and sleeping. Tomorrow is it. Tomorrow I see if I still have a shot or not. Every day my ankle has hurt less, telling me that's a good sign.

My phone pings as I finish packing the small carry-on I'm taking on my flight to LA later.

MEREDITH: This is bullshit, Charlie. CALL ME!
CHARLIE: I'll call you later.
MEREDITH: No, you won't.
CHARLIE: What do you want me to say, Meredith?
MEREDITH: I'm calling and you better fucking answer.

My phone rings, a silly selfie of Meredith popping up. My thumb immediately moves to decline but I pause just before I hit the button, shifting to green.

"H-hello?" My voice feels rusty from lack of use. I haven't had much to say and it's not like anyone around me cares to hear it anyway.

"Fucking finally, woman!" A sad smile crosses my lips at her exclamation. "I thought you would never pick up your phone."

I stay silent and she sighs.

"Talk to me."

"I-I don't know how."

"Charlie." The sadness in her voice burns my throat.

"If this is what a relationship is about, I don't want it. I don't want to feel like this anymore."

"It's not, babe."

"It was for my parents. For years. It was that way for you too, with Daniel."

Meredith's breath hisses out at the mention of her ex's name.

"Relationships are a lie, Mer. True love doesn't exist. And I can't. I can't compete with those other girls. The ones in the pictures."

"You don't have to compete, Charlie. It's not a competition to Jax. He cares about you."

I scoff. "He has an interesting way of showing it."

"He's a good guy, Charlie, but he's still a guy. They're pretty clueless sometimes." I can hear the smile in her voice. "I know he misses you. Every day. He's a sad puppy moping around here."

I can't picture that. Do I even want to? "What if I'm not enough? What if I give him another chance and he proves me right again? What if he breaks my heart? What's that saying? Fool me once?"

"What if he doesn't?" she counters immediately, and I know she's been thinking about this. "Look, if you want to end it with Jax, that's your choice. But don't you owe it to yourself to have a conversation with him? To tell him how you feel?"

Uncertainty lashes through me. "I don't know if I can."

"Charlotte Grace Walker. You can. Think of all the things you've done just by saying what you think, what you feel, by busting your ass. No more hiding. Do it. I promise you, you'll feel better if you do." Her voice muffles on the other end. "Of course. I finally get you on the phone and I have to go. Something about the way they're packing up our stuff."

"Okay."

"Answer next time I call, okay?"

"I will."

"Love you."

"Love you too."

She disconnects and I lower the phone, clicking on the text messages and re-reading through the ones Jackson has sent this week. It's like our conversations from before but one sided. Interspersed through those are songs he thinks I'll like, songs that remind him of me. Ed Sheeran's *Give Me Love* is the latest one. I play it, a sad smile twisting my lips as I listen to the lyrics. I'm so close to falling in love with him. If I let go.

I keep scrolling to a selfie he sent me, this one also from in front of the Bellagio. Our pose is almost identical to the one I have but he's kissing my cheek in the photo. The last text is one he sent today. A selfie where he's holding a piece of paper with its own message. *Can I call you?* His normally vibrant green eyes are dimmed, dark circles visible underneath, and my fingers automatically move to trace the circles lightly. This week hasn't been easy on him either. Before I can talk myself out of it, I hit reply.

CHARLOTTE: Yes.

My phone rings within seconds.

"Hey."

"Hey." His voice cracks and he clears his throat. "I was surprised to get your text."

"I surprised myself. I guess I'm ready to talk." My eyes fill with tears at the drawl in his voice, familiar and not after the last week.

"Gorgeous." Pain lances my heart at the use of his nickname for me, tears flowing faster. "I'm so sorry. One second Meredith and I were out on the dance floor and then we heard my song as a remix, and everything got—"

"Fuzzy," I supply blankly, recalling the story he told me about his birthday during our ride from the airport.

"Charlotte, baby, fuck. I swear to God, I swear on my guitar, those pictures are not what they looked like."

I want to believe him. At least, the small piece of my heart that doesn't feel bruised by all this wants to. The rest of me, the pieces of my heart that shattered when I saw those pictures, try desperately to protect me. "I don't know, Jackson, you looked pretty cozy with Ms. Supermodel. Her hand was like right there. I'm not stupid." My voice breaks on the last word, my choppy breaths betraying my tears.

"Gorgeous, Charlotte, please don't cry. I'm so sorry. What can I do to show you I'm sorry? How do I fix this?" Anxiety colors his voice and I have to take several deep breaths before I can answer.

"I don't know, Jackson."

"Baby—"

"I don't know if this is fixable. Maybe this is the universe saying this isn't going to work. We have two very different lives. Two very different dreams. Maybe...maybe we should stop—"

"No, baby. This was me being a dumb ass. I'm an idiot. But I need you in my life. I-I'm starting to fall for you." Sharp pain steals my breath at his quiet admission. "Please. Please. I'm begging you. Please give us another chance."

Rubbing my forehead, I wish I could erase the memories of all those headlines that seem lodged in my brain. If I didn't feel something for him, if I wasn't falling for him, it wouldn't hurt this bad. Right?

"You can't erase what happened, Jackson, it's not possible. You can't erase what happened any more than I can erase how I feel because of those pictures—"

"I'm so—" He tries to interrupt me, but I keep going.

"I know you're sorry. But I also know that you hurt me, and a big part of my brain is telling me to run, to protect myself from the potential you have to hurt me anymore." His breath hisses through his teeth, and I know my words hurt him even though that's not my intent. "The other part of me is saying to keep trying with you. To give us a chance to work. I'm terrified that how I feel about you, what you make me feel, is going to destroy me."

"I never meant to hurt you, Charlotte, I promise. I promise I'm never going to hurt you again. I meant what I said earlier. I'm falling in love with you."

"If you're with me, you're with me. No more pictures like the one I saw. Us."

"Fuck the label." I smile hearing him repeat back what we said when we started this path.

"I-I'm falling for you too, Jackson." As scary as it is to admit, it's true. Doubts still sit in the back of my mind, reminding me that we're two very different people. That he has a lot of opportunity to find someone else. That he doesn't have to be in this. "Don't break my heart."

"I promise."

If I believe him, why does ice still run through my veins?

CHAPTER 19

CHARLIE

The music stops, and I nail the final move in the audition I've been working on for the last several weeks. Holding the pose until the last notes fade and a few seconds after, I blink, the room coming back into focus after spending the last several minutes lost in the melody.

"Charlotte, ma chérie, c'est magnifique." Madame kisses both my cheeks, her jasmine scent a warm reminder of all the work she's helped me complete—both over the years since I started dancing for her and, more specifically, these last several weeks. It had been a surprise to see her when I showed up to the audition this morning, but she'd explained that she wanted to see Meric again. Secretly, I think she wanted to keep an eye on me.

Lowering my head to my chest, my hair hides the warmth staining my cheeks. "Thank you, Madame."

Two men join us in the middle of the room, one a younger man with sandy brown hair and glasses and the other a man closer to Madame's age with salt and pepper hair and a patrician nose.

"Charlie, right?" At my nod, the younger man continues. "Nice to meet you, I'm Garrett Harrison."

Before I can say anything else, the older gentleman takes my hand out of Garrett's, both of his wrapping warmly around mine.

"Très jolie, Charlotte." His accented words flow together and create a unique song. When Madame had mentioned a friend, I hadn't realized he would be French too. "Meric Toussaint."

He places a kiss on the back of my hand before turning to Madame Laurent, speaking rapid-fire French, but I recognize danseuse—dancer—and belle—beautiful. Heart racing in my chest, I try to keep my imagination from running away with me.

"Meric, we are being rude." Madame gestures to Garrett and me, both of us watching their exchange. If their words had been music, their hands were the dance, moving gracefully with their conversation.

"Excusez-nous," Meric apologizes.

I shake my head. "It's fine."

Garrett grins. "I'm used to it."

Laughing, Meric rolls his eyes but doesn't address Garrett's comment.

"So, Charlie," Garrett turns to me, his blue eyes appraising me. "Are you really dating Jax Bryant?"

Stomach sinking, I nod. "I am—we are. But I've also been dancing for years. I'm professionally trained at—"

Garrett holds up a hand. "Madame gave us a rundown of your credentials already. I was just curious."

Is that a good thing or not? I twist my lips in a passable smile —or as close to one as I can get it. Jackson and I are...complicated for lack of a better word. But Garrett, Meric, Madame—none of them care about my current relationship status. Not really.

"My good friend is also the lead choreographer on his tour.

She and I danced together in New York while I was there." Garrett smiles and nods.

"I've seen Jax's show when he was in LA recently. That choreography is great—a serious workout."

With a laugh, I commit his comment to memory to share with Meredith later. She'll love that.

"So, Charlotte. Claudine tells me you were injured? Last year?" Meric asks.

I nod. "Yes. Several stress fractures in my right foot and ankle."

"Chirurgie?" Meric shakes his head. "Surgery?"

"Yes, I've spent the last year recovering and rebuilding."

Meric and Garrett share a look, leaving me questioning my chances. "Garrett and I have several other auditions lined up today." I nod. This is it. The rejection. "Once we have concluded the auditions, Garrett will be letting you know if you receive a call back."

My knees almost buckle at the relief that washes through me, my muscles screaming when I have to lock them to keep myself upright. Looking at Garrett, he nods.

"You should hear something tomorrow at the latest. The artist is...anxious to get started. This process has taken longer than he anticipated."

I nod like I understand what he's talking about when I don't even know who the artist is. The name is being kept confidential for now. After shaking hands with Garrett and Meric and saying goodbye to Madame, I grab my bag and change in the dressing room. As I'm leaving, I see a third man enter the audition space from another door. He looks familiar and I wonder if I know him from school. Shaking my head, I push out to the warm California weather.

Adrenaline flags as I close the studio door behind me, the aches and pains in my body reminding me that I pushed myself to the limit to get prepared for today. But at least I know that I couldn't have done anything more for the audition. Leaning against the building, I order a Lyft back to Meredith's. When her parents had heard about my audition nearly a month ago, they'd insisted that I stay with them, telling me I'd have my own space since I was staying in the guest house which they'd converted into an apartment for Meredith.

My phone rings as soon as I close the front door.

"Hello?"

"How'd it go?" Mom asks, and I can hear Bella playing in the background.

I bite back a groan when I sink into the soft couch cushions. "Okay, I think."

"Tell us about it."

"Us?"

"You're on speaker with your dad and me."

"I dunno." I pause, thinking back to the look that passed between Garrett and Meric when we discussed my injury, my stomach churning. "I *think* it went okay. My injury came up so it's hard to tell. The one guy, Meric, is a friend of Madame's from way back."

"When will you find out if you got it?"

"I won't know for sure I got it until after the round of call backs. But I should hear about that no later than tomorrow according to Meric's assistant." I'm not sure that's what Garrett actually is, but it seems like the title Mom and Dad will most likely understand.

"Well, let us know, okay? Take a few days off." Mom laughs a little and I smile. I desperately need to give my body a break.

"I will." We say goodbye and I lean my head back against the couch, letting my mind drift. I'm nearly asleep when my phone rings again. I don't even open my eyes as I answer.

"Hello?"

"Hey, gorgeous, how'd it go this morning?"

"I think it went really well. I hope so." I explain the audition and that I'll get a call back in the next day or two.

"I'll keep my fingers crossed for you, but you don't need luck. They'd be idiots not to pick you," Jackson assures me.

I shrug, twirling a section of hair around my fingers. "I hope they pick me. But it's still just for a callback."

"This time." Sound picks up on his end of the line followed by a growl. "Damnit, I wish I had more time to talk to you."

"It's okay." I know he has a life too.

"The guys all just piled back on the bus and I promised I'd play video games earlier."

I hear the laughter. "Did they just call you *Jackie*?"

"Ugh. Yes." His voice muffles when he says, "Assholes, you're lucky I'm on the phone otherwise I'd kick your asses. Yes, all of them. Fuck."

There's some scuffling and then the line goes dead, followed by a picture of two guys sitting on top of Jackson on the couch in the front of his bus.

JACKSON: He'll call you later.

♪♪♪♪♪♪

When my phone rings a few hours later, I grab it, fully expecting to see Jackson finally calling me back. Instead, an unknown phone number flashes Los Angeles at me and my palms grow clammy.

"H-hello?"

"Charlie?"

"This is she."

"Hey, Charlie, it's Garrett. Harrison. From this morning?"

"Hi, yes, Garrett. How's it going?"

"It's good. Been a long day but I'm sure you don't really care about that," he laughs.

"I'm sure it has been." I don't know what else to say since I don't know exactly how many auditions they had after mine.

"I'm kidding. Charlie, Meric was so happy to have you audition for the video today," he starts. And here comes the easy let down. They send the nice guy to do it. "And while we didn't say anything to you, the artist was watching from another room. He loved you. He doesn't want to do call backs, he wants to offer you the role."

"What?" Pulling the phone away from my ear, I blink at it.

"If you want it, the role is yours."

"Oh my gosh, yes! Yes, I want it. When are rehearsals? What's the schedule?"

Garrett laughs. "Welcome aboard. No rehearsals. The artist has been pretty specific—he wants it improvised. He thinks you're the perfect fit."

"He?"

"Unfortunately, I'm still not at liberty to disclose that until you sign the contract and non-disclosure agreement. I hope that won't be a problem?"

I'm hesitant, but in the end, I know Meredith's dad, Mike, will review everything for me since he has a background in entertainment law. "Okay."

I vaguely hear Garrett tell me he'll send me an email with the details, and they'll see me in a few weeks for the video shoot.

Plans swirl in my mind and I immediately open my phone app, pressing on the contact, waiting anxiously for it to ring.

"Hello?"

♪♪♪♪♪

After squealing my news to Meredith and making plans to continue to crash at her house until the video shoot, I hung up, intent on reading for the rest of the afternoon. Instead, Val, Meredith's mom, had knocked on the door, insisting that we go celebrate my job with dinner while Mike reviewed the paperwork.

Now it's dark and I'm lounging on the couch with a full stomach.

JACKSON: Hey, gorgeous
CHARLOTTE: You live! LOL
JACKSON: Haha. Funny. Those guys are assholes.
CHARLOTTE: Did you at least have fun?
JACKSON: A little bit. *wink emoji*
JACKSON: Took me for-fucking-ever to find my phone.
CHARLOTTE: They hid it?
JACKSON: *eyeroll emoji* Yep.
JACKSON: Long story short, it was hidden in a cupboard.
CHARLOTTE: *laughing emoji*
JACKSON: So I heard your news! CONGRATULATIONS! I knew you could do it!
CHARLOTTE: Thanks *blushing emoji*
JACKSON: I'm so proud of you. How excited are you?
CHARLOTTE: I keep thinking this is a dream and I'm going to wake up.
CHARLOTTE: I even pinched myself earlier.
JACKSON: Don't hurt yourself.
CHARLOTTE: Nope. Just enough to make sure I was awake.
JACKSON: Good
JACKSON: Can I ask you something?
JACKSON: Why didn't you tell me your news?

Nibbling on my lip, I re-read Jackson's question, hoping to come up with an answer. But I don't have one, so I type the truth.

CHARLOTTE: I don't know
JACKSON: Can I be honest with you?
CHARLOTTE: Okaaaayyyyy

Nerves flutter in my stomach, wondering what else he hasn't been honest about.

JACKSON: I'm scared.
What? His response surprises me.
CHARLOTTE: Of what?
JACKSON: That you didn't call me because of what happened in Chicago.
CHARLOTTE: Oh.
JACKSON: ?
CHARLOTTE: I don't think that has anything to do with it.

Does it? I'm not sure. But I really wasn't thinking about Chicago when I called Meredith instead of Jackson.

JACKSON: You don't think?
CHARLOTTE: Maybe a little? It wasn't a conscious thought. I called Meredith to talk about a place to stay.
JACKSON: I'm sorry. I let you down.
CHARLOTTE: I accepted your apology.
JACKSON: I know you did. It just...
CHARLOTTE: It just what?
JACKSON: It feels like you're holding back.
CHARLOTTE: Holding back?
JACKSON: Yeah.
JACKSON: How do I fix this?
CHARLOTTE: There's nothing you can do, Jackson. I just... time. We'll be fine.
JACKSON: Promise?
CHARLOTTE: Promise.
JACKSON: Fuck the label.

I giggle, sending him a GIF of a laughing baby so he knows he succeeded in making me smile.

CHARLOTTE: I'm exhausted. Going to head to bed I think.
JACKSON: I wish I was there.
CHARLOTTE: I know. Me too.
JACKSON: Goodnight, gorgeous
CHARLOTTE: Night. *kiss emoji*

Guilt and questions prick at me once I'm in bed. Am I still blaming Jackson for Chicago?

I fall asleep before I discover the answer to that question. Waking up the next morning, I discover a new text from him.

JACKSON: I got you something.
CHARLOTTE: You did? What?
JACKSON: Be at this address at 4.
I get an address in LA but not what it is.
CHARLOTTE: Where am I going?
JACKSON: Wear comfy clothes.
CHARLOTTE: ?
JACKSON: You'll see.
CHARLOTTE: Okaaaayyyyy
JACKSON: You'll like it.
JACKSON: Promise.
JACKSON: This is a good surprise.

The surprise is an upscale spa that's so fancy it has a circular drive with a fountain in the center. Standing outside the building, I grab my phone, opening Jackson's contact.

CHARLOTTE: Jackson, what on earth?
JACKSON: What?
CHARLOTTE: What is this place?
JACKSON: I thought it was a spa? That's what it said online.
CHARLOTTE: *eyeroll emoji* It IS a spa. But it looks really nice.

CHARLOTTE: Expensive.
JACKSON: Don't worry about it.
CHARLOTTE: Jackson.
JACKSON: I wanted to treat you after all your hard work. Val recommended it.
JACKSON: You deserve it. *kiss emoji*
JACKSON: Just say thank you, Charlotte.
CHARLOTTE: Thank you, Jackson.
JACKSON: You're welcome, gorgeous. *wink emoji*

The lobby smells lightly floral and of fresh linen. I approach the marble counter slowly, and the woman behind it looks up, smiling, when I'm still a few feet away.

"May I help you, miss?" Even her voice is relaxing.

"Um, I think I have an appointment? My...boyfriend booked it?" I stumble slightly on the term because it still feels foreign on my tongue. Boyfriend.

"Name?"

"Charlotte Walker?" Everything I respond with sounds like a question and I clear my throat. I know my name is Charlotte Walker. Why am I asking her?

Typing into her computer, she nods. "Yes, right here. You've been booked for a one hour hot-stone and aromatherapy massage. Would you like to have a seat?"

Nodding, I move to an overstuffed couch, taking a seat, and snag my phone out of my bag.

CHARLOTTE: What did you get me into?
JACKSON: LOL. The massage?
CHARLOTTE: It sounded like I just ordered a drink at a coffee shop.
JACKSON: *laughing emoji* Enjoy it.

The massage is amazing. I'm so relaxed afterwards, I'm glad

I'm not driving because I end up practically comatose in the backseat of the car. Pulling up to Meredith's mom and dad's, I head for the main house since Val had told me earlier to come see her when I got back. Now I know what her smile was about—she'd given Jackson the recommendation for the spa surprise.

When I knock and ease the door open, the sound of laughter greets me and makes me smile.

"Val?" I hesitate to walk any further, wondering if they have company.

"Hey, gorgeous." My body seizes in fight or flight mode as a voice I'm not expecting causes my everything to go on red alert. Finally, the ringing in my ears dies down enough for me to process and I'm turning around, rushing in the direction of that slight southern drawl.

"Jackson! What are you doing here?" Once in his arms, his hug lifts me slightly off the ground. For the first time since I saw those pictures, a sense of hope flares. Everything will be okay.

"I told my tour manager there was a family emergency. I just had a radio thing I had to get out of." He shrugs, green eyes sparkling as he takes me in. "I had to see you. To tell you in person, congratulations." My heart rate picks up when he places a soft kiss on my forehead.

Val stands in the doorway, smiling as she takes us in. "How'd you like your massage, Charlie?"

I close my eyes, sighing. "It was amazing."

She nods. "Good. They do an amazing job there, so I knew anyone you saw would treat you right." She looks between Jackson and me before cracking up. "Okay, I can tell you two would rather be anywhere else but here. Jackson, I'll tell Mike you said goodbye. Goodbye."

With an exaggerated wave, she leaves the room. Jackson's hand tangles around mine, tugging me out the front door.

"Come with me?" He moves until I'm backed against the door

and my core throbs at the intense way his gaze rakes me from head to foot.

Nodding, I step forward, my chest pressing against his. “Let’s go.”

♪♪♪♪♪♪

The hotel that Jackson has a room at reminds me of the spa earlier.

“Thank you for my massage today.” I glance at him as we walk through the cool marble lobby toward the elevators. We stopped and grabbed my bag before hopping in Jackson’s rental car. While one hand currently grips the bag, his other is wrapped around mine, a finger skimming the erratic pulse that flutters at my wrist.

He presses the call button before turning to me. “You’re welcome. Did you like it?” His voice is low, a whisper between the two of us.

“I did.” I nod, wrinkling my nose. “It was weird at first though.”

“What was?”

“I’d never had a massage before.” I shrug as the elevator dings its arrival.

“Why was that weird?” He’s still as he waits for my response. Does he know what I’m going to say?

“Y-you’ve been the only one to touch me.”

“Touch you? Those unprofessional—” The look on his face has me backtracking.

“No, not like that. They were fine. It’s just, it made me think about you.” His tongue drags across his lip as his lids lower, causing my thighs to clench in response.

“Did it?” His voice is gravel-filled, a raspy whisper in the elevator. “What about me?”

The elevator doors open on our floor. Exiting, I nod, not

answering his second question, but my eyes track his Adam's apple as it bobs with his swallow. His long stride moves him to his room ahead of me, and he opens the door to usher me inside.

The space is a haven of relaxation and comfort. Neutral tones with splashes of soft green and blue greet me in a room dominated by a king size bed that looks like a massive pillow. Another door leads to the bathroom with a large jetted soaking tub.

The door closes behind us and I tense, waiting. Ready. The flirting in the elevator has caused my body to combust.

The bag falling from Jackson's hand is my first signal, the sound muted by the thick plush carpet.

His voice vibrates against the shell of my ear before his arms circle me and draw me closer to his heat. "I missed you."

I turn my head and my eyes lock with his. "I missed you too."

Spinning me, his arms constrict until I sink into him.

"Jackson?" My voice is muffled by the soft cotton of his t-shirt.

"Hmmm?"

I lean back to look him in the eyes. "Are you sure it was okay to skip out on your radio thing?"

He nods. "I made the right choice. I needed to see you."

"But—"

He lays a finger against my lips, stopping my protest, the touch creating another spark. "Us." His eyes darken, growing hooded the longer we stare at each other.

I try to speak around his finger, but he adds pressure, causing a pleasurable ache to build.

"Fuck the label." It's all growl before his mouth covers mine. Our kiss ignites an inferno with the first brush of his tongue.

This. This feeling is what has been missing. He lifts me off my toes, deepening the kiss as his tongue sweeps between my lips. With another boost, I wrap my legs around his waist, groaning into his mouth as his hands knead my butt through the thin material of my yoga pants. My whimper when he breaks the kiss shifts to a moan as his lips move down my jaw, along the column of my throat. Tilting my head, I give him better access. My fingers scrape into his hair as I clench my thighs around his hips. He nips at the juncture of my neck and collarbone, groaning against the skin.

Maneuvering to the bed, he drops me when his knees hit the edge. I bounce once, looking up at him.

"I-I didn't come here for this." He looks torn, his muscles locked with indecision.

"I know." Sitting up on my knees, I loop my arms around his neck, yanking him down with me. "I want you. Make me forget, Jackson."

Make me forget the memories of those pictures. I don't say it out loud, but I might as well have.

"Not forget, baby. Remember. Us. My lips on your skin as I make you come."

Pressing a kiss to his stubbled cheek, I watch his eyes close, long lashes resting against his cheekbones. Another kiss lands closer to his lips and I breathe in the spicy scent of his cologne, remembering. "Fuck," he growls.

His eyes blaze green fire when they meet mine.

"What's wrong?" I ask.

"I...I just want you so much." His words are slow, like they're ripping out of him without his permission.

"Kiss me." My whisper against his lips is met with his arms tugging me impossibly closer. His hips flex into mine as the emotions underlying his words cause goosebumps to shiver down my spine. Lifting my hips, I thread my fingers through his hair. "Make love to me."

One of my hands boldly finds the bulge that presses against his zipper. I need his hands on my body. His mouth once more slants against mine as I rub him through his jeans, his fingers flexing into my hips as his tongue plunders my mouth. Those long, skilled fingers move, finding the edge of my yoga pants under the oversized t-shirt, tracing along the skin there, making the need edgier than before. He rolls me under him, his erection rubbing against the seam of my pants until I groan at the friction.

I break our kiss, tugging at his t-shirt so he helps me take it off before we discard my own. My desperation makes my fingers shaky. Jackson leans down, licking and kissing my exposed collarbone before moving south, biting the swell of one of my breasts as his fingers swirl closer to the pebbled nipple on the other one.

"No bra, baby?" Heat skates across my skin at the vibrations of his voice as he growls against me.

"Didn't think I'd need one." His other hand is still rubbing those maddening patterns along the waistband of my pants and my hips push against him. "Jackson."

I whisper his name before his lips finally make contact with my nipple, laving it with his skilled tongue before sucking it into his mouth. My fingers scramble and twist in the sheets beneath me, and my panties are damp with the need to have him inside me. No more waiting. He straightens and grabs my hands to kiss my fingers before he lays me back down on the bed. His hands move to the waistband of my pants.

"Don't tease me," I protest.

He doesn't stop, drawing down both my pants and panties together until they tangle around my ankles where I can kick them off. From his position, he leans over the bed, arms flexing as they hold him above me, muscles defined by his effort.

"Fucking beautiful." Hot kisses press against my lips but he leans back up far too soon for my taste. As he retreats, I lift my hands, ready to call him back. He pulls my legs with him, my hips resting on the edge of the bed. The heat of his gaze singes my inner thighs as he spreads them. The lick of his lips is the only warning I get before he dives tongue first into me. My fingers fist in his hair as he wrings unintelligible words from my lips, his tongue circling and sucking at my clit. Two fingers stretch me, pumping in a counterpoint to the swirl of his tongue. My legs tense against his shoulders as the orgasm shimmers at the edges.

"Come for me, gorgeous." Nibbling the bundle of nerves his tongue has been tracing, he scissors his fingers. My orgasm lights up every nerve, tightening every relaxed muscle as I cry out, the release washing over me until the only thought I have is Jackson's name.

My vision is hazy as I come back to earth and I watch him straighten from his knelt position, shucking his jeans and boxers before he climbs onto the bed.

"Hey."

Smiling, I trace his scruff with my palms. "Hi."

He nuzzles my throat as my hands roam his back, clutching at his hips to bring him closer to me. "Jackson, please."

His hard cock nudges my entrance and we both moan at the way he glides effortlessly through my slick folds. I try to lift my hips, to deepen the connection, but he holds me still.

"Baby, I need to grab a condom." His tip inches forward and I moan.

"I'm..." I lick my lips. "I started birth control."

On a groan, Jackson's forehead meets mine. "I'm clean, gorgeous. Tested right before the tour started. There wasn't... there wasn't anyone between then and you."

"I want to feel you." He's ignited this fire and I need him to put it out. Now.

A war battles behind his eyes until he focuses back on my lips, his mouth quirking to a sexy smirk. "Do you trust me?"

The question is loaded with meaning. If we're going to move forward, I have to trust him. His head presses further into my entrance with my nod, moving inch by slow inch. My head crashes side to side with the overwhelming sensations. I try to shift my hips or drag him closer. "Faster. Please."

"Slow," Jackson growls into my ear, his tongue tracing the rim. When he's fully seated, he pulls back so only the tip remains. My nails pinch into his hips at the slow torture driving me higher to a second orgasm. A snap of his hips fills me again, my groan echoed by his as he repeats the slow retreat followed by the quick thrust of his hips.

"Jackson." I watch sweat bead and roll down his temple. "Please."

His name, coupled with my plea, severs the iron thread he maintains over his control. His pace picks up, the sound of our bodies slapping against each other harmonizing with broken breathing and mixed groans.

"I'm close. Oh god. Jackson." My fingers grip his biceps, slipping on the sheen of sweat that covers us both. He shifts until he can draw my nipple into his mouth. Using his teeth, he bites down, simultaneously swirling his tongue around the sting. My movements lose their grace as every muscle locks in response to the powerful orgasm that shatters through me. I cry out as my muscles spasm around him, and his own pace increases until he freezes, pulsing his release.

His eyes blink open, half a smile forming in a lopsided grin.

"Okay?" he asks.

I nod at his question, his smirk growing until both dimples bracket his mouth.

"Good. Because.that.was.the.sexiest.fucking.experience.of.my.life." He punctuates each word with a quick kiss to my lips. I smile against them, loving his playfulness.

"C'mon." He stands, towing me with him to the shower.

Once we're clean and dry, we crawl back in bed. Jackson tucks me into him, his heartbeat thudding in a familiar pattern.

"I'm so tired," I yawn, rubbing against his chest, my damp hair cool where it tickles my shoulder.

His hands rub along my arms. "Sleep, baby."

"I-I don't want to." I blink, trying to stay awake.

He chuckles, fingers resuming paths along my shoulder. "Why?"

"Don't want this to be a…dream." I'm still blinking, trying to stay awake.

"It's not a dream, baby. I'm here." His lips press against my hair.

"Jackson, I—I love you." His chest rumbles a response, but sleep claims me, luring me down where the music times to heart-beats and green eyes light up with warmth as we dance.

CHAPTER 20

JAX

"What in the actual fuck were you thinking?" Nick sounds like he's about ready to explode. "Do you have any idea what shit you've started this time?"

Pinching the bridge of my nose, I blow out a breath through my mouth. Once Charlotte fell asleep earlier, I had no choice but to answer when Nick's ringtone started playing from the pocket of my jeans. "You told me to get with Charlotte and 'get something good.'"

It had been good, even if it wasn't seen. Feeling her come around me, nothing between us, her sleepy admission that even now has my heart pounding in my chest. She loves me. I have no idea what I did to deserve her love, but it's there. Somewhere along this fucked up path to our relationship, she fell in love with me just like I've fallen in love with her.

Holy shit. I sit up as the realization hits me. I love her.

"Are you listening to me?"

I have no idea what he just said. "Didn't you tell me that? To get with Charlotte?"

Reminding him is not my smartest move. Nick's teeth click audibly. "I told you to do that because she's good for your image, Jax. But not when you fucking cancel shit to do it!"

"I was just recording call signs. I can do that any time."

"That's what you think," Nick growls. "What did you tell Russ?"

"I said it was an emergency."

"Was someone dead?"

"Well, no."

"Dying? Hospitalized?" Nick barrels through my silence. "Jackson, if you don't want to do this anymore, you don't need to torpedo both our careers. I can find you a different exit strategy."

"No, I do want this." Panic stiffens my grip on the phone.

"You have a fucking fantastic way of showing it," Nick sighs. "Two words for you. Impulse fucking control. Yes, I wanted you to fix this mess you made in Chicago, but this was not the way to do it. This fuels rumors, it doesn't extinguish them. Randa is pissed, dude. Like if you hadn't sold out the remaining shows on your tour, you'd already be out on your ass."

The news that I've sold out the rest of my tour should be exciting, but it's buried in the mess I continue to create for myself. Every time I try to fix one thing, I end up making something else worse. "Fuck."

Movement in the doorway catches my attention. Charlotte peeks at me, her eyes sleepy, hair messy from the pillow. I smile and motion her forward, drawing her into my lap while I wait for Nick to wind down.

"Couldn't have said it better myself. It doesn't help that they've seen and heard nothing about your next album."

"I thought I had until after the tour was done?" Uneasiness prickles at my skin like a bunch of fire ants. My fingers flex against Charlotte's hip and she squirms in my lap.

"Tour's up in a few weeks. Do you have anything ready?"

"Not exactly."

Nick blows out a breath. "Look, I get it. I know the pressure that comes along with label demands. I've been in this industry longer than you, so I've seen the underbelly of the beast, kid. I'm going to give you some advice."

Rolling my eyes, I try to keep my voice even. "Okay."

"You need to be the poster-child of good behavior for the rest of the tour and until after the album's cut. Like, they don't even say jump and you pretend to ride a fucking pogo stick. You get me?"

Glancing at Charlotte, I console myself by running my hand along her smooth thigh. Her hands lift, rubbing across the back of my neck. I've got to figure this out. For her, for me, for the label. "Okay."

"Otherwise, dude, it's gone. Your contract, your songs, the money, all of it."

"I understand."

"You think that's enough?" Nick's laugh is bitter. "Do you want it?"

Thinking for a moment, my eyes find Charlotte's, locking on hers. "Yes."

"Then you better hear what I'm telling you—no more fucking up."

"Okay, okay."

"I'm serious."

"Nick, Jesus Christ, I said okay."

With a click, he's gone, and I toss my phone onto the table.

"Everything okay?" Charlotte's arms loop around my neck.

"I'm not sure."

Scrubbing my hands down my face, I shift, my hands circling her waist, drawing solace from the way she lays her head against my shoulder. She fits like she's always been there. She mumbles something that I don't quite catch. "What was that?"

"D-did you hear what I said earlier?"

Her sleepy declaration comes back to me, forgotten under Nick's pressure. The warm breath of admission against my chest before her body melted against mine.

"I heard you." My voice is soft, my arms wrapping around her automatically. Her body heats with a blush that I watch burn up her neck into her cheeks. Normally, I'd be able to see it sooner, but my t-shirt hides her collarbone.

"You did?" She starts to shift off, but my arms wrap tighter, cementing her to me.

"Hey, don't run away." I kiss the skin on her neck that I can reach. "Talk to me." She makes a non-committal noise, attempting to hide behind her hair. Locking both her wrists in one hand, I use the other to tuck her hair behind her ears. "Why are you hiding?"

"I'm embarrassed."

Biting back my laugh at the look on her face, I lift my head, kissing the tip of her nose.

"About what?"

"That I said…" She trails off, eyes darting around the room.

"That you said…?" I prompt, kissing the underside of her jaw.

"You didn't respond. I said…I…love you." Her admission gusts out in a sigh and I smile. Her eyes are closed, like if she can't see me, I can't see her. Fuck, she's cute. "And…and I don't expect you to say it back. I know it's fast or too soon or whatever, but I just can't deny what I feel."

"Charlotte. Baby, look at me." Her eyes don't open, and I try again. "Open those eyes, gorgeous."

Slowly, one peeks open, followed by the other. I wait until they are both trained on me before continuing. "I love you too."

Her eyes widen, searching mine. "You do?"

I nod. "Never in my wildest dreams did I think I could have music and love. But, with you, I get both. I love you."

Her smile lights up the entire room before her lips brush mine. "I love you."

"I'm not going to get tired of hearing you say that."

She giggles, mouth inches from mine, and I lean up, capturing her lips again. My tongue delves in to stroke hers and I feel my cock harden against her hip. I shift her to straddle me and move my fingers to tangle in the ends of her hair, tugging slightly to move her mouth where I want it. Her fingers flex against my shoulders while my hands sweep large circles along the soft cotton over her back. I can feel the damp heat of her through my boxers and realize she isn't wearing anything other than my shirt.

"Baby." I nip her chin and she gasps.

"Hmmm?" Her head tilts back, exposing her throat and my lips press against the pulse point fluttering there.

"Are you wearing panties?" I want to hear her tell me.

She shakes her head, the ends of her hair tickling my thighs. My cock kicks in response to her answer. "No."

"Fuck." My fingers pluck at the hem of the shirt, moving it up and out of my way, hands smoothing down to the insides of her thighs, feeling her squirm as I glide a finger against her. "So wet for me baby. Always."

"Jackson." Her fingers thread through my hair, nails scraping as her hips move against me. My lips trace her jawline, moving down as they reach her neck, licking and sucking my way down the column of her throat, teeth sinking in roughly where her neck and shoulder meet.

She cries out and tilts her head to give me better access. Grinning, I fist the hem of my shirt, debating ripping it off of her but hesitate. Instead, I tug, pulling the shirt up her stomach and breasts, and watch her nipples pucker in the cool air from the air conditioner.

"Beautiful." I layer soft kisses along her collarbone. Lifting my hand, I trace a finger along smooth skin to spiral around her breast, starting on the outside and working my way closer to the pink tip. Never touching it.

"Jackson."

It's a groan at the teasing caress and I smile, blowing out a breath, the sigh tightening her nipple further. My hand moves to her other breast, never fully connecting with her nipple as my lips keep going, gliding from her collarbone to the swell of one peak.

"Please." Her whispered moan is loud in our quiet room. I lift her to her knees, capturing a beaded tip in my mouth as I suck and lave at the hardened point before nibbling lightly. Her back arches, pressing her closer to me, while she holds my head against her.

Moving my fingers, I draw patterns along the insides of her thighs until her hips move restlessly with the touches. Sliding easily between her wet folds, I find her clit, circling before pressing a finger inside. We both groan, her hips moving up and down as she tries to ride my finger.

"Fuck, baby, I can feel you. You're fucking close, aren't you?"

A second finger joins the first and she moans her agreement into my mouth. I stand swiftly, my fingers leaving the warmth of her pussy. She starts to protest but my lips silence her as I lay her down on the couch, pushing my boxers down before kneeling next to her, sliding her thighs open, her arousal thick in the air. "Mine."

My voice is a growl as I bend forward, sliding my tongue up her center before circling her clit. I slide two fingers back in and pump them, my lips closing around the bundle of nerves as her legs shake around me.

"Jackson." Her hips press against me and I bite down gently, watching her shatter into a million pieces. Not pausing, I shift us again, settling her back into a straddling position over me, pushing at her entrance, inch by inch until our hips meet. Leaning back against the couch, I groan as her aftershocks pulse around me.

Charlotte moves in my stillness, lifting up and down slowly at first before picking up speed, her movements losing their gracefulness as her muscles clench around me. I take over then, pumping into her. My thumb circles once, twice, around her clit before applying pressure.

Her second orgasm spasms around me and my own hits like a bolt of lightning, pleasure taking over in a shatter of lights that pulse with every pump of blood through my body.

"I love you." My breath saws in and out of my lungs as I attempt to regain consciousness.

"I love you."

I'll never get tired of hearing those words, the sound of them lighting up my chest.

♪♪♪♪♪

Her shoulder is warm with sleep as my lips press against it and I watch her eyes flutter open with my touch.

"Good morning, gorgeous." Teasing a quick kiss on her lips I back away before it can ignite beyond the chaste one I intend to deliver. Unfortunately, I don't have time to indulge in any more of her body this morning.

It's early but my plane takes off in less than two hours, so I've had to get up, shower and dress while she slept peacefully, the sheets tangled around her hips in an image that has burned itself in my brain. It took every ounce of willpower to get up when my alarm went off this morning, my fingers itching to turn it off, to trace the warm curves snuggled next to me instead.

"Mmmm. You smell good." She stretches, arms raised above her, the sheet pooling below her breasts. She is temptation incarnate, but I have to resist. "What time is it?"

Finished stretching, the sheet settles back over her, and I can breathe fully again despite my zipper digging into the ridge of my hard-on. "It's still early. I didn't want to wake you, but your next surprise should be here soon. Do you want a shower and some coffee before?"

Her eyes clear more, softening as they look at me. "That sounds amazing." A groan escapes her as she moves off the bed, keeping the sheet in place.

"Sore, baby?"

She nods and I don't hide my smirk. The universe serves karma right back to me when the sheet falls to her waist, her nipples tightening in the cool air. My eyes heat but I stay where I am. She's not in the shower very long, coming back in the room wrapped in a towel, a cloud of coconut scented steam wrapped around her. Drops of water disappear into the shadow of her cleavage, and the need to trace the path with my tongue claws at me. I've brewed two cups of coffee while I wait for her, but forget what I was doing as she steps out of the bathroom. Closing my eyes, I fight the urge to walk over to her and trace the water with my tongue. Moving a hand to the bulge in my jeans I adjust myself, hoping to relieve the ache. "Fuck, gorgeous."

"I'm sorry." Her laugh doesn't sound sorry. "I forgot clothes."

I keep my eyes closed while she dresses, knowing that if I open them to watch her, my intentions to get to the plane on time will go to hell. I can sense the wheels spinning in her brain and take a guess.

"If it were up to me and I opened my eyes right now, neither of us would need clothes for the rest of the day."

She squeaks at my deep voice and I chuckle.

"Okay, you can open your eyes now," she says.

My eyes open, widening in surprise when I see her inches away, dressed in shorts and a tank top. Stepping on her tiptoes, her lips are whisper soft against mine. A knock on the door has her lowering back down faster than I would like.

"Room service?"

Shaking my head, I bite my lip to try to keep my smile from giving away her surprise. "I didn't order anything. Why don't you answer it?"

Her brows lift in curiosity, but she still moves to the door.

Once she opens it, she squeals. Meredith steps in and wraps her in a tight hug.

"Mer, holy crap, what are you doing here?"

"Jax suggested it. This way we can do California up right while we wait for your video. OMG." She laughs, wrapping an arm around Charlotte.

"You did this?" She turns back toward me and I nod.

"Yeah." I continue with a shrug. "I'd love to stay here, show you my favorite spots, but I have to get back. Meredith can take a few days off before returning for the last few shows."

She rushes me, jumping and squeezing me in a full body hug as my hands grip her hips. "You are the most thoughtful person."

I squeeze her back, my whispered words meant for her ears only. "There are so many things I want to show you."

She blushes, her pupils dilating as she catches my meaning. I'm not talking about the beach.

"Wow, okay, glad I don't know what he just said to you." Meredith grins while she checks out the room.

My phone chimes, my face falling when I see the message. "I need to go."

Charlotte slides down my body, eyes watching as I put on my baseball cap and grab the small backpack I'd brought with me for the trip. "Already?"

I tug her to me. "I'm sorry, gorgeous. I need to head out to make my next show on time."

Her nose buries in my chest as she snuggles into me. "I know. I'm going to miss you."

My lips graze her hair. "I'll miss you too." Fingers gentle, I bring her face up to look at me. My lips touch hers and my tongue licks inside before my phone interrupts us again. I pull back with a groan. "I love you."

She nods and her eyes turn liquid gold with the tears that swim in them. "Love you too."

CHAPTER 21

CHARLIE

"That was fucking hot earlier." Meredith fans herself as the two of us lay next to her pool, listening to music on a drowsy afternoon. She cackles with laughter as I hide my face in my hands. I hadn't meant to put on a show, but whenever Jackson and I kiss, everything else fades. It's the two of us, the slow slide of his lips against mine, his fingers digging into my hips—I break off that line of thinking before my breathing gives away the NSFW trail my thoughts are taking. "Seriously though, Char, you guys are the cutest couple I think I've ever seen."

Happiness bubbles out of me, the smile growing on my face. "Mer, he's the most amazing, sweetest guy I've ever met. I'm so in love with him."

Her head jerks in my direction as she yanks off her sunglasses. "Love? Have you told him yet?"

"Well…" I chew on my lip, embarrassment lodging in my shoulder blades when I remember my sleepy confession. But he'd said it back. Multiple times. I nod.

"Last night as I was drifting off to sleep, I let it slip."

"Really?"

I nod again, sharing the story of my first admission of love, followed by the conversation when Jackson told me he felt the same.

Meredith is quiet as I finish the story, lip caught between her teeth. "Don't you guys think this is moving a little fast?"

"Is there a time limit for falling in love?" Hurt creeps into my voice, my defenses rising. I thought she would be happy for us. She's the one that pushed us to date anyway, right?

"No, Charlie, shit that wasn't what I meant." She reaches out, rubbing my leg. "I just meant...I love you. I love Jax. I don't want to see either of you get hurt."

"Hurt?" Confusion scrambles my thoughts.

"It's just—It's—I don't want to see you get caught up in a story the label is selling. Jax is used to this world, to their crazy demands. You're not."

I shake my head. "We talked about that. Way in the beginning. We said that we were going to focus on us and didn't care what the label said or did." Fuck the label. Jackson's gravelly voice drifts into my consciousness, and a shiver dances down my spine.

"So he told you how much trouble he's in?"

Trouble? I'd heard a lot of Jackson's side of the phone conversation but couldn't tell what the other person was saying. I'd spent a few minutes after waking up laying there, listening to Jackson heatedly speak to whoever was on the other end of the line.

Nick. I remember Jackson saying his name. When I'd poked my head around the corner, he'd been leaning back on the couch, frustration and defeat rolling off of him in waves. He'd glanced up then, seeing me, his eyes the color of spring as he'd looked at me, motioned me forward.

Nausea creeps through my stomach.

"Not really?" I hope Meredith will explain. "What kind of trouble?"

She sighs. "I wanted him to tell you."

"Well, he didn't and you're here," I fire back.

"The Chicago thing went really bad. His label rep—"

"Nick?"

"Nick the dick." She rolls her eyes. "He told him that Jax needed to get some positive spin with you. Like fly you to the next concert or another romantic getaway or some shit like that."

Is that what yesterday was? Doubt creeps in, dampening the happiness I had felt a few minutes ago. "So you think yesterday was...?" I can't bring myself to say it.

"No, or at least, not the main reason," Meredith amends. "I know Jax cares about you." Cares about me is a lot different than love. "I just—I don't think the label thought him blowing off an appearance to come see you was the best idea. It definitely wasn't their suggestion."

"Oh."

"Charlie, he could lose a lot if he doesn't play by their rules."

"I know."

"You do?"

"He told me. He'd lose his songs, he'd owe money back..." I trail off and Meredith nods.

"He's got to be on really good behavior."

I'd heard Nick through Jackson's phone last night. *Pretend.*

"Especially since he's been given the opportunity to present at this year's awards show," she continues.

"He did?" Why hadn't he shared that with me?

"His last few tours weren't great."

"Yeah, he told me." At least, I think he'd told me everything. What if there was more?

"Well after that shit, the head of Reverb told Jax to not bother going. She'd make sure he didn't get invited."

"She said that?" Just who is Jackson dealing with?

Meredith shrugs. "Through Nick."

"When is the awards show?"

"Next weekend. Here."

My shoot is next Friday, so I'd planned to head home next weekend. With nothing going on, what if I stayed here to surprise Jackson? Would that make his label happy?

"Do you think Jackson can take a date?" Meredith nods, catching my idea. "I want this to be a surprise, though."

Meredith mimes zipping her lips and I roll my eyes. She can't keep secrets to save her life. Grabbing her phone, her fingers move over the screen. "I at least need to tell Derek. He can help us find you a dress."

When her phone chimes, she squeals, and I barely suppress a groan. What sort of makeover monsters have I created this time?

♪♪ ♪♪♪

All day I kept expecting to hear from Jackson, even if it was just a quick text. But by later that night I still haven't heard from him. He's traveling, trying to play catch up for the two days of hooky he played to come see me. Guilt pushes at me, making my fingers clumsy as I text him.

CHARLOTTE: Make it back yet? Miss you. <3

"Texting Lover Boy?" Meredith startles me from her position in the doorway. She waggles her eyebrows and sticks out her tongue.

"Don't be a dork." We share a giggle, but I can't help but wonder why I haven't heard back from him. *Remember the last time you didn't hear back from him?* My helpful brain flashes a slideshow of pictures from Chicago, hurt and doubt pricking when I think about those. Taking a deep breath, I push them away. He loves me. He said so.

CHARLOTTE: Goodnight.

Meredith leaves and I turn out the light, staring at the dark ceiling. My second text still doesn't have a response. My breath stalls when I think about the bits and pieces I'd overheard last night, my conversation with Meredith replaying in my mind. How much trouble is he in, and am I worth it?

CHAPTER 22

JAX

A somber mood permeates the air when I get back to the tour in New York. Normally, I would crack a joke and ask who died, but I already know. My career is at death's door, the livelihood of everyone here threatened by my actions. Again. Guilt gnaws a hole in my stomach, warring with the frustration that's been burning there after every good thing I did went unnoticed.

It's as if the last year of good behavior has been erased. News of my skipping out on the tour has caused all sorts of rumors to circulate. Everything from my being in rehab—seriously, where do they come up with this shit?—to dying in a tragic car accident. Walking backstage, conversations stop, people side-eye me, trying to figure out which rumor is true. Obviously, I'm not dead, but who knows what else has made the rounds. Squeezing the back of my neck, I keep my head down, unwilling to meet anyone's eyes as I walk quickly through the venue heading to my bus.

"Fucking finally."

That voice stops me in my tracks as I'm about to head up the steps.

"Nick." My eyes widen, knowing what his presence here means. Shit. "What are you doing here?"

"Is that any way to greet the person whose ass you should be kissing right now?" Nick's slick three piece suit looks out of place surrounded by threadbare denim and faded t-shirts.

"Uhhhh." Nick's smirk causes my stomach to ripple with apprehension and the hairs on the back of my neck stand up. He descends the steps until he and I are eye level with each other.

"Since you can't seem to make solid decisions when someone's not here to baby-sit you, consider us conjoined twins now, asshole. For the duration of your tour, I will be the Jiminy Cricket to your Pinocchio."

Though I had been expecting something, I hadn't anticipated this. "What the fuck?"

"Exactly. That's exactly what I've been asking myself since Chicago. I thought we understood each other then. Until you blew off one of the biggest set of radio stations in the country—fuck, they own stations in all the major markets. I figured before you screw both of us out of a job or get yourself sued for breach of contract, I'd swoop in to the rescue." Puffing out his chest, he looks down. "I'm thinking of getting an S here. Super Nick. Or shadow. While I'm here, consider me your shadow."

Dread settles over me like a straitjacket at the dark twist to his lips.

I should know better than to not take Nick literally. For the rest of the day, wherever I go, Nick follows like a sharply dressed, out of place shadow. I'm amazed that he doesn't follow me into the bathroom since, even on my bus after the concert and after-party, I'm not safe.

CHARLOTTE: Make it back yet? Miss you. <3

CHARLOTTE: Goodnight.

Charlotte sent the texts hours ago. Frustration eats at me that I missed my chance to talk to her tonight. Nick hovered around me during the entire meet and greet after the show and I'd had no choice but to stay the whole time. I'd stuck to water, further fueling rumors that I had been in rehab, exhaustion catching up to me after the last few days. I wanted to scream 'Newsflash—rehab is more than two days' but I didn't bother.

My fingers hover over the keyboard, ready to send something that Charlotte will see when she wakes up, but a sharp rap on my door followed by the knob immediately turning interrupts what I want to say.

"What the hell, Nick?" I toss my phone down on the little shelf next to me, running my hands through my hair. "Go away."

"Aw, c'mon, Jax. You don't mean that." Finally changing out his stupid looking suit, Nick's in basketball shorts and a t-shirt, an outfit that makes him almost look human.

"Actually, I do. As you can see," I gesture to the bedroom where it's just me, my phone, and my guitar. "I'm not fucking anything up in here, and all I want to do, since I can't call Charlotte, is go the hell to sleep."

"Call her."

"Dude! It's fucking midnight where she's at." And her body needs to recharge after the last few weeks of brutal pressure she'd put it under to prepare for the audition.

Groaning, I let my head fall back against the wall behind me.

"What do you want now?" Keeping my eyes closed, I fight the claustrophobic feeling squeezing around my neck like a noose.

"Two things. Listen, J, I know I've been—"

"Riding my ass?" I supply helpfully.

"Focused on your success," he corrects. "But you have a really good chance that most people never get. You nearly fucked it up once and you won't get a third chance. I don't want to see you lose everything you've worked for."

I crack one eye open. He almost sounds like he cares. Where does the experience I hear in his voice come from?

"Another thing." He tosses me his phone. "Call Michaela."

Shit. "Why?"

Michaela's an artist Reverb recently signed, and we'd met in Chicago. Why is he telling me to call her after the Chicago fiasco? She was the one whose picture Charlotte sent to me.

"The awards show next weekend?"

Wariness has words sticking in my throat before I'm finally able to croak out, "Yeah?"

"You're walking the red carpet together."

"What? Why? What about Charlotte?"

Nick shrugs. "We want to build some buzz on the duet. It's releasing the same night. This will be good for photo ops and the chance to build some excitement."

"Okay, but what about Charlotte?" I'd briefly considered asking her but hadn't gotten around to it yet. Maybe she'd still be in LA—

"Do you really want Charlie to have to come in the back door while you walk the carpet? Make up something. Tell them Charlie couldn't come, whatever. I don't fucking care. But you *will* be doing the red carpet with Michaela." Nick interrupts my thoughts, "Pogo stick, remember?"

FUCK. Swallowing, I nod. "I remember."

Glancing at Nick's phone, I see it's already queued up to Michaela's number. "Where is she?"

"St. Louis."

Clicking on the contact, my stomach churns as I wait for her to pick up. I just got Charlotte back, I don't want to fuck this up again. Nick stares at me, sensing how close I am to hanging up the phone. How the hell am I going to tell Charlotte about this?

"Hello?"

♪♫♪♫♪

Nick's presence is making me crazier by the day. His hovering and spouting of label ideology is trying the patience I've discovered doesn't exist with his constant helicopter style. His shadow-like state is pushing me past the breaking point. Dragging my hands through my hair, I blow out a breath. How the fuck do I get him off my case? Better yet, how do I get him and the label off my back?

We're halfway through the week and anytime I've picked up my phone to call Charlotte, Nick has been there to yank my attention to something else. We're at the last concert leading up to the awards show and guilt burns like acid in my stomach. I still haven't told Charlotte about Michaela. I need to. If things were different, I'd be taking Charlotte instead.

Nick's in one of the empty chairs of the stadium, reading through emails, cowboy boots tapping against the chair in front of him in a way that makes my molars grind together. The cowboy boots are new, but something tells me he's more comfortable in them than he lets on. I can't wait until he has to go bother his next "favorite" artist.

My head pounds with an ever-present headache while I run through sound check. Finished, I rush back to the bus, downing two aspirin in an effort to alleviate the jackhammering in my skull. Christ, I'm so fucking tired of this. Nick always up my ass. Not talking to Charlotte. Not sleeping because everything feels like it's falling apart, and guilt that I'm not being honest with her.

There's a new email from the awards producers to discuss the logistics of my arrival with Michaela, the award presentation, and who I'm going to be presenting with. I should be excited. Instead, the email just makes me more tired than I was before. Taking advantage of the peace and quiet while Nick is occupied elsewhere, I click on the phone icon. Finally, time to call Charlotte. Before I can even unlock the screen, Nick is opening the door.

"Don't you *ever* knock?" I toss my phone down on the bed, clasping my hands behind my neck, breathing flames.

"Meh." Nick shrugs. "Sometimes."

"Out." I've had enough. Would it kill him to give me five goddamned minutes to myself? To give me privacy so I can call my girlfriend?

"Is that any way to treat your favorite label rep?"

"You're my only label rep," I snarl back.

"Potato, tomato." Nick smirks. The desire to punch him in the face overwhelms me so much I have to clench my hand by my side. "Guess who I just got off the phone with."

Glaring at him, I raise my eyebrows, hoping he'll just get it over with.

"The awards show producers. An act cancelled on them—something about a broken collarbone. They want to know if you're interested."

I nearly fumble the water bottle in my hand with his announcement. "Seriously?"

Smiling feels foreign after the last several days of not having a reason to. This is a huge opportunity.

"Told you I was your favorite."

"This is…this is incredible."

"Randa is pleased. They want you and Michaela to debut the duet that's coming out on her album." My happiness dims at his words. Of course, Randa wants to dictate this too. Before I can share my reservations—namely that I think my girlfriend will kick my ass to the curb—he leaves, making a comment about figuring out some plans.

Charlotte is the first person on my mind to tell. Shutting my door, I click on her number.

"Hello?"

"Hey, gorgeous."

"Jackson." My name catches in her voice, the sound a balm to my battered soul. Fuck, I miss her.

"I miss you. You guys having fun?" She's been texting me off and on, but I don't even have time for more than a few responses before I'm being carted somewhere else by "Super" Nick, my shadow.

"We are. We've hit the beach a few times and Meredith took me sightseeing. I miss you too." There are muffled voices on her end, and she comes back. "Meredith says that she'll see you next week."

I chuckle. "Okay. Well, that's why I was calling."

"Is everything okay? You still get to present, right?"

"I do. Even better. Guess who gets to perform at the show on Sunday?"

"Ummm…Luke Bryan?" My eyebrows raise, impressed that she's more familiar with different artists.

"Haha. Funny girl. Guess again."

Charlotte giggles. "You're really performing?"

Swallowing the guilt, I rub the back of my neck. "Looks like it. It'll be a duet I collaborated with on another singer's debut album." That's mostly the truth.

"That's so amazing, Jackson. So, you'll need Meredith this weekend?"

Nodding even though she can't see me, I respond. "Yeah. I'm not breaking up any plans for you two, right?"

"No, I was going to head back to Colorado after the shoot anyway." Disappointment crashes the excitement. Even if I couldn't take her to the ceremony, I had still hoped to see her since the awards show was going to be in LA.

"You are?"

She sighs. "I've been gone for two weeks. There's no other reason to stay in LA after the shoot."

"I don't know. What if they need to do a re-shoot or you get another job?" I really want to see her this weekend.

"I'll figure it out. Why, is there a reason *you* want me to stay in LA?"

It's better if she's not there. She'll be less likely to see any coverage of the awards show from home. "No. You're right."

"Oh." Her voice bleeds disappointment. Shame tightens my chest and I rub at it to relieve the ache.

"Jax!" Fuck Nick and fuck his fucking timing.

"Shit, gorgeous, I have to go. Can I try to call you later?"

"Sure, okay. But don't worry if you can't." Her voice is softer than normal, worry evident in the cadence. "Try to rest a bit."

"No rest for the wicked, Charlotte. Remember?" It feels like a lifetime since I said those words to her the first time.

"I remember." She clears her throat. "Break a leg tonight. I love you."

Those three words make my heart beat faster, even as guilt still nibbles in the back of my mind. I need to tell her. Tonight. "I love you too, gorgeous."

I *will* call her tonight. I have to tell her.

CHAPTER 23

CHARLIE

The last week in LA has been so much fun. Meredith and I have been all over the city, from the beach to Griffith Observatory. Every new place we go inspires a new image of Jackson and me here together. Of maybe making a life here. Together.

Since he's traveled back to rejoin the tour, he's been distant, and most of our communication has been through short text messages on his part. Hearing from him yesterday was a good surprise as Meredith and I lounged on the beach.

I giggle, remembering how disappointed he sounded when I told him I was going home after the shoot. This time it's my turn to surprise him.

"What's that little chuckle about?" Meredith plops down on the couch next to me.

"How sad Jackson sounded yesterday. He really has no idea, does he?" Is it possible that Meredith has actually learned to keep a secret?

Meredith snorts. "He's such a baby."

My phone rings, interrupting our laughter.

"Hello?"

"Hey, Charlie, it's Garrett."

"Oh, hey, Garrett, what's up?"

"I'm calling to let you know we need to reschedule the shoot. The artist had a family emergency and is out of the country right now."

Out of the country? Who exactly am I recording with? "Oh, okay."

Meredith gives me a questioning look and I hold up a finger.

"Right now, the artist isn't sure when he'll be back, but he said he'd call me when he's able to reschedule. So, for now, we're on hold."

"Oh." Does this mean that the shoot might not happen? Disappointment saps me and I slouch into the cushions.

"Don't worry. He did say he wants to get it recorded still, but probably about a month or so from now. Will that still work for your schedule?"

"Yeah, yes. Absolutely." All I have planned at home is watching Bella since I stopped teaching classes at the studio, not wanting to leave Madame in a lurch when I left for LA. My schedule is wide open.

"Great. I'll keep you posted. Thanks, Charlie."

"Yeah, sure, no problem."

We hang up and Meredith pounces.

"What happened? What's going on?"

"Shoot got rescheduled." I shrug. "Something about the artist having a family emergency."

"Who?"

Chewing on my lip, I flip through the possibilities. Garrett had sent me an instrumental version of the music so I could get a feel for the song, but they've been so tight-lipped that I still have no idea. "I'm not sure. He said 'he' so obviously a guy. But it's like no song I've heard before."

"Ugh. That's frustrating."

A knock on the door is followed by Meredith's mom poking her head in. "Hey, girls, Dad and I are heading to dinner. You wanna come?"

"Where are you going?" Meredith sits up, the thought of food a temptation I know she won't ignore.

"We thought we'd try that new steak place."

"We're in." Standing, she yanks me up as we follow her mom to the car.

Meredith's parents are more relaxed than my own. If Meredith and I would have said no, Val would have shrugged and left. Even when I was the only one here, she and Mike would check on me, but otherwise I was left to do what I wanted when I wanted. It's been different. Refreshing. I wonder if I can keep this up in Colorado when I go home. Mom and Dad had started to relax a little, but I still hesitate, wondering if things will go back to "normal" when I get back.

Meredith starts tossing names of artists at me, and when I don't recognize some of the names, she plays songs. By the time we get to the restaurant, I've forgotten all about returning to Colorado and what it'll be like after being here.

♫♪♫♪♫

My phone rings, waking me up the next morning.

"Hello?"

"Charlie? You're still asleep? I'm sorry."

Sitting up, the room spins, and I lay back down. "That's okay, Mom. I must have been tired."

"Are you feeling alright? You're not sick, are you?"

"Yeah. No. I don't feel sick. Just tired."

"I thought you were taking it easy out there?"

Smiling, I try to reassure her, "I am. And we don't have anything planned today. We just stayed up late last night watching movies."

"Your shoot is tomorrow, right?"

I explain that it got rescheduled.

"So, you'll be coming home soon?"

"Ummm..." I'd been thinking about maybe taking the time to travel with Meredith and Jackson for the last few stops on his tour. Garrett has my cell phone and the tour wraps before I'd have to be back. "I'm not sure." I explain the surprise that Meredith and I have planned for Jackson and that I may end up traveling with the tour for a few weeks.

"If you're sure," she says warily.

"I still have to talk to Jackson, but I'll keep you posted."

"Alright, Charlie. Oh shoot, I have a meeting in five minutes. We'll talk again this weekend?"

"Okay."

"Have fun and be safe. Love you, baby."

"Love you too, Mom."

Now, I just need to get through the nervous excitement coursing through me at the thought of my surprise for Jackson.

♪♪♪♪♪♪

"I don't feel so good." These aren't butterflies fluttering serenely in my stomach, these are kamikaze butterflies dancing chaotically while dive-bombing into my throat.

Pressing a hand against the tulle overlay of the dress I'm wearing, I hope to stave off actually throwing up. It's not like I've eaten anything—I was too nervous to eat earlier, but my hands are shaking like a caffeine junkie on a quad shot of espresso regardless.

The crowd ebbs and flows around us, attendees for the awards show entering the large foyer of the venue where they're being hosted. The din is a constant vibration as people filter in from the red carpet, noise levels rising whenever the doors open to admit someone new.

Fans and reporters line the carpet, cheers and screams growing louder as their favorite artists walk less than fifty feet in front of them. I'm relieved that Meredith brought me in the back entrance, but even that was chaos, dancers and stagehands hustling in preparation for the show tonight.

"Jax is going to trip over his tongue." Meredith bounces next to me, absorbing the energy of the crowd while I just want to find a quiet corner and hide. This was a stupid idea. I'm not a fan of being in crowds of people. On stage is one thing. This is something entirely different. Derek stands on the other side of me, eyes agog at all the celebrities around us. I'd call him out on it since he does work with celebrities every day, but I worry that if I open my mouth, it won't be to speak.

He grabs one of my shaky hands in his, the squeeze reassuring, while his other hand fluffs the skirt on my dress. "Chér, you are a vision. Don't chew off your lipstick."

Releasing my lip from my teeth, I'm afraid to move in case I do any more damage. Despite the nerves threatening to topple me, I've never felt more like a princess, the blush pink A-line dress made of a soft tulle whispers as I move. The top of the dress has a delicate floral lace overlay—it's initially what drew me to the dress when Derek sent me the picture.

My fairy godfather even found a matching pair of heels that aren't so tall they make my ankle scream. Once I was dressed, Derek and Meredith had done my hair in a messy, elegant updo that leaves wisps moving against my face in the air conditioning. My make-up is subtle and soft, making me more recognizable when I looked in the mirror, but also giving me a glimmer of confidence in this otherwise tumultuous evening.

"Sorry," I mumble. Meredith looks ready to jump into the party at any second. "What time again?"

"Anytime now," she says.

Jackson had agreed to meet her at a set time under the guise of discussing the performance. Instead of meeting Meredith, I plan on surprising him. Knots twist my stomach while we wait. Should I have given him a clue that I was coming? When? He has been hard to get a hold of since the stolen day when I first got out here.

Fidgeting with a delicate bracelet, I roll it against my wrist, watching as celebrity attendees mingle with one another in glittering dresses and matte suits or tuxedos. We're partially hidden in an alcove off to the side of the bigger room. Watching all of them, I'd probably be more starstruck if I wasn't so nervous. Meredith's phone chimes, startling me.

"Relax." Squeezing my hand, she smiles at me. I feel bad for her, knowing my hand is clammy. "Okay, this is him. He's here. Breathe, Char."

I try to focus on her as much to calm the lightheadedness as to hear what she's saying over the crowd. The doors open and I can hear fans screaming Jackson's name. My heart rate picks up, reacting to the excitement, to the screams. Thank goodness for our hiding spot. The best feature of this little alcove is that, with a quick move, we can watch Jackson walking the red carpet before intercepting him at the door while also staying out of the spotlight.

My body heats, fingers itching to tangle with his, to feel the callouses there and hear his southern drawl whisper my name. I picture his face when he sees me, his green eyes brightening, the smile that makes me happy in return.

He looks amazing and relaxed, answering reporters' questions, smiling and signing autographs for fans lucky enough to be close to the ropes and able to interact. His dark suit and stark white shirt contrast nicely and add a debonair attitude with his dark hair combed back. The beginnings of a five o'clock shadow soften his jaw, adding to the mix of polished and scruffy sexiness.

My heart trips in my chest and fire skates along my skin to my core and burns the nerves away. The butterflies flap more furiously as I try to breathe through all the sensations buffeting my body. Soon. Minutes from now, we'll be reunited.

Jackson finishes an autograph and his hand stretches, moving, resting on a back bedecked in red silk. The world spins to slow motion and a buzzing starts in my ears. He stands next to the blonde as a camera flash goes off, and I flinch at the bright light. They turn, graceful and in sync, heading toward the entrance. Picture-perfect in bold colors as my face goes cold.

"Charlie? Charlie? Are you okay? Charlie? You just turned gray. Oh shit." Meredith sounds like she's underwater. Or possibly I am.

The woman with Jackson is heartbreakingly familiar or maybe it's just because I've spent hours staring at her picture, her hand on Jackson's thigh. I can't forget the features of the supermodel-like face that had smiled as she leaned her head against his chest.

My mind stutters, everything coming at me in flashes of consciousness while it shuts down. It's hard to get breath in my lungs, the air burning on every inhale, stalling on every exhale. Is this why I haven't heard from him? Was I right to not trust him? Was I really not worth the trouble he had gotten into?

"Mer, they're almost here." Derek's voice is clear, panic edging into the normally teasing accent.

"Charlie. Charlie, don't. C'mon, let's go."

I'm outside my body, watching events unfold. Meredith and Derek are trying to turn me to head in the opposite direction of Jackson and his date, but I'm frozen, glued to the floor, staring as they come closer to the door, closer to discovering what a complete, naïve idiot I've been.

Jackson leans over, whispering something to her. She throws her head back, her bright red lips parting with her throaty laugh, and he grins in response. It's that colorful image in a black and white world that wakes me up.

Setting my feet, I shake off Derek and Meredith, moving to stand so that Jackson will see me as soon as he opens the door. They get stopped just before they reach the door and my confidence falters.

As if the universe senses that waver, Jackson shifts, his eyes connecting with mine through the glass. The green orbs widen in what would normally be a comical way, his mouth moving and forming words that I can't make out through the noise. Excusing himself from the conversation with his date and a reporter, he rushes inside.

"Gorgeous—"

I hold up a hand to stop him from coming closer. "Don't you dare." My voice wobbles and I swallow the lump building in my throat. "I trusted you."

People nearby notice the drama unfolding and Jackson glances around, trying to motion me back into the alcove. "Gorgeous, the label set this up. We're just friends. I had to—"

His voice is quiet, like he's trying to mesmerize me into following him into the quieter, more private setting. Like he's trying to get me to fall for his lies. *Again.* "Bullshit." I feel Meredith and Derek on either side of me, Meredith's heat lending me strength. "You're a liar and I'm an idiot for believing you."

"Baby—"

"NO." My voice is louder, drawing more attention. "You don't get to call me that. Not anymore."

Jackson's date steps into our circle, her bright blue eyes ping-ponging apprehensively between Jackson and me. "Jax? Is everything okay?"

I've never wanted to hit someone as badly as I want to hit both her and him. Turning my gaze to her, I concede. I'm not going to do this anymore. "You can have him."

"What?" She looks confused and opens her mouth to say something else, but Jackson motions at her to be quiet.

"Gorgeous, Charlotte, wait. Let me explain."

Shaking my head, I keep my hand held up when he starts to step forward again. If he comes near me, I'll shatter. "I fell for it once, shame on you. I fell for it twice, shame on me. I refuse to give you another chance to lie to me. Fuck you, Jackson. Go to hell."

Spinning, I walk away with no destination in mind other than not near Jackson. Meredith's voice carries in the cavernous room, so I hear her when she chimes in behind me.

"I quit, asshole." Meredith and Derek flank me as I make my way to the back hallway. Fortunately, Jackson doesn't follow us. Once through a door, the adrenaline leaves my body in a rush and my knees buckle. Derek swoops in before I fall completely, slipping his strong arms around my waist.

"It's okay, little one, I've got you."

Numbness beckons and I give in, trying to ignore the murderous rage on Meredith's face and the pity in Derek's kind eyes as they both bear witness to my stupidity. Instead of my fairytale moment, the clock is striking midnight. My heart cracks, tears streaming unchecked down my face.

Everything blurs.

I'm curled in my bed at Meredith's. She and Derek managed to get me here without her parents noticing. They'd turned on the light for me before moving back out to the living room. Even though the door is mostly closed, I can still hear them. My eyes are gritty and swollen but the tears don't stop. Shouldn't I have run out of tears by now?

Hushed whispers hover at the edge of my awareness.

"Why the fuck did you quit?!" Derek whisper yells to Meredith. Or, more accurately, yells at Meredith. If he was trying to be quiet, he's failed miserably.

"I won't work with him, Derek. He's not the same guy I grew

up with, because that guy would never have broken my best friend."

Am I broken? Is that what this feeling is?

"You were there, Derek. I've never seen her that way—ever. I should have junk punched him when I quit."

"Whoa, tiger. Sit back down. You don't need to go finish that job."

No emotion registers anymore. The numbness is scary, an abyss I'm not sure I understand, but still welcome. The ache where my heart used to beat isn't ripping me apart anymore.

"I saw her. She hasn't stopped crying. There's no sound. Just tears. It's creepy as fuck." Derek's voice is lower, confused. I want to tell him not to worry about me, but if I open my mouth now, I'm worried the numbness will leave, scared off by the screams waiting to escape.

"Char?" Meredith comes into the dim room and sits on the edge of the bed. I blink but otherwise don't move, fatigue weighing down on me. "Let's get you in the shower, girl."

Meredith leads me to the bathroom where the harsh mirror shows tracks of mascara around red-rimmed, swollen eyes, tears making fresh paths through the streaks of black. My hair has come out of its updo, a massive tangle around my pale face.

The one thing that doesn't look like a complete disaster is the dress that made me feel like a princess when I first put it on tonight. It's rumpled from laying on the bed, but otherwise looks the same. The only difference is, it's not magical anymore.

Meredith turns on and adjusts the water for me, then unzips the dress, helping me remove it.

"I'll be right outside," she whispers, pulling the door mostly shut when she leaves.

I'm cold. Not the normal winter in Colorado cold, but deeper, as if all my organs are frozen, made of ice, and don't know what heat has ever felt like. Not bothering to take off my panties or strapless bra I climb into the shower, cranking up the hot water.

The heat hits my skin and I sink to my knees. Deep, wrenching sobs rack my body as the water scalds my skin from gray to pink to angry red.

Memories swamp me of Jackson, shattering like mirrors as I try to push each one away. This pain is unbearable. I cry for the disappearance of the numbness, frightened away by the hot water. I cry for the pain that follows, feeling like millions of shallow cuts along my skin. I cry for the broken fairytale I dared to believe in.

Time loses meaning, but eventually Meredith comes back in, helping me up from where I sit on the floor of the shower. She turns off the water and wraps me in a fluffy towel. Helping me out of my soaking underwear and into dry pajamas, she sits me on the bed, brushing the snarls from my hair like I would for Bella. Her sad eyes take me in when she tucks me into bed.

"Get some sleep, Char."

She turns off the light and I close my eyes, begging sleep to come and stop the nightmare I'm currently surviving in.

CHAPTER 24

CHARLIE

Sometime in the middle of the night I make a decision. This feeling, this bottomless darkness that has snuffed out the ability to breathe is because I tried to go after what I wanted. I decided to pursue my relationship with Jackson, I told him it was *us* without realizing it was *me* putting myself out there alone and that, by doing so, it's my fault the hole exists where my heart used to beat.

I was better off before. Was it frustrating to feel like I was settling for a life I didn't want? Yes. But I didn't feel like my entire world had imploded either.

Throughout the night, I watch the shadows crawl across the walls as the day draws near, making a plan to survive.

"Charlie?" Meredith's raspy voice reaches out in the semi darkness of the morning, startling me from my thoughts. Pain pierces my stomach. It shouldn't be Meredith's voice I hear first thing this morning, but it is. "Did you sleep?"

Shaking my head, I tell the truth, and Meredith's eyes fill with sadness at my response. "I've been thinking."

"What have you been thinking about all night?" She speaks softly like she's afraid to ask me the question.

"I'm going home." My voice is flat, emotionless. Resigned.

"But you're coming back out for the video shoot, right?"

"I don't really know—" My voice cracks.

"Charlie, no. Don't say that. You earned it." She looks at me, her own eyes brimming with tears. "It's your dream."

I shrug, tired of putting in the effort to hope. To dream. It's easier not to. On all counts.

♫♪♫♪♫

Time passes, days blurring together. One minute I'm in LA, waiting for Jackson to walk through the doors and meet me, and the next, I'm back home in my parents' house in Boulder. My room has become my haven, curtains closed against the world.

The sunlight that currently filters around them tells me it's daytime. Jackson has called and texted, but I don't respond, choosing not to read the messages. The hardest part is when the notifications about the wrap-up of his tour ping my newsfeed.

Bryant Wraps Successful Tour

What's Next for Jax Bryant?

Bryant's Breakout Tour

There's been no mention of me in any of the articles, the reporters having moved on from our love story the label wanted to spin.

My phone rings, a welcome reprieve from thoughts of Jackson and the woman in red.

"Hello?"

"Hey, Charlie, it's Garrett." My last call with him feels like a lifetime ago. Has it really only been a week?

"Hi, yes, Garrett, how's it going?"

"We're finally back on schedule. The artist called me yesterday. He'll be back in town in two weeks. That work for you?"

"Sorry, what?" Shaking my head, I try to clear the fog to process what he is telling me.

He laughs. "Two weeks. You want to shoot a video?"

"Okay." Nodding, the idea starts to gain ground. "Yes. I'll be there."

I need to start living again, to actually make some money since I'm now jobless. My parents haven't said anything to me about watching Bella, but since they weren't sure when I would be home, they'd already made plans for her for this week. I had planned on calling Madame but hadn't gotten around to it yet. Garrett gives me the details, telling me he'll email the contract to me before disconnecting.

"Charlie?" Mom's voice calls up the stairs. "Do you want some tea?"

Nausea has been my constant companion this week, my body rejecting anything I've tried to eat. I head downstairs anyway, hoping the tea will help settle my stomach.

Mom eyes me, taking in my messy ponytail and oversized t-shirt paired with beat-up yoga pants. It's been my uniform this week and it's not likely to change soon. Dad sits at the table, eyes glued to his phone.

"You okay?"

Sitting down at the table, I avoid the question. "They rescheduled the shoot."

Mom's smile stretches across her face. "Oh, honey, they did? That's so exciting."

Coming over, she loops an arm around my shoulders, squeezing me into a hug.

"You don't seem very happy."

I shrug. "I'm not sure I should do it. Maybe I should just call Madame and see if I can get back on at the studio?" Surely, she'd let me come back.

"Charlotte Grace Walker. No." Mom sets a cup of tea in front of me, sitting down with one of her own. "You're doing this video. Your dad and I have some things to say to you."

Stomach churning, I stare into my tea. "Okay?" I look up and search for some sort of sign telling me what they want to talk about. Dad seems really awkward—more so than normal. What could possibly have him looking like that?

"Charlie, we—you—we—" At least I know where I got my great articulation skills. My mom stumbles before continuing, "We...wanted to apologize to you."

Bewildered, my eyes ping between them. I want to ask Mom to repeat that, but I think they might not understand why I'm asking them to say it again.

"We owe you an apology for a lot," Dad echoes.

Gaping at Dad, I want to pinch myself. Is this a dream?

"When your dad and I first got back together, there was a lot to get through. We...um...well, we saw a therapist for the first year after Bella was born."

Dad picks up where Mom stops. "We dealt with our issues." He gestures between the two of them. "But chose to forget that you were there for a lot of it." Clearing his throat, he continues, "What I said about your mother during those years, Charlie, that was wrong. To say them to you? I'm embarrassed every time I think about it."

Mom's eyes fill with tears. "We both said things we regret. But we regret hurting you by fighting more. By not acknowledging that to you. By not acknowledging you." Tears roll down her cheeks, and I feel my own eyes sting.

"I need to apologize for what I said the other night too." Dad draws my attention back to him. "I had no right to discount the work you've put into dance, into recovering from that injury.

You're right, we weren't there for the surgery, but getting that call? Knowing you were going into surgery? That scared the hell out of me. I don't want to see you hurt."

"But watching you dance, baby? That's been one of the best things to witness. You just…you light up when you dance." Mom's voice is quiet, her eyes bright.

I nod, not trusting myself to speak.

"Which is why we're firing you. Permanently." Dad's smile softens his words. "No more watching Bella unless you volunteer."

"What?" I ask.

He chuckles. "It's time. We got Bella set up in a preschool because we don't want you to settle. We want you to chase your dream, Charlie. The world is hard enough. We don't need to make it harder."

"We love you. You're our first baby. Even if you are all grown up now." Mom reaches out, running a hand through my hair. "We'll support whatever dream you want. Help you however we can."

"Really? You think I can do it?" Dad nods and I throw my arms around him, hugging him as tears stream down my cheeks, the enormity of everything they said hitting me. From this angle, I can see the Candy Crush app open on his phone and I laugh through the tears. Dad looks at it too, chuckling.

"It's addicting." I laugh at his embarrassed explanation, still snickering when Bella comes into the kitchen.

"Chawie, juice?"

"Mommy will get it, Bella." Mom starts to get up, and I hold up my hand.

"That's okay, Mom, I'll get it. You sit." Opening the fridge, I lean over, a wave of vertigo hitting me so hard I fall forward, the world spinning around me in a blurry wheel before fading to black.

"Charlie? Charlie? Honey?" I'm lying on the floor looking up at Mom when I blink my eyes open.

"Mom?" I try to sit up, my head throbbing.

"Easy, baby." Dad helps me up into a chair. "You fainted."

"What?" I don't remember fainting but that would explain why one second I remember grabbing for Bella's juice box and the next I was looking up at Mom leaning over me.

"Enough is enough. You haven't been able to eat all week and now this. We're going to the ER."

"Mom, I'm fine." But her look tells me she thinks otherwise.

"No arguing. I should have taken you earlier this week. I just chalked it up to traveling."

Dad nods. "I'll stay here with Bella. You go."

Getting to the hospital, Mom sends me back to the room myself.

"This way you'll have privacy." When I understand her meaning—that Mom realizes I'm no longer a virgin—I can't help the heat that lights up my face. She laughs, pushing me to go with the nurse when my name is called. "I was young once too, Charlie."

The nurse shows me to a room with instructions to put on a gown. The bed is relatively comfortable for it being in a hospital, but I still twist my phone in my hands waiting for the next part.

"Charlotte Walker?" Scrubbing a hand over my eyes, another nurse walks in to take down my symptoms and medical history. Transcribing my responses into her electronic chart, she clicks on her screen. "Date of your last menstrual cycle?"

I hesitate. After my whirlwind relationship and subsequent crash and burn with Jackson, I can't place the date.

"I-I'm not sure."

"Are you sexually active?"

My face flames at the question. "I-I was. But it didn't work out so I'm not now?" Probably more information than she needs, but she doesn't look up from keying notes into her computer. What does she write?

"Is there a possibility that you could be pregnant?"

"I-I-I-" We used birth control. And condoms until recently. It's not possible. Right?

The nurse hands me a specimen cup before I can fully craft a response. "It's a normal procedure for women who are sexually active."

I nod, the urge to drop the cup and run out of the building pounding through my blood. But even now, nausea swamps my stomach, draining me physically and mentally. I leave the cup in the little door of the bathroom, my mind spinning chaotically as I climb back into the bed.

I take several deep breaths, closing my eyes. A perfunctory knock interrupts my attempt to calm my heart rate, and a young doctor enters the room.

"Good afternoon, my name is Dr. Langley."

Shaking her hand, I nod. "Hi, I'm Charlotte. Charlie. Walker." Will I ever be able to say my full name again without being reminded of the sound of it from Jackson's lips with his slight drawl?

"Tell me about your symptoms, Charlie." She listens intently before finding my chart on her computer. The silence as she reviews the chart causes my fingers to twist in the gown on my lap. It feels like the longest five minutes of my life as she stares at the computer before looking back at me.

"Charlie, your test came back positive. You're pregnant."

Air whooshes in and out of my ears, making it sound like I'm in a windstorm. "Pregnant?"

The doctor nods.

"But...but we used protection." Pregnant?

"Condoms?"

I nod. "And birth control."

"While condoms may advertise being 98% effective, the odds

are closer to 85%. And if you had just started birth control or weren't consistent with your dose?"

"I-I'd just started."

She nods. "Usually, they tell you to stay on another form of contraception as you start your prescription."

Had anyone told me that? I can't remember. The deep breath I'm trying to take keeps getting stalled part way into my lungs. Pregnant?

"I read in your chart that you've been experiencing some extreme nausea?" I nod. "Have you been able to keep any food down? Water?"

I shake my head.

"I'm willing to bet you have Hyperemesis Gravidarum. It's an extreme version of morning sickness."

"The thing that Princess Kate had?" Dr. Langley nods again.

"Exactly. Hyperemesis Gravidarum starts earlier and sticks around longer than normal morning sickness, usually requiring more careful monitoring of the pregnancy. We need to make sure you're getting enough nutrition and staying hydrated. I want to get you some IV fluids now and send you home with a prescription that should help with the nausea and vomiting. I'm also going to give you some instructions on a diet that includes ginger or adding a B6 supplement besides the standard prenatal vitamins. Finally"—she pauses again, her face serious—"stress is going to exacerbate the condition. Try to stay calm, take it easy. HEG—the short way to say all that—can cause dizziness and fainting so it's important to get it under control and keep it that way."

I nod, trying to absorb everything she has shared.

"I'll send a nurse in with the IV and once we're done getting you some fluids, you'll be ready to head home."

She excuses herself and my eyes drift to my still flat stomach. It doesn't look like I'm pregnant. My hands hover over my middle, almost afraid to touch it. My baby. Jackson's baby. Jackson. One trembling hand rests lightly against the warm skin while other falls to my side. I lean my head back and close my eyes.

"What am I gonna do?" I have to tell him. I know that. Picking up my phone, I open my contacts to stare at the list of favorites I have stored. Meredith. Mom. Dad. Jackson. Closing out of that app, I open my pictures, thumbing through selfies that Meredith and I took sightseeing in California, slowing on images of Jackson.

How are my parents going to react to hearing they're about to be grandparents? They were younger than I am now when they had me. Will that help soften the news?

First things first, I need to tell Jackson. Closing my eyes, I picture his smile. It's so easy to imagine the way his emerald eyes would spark when he looked at me. The images fade and I see him swaggering confidently on the red carpet, the instant his hand connects with red silk. The same slash of hurt rears up sharper than ever. What will his reaction to the baby be?

After getting a round of IV fluids, I make my way back out to the waiting room where Mom looks up from her phone.

"Everything okay?"

I nod. "Just dehydrated."

Mom raises an eyebrow. "That's all it was?"

I shrug. "That's what the doctor said." Among other things.

Mom stands, grabbing her jacket and purse, and we walk to her car.

"Have you heard from Meredith yet?" Her voice startles me from my thoughts as we head home.

"Meredith?"

"Yeah, I thought you'd have told her about the video being rescheduled and want to stay with her?"

"Oh, yeah, right. I guess I just wasn't thinking straight." Can I still do the video shoot now that I know I'm pregnant?

I can—I'm not showing and won't for some time. One of Dr.

Langley's instructions was to find an OB soon. When I get back from the video shoot, that'll be first on my list. First, call Meredith about the video shoot. Second, do the shoot. Third, tell Jackson about the baby. I can't tell Meredith right now, I've already put her too far in the middle of my relationship with Jackson.

Don't worry, baby, I'll be our voice in the world.

I'll build that fire back up. If not for me, then for us. No more settling, no more rolling over. It's time to go after what I want. I may not be saying it out loud, but inside it's a tribal yell. A small smile touches my lips.

A mother's yell.

CHAPTER 25

JAX

The final concert in Philadelphia was not the best of my tour. If I'm honest with myself, I think it had been the worst in my history—and that's including concerts from the last tour that I don't remember, so out of it that I nearly got my record deal revoked. I couldn't focus tonight, relying on autopilot, my brain still stuck on images of Charlotte, standing there in a beautiful dress, her eyes dim with hurt but still flashing with fire.

She hasn't responded to any of my texts or picked up when I've called her. *Do you blame her, dumb ass?* Her image is burned into my brain as are her parting words to me. Fuck you, Jackson. Go to hell. Rubbing at the ache burning in my chest, I take the shot someone hands me. I've made it, the final after-party.

"To the finish line!" With the crowd cheering me on, I toss it back, grimacing as the burn traces the path to my stomach, stealing the ache in my chest with it. I didn't ask what it was, I don't care. I just want my memories to leave me alone for tonight.

"Hey, Jax." Michaela sits next to me on the couch.

"Michaela, what brings you to Philly?" I hadn't expected to see her again, especially after the awards show train wreck.

"Visiting my parents for the weekend and thought I'd come say hey. The other night was...interesting." I'm torn between not trusting that she's telling me the truth—Chicago, the awards show, and Philly all feel too coincidental—and wanting to give her advice about hiding the emotion so prominently displayed on her face. Emotions don't work in our reality, they'll just chew her up and spit her out.

Rubbing my neck, I relax as the effects of the shot blur the edges of my vision. Or maybe it's the three other shots I've already had. "Yeah, sorry about that."

The warmth of her hand transfers through my jeans where she rests it on my thigh, leaning forward slightly in an effort to be heard over all the noise surging in the room. "I understand. I feel bad that I pissed off your girlfriend. Or is she your ex-girlfriend now?"

I smirk and choose not to respond, instead, I take a pull on the beer that someone's handed me, Another shot glass is passed to me with a similar toast as before, the warmth sliding down a little smoother. Michaela takes a shot and grimaces, coughing. Raising my eyebrows at her devious grin, I shake my head.

"Are you even old enough to drink that?"

"Almost." She winks at me. "I'll be twenty-one in a few months."

Fuck, she's younger than I was when I started in this industry. At twenty-one I'd been hanging out with my friends on campus, finishing up college. It wasn't until after graduation that I'd been free to pursue music. Now it feels like I've lived a hundred lifetimes at the ripe old age of twenty-six. As the party progresses around us, Michaela and I talk about music, playing guitar, our favorite artists, favorite covers. It's an easy conversation overlaid with a lot of flirtation, her leg pressing against mine as she's gotten closer and closer on the couch, practically sitting in my lap. The liquor keeps flowing and my vision grows fuzzier.

"I'm gonna g'some air." I stand, unsteady on my feet, and weave through the crowd who all chant my name. Squinting, I head to a gray metal door, cool air rushing in. A-ha! I take a deep breath and collapse against the wall outside the exit, stars dancing in front of my eyes while the fresh air blows against my overheated skin.

The door clangs next to me. Who is interrupting my peace?

"Air sounded like a good idea." Michaela's eyes are hazy, and a lucid thought sneaks through the buzz fogging my brain—I shouldn't have let her drink so much. The rest of me punches that logical thought in the dick. Don't be such a pussy.

I let my eyes travel her body as she stands across from me. Blonde haired and blue eyed, she's wearing a top that shows off a sliver of toned, tanned stomach above a short denim skirt. Her face lifts and she looks up to the sky. "Can't really see much tonight."

She staggers backward and I grab her arm to keep her from falling over the short railing she has leaned against. "Careful there."

She giggles. "Whoops."

Her gaze collides with mine. Belatedly, the fact that I've still got my hands wrapped around her arms filters into my consciousness. The skin under my fingers is soft and warm. Had she moved or did I pull her closer? My eyes track the pink tongue that darts out, watching as her attention flicks from my lips to my eyes and back again. Time stretches as I lean down and her lids slide shut.

Her lips are soft, the vanilla taste reminding me of vanilla ice cream. I keep waiting for the smell of roses and coconuts to hit my nose, so I deepen the kiss, desperate for the smell, dragging her close and licking into her mouth. Fingers dig into my chest instead of drifting up to tangle in the ends of my hair, and it hits me. The kiss doesn't feel right, it doesn't taste right. This isn't Charlotte.

"Fuck." I break away, falling back against the wall and closing my eyes as I ram my head into the brick behind me. "I'm sorry."

"Yeah, me too." The defeated tone in her voice has me opening one eye. Michaela's grin is rueful. "That was like kissing my cousin."

That surprises a laugh from me. "Gee, thanks."

"Oh, shit, sorry." The blush that settles in her cheeks reminds me of Charlotte. "Not like that."

"I didn't think to ask if you had a boyfriend." The thought punches me in the gut.

"It's complicated." Her delicate shoulders shrug and a pained expression passes over her face.

"Fuck do I understand that." Sighing, I lean my head back into the brick again.

"Love's a bitch." Michaela's sigh echoes my own as she wrenches open the heavy fire door. "I'm gonna head home. Get some sleep. You should too."

"Michaela?"

She pauses halfway through the door.

"Thanks." She nods, her eyes meeting mine before heading inside. The door whooshes shut leaving me alone with my thoughts, disturbing company as I make my way back to the bus.

Wobbling up to the last step, I grab for the rail, the room spinning. What is that ringing sound? Oh. I fish my phone out of my pocket.

"Thought you weren't speaking to me?" I slur.

"Don't be so melodramatic, dummy." Jessie's voice is welcome in the silent bus. Heading back to my room, I flop on the bed, toeing off my shoes.

"Me?" I snort.

"What's wrong with you?" Jessie is exactly like our mom, a fucking bloodhound. "Are you drunk?"

"Yep." I pop the p, vaguely aware that I shouldn't have admitted that to my much younger sister.

"You're a bigger idiot than you look like then, Jackson. Isn't that what landed you in hot water before?"

Opening an eye, curiosity gets the better of me. "What do you know about all that?"

"I'm sixteen, not six. And you were all over social media with your shit."

"Oooooh, I'm gonna tell Mama you said a bad word."

I can hear her roll her eyes through the phone. "Whatever. You hadn't been lately. Well, except for Chicago which I am still pissed about. What's going on, big brother? Tell Jessie about it."

So, I find myself spilling my story to my baby sister who, unfortunately, only tells me to stop being a dumb ass before she hangs up on me. How the hell do I do that?

♫♪♫♪♫♪

"I want to be with you too, Jackson. Label or not. Forget about them. Let's be us and they can do whatever they want."

Those unique eyes—they're a lioness. Watching me. Telling me everything I need to hear.

The way Charlotte looked at me that night—our first night in Vegas—is a constant burn. I will win her back. But first, I need to show her I've changed. No more impulsive decisions.

"Holy shit." I can read Nick's lips in the booth as the final notes of the song ring through my headphones. His grin is infectious. It's the first time I've cracked a smile in nearly a month. In my plan to win back Charlotte, my single-minded focus has been in pouring my soul into songs and recording them for the next album release. If I'm tired enough when I lay down at night, I don't miss the feel of her against me, my body aching in counterpoint to my heart, sleep far behind. Swallowing what's left in my water bottle, I'm convinced that it's only my throat being irritated that causes it to burn.

"Dude." Nick bursts into the studio, laughing and taking turns fist bumping me and the other musicians. I've never seen him this happy. He'd shown up this morning telling me Randa had sent him to see if I was fucking up again. But something about how he said it didn't ring true. Since the awards show, he's been more observant. If I didn't know better, I'd almost say he's appointed himself my big brother.

"I take it you liked that?" My voice is full of laughter at the look on his face, and I almost grab my phone to take a picture.

"I've never seen anything like that. You're a fucking beast."

Squeezing the back of my neck, I try to avoid Nick's assessment. The truth is, I need something to occupy my mind. Songs seem to explode from me as soon as my pen hits the paper. Every day my fingers itch to call Charlotte, my ears beg for one more chance to hear her voice.

I've spent hours staring at our text screen, starting to type something out when the temptation gets to be too much, ready to send her a song that reminds me of her before I have to delete whatever it is I'd been prepared to send. It's like my finger and her contact name in my phone are opposing magnets, an invisible force preventing me from moving the few millimeters to call her. I've started leaving my phone at home to avoid the urges.

"Thanks, man." I shake my head to wrench myself away from those morose thoughts. Chronologically, it's been a month, so why does everything still hurt like it happened yesterday? It's time to start my war to win her back. "You think Randa and the other execs will like it?"

"Well..."

Nick's hesitation spikes panic in my chest. Was this month

just a waste of time? Maybe I've screwed up too badly, maybe what I've recorded isn't what they want. Without music and Charlotte, what am I going to do?

"I sent them the majority of the files yesterday. They haven't heard the final version of the song today."

"Nick, spit it out." My muscles tense as I steel myself for the bad news he acts like he has to deliver.

His head falls to his chest before he pops back up, wearing the biggest shit eating grin I've ever seen. "They fucking loved it. They already know what song they want to release first."

"Seriously?"

Nick nods. "And…"

"And?" I prompt, eyebrows raised. I'm going to throat punch him if he keeps messing with me like this. "For real, quit sandbagging whatever it is you have to say before I deck you."

Nick laughs. Actually laughs. "We want to produce a video for 'Dreamer.' The song is still sitting in the Top 100 and has gotten more traction since the tour ended."

"Holy shit." Is this really happening? My personal life may be a fucked-up mess, but professionally, I've never imagined anything this good. I want to call Charlotte and tell her the news. The fact that I can't settles like an icy rock in my stomach.

Even hours later, that glacier hasn't melted. Sitting on the deck of the condo Reverb has put me up in while I'm recording in LA, the sunset is an artist's work against the ocean, but memories of Charlotte swamp me, her voice echoing in my head, pricking like thousands of needles against my skin.

"I don't know who Charlie Daniels is." She smiles, wrinkling her nose slightly.

"Hi." Pink spreads across her cheeks, her chest rising and falling as she tries to catch her breath.

"Jackson, I—I love you."

So many memories swirl, louder when I'm not busy.

"Wanna grab a drink?" Nick pokes his head outside,

distracting me from my thoughts and the golden orange sunset in front of me. He has decided he likes this condo better than his apartment, so he's spent a lot of time here with me.

"Nah." Even the thought turns my stomach.

"Dude. You're done with the album. That was your excuse before." I haven't ventured out since the last after-party, using recording as an excuse to avoid going anywhere, but Nick's right, the album's done and I can't use that reason anymore.

"Nah," I repeat. "I'm not feeling it."

He disappears back inside before re-emerging a few minutes later, a couple of beers gripped in his fingers. Handing me one, he sits in the chair next to mine and we both stare at the water while the sun dips lower.

"Seems Randa finally got the stick out of her ass where you're concerned."

Great. Glad I could make *her* happy. Finally. Too bad that news doesn't ease the ache in my chest.

"She has a few ideas for directors," he continues.

"Cool."

He takes a pull of his beer while mine condenses in my hand. Part of me wants to dive into the bottle headfirst, but the other part hesitates, reminding me that the last time I had a drink, I screwed up. Again. My stomach churns, prompting me to put the untouched bottle down next to my chair. Nick glances at it before looking at me, the weight of his stare causing me to shift in my seat.

"No beer?" I shake my head. He wouldn't get it and I don't feel like wasting the energy trying to explain it. "Not the right kind?"

"I've had it before. It's pretty good. Just don't want it."

The sun's almost gone, merely a sliver of orange and pink against the silver-tipped ocean. Another day ending without Charlotte. How can I miss her so much when I only knew her for such a short time?

"Is this about Charlie?" His question startles me from my

ocean vista musings. His eyes are curious when I meet his gaze. Even hearing her name is a knife in my chest, the ache acute as I rub at it, hoping it'll go away if I don't say anything. "I'm worried about you. That's why I've been hanging around so much."

I scoff at his sudden bout of emotion. "Yeah, okay."

"Look, I understand the pressure you're under. I get it. I remember wishing I had someone who understood. I'm here to talk, if you want."

"It's fine." He doesn't have a clue.

"Did you know I used to be engaged?" Nick's question surprises me for the second time in as many minutes.

"No shit?" I shake my head. "Who's the lucky girl?"

"Emphasis on the used to be part." His laugh is mirthless. "Em —Emily—and I were high school sweethearts." He takes a deep breath, letting it out before taking another drink of his beer. "When we graduated, I loaded up my truck and headed here. God, I was the biggest fucking redneck back then. True small-town stereotype. Just me, my beater of a truck, and an equally beat-up guitar." He shakes his head. "The day I left, Em gave me a kiss, wished me luck, and I watched her get smaller and smaller in that rearview mirror before she disappeared."

"We had these plans—I was gonna get a contract and sing all the songs I'd written for her."

"You write songs?" My mouth drops open in shock. He flips me the bird but continues.

"It wasn't as easy as we'd dreamed it would be. I must have sent in hundreds of demos. Tried every angle I could think of. I'd call Em, depressed as hell that it wasn't working out, and she'd build me back up and promise that someday we'd laugh about all the work I was doing. She got it but she didn't really know, y'know?" Nick tips the beer bottle up to his lips, grimacing when he realizes it's empty. "She never once believed I wouldn't make it."

My heart pounds. Can he hear it? He's preoccupied picking

the label off his bottle. "When I was finally signed, she was over the fucking moon. After I recorded my first EP, I was gonna go back, pack her up, and we were gonna live happily ever after."

"W-what happened?" Licking my lips, I wait for his story to continue. Something tells me this isn't a fairytale he's telling me.

"I was in the studio when my cell phone rang, so I couldn't answer it right away. We took a break, and I noticed my mom'd called." His swallow is audible, the label from his bottle nothing but flecks of paper all over the deck, spinning in the breeze kicking up off the ocean. "She never called. So I think I knew before she answered. There'd been an accident. A truck'd crossed the center line and hit Em headon. She died on impact."

My whole body goes cold at the tone of his voice. "Nick."

I want to tell him I'm sorry about Emily. I didn't know her, but no one deserves the pain that still lives in his voice. He waves me off, staring at the gray-blue sky of twilight.

"I couldn't after that. I couldn't do it. I got off the phone with my mom and I…stood there, staring at the studio that had been familiar to me a few minutes before and realizing I had no idea where I was. The guy I was working with at the time, my Nick you could say, told me to suck it up. Shit happened and life wasn't fair."

"What the fuck?"

He smirks. "I was a little more crass than that. Then I walked out. Left everything right where it was and drove straight home to Nebraska that night."

"You came back though?"

He nods. "I was home about a month. We'd buried Em in the little cemetery at the edge of town and I just…drifted. Nothing mattered anymore. I lost the song the second I lost her. At the end of that first month, I heard from Reverb execs. They'd heard from my rep that I couldn't hack it. That I'd walked out for no reason and they were calling to tell me I was in breach of contract. No one knew about Emily until I told them. They offered to bring me back out, have me start recording again. I turned 'em down, telling them I didn't sing anymore. Hung up on them actually." Nick's smile is a cross between a grimace and a smirk.

"They called me back twice more. Each time I turned 'em down flat. Figured after the second time they wouldn't try again. Until the day Randa showed up at my parents' farm."

My eyebrows hit my hairline with that news. "No shit?"

"No shit. She said she understood my reluctance to come back to LA, but figured I could be of use to her as a rep. They'd fired mine—thank fucking god—and needed someone who would understand artists. She'd figured I'd be good at that since that's where I started. Fuck, I'd only ever wanted to sing so I figured I better find something since I didn't see myself growing old on the farm."

I nod even though, as my rep, he's mostly been a pain in the ass.

"You're probably wondering why I told you all this now." I nod again, still not sure I understand whatever lesson he's trying to impart. "If I could do it over again, I'd have chosen differently. I'd have picked Em. Asked her to come with me when I first left. Instead, I was so focused on 'making it' that I lost her."

Nick heads inside without another word, my attention moving back to the waves I can still see in the growing darkness. Pulling out my phone, I tap out a message, pressing send without hesitation.

JACKSON: I miss you.

CHAPTER 26

CHARLIE

Swallowing the nerves that threaten to punch their way out of my throat, I make my way into the nondescript building that houses the sound stage for the video shoot. It takes a minute for my eyes to adjust to the lack of light after the bright sunshine outside, and I blink, trying to clear my vision before moving into the cavernous room. My hand presses against my stomach, calming the nerves that are making the nausea more intense than it has been lately.

"Charlie, welcome, glad you made it." Garrett's smile is warm, his gait confident as he moves from the middle of the large room to where I stand at the edge of the hallway.

"Um, thanks?" My answering expression is less warm and more nervous than anything. Butterflies are a strong competition with the nausea this morning.

Since being diagnosed with HEG a month ago, I've learned that small, frequent meals and ginger ale keep the nausea in check, otherwise I can take the medication the doctor prescribed. Nothing is going to help today, though.

Garrett laughs, sensing my anxiety. "Don't worry, you're going to be great. Meric and I are super excited to work with this director. You're going to love her and Dylan, our artist."

"Dylan?"

"Dylan Graves. Have you heard of him?" I nod, my vision tunneling with Garrett's announcement. Dylan Graves is one of the hottest rock stars with multiple current releases topping the charts. Never in a million years did I think the instrumental song I'd listened to would be from him.

Meredith is going to be so jealous when I tell her who the video is for. Glancing around the soundstage, cameras face in a semi-circle around a darkened section shrouded in shadow. Crew members cluster in groups talking to each other, either by the cameras or a massive table full of food. I skip over that table, my eyes still traveling. Meric is talking to someone not much older than me but the authority she exudes is hard to miss. The director maybe? The door behind me bangs open and I jump, whirling around, heart pounding. A shadowy figure centers in the doorway, backlit by the nearly white sunlight outside.

"Speaking of Dylan, here he is now." Garrett turns toward the newcomer, while Meric and the woman move in our direction.

"Dylan, nice to see you again." Meric shakes hands with the blonde Viking look-alike before turning to the director. "Claire Shaffer, director, meet Dylan Graves, artist."

Dylan smirks as the two shake hands. Claire responds with a professional smile to his panty-melting grin. "Dylan, looking forward to working with you. I can't wait to get started on making your concept reality."

Dylan nods at the petite blonde. "Thank you. I'm looking forward to your capture of it."

I notice he stresses the word your but then it registers, my knees wobbling at his crisp British accent. How had I not known that he's British? And what concept? I'm relatively unsure of the day's events other than I'm going to be improvising and dancing in a music video—with Dylan Graves. My hand moves to my stomach again, willing the nausea to stay unnoticed.

"Dylan, Claire, this is Charlie. You probably recognize her."

Dylan turns bright blue—almost violet—eyes to me. There's an astuteness in their depths that I don't expect. Can he read my mind? Wait.

"You look familiar. Were you at the audition a few weeks ago?" The momentary glimpse of the third man that had joined Meric, Garrett, and Madame emerges. That's why he had looked familiar—he was freaking famous.

He nods. "I wanted to watch, but Meric suggested I observe from a different room. Charlie, was it? How do you do?" Dylan's smile continues to add to his appeal. His voice is like smoked honey, those lavender eyes intelligent and observant. The scruff on his jaw, combined with spiky light brown hair, gives him a bad boy vibe supported by a black leather jacket over a white t-shit and ripped blue jeans. Scuffed motorcycle boots complete his look.

Does he have a motorcycle outside or just like the biker look? It feels too hot to be wearing a jacket like that just for show. My cheeks flush when he catches me cataloging him from head to foot, a perfectly sculpted eyebrow lifts slowly at my blatant perusal. Sadly, his good looks don't cause my pulse to spike, cementing the fact that I'm well and truly still in love with someone else.

"Mr. Graves, it's—it's, uh, nice to meet you. Thank you for giving me this opportunity," I stammer my way through the introduction, Dylan's grin deepens at my ramble. I notice he doesn't have dimples like—*stop it, Charlie.*

"Please, love, call me Dylan. I'm not giving you anything you didn't earn. Are you professionally trained?"

I nod and, out of the corner of my eye, see Meric, Garrett, and

Claire head for one of the cameras. Dylan and I chat for a moment—he recognizes the school I attended in New York, even knows a few of my former classmates. As he shares bits and pieces of his own upbringing in England, I relax. His friendly demeanor makes him easy to talk to.

"Charlie, is that short for anything, love?"

"Charlotte. I couldn't say my whole name when I was little, so I ended up with my nickname." A blush warms its way into my cheeks.

"Charlotte, like a princess." No funny remarks about a classic country artist. I should be happy. I miss Jackson.

"Okay, guys, let's get started. Charlie and Dylan, head to wardrobe and then we'll discuss the plans for the shoot."

He nods as lights start to flash on. Anxiety skitters through me by what they reveal. A gigantic bed with billowy, gauzy white curtains around the four posters is dead center of the cameras. "Ummmm."

He turns to where I've frozen after a few steps. "You all right, Charlie?"

Closing my eyes, I take a deep breath before opening them again. "I've heard the instrumental and I know this is mostly improv dance, but everything else is..." I shrug, trailing off.

He chuckles. "Has no one shared my concept with you?"

"No?" Should they have? Did they and maybe I wasn't paying attention? Crap.

His smile is lopsided, genuine. "I apologize. It wasn't any big secret and I thought they'd shared it with you after you accepted the job. Here, listen to this." Dylan grabs his phone and plays the full version of the song we're shooting the video for.

It's a love song, the slow ballad not like his other songs. The haunting melody fits with lyrics that move from happy memories of a new relationship to despair at its end. Holy crap, this song is my anthem. Tears brim before rolling down my cheeks as the music ends. He watches me curiously, his eyes solemn. "You feel that? That happier emotion?"

Nodding, I swipe at the errant tracks on my face.

"We'll be dancing together either there"—he points to an area that resembles a club dance floor—"or there."

The bed. He'd pointed at the bed. Panic ices across my skin and must reflect on my face because he squeezes my arm with a laugh. "Fully clothed, love."

His reassurance allows my breathing to return to a normal rate. "Okay."

"Yes?" Those violet eyes search mine. What do they see?

"I'm...I'm not very experienced with all of this." Shrugging, I admit my inexperience.

Dylan's expression is warm, a friendly face in a sea of unknown. "You'll be perfect. You'll see."

Tossing an arm around my shoulders, he leads me toward wardrobe. What if I'm not?

♫♪♫♪♫

We spend several hours going through Claire's plan for shooting. Throughout the discussion, Dylan makes faces or comments that have me laughing and I'm relaxed by the time we get to the dancing piece of the day.

The white dress I wear for the shoot is soft, the material smooth under my fingers. The higher neck reaches my collarbone, preventing any significant wardrobe malfunctions, but the dress stretches snugger across my breasts, the weight I've gained evident as I'd stared at myself in the mirror.

While the front of the dress is high, the back is completely open so that the air conditioning ripples goosebumps down my back and arms. The dress is short, the skirt layers of the same gauzy material as the curtains. It's beautiful and, after spending time in hair and make-up, I feel my confidence grow. I can do this. The music starts and I take the mark that Claire indicated earlier, my body itching to move as the melody beats through the room.

"ACTION." Claire's voice is clear, and my pulse jumps at her words, but my body is already in motion. My hair flies with me as I spin, curls wrapping around Dylan when he pulls me into his arms. He moves us in a slow dance until he twists me, his head finding the curve of my neck. It's a reminder of another dance in another room. Taking a deep breath, I push those emotions down, unwilling to think about them while I try to move forward.

Dancing for a video shoot is different than any other performance I've done. Minutes of dancing are broken up with scene changes and retakes, allowing breaks where I get to know Dylan more. His dry sense of humor is hysterical, and I find myself giggling more than once on a break while he tells me different jokes or stories. At one point, he tows me to the craft services table.

"I'm famished." Dylan dives in, grabbing handfuls of different foods even while he fixes himself a plate. "Love?"

"Oh, um, I'm not sure." Fruit should be safe—it is at home—so I grab a small bowl.

"Cuppa?" Dylan holds out a basket of tea selections and I shake my head when I don't spy any peppermint or ginger. Caffeine has not agreed with my being pregnant. Grabbing a water bottle, I motion to some chairs near the table.

"I'm good," I say.

Dylan nods, joining me a few minutes later, his plate bowed under the weight of food, a hot cup of tea balanced in the other hand.

"How do you eat all that and look like you do?" I cover my mouth with my hand as if I can force the words back inside.

"How is it that I look?" Dylan smirks at me before bursting into laughter. "Sorry, sorry, couldn't resist. It all burns off. Has since I was a kid. It takes a lot to look like this and not some skinny rail."

Dylan is still shirtless after the latest scene we just filmed, muscles defined on his shoulders and chest tapering down to a crazy amount of abs. A large phoenix tattoo takes up a significant portion of his shoulder and chest. His eyes catch me staring at it, mesmerized by the blurred colors.

"I got it recently." The colors are vibrant, the tattoo blending expertly.

"What's it for?"

"That's a story for another time, love. And that time must involve a pint or two first." Dylan smiles, removing the sting from his words. "But the one on my back is my first."

Tossing his empty plate into the trash, he stands up, turning around to reveal a comet of music notes in between his shoulder blades.

"Notes?" I ask.

Dylan's back vibrates with his laughter. "Music always felt like heaven to me. So, I created a way to keep that celestial concept close."

As he turns, he smiles another lopsided grin that I return. He lifts a piece of hair out of the way of my plate where it hangs over the sticky juice left from the fruit. Tucking it behind my ear, his fingers drag down my nose in a flirty caress.

"What the fuck!" It's a blur of motion but the accent in those words is one I can't forget, no matter how much I want to. "Hands off, asshole."

Jackson stands in front of me, chest heaving while he glares daggers at Dylan.

"What the hell, mate?" Dylan's eyes flash, his fingers clenching at his side.

Trying to stand, I have to finally push my chair back since Jackson isn't moving. When I try to walk around him, he palms my wrist.

"Jackson, what are you doing here? Stop." I struggle against his grip, watching Dylan's eyes ice over when they shift to where I'm trying to sever the contact.

"Me? Nick set up a meeting for us with Claire." His eyes move over my features. "Charlotte, what are you doing here?"

"You two know each other?" Dylan asks, feet planted wide, still ready to fight.

"Considering she's my girlfriend, yes." Jackson bites out his response, jaw ticking.

"I'm not your girlfriend, Jackson." He deflates at my words, but only enough that I notice.

"Look, why don't you two go sort yourselves? I'll be right here…" His eyes lock on mine in a question. I nod in response. "Waiting."

CHAPTER 27

JAX

The guy—holy shit, that's Dylan Graves—that had just been touching Charlotte gives me a look, questioning my sanity. Join the club, dude. Chancing a glance at Nick, whose eyes are bugging out at my actions, I see he's trying to placate an older gentleman and a young blonde woman.

Charlotte trails behind me and I find a relatively private spot on the other side of the stage, a wall between us and everyone else. Red still clouds my vision as I notice the large bed on this side of the wall. But Charlotte's here, right in front of me. I'm touching her, reveling in the soft feel of her skin and breathing in her roses and coconut scent. It's like the universe has granted me my wish.

"Have you lost your damned mind?" Her beautiful caramel eyes flash molten fire at me, her use of a cuss word tipping me off to how much anger radiates through her petite frame.

"I-I'm sorry. I just, I watched him touch you like that…I didn't know it was you until I did, and then I just saw fucking red. I wanted him to get away from you." I run my hands through my hair before I grab my neck. Embarrassment and frustration now fight for command of my brain.

"I can't do this right now, Jackson. I'm working. And what you just did? That made me look completely unprofessional." I start to apologize again, but she holds up her hand, stopping me. "No. You and I aren't together anymore. You don't get to charge between me and someone else like a bull on the warpath. God, I'm so embarrassed right now." She closes her eyes, leaning her head back against the wall.

I groan at the guilt that starts to show up, late to the party as always when it comes to my impulsive behavior. "Would you believe me if I said I didn't mean to embarrass you?"

Her body relaxes incrementally on a sigh. "I know you didn't mean to."

Stepping forward, I bring my forehead to hers. "Thank you."

A second is all I get to feel whole, one brief moment, before she tries to duck beside me, retreating until her body is flush against the wall behind us. "It still doesn't excuse your behavior. We're not together anymore, Jackson."

"I want to be though." My admission is a whisper between us.

"Jackson." She pushes at me. "I can't do this right now."

I search her eyes, desperate to find something I can latch onto, some spark of hope. "Charlotte, please."

"I can't. You know I can't." She closes her eyes, her face twisted in pain and something else I can't puzzle out.

My breath brushes against her mouth, given our proximity. "Please. Give me another chance."

I don't give her time to respond, trying to convince her of how I feel with more than words. My lips cover hers as I pour every emotion inside me into this opportunity. My last chance. She hesitates, my heart sinking, until her mouth opens under mine, her fingers diving into my hair. I sweep my tongue inside her mouth, igniting the flame between us. My erection digs painfully into my zipper and my fingers flex where they grip her hips.

"Charlotte." Groaning, I break the connection of our lips, tracing her jawline with nipping kisses. I feel her freeze before she pushes me away.

"No."

Fuck. Do I have such little self-control that I can't spend five minutes talking to her before I'm trying to push for more? The taste of her is strong on my lips. I reach toward her, a frustrated growl escaping as she side-steps my touch, my hands falling empty. She shakes her head, those mahogany waves following the movement.

"Please, I can't do this." Turning, she starts to walk away from me. *Stop her!*

"Charlotte." She freezes and my mind races in anticipation of her turning around. But instead of it playing out like it just did in my mind's eye, her body begins buckling, collapsing to the ground. "Charlotte! Somebody help!"

I catch her before she can crash, cradling her in my arms.

Shirtless blonde guy—okay fine, *Dylan*—is the first behind the wall. "Charlie? What the fuck did you do?"

My heart jackhammers in my chest and I shake my head. "Nothing. She just, one second she was walking away and the next..."

Nick shows up next, alerted by the sound of my voice, and blanches. It's only for a second and, if I didn't know his story, I wouldn't have known to look for it. I shift my attention back to Charlotte, the flutter of her pulse where my fingers press nearly toppling me with relief. She's pale—so pale her skin is nearly translucent.

"Come on, gorgeous, open those beautiful eyes of yours for me." My request is whispered against the skin of her forehead, lips brushing against the cool skin.

"Why don't we take her to lie down?" A younger guy with

glasses suggests. I don't let her go, standing and shifting her slight weight against me.

"Show me where to go." I'm not leaving her again.

♪♪♪♪♪♪

Please let her be okay. Please let her be okay.

"Wake up, gorgeous." Taking her hand in mine, I press the cool skin to my lips. "Please."

My thumb takes up a pattern, rubbing over her fingers, willing her to wake up. This is the longest five minutes of my life.

"I just want to talk to you, baby. Please wake up, you're scaring me." Her fingers twitching against mine is the first sensation she's finally coming to. I watch long lashes flutter against her cheek before they open, her eyes hazy and confused.

"You're awake." I smile, relishing the feel of her hand squeezing mine. She nods, a panicked expression following as she motions for the trash can near me. Handing it to her, she leans over, stomach heaving. Using one hand, I rub her back while the other keeps her hair out of the way. When she's finished, I take the can back from her, setting it off to the side. "Are you okay now?'

She nods, still looking greener than is good for my sanity. "W-what happened?"

Sitting up, her feet move to the floor and I shift from my kneeling position in front of her to sit next to her on the couch.

"It's my fault." Guilt churns in my stomach. "We were talking, and I-I saw you start to go down. You just...crumpled." My thumb resumes the pattern on her fingers, soothing me when my fear spikes again. "I...managed to catch you. Before you fell, I mean."

"Thank-you." She takes a deep breath, chewing on her lip. "Jackson, I need to tell you something."

"Charlotte, what's going on? Why did you faint? Are you okay?"

We speak over each other, my fingers tightening around hers. Is she sick? Please, God, let her not be sick.

"I'm pregnant." The word hangs in the air between us.

"Pregnant?"

"Uh-huh." She looks calm about the situation, like this isn't news to her.

"You've known about this?" I motion to her stomach.

"I found out about a month ago."

"Holy shit. A month?" I blink, trying to process the news as quickly as I can. "It's mine."

It's a statement, not a question, but she nods anyway, her shoulders relaxing on a deep sigh. Was she worried that I would question that?

"But…but condoms and birth control?" Her face tells me she's already thought about that.

"Apparently there's still a chance. Neither is one hundred percent effective. Condoms are only like eighty-five percent." What. The. Fuck? My eyes widen with that piece of knowledge. Swallowing is painful around the massive lump in my throat, my Adam's apple feeling like it's sticking partway down. A baby. My baby. Charlotte. Our baby. A huge grin takes over my face.

"You're happy?" She sounds unsure.

"You're keeping the baby?" My smile dims when I consider the fact that it's not the only option in front of her. When she nods, my happiness returns to full wattage and my lips brush against her cheek. "I'm fucking ecstatic. We can be a family now."

Confusion knits her brows. "What?"

"A family. You're having my baby. We can get a house somewhere—Boulder, maybe? Or here? Marry me."

She stands suddenly, swaying on her feet. "Whoa, Jackson. Who said anything about being together? Just because I'm pregnant doesn't mean we're together. Think about this."

Reaching out a hand to steady her, it hurts when she recoils. "I am thinking about this. I love you."

She shakes her head, like she doesn't believe me. Panic flares. I need her to believe me. To believe in us. "We have two very different lives, Jackson. Two very different dreams."

Fuck. This sounds familiar.

"You're my dream. My life, Charlotte. Please." I clear the burning sensation from my throat. I can't lose her. "I love you."

"Do you love Michaela too?" Taking a deep breath, she stands tall, a hand flat against her stomach.

"What?" Now I'm confused.

"I saw you." Her voice is quiet, eyes closed as she stands there.

"I know, and I'm so—"

"Not the awards show, Jackson. Online. In a story about you. You and Michaela were kissing. After the awards show," she bites out the words, like they hurt her physically. Shit.

"Char—"

"You can't deny what I saw with my own eyes, Jackson. Tell me you didn't kiss her." I want to lie. I want it to be untrue. But I nod instead.

"It was the last concert. We were celebrating, doing shots and stuff and she was there. We talked for a while and..." My breathing is short and choppy, panic paralyzing my vocal cords.

"And you kissed her." She backs away from me, eyes stricken, disappointed.

Reaching out, I try to palm her wrist. "It didn't mean anything."

The swirling gold of her eyes hardens, flattens, loses its sparkle. "I don't believe you. You told me before that it didn't mean anything. That her being in Chicago meant nothing. Then you show up with her to the awards show—without telling me—"

"I didn't want to upset you," I try to interrupt, but she keeps talking.

"Take a look, Jackson. I'm still upset, even though you didn't tell me. Were you even planning on telling me? Or am I still just a tool for you to use for good PR? Wouldn't it look good—Jax Bryant, family man?" Her voice cracks and I stand, taking a step toward her.

"Charlotte—"

"No. We weren't meant to be. We were always pretend. You realized it, which is why you kept things from me. It didn't matter to you if you told me or not. Now you're back and I can only assume it means that something else has hurt your reputation and you need me to fix it. Maybe you're bored since your tour ended. I don't know. But you knew we weren't real first. We can't work. And I know it now."

Pulling her arm out of my grasp, she spins, walking quickly toward the door.

"Charlotte—"

"I have work to do, Jackson. Work that doesn't involve you. We'll figure out the baby, but not here, not now. Please leave." Grabbing the door handle, she walks out, taking my heart with her. Shit. What the fuck do I do now?

♪♪♪♪♪

I wipe sweaty palms against my cargo shorts while the temperate sunshine warms my shoulders the same way the sun and a magnifying glass warm a dry piece of grass. Lifting my hand to knock on the door is one of the hardest things I've ever had to do. Nerves kick in and I shift my weight from foot to foot realizing that, for the first time in as long as I can remember, I've knocked on this door rather than just walk in.

"Jackson!" Val's hug is warm and coupled with a weird look, but she doesn't call me out on the knocking. "What a pleasant surprise. Meredith didn't tell us you were in town."

"Hey, Val." Returning her hug, I'm reminded of Mama, and the fact that she's going to be a grandma. "No, it's a surprise for her too."

"I'm sure she'll love that since she ended up not making your last show." Val pulls me into the house, still talking, so much like her daughter that guilt pricks uncomfortably. "She said that she needed to help Charlie, but Charlie was in Boulder. But she's back now. Oh shoot, she's not here right now. She's filming her video today. So exciting."

My eyebrows crawl under my baseball cap. With the way Val is treating me, what she's saying, it's clear she has no idea what my relationship status is with Charlotte or Meredith's reason for leaving the tour.

"Action Jackson, how are you, son?" Mike stands, shaking my hand as he ignores the TV. ESPN blares some replay of a football game from the eighties if the uniforms are anything to go by.

"I'm good. Glad to unwind a bit."

Their reaction to me—unchanged from the last time they saw me a few weeks ago—makes acid churn in my stomach. I'm a fraud.

"Now, Jackson, you must be hungry? Thirsty?" Val pushes me into the kitchen.

"If you're asking, I am," Mike's voice booms after us.

Ducking her head back into the other room, Val calls him out, the familiarity making me smile. "You live here. Your legs aren't broken."

He laughs and I shake my head when Val turns back to me. "Right, anything? Water? Soda?"

I have no idea how long I'll be staying—or living—after Meredith sees me. Val grins, taking pity on me but not for the reason I wish she would. "Okay, okay, you've spent the requisite time with the old folks. Go ahead. Go find Meredith." She shoos me to the back door. "She was by the pool earlier."

Nerves lump in my throat and my hand slips off the cool metal of the door handle. Is this how inmates feel on death row as they walk towards the execution chamber? The dread in the pit of their stomachs? A small glimmer of hope that there'll be a reprieve?

Strains of music float on the light breeze that hits me as soon as I step out onto the back patio. Meredith's eyes narrow as she glances up at the sound of the door shutting.

"You have some fucking nerve."

"Mer, I just want to talk." Holding up my hands, I wish I had a white flag to wave instead. "Please. Five minutes."

"I have nothing to say to you, jack-ass." She jumps up quickly, intent on escaping to her house.

"Please, Mer." I put my hand lightly on her arm. When she doesn't keep walking away, I take a deep breath. One hurdle down, seven hundred and eight more to go.

"Five minutes." She crosses her arms, glaring at me.

"Do you, ah, want to sit?" I motion to her vacant pool lounger and the one next to it.

"Four minutes and forty-five seconds." She looks at her wrist pointedly but since she doesn't wear a watch, it's a little funny too.

"I'll take that as a no then." I try to smile. Her facial expression doesn't change from the blank slate currently staring at me. Correction, through me. "I know I hurt you, Mer. Not deliberately, not intentionally, but because you told Charlotte she could trust me, and I let her down. I let you down." I rub my hands on the sides of my shorts again. "If I could change it, I would. I just…God…I'm so fucking sorry. Which is such an inadequate word, and if there's a different one that I'm not thinking about, feel free to chime in. I'm sorry I hurt her. Christ, am I sorry about that. I'm trying to fix it because, without her, my life doesn't make any sense. It's like everything in my universe harmonized the minute I walked into the rehearsal room and found her that day."

Tugging off my baseball cap, I run a hand through my hair

before shoving the hat back on. Is anything I'm saying getting through to her?

"I saw her this morning." Her eyes widen at the piece of news, but I keep talking. "I walked into the soundstage where she was dancing, and my entire world stopped and started in that moment. I felt like I saw everything—I saw her—clearly for the first time. She's fucking beautiful normally, but today she was... ethereal...mesmerizing..." My words trail off as I blow out a breath. "I'm pretty sure my five minutes are up, and I understand you're still pissed at me, but I miss you, Mer. I miss my goofy friend who was also my biggest cheerleader. The one who keeps me grounded but also encourages me to do crazy things at the same time. I miss you, Mer, and I want us to be friends again. I want to be able to text you random things and know that you'll understand them because you always do."

"Like the weird SpongeBob GIF you sent me," she supplies, uncrossing her arms. Hope ignites in my chest. At the beginning of the tour, I'd sent her a GIF of SpongeBob in a baseball hat.

I grin. "I knew you'd get that I wanted a peanut butter sandwich if I sent you SpongeBob in a Goofy Goober hat." She rolls her eyes, but her lips twitch as she tries to contain her reaction. "Can we be friends again?"

My eyes search hers, hoping that since she hasn't walked away yet, we might be on the right track. Her silence ages me five years until she finally nods.

"I've missed you, you know." She smiles, but just as quickly turns serious. "I couldn't believe what I saw that night. I never, ever would have predicted that. I kept telling Charlie over and over again that you were someone she could trust. Someone she could rely on."

"Mer—" I groan, squeezing the back of my neck, remembering Charlotte's face.

"Jax, she was fucking wrecked that night. I was wrecked for her. She didn't speak at all. I wouldn't wish that level of heartbreak on anyone, even if I have experienced it myself." She shushes me when I open my mouth. "Forget I said that. We're not talking about me right now."

I nod, agreeing to let my question drop…for now.

"I want her back, Meredith. What do I do?"

"She's scared, Jax." She looks at me and I see residual flickers of her anger. Charlotte has every right to be scared that I'm going to fuck it up again. "She's afraid she's not enough for you."

What? She shouldn't be scared of that. I'm the dumb ass, not her. "She's fucking everything to me." My voice rises and I blow out a breath. "I know I'm not good enough for her, but it's beyond want, Mer. I need her."

She looks at me, brown eyes judging, measuring me, before she nods. "Are you willing to fight for her? It's not going to be easy this time around."

I nod.

"I need you to be one hundred percent sure, Jax. You won't get any more chances after this—from me or from her. Don't fuck it up."

CHAPTER 28

CHARLIE

Closing my eyes, I take a deep breath and let the music wash over me. I begin moving with the melody—slowly, building power, faster, pushing myself. The lights on the scene are soft, a mix of blue and pale. The music shifts, changing, and a strong hand wraps around my waist, pulling me close, two individual heartbeats melding into a single harmony.

His head lowers, nuzzling the place where my shoulder and neck connect, and I lean my head back against a strong chest, reaching up and threading my fingers through light brown hair. In the next minute, I'm spinning away, pirouetting until I'm on my own in front of the mirrors and the barre, gauzy white curtains blowing in a simulated breeze as I dance to Dylan's painful lyrics about being separated from the love of his life.

The music crescendos and I move my body in time to the rising harmony until it starts to fade. Moving myself to a prop window, I reach out one hand to the white curtain, the other hand curling around the smooth wood in front of me.

"CUT!" The music fades to silence and Claire's voice cuts through, breaking me from the spell.

I blink, the rest of the room coming back into focus. My heart pounds, my chest rising and falling as I work to catch my breath.

"That was bloody brilliant, love." Dylan walks up, lifting and spinning me around in a gigantic circle that has me gasping and laughing at the same time. "Absolutely fucking brilliant."

The adrenaline is beginning to fade after the busy day of filming—including Jackson's interruption and my fainting episode. Relief floods me when Garrett tells me they have what they need and I can head out.

♪♪♪♪♪♪

I'm still tired the next day, but fortunately, the only thing on my agenda is sitting by the pool and relaxing. Meredith had to run an errand with her mom earlier so I'm enjoying the quiet sunshine alone. My phone chimes next to the pool lounger and I grab it, shading the screen with my hand.

JACKSON: Hi

I should be surprised to hear from him, but I'm not. Not after yesterday. I'd expected something different, so his casual text catches me off guard. My fingers hesitate on the keyboard, residual anger and embarrassment lingering. No one mentioned anything to me, but I noticed Dylan's eyes were on me more *after* Jackson left than before. I sigh and remember my promise that we could talk about the baby. Now is as good a time as any, I guess.

CHARLOTTE: Hi?
JACKSON: How are you today?

The excitement that comes with his question is a muscle memory—is emotional memory a thing?—until I realize he's not necessarily asking about me, but the baby.

CHARLOTTE: I'm okay. Tired. But okay.
JACKSON: Are you taking it easy?
CHARLOTTE: I'm currently kicked back poolside, so yes?
JACKSON: You look beautiful.

"You do look beautiful." The deep voice behind me interrupts the text I'm reading, nearly causing me to drop my phone.

I look over my shoulder to find Jackson as he stands behind me in swim trunks, a t-shirt, and flip flops. A towel is looped around his neck.

"W-what are you doing here?" My voice has a breathless quality even though I've done nothing but sit in this lounger since breakfast.

"I wanted to see you."

"Oh." His words shouldn't cause my pulse to pick up or a flush to spread to my cheeks, but my traitorous body is obviously on Team Jackson.

"Is it okay that I'm here?"

I shrug. It's not my house and I'm sure Val and Mike don't care. "Y-yeah."

He sets his towel on the lounger next to mine before slowly sinking down, playing around on his phone for a minute before music starts. It's peaceful and quiet, so it should help me get back to the relaxed state of mind I had a few minutes ago but, even though a table sits between us, I feel Jackson shift slightly in his chair, trying to get comfortable. My whole body is tuned to his, aware of every shift and deep breath in and out, the butterflies swirling in my stomach equal parts delicious and nerve inducing.

"Meredith around?"

"No, she had an appointment." I haven't been this nervous

around Jackson since the first time I met him in Denver. My nerves feel more intense now than they did then. I give up trying to swallow around the dryness of my throat and grab my bottle of water. "What are you doing here?"

"I was hoping to talk to you." He settles back, and I try to mirror his pose, but I can't get anywhere near the relaxation he's exuding.

"You were?" He hums his assent, the sound sending shivers down my spine until I remember. "Right, I promised you yesterday. We need to talk about the baby."

Cracking an eye open, he watches me in silence for several minutes before he responds, "No. Well, yes. Eventually. First, I wanted to apologize to you."

"Apologize?"

"How I acted yesterday." Jackson has the grace to look embarrassed. "That was stupid."

"Why were you there yesterday?"

"Nick told me that Claire is the director they want to film a video for 'Dreamer.'" My eyes widen with his news. I watch a smile grow across his face, his dimples bringing my attention to his lips.

"Jackson, that's amazing." My face mirrors his. I'm so proud of him. Even if I don't have the right to be anymore.

"Nick's pretty excited."

"And you too?"

He nods. "I can't believe it's happening. I wanted to call you, as soon as I knew."

His admission leaves my skin tingling. "You did?"

He nods, sitting up more so he can fully face me. "You're the first person I thought of."

"Oh." His eyes burn into mine and I turn my head, breaking the spell, to stare at the cool blue of the water.

"I was serious, you know." My gaze swings back to him. "I want another chance for us."

"Jackson." His name escapes me on a sigh.

"I know, I know," he continues. "I don't want to rush you, but I don't want to hide that from you either. I'm done with that."

"Done with what?"

"Keeping things from you."

"Oh." Blushing, I catch his smirk out of the corner of my eye as he leans back against his chair.

"How are you feeling?" His voice is calm, but there's a tension in his body that reminds me of a predator who waits patiently to pounce.

"Okay."

"Really?"

I nod. "I've been trying to take it easy. Yesterday was…an anomaly."

"You fainted."

Huffing, I nod. "I know. I was diagnosed with Hyperemesis Gravidarum."

"Hyper-what-mia?" Jackson's eyebrows furrow in confusion.

"It's an extreme version of morning sickness. I was really sick for a while. Nothing wanted to stay down. I'm on medication now and they've given me a special diet and some other tricks to help so it's manageable. But the HEG—that's the abbreviation—can get worse with stress and that's why I fainted yesterday."

"Stress?" Jackson pales and I have a feeling he's blaming himself.

"Dancing at that level, traveling, both elevate stress."

"And my dumb ass caveman antics."

"Well…" I shrug. "I wasn't going to point it out…"

Jackson laughs, rubbing the back of his neck. "Fuck, I'm sorry."

I shrug. "You didn't know."

"Now that I do know, I'm going to make sure you take care of yourself. And take care of Peanut."

"Peanut?"

"I didn't want to just say 'the baby.' I got online last night and was looking at different websites. It says the baby is about the size of a peanut right now. So...Peanut." The soft smile on his lips, coupled with the fact that he's nicknamed the baby, causes me to melt like a hot grilled cheese.

His hands shift to the hem of his shirt, tugging up, the heather gray material revealing his toned stomach and chest before moving over his head. My eyes are hidden by sunglasses so the fact that they travel the lines that I've tasted is my secret. My tongue rats me out though, moistening my suddenly dry lips.

"See anything you like?"

My eyes move from where they've been stuck on his chest and abs back to his face. His amusement tells me he's busted me. The heat of a blush steals up my neck at being caught. Leaning back, I ignore his question and light chuckle.

"Sorry, it's just warmer out here than I thought. If it makes you uncomfortable, I can put it back on." Jackson gestures to the shirt still in his hands.

Shaking my head, I pretend to be unaffected, even though we both know that's a lie. "It's fine."

He doesn't say anything else and neither do I. The sun is getting warm and I think about cooling off in the pool. My tank top pulls off easily enough, but I need to lift my hips to shuffle off my shorts.

"What are you doing?" Jackson's voice is strained and I glance over.

"I'm gonna hop in the pool for a bit."

The water is cold after the heat of the sun and chemistry with Jackson. The change in temperature creates a shiver as goosebumps break out when I wade slowly into the cool water. I wade farther in and the water laps against my chest, causing my nipples to harden.

Jackson is silent but I still feel the heat of his eyes tracking me. Leaning back, I lift my legs, floating on my back as warm California sunshine on my face mingles with the temperate water under me. I close my eyes to focus on breathing, on keeping myself afloat. The music is muffled so all I hear are the occasional notes through the water while the smell of chlorine tickles my nose.

My head bumps into something hard and I start, throwing an arm up as I lose my ability to float. Strong hands grip my waist before I can sink under water.

"Sorry. Didn't mean to startle you." Jackson's drawl whispers against my ear. I find my feet to stand and he releases me. Immediately, I miss the warmth of his hands on my hips and I shiver when the cold water rushes in the space between us.

"S'okay." He's close. Close enough that I can smell the tangy scent of sun-warmed, sweat dampened skin mixing with his cologne. Close enough that he reaches out and brushes a wet strand of hair behind my ear. My eyes close, absorbing the feel of his fingers along my jaw. He drags his hand back, eliciting a shiver of awareness down my spine. Desperation to lean into his touch wars with fear, and I'm not sure which one is going to win.

"Charlotte." My name is a breathy exhale between us, and I blink my eyes open, thankful for my sunglasses.

My lips part at the look on his face. Pain, resignation, hope, desire all combine, speaking to me on a primal level. "Y-yes?"

"One date. Please." His green eyes burn as they search my face. "One more chance."

"Jackson—"

"Jackson, I didn't know you were here."

We surge away from each other, our sharp movements creating waves that make the situation even more awkward and obvious. Val doesn't say anything, but I also don't miss the smirk that highlights her face the closer she gets.

"I'm not giving up." Jackson's voice is a low murmur as I wade past him to the stairs. Anticipation shivers through me again and suddenly I'm looking forward to Jackson's pursuit.

CHAPTER 29

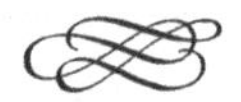

JAX

JACKSON: I never got your answer earlier.
CHARLOTTE: What was the question?
JACKSON: Come out with me.
CHARLOTTE: Jackson.
CHARLOTTE: We've been over this.
CHARLOTTE: I have to stop believing in fairytales.

Ouch. That text fucking hurts. Once upon a time, she leaned her head against my shoulder. *"I feel like Cinderella at midnight."* Fuck, if I could go back in time, I would do so many things differently. But I don't have a time machine.

JACKSON: You're right.
CHARLOTTE: I am?
JACKSON: You shouldn't believe in fairytales.
CHARLOTTE: I know.
JACKSON: Fairytales are easy. They're the flash. Real life is

harder, but it's worth it. You can still have your happily ever after.
JACKSON: One dinner.
JACKSON: If I don't convince you with one dinner, I won't ask again. I'll accept the friend zone.
CHARLOTTE: I don't know.

It's not the "no" I got from her before. Smiling, I'll accept the progress I'm making.

JACKSON: That's not a no.
CHARLOTTE: It's not.
JACKSON: So does that mean it's a yes?

My phone ringing means I don't get to watch Charlotte respond. Irritated, I answer Nick's call.

"What?"

"I'm sending you a link, click on it." Rolling my eyes at Nick's amazing phone etiquette, I wait patiently for the text, clicking on the link as soon as it pops through.

> *Daddy Jax? Sources say yes. First came love for our golden boy, steaming up stories with Denver Delight, Charlie Walker. A source at a Boulder hospital recently identified Charlie was admitted for a visit, confirming that our tiny dancer has a tiny baby bump and Hyperemesis Gravidarum (HEG). Readers may recall this is the same condition that Princess Kate had with her three pregnancies. But Charlie looked fit as a fiddle leaving a Los Angeles sound stage earlier this week. Dare we say glowing?*

"Fuck." I need to call Charlotte.

"Is it true?"

"Well…" I haven't even had the chance to tell my family. She and I didn't talk about that after our near kiss in the pool or when I stayed for dinner with her and the Pryces. One thing was certain—she hadn't told Meredith yet either. "Yeah. I found out earlier this week."

"Okay." Nick sounds distracted, probably trying to think of about a million ways to spin this news. "Okay, let me think."

"Nick." I try breaking through his brainstorm.

"Obviously this was illegal. A HIPAA violation? Wonder if the attorneys can get it down."

"Nick."

"No, that won't work. It's already out there now."

"Nick."

"A discredited source? Legal action is still necessary. Piece of shit 'source,'" he scoffs.

"NICK!"

"Sorry, what?" His little freak out has been amusing, but I know what I need to do. No more shit the press can spin to fit their own agenda. It's time I told my side of the story.

"Do you know anybody—anybody reputable I mean—who would want an exclusive interview? On TV?"

"What?" He sounds confused, which given our positions, I would have laughed at before.

"I'll give an exclusive to whoever you recommend. All of it. Every question is free rein—last tour, Charlotte, the baby, everything." Since my favorite response is no comment, this should generate some interest.

"It's about fucking time." I can hear the smirk in Nick's voice. He's done everything but demand this type of interview since I signed my first record deal. "You're sure?"

"Positive." No more flying by the seat of my pants. This is for Charlotte. For Peanut. And I refuse to let them down again.

Once I lay out my plans with Nick, I click back on my texts with Charlotte.

CHARLOTTE: I don't know that either.

I have to scroll up and remember. Her response wasn't a no or a yes to my request for one dinner. One more chance.

JACKSON: Sorry, Nick called. Hi
CHARLOTTE: Hi
JACKSON: I need to talk to you. Can I call you?
CHARLOTTE: Ok?

She picks up on the first ring. "Jackson?"

"It's me." Rubbing the back of my neck, I have no idea how she's going to take this news.

"Is everything okay?" Worry laces her tone and her breathing is choppy.

"It's fine. It's going to be fine. Take a deep breath for me." When I hear her let it out, I keep going. "Fuck, I'm sorry. I don't want to stress you out."

"I don't usually get texts from you asking to talk to me," she reminds me.

"I know. I was going to text you, but I thought I should tell you over the phone. I'd drive over there but I know it's late."

"What is it?" Anxiety creeps back into her voice. Get to the fucking point.

"Nick just called me. There's a new story on us. Someone in Boulder leaked that you're pregnant."

"What?" Her voice is a high-pitched squeak. "But-but-but I haven't told Meredith…or my parents. Oh shit."

"I was wondering if you'd told them." My voice is quiet, calm, trying to get her to relax.

"I-I didn't want them to be the next to know. I wanted you to know first."

The fact that she waited to tell everyone, that she wanted me to be the first to know, shouldn't make my dick kick against my zipper. But fuck if it doesn't.

"Do you have any idea how that makes me feel?" My voice is low, a growl into the phone.

"No?" Her voice is breathless.

"I love you."

She laughs, the sound tight with stress. "Not where I thought you were going with that statement."

I chuckle in response. "Not where I was going originally. But I wanted you to know that. I love you. We're in this together. Do you want to tell Meredith together? Or your parents? My parents?"

"I'll talk to Meredith. She'll know soon enough anyway if she doesn't by now." I can hear her deep breath blow across the phone. "But can we talk about how we're going to tell my parents and yours?"

"Absolutely. Whatever you want, I'm here for."

"Thank you, Jackson."

"Anytime."

"Jackson?"

"Yeah, Charlotte?"

"Thanks for letting me know about this too. For talking to me about a plan." Grinning like a fool, I try to keep the hope manageable in my chest.

"You're welcome, gor—Charlotte. Get some sleep, okay? Let's talk tomorrow and get our plan set up."

"Okay. Goodnight, Jackson."

"Sweet dreams, Charlotte."

My phone ringing as soon as I hang up makes me think that Charlotte forgot to mention something.

"Forget something?"

"Jackson Matthew Bryant."

Oh shit. The triple name.

"Mama?"

"Don't you 'Mama' me." I can hear her attitude through the phone and can only be grateful she's not in person to grab my ear. It aches just thinking about all those times she did it growing up. "What in the heck fire is going on? Why is Jessie telling me I'm gonna be a grandma and giving your dad a heart attack?"

"Jessie said what?" Leave it up to my kid sister to run to Mama and Dad to tattle.

"She showed me the story, Jackson Matthew. And it wasn't in some *Enquirer* wannabe either."

Rubbing the back of my neck, I groan, "Mama."

"Am I getting a grand baby?"

"Mama. I was gonna call you tomorrow. We were," I amend.

"We?" Mama's voice softens. "Charlie?"

I hadn't even had the chance to tell her about dating Charlotte before all hell broke loose. Now this. Christ.

"Charlotte, yes, ma'am." Smiling, I remember the question I posed to her. "I asked her if she was named after Charlie Daniels when I first met her."

Mama laughs just like I hoped she would.

"You'll bring her to Austin." It's a demand, not a request.

"Mama—"

"Either you two come here or we'll be coming there. Your choice, Jackson Matthew."

Fuck. "Yes, ma'am."

"Now that I've had all my excitement today, I'm going to bed. A grand baby." She sighs. "Goodnight, baby. Love you."

"Love you too, Mama."

This is spiraling out of control quickly. Knowing Mama, she'll make good on her threat and Dad hates to travel.

"It's time to win back my girl."

CHAPTER 30

CHARLIE

"Pregnant?" Meredith's voice is a high-pitched squeak the next morning as she sips on her coffee. I breathe through my mouth, upset that even the smell of it makes me nauseous anymore. "Does Jax know?"

I nod. "Thank goodness too since someone from Boulder leaked it."

Jackson told me this morning that the label's attorneys are working on finding out who so they can address it. I guess this is the price of dating—and getting pregnant by—someone who's famous.

"I didn't think I needed to have the protection talk with you, young lady," Meredith scolds, a teasing glint in her eye.

"Haha," I respond. "Just so you know, condoms are not foolproof."

"Really?" Her eyes widen again.

"Nope." I pop the p and watch her face for a reaction. She's an excellent poker player so nothing to tease her about.

"Good to know." She nods. "So, I'm gonna be an auntie?"

Laughing, I shrug. "I guess?"

"Yay." She swoops me into a hug, a big smile on her face. "We're gonna spoil this baby."

"That's exactly what I'm afraid of," I respond with a groan.

"What about you and Jax?"

I shrug. "He wants to try again."

"He told me that." Meredith's voice is quiet, her eyes watchful.

"He did?"

"The day of your shoot. He came over here so we could talk." Meredith huffs out a breath. "I think you're it for him, Char. You're his person."

Shaking my head, I try to think realistically. No more make-believe. "It's not real."

This time it's her turn to deny what I'm saying. "I've known Jax a long time, Charlie. Probably know him better than anyone else. When I say you're his person, it's because you are."

I mull over her words, eating breakfast in silence while she talks to her mom and dad about the upcoming football season.

"Charlie?" Meredith's voice interrupts my thoughts, like she's been trying to get my attention for a while.

"Sorry, what?"

"I have to run somewhere. Are you cool here by yourself for a bit?"

"Of course." I nod. "I'm going to research flights home."

Ignoring her pout—if it were up to her I'd move here permanently—I head for her place and my computer.

♪♪♪♪♪♪

My relationship with Jackson stays on my mind all day, wearing me out to the point where I end up falling asleep on the couch still without any idea about whether we move forward together or if I should continue to keep him as just a friend.

"Charlie? Charlie, wake up." Meredith nudges my shoulder and I blink my eyes open.

"Hey," I yawn. "Sorry, must have been more tired than I thought. What time is it?"

"Around three, I think." Meredith chews on her lip, her eyes bouncing with nerves.

"Mer, everything okay?"

"Jax is gonna kill me," she mutters. "But I told him to tell you."

"What?"

"I want to show something to you." Meredith fidgets with the phone in her hand. "But I don't think I'm supposed to."

Nerves settle like ice, freezing the blood in my veins. "What do you mean?"

"Jax said if he wanted you to know then he would have told you, but he was afraid you'd think it wasn't real." She's talking in circles.

"What wasn't real?"

"Exactly," she huffs.

"Meredith, what are you not supposed to show me?" She grins, that Cheshire Cat smile that should worry me, but this time it doesn't. Meredith uses her fairy godmother powers for good most of the time, after all.

"Here." Clicking on her phone, mine immediately chimes with a text. "Watch this."

She gets up and walks away, leaving before I can say anything. Opening the text, it's a link for a video shot earlier that day.

"Welcome back, everyone. Christy Carlisle here with a special guest today. A last-minute, special guest." I've seen this show a few times. Why does Meredith want me to see this? "Jax, how are you?"

The camera pans to his face, a light scruff setting off his bright green eyes. He's not wearing a baseball cap today and his hair is styled. He looks nervous and my fingers ache to smooth the furrow between his brows, the tension I see in his shoulders.

"Well, honestly, Christy, I'm a little nervous." He laughs, rubbing the back of his neck.

"Why nervous?"

Jackson's grin is lopsided. "I have a lot to say and I'm not sure where to start."

Christy smiles at him. "I find that starting from the beginning is always a good idea."

Jackson laughs again, taking a deep breath. "I like that idea." He nods before continuing. "Several months ago, I met the most amazing woman. Just as beautiful inside as out."

"You're talking about Charlie?"

Jackson nods. "Charlotte, yes."

My heart races, not sure why he's on this show mentioning my name.

"You two started dating, right?"

"We did. Dating long distance sucks. I can honestly say that. Especially when part of you loves what you're doing but the other part is begging you to go back." He swallows. "I'm not known for being Mr. Plan Everything Out. I'm a little more laid back than that. More like Mr. Impulsive. And, ultimately, that hurt her. I hurt her. Because I'm human, not perfect, I made some boneheaded mistakes."

"Your fans weren't particularly happy with you."

Jackson shakes his head. "They weren't. I wasn't happy with myself either. Charlotte is the best thing that has ever happened to me. We fell in love." He clears his throat. "But I didn't earn her love so much as she gave me everything—whatever I asked for, if it was in her power—she did it to make me happy. Before her, I didn't think I could have music and a relationship. But with her, I wanted to. I wanted to be better for her. I wanted it all. With her. For her."

"Sounds like quite the girl."

"She is. And I don't deserve her. I've made some really stupid mistakes in the past. But I'd like to think that everyone is human, we all make mistakes." Christy nods. "Those mistakes cost me the woman I fell in love with. The one I'm desperate to get back. If I could wish for anything in my life, it would be for another chance with her."

"So, what about these recent reports? Are you going to be a dad?"

"You know, Christy, I know I said I'd answer all your questions, but I have to go with no comment on that one."

"Now, Jax—" Christy starts before he interrupts.

"When I have something to share, you'll be the first to know." Jackson's expression is radiant. "For now, I just wanted to open up about my past, get rid of any lingering secrets. So I can move forward."

"With Charlotte?"

"I hope so," he murmurs.

"Is she watching today? What do you want to say to her?"

"I didn't tell her I was coming to do this." He laughs.

"Anything to say to her?"

Jackson shakes his head. "I'll keep that for when I see her next time."

The video ends, it's a brief clip of the longer show and I make a note to watch the entire thing later. Taking a deep breath, I let it out. Is he serious? Do I dare risk my heart one more time? There's only one way to find out, I guess. My fingers shake on my phone and I nearly throw the thing since it takes several attempts to get the text right.

CHARLOTTE: Meet me at El Matador Beach. 7 PM.

CHAPTER 31

JAX

Re-reading Charlotte's text, I look for any hidden meanings and come up with nothing.

CHARLOTTE: Meet me at El Matador Beach. 7 PM.

I'd gotten her message shortly after I finished my interview. While Christy was reputable, her questions had covered a lot and I felt like I had just been to confession even though I wasn't Catholic. Nick had worked wonders, getting me on with her so I could set the record straight. I was in love with Charlotte and didn't want any more secrets to sabotage my chance with her. I fucked up, but I wanted her back desperately.

Is that what this is about? Why she wanted to meet me at the beach? Was she ready to give us another try? Did she see my interview? These questions swirl as I sit on the hood of my car, mesmerized by the waves rolling in as I wait for her.

"Hey." Her voice is quiet behind me, nearly drowned out by

the waves and the gulls. But even if I couldn't hear her, the pinprick of awareness would have told me she was here.

"Hey." I smile at her. She's wearing a pair of cutoff shorts and a white tank top sprinkled with pink flowers, a pair of flip flops on her feet. Beautiful.

"Thanks for meeting me." She steps closer, close enough that her unique smell blends with those from the beach. Home.

"I'm glad you texted." I motion for us to walk toward the beach and she nods. Grabbing my guitar case from the back of the car, I lock up, relief flooding when she lets me tangle our fingers together. The crowd is pretty thin, most beachgoers going to grab dinner or heading home, and it's too early for any bonfires to bring in the evening crowd. We both kick off our flip flops and I tuck them into a pocket of my shorts as we make our way to the ocean's edge near a rocky outcropping.

Stepping into the cool surf messes with Charlotte's balance and she grips my hand. Chuckling, I tuck her into my side. "I've got you."

She nods and my nerves swirl as I try to decipher the meaning, but we keep walking, the sun coming closer to the horizon, turning the sky shades of orange and pink. The outcropping leads to a quiet cove and we both stop, enjoying the peacefulness and the feeling like we're the only two people on a deserted section of beach.

Sinking down slowly, I lower her with me, situating her in front of me, her back to my chest.

"I saw your interview." The wind whips her words toward the ocean, and I have to strain to hear her.

"You did?" My heart speeds up. "What did—what did you think?"

Turning her head, her eyes capture mine. "Were you serious?"

The fact that she feels like she still has to ask me that question sucks, but I expect it to. For me, how I feel about her is certain. Absolute. But I've done little to prove how I feel to her.

"I was."

Her head swivels back to our vista and my lips brush her bare shoulder. My arms wrap around her stomach to rest on the flat expanse where our baby currently grows.

"How do I know it's true? You've told me before. What's different now?"

"I'm scared," I admit.

Confusion wrinkles her nose. "Scared of what?"

"Never being able to do this again." My arms wrap tighter around her, my gaze moving to the ocean before meeting those tiger's-eye-colored irises again. "I'm afraid that I've lost you. That I pushed you away. Permanently."

She pushes her hair out of her face, tucking it behind her ears, staying silent before she turns to face me. "I'm scared too."

My words echo her question to me. "Scared of what?"

She takes a deep breath and exhales it, her eyes dropping to the sand under us before she looks back up. "I'm scared of taking a chance. I don't think I can do it again. Not without knowing that this is it for you. That you're one hundred percent focused on us. That you're in this just as much as I am. But if not, if this is just about the baby—"

"It's not about Peanut," I interrupt. "It's about how I feel about you. I know you need assurances that I'm different. I don't want to ask you what I need to do because I need to know that for myself. To prove it to you."

She nods.

"I'm tired of living my life without you, gorgeous. I'm tired of feeling like I'm lost. You're it for me. You're my home. And I want to create that with you."

"What?" She shakes her head like she doesn't understand.

"I want to put down roots. Austin, Boulder, here, Timbuktu. I want you to be a part of that." I reach up and cup her cheek in my hand.

"I don't know what my future holds." Her finger traces over the scar on her ankle and mine drop to trail hers.

"Whatever your future holds, I want to be your biggest cheerleader. I want to support you, for us to support each other. I saw you dance. That's your future and I'll help you get there however I can."

"It sounds like a fairytale."

"It's real," I promise her. "No more treating you like a damsel in distress though. You're a rock star."

She laughs. "You're crazy."

"For you," I tell her. "Can I play something for you?"

Her attention shifts to the guitar case that lays all but forgotten next to me. Finally, she nods.

The zipper is loud in the silence but still muted by the sound of the waves in front of us. Adjusting the guitar in my lap, I begin to play. A man asking for forgiveness, realizing he's lost pieces of himself, the best thing in his life, willing to do anything for another minute of time with her. The fact that Nick helped me write it makes the song bittersweet, but I pour myself into it the same way he and I did when we worked on it one night at the condo.

When I grabbed the guitar from the car, I wasn't aware I was going to share the whole song with her yet, but my fingers have a mind of their own, playing to the end of the song. Charlotte's eyes brim with tears. Reaching up, I capture one as it traces down her cheek.

"Don't cry, gorgeous."

"Jackson, that was...oh my god, that was incredible."

Smiling at her praise, the hints of awe in her voice, I share my admission. "It's for you." I state simply, the only explanation I can give her.

"For me?"

I nod. "Every song I wrote...fuck, any time I put pen to paper, words poured out of me. About you. About us. About how I feel about you. I know I've done a shit job of showing you, but if you give me another chance, I will. I'll show you every day what you mean to me." Those beautiful eyes—the ones that hooked me from that first night—lock on me as I stand up to pace in front of her. "I need to apologize to you."

"Jackson, you've already apologized."

"I never apologized for keeping you in the dark. For not telling you the decisions I was making that could impact you too. For not treating you like your opinion, your thoughts about our relationship, mattered. I thought I could handle everything on my own. That I could play Prince Charming. But that wasn't fair to you. That way of thinking didn't bring you closer, it pushed you away."

I sit back down in front of her.

"Charlotte." The words all push at my lips at once, and I take a breath to organize my thoughts. "You've captured me, gorgeous. From that moment I watched you dancing in that rehearsal room in Denver, I've fallen deeper and deeper under your spell. And I kept screwing up, pushing you away when all I wanted to do was pull you closer. God knows I don't deserve another chance with you, but I'm begging you anyway. Please. Be with me. I won't make an empty promise not to hurt you again, but I can promise you this. You own me. You've taken my heart and soul and they're yours if you want them. I-I love you, Charlotte."

I swallow around the lump in my throat, searching her eyes with mine in the deepening twilight. Hoping I'm not too late.

"You love me." She reaches out, laying a hand against my chest. My hand covers hers to press it more fully into me, willing her to feel the way my heart pounds under her palm. It hits me then.

"You believe me?"

"I want to."

I squeeze her fingers. "I love you, gorgeous."

Leaning forward, I brush my thumb against her lower lip

before dipping further, capturing her lips with mine, my fingers threading through her hair as my mouth slants over hers, deepening the kiss, pouring every emotion coursing through me into that connection.

I've tried to tell myself to go slowly, especially since finding out about Peanut, wanting to convince her that she is what I want more than anything, and Peanut is just a bonus—like winning two Grammys for the same song. I soften the kiss before breaking the connection, watching Charlotte's mesmerizing eyes blink open.

"If—if this is about the baby…" she begins.

"It's not. Baby or no, I love you. I love you for you, because of who you are and what your heart says to mine, whether I'm right next to you or separated from you by thousands of miles. I love you. I'm not going to lie either, though. The second you told me, I have loved both of you with every ounce of who I am."

My head drops to her lap so that my lips brush her shirt. "Do you hear that, Peanut? I love you and your mother so fucking—freaking—much."

She nibbles on her lower lip, eyes focused on where my mouth moves next to her stomach. Those moments in the silence are an eternity. Slowly, her eyes clear and her shoulders straighten. Her entire body relaxes and she clears her throat.

"I—" I look up, meeting her eyes, waiting. I'd wait forever for her if I had to, but she doesn't make me wait that long. "If you're in this, I am too. I…I want to be with you, Jackson. One hundred percent. I love you too."

Grinning, I sit up and claim her mouth again in a breathtaking blur, my tongue running along her lips until she opens for me. The rest of the world fades away as Charlotte gives herself to me, offering me her heart as she returns my kiss.

I sink back into the sand with her still wrapped in my arms, burying my fingers in her silky hair while her hands rest against my chest. When I break our kiss, her forehead leans against my shoulder.

"You love me?" I ask. My hands rub along her back.

"I love you." She reaffirms, pressing a kiss against my scruff-covered jaw.

"I love you, gorgeous. So much." My lips find a spot behind her earlobe and I groan. "We should go."

"Go?" She snuggles into my embrace.

"I want to take you somewhere."

"Where?"

"Somewhere I can show you how much I love you." Her body melts into mine and I know, if I don't get up now, I won't. But it doesn't stop my arms from staying around her as I gaze at the sky.

CHAPTER 32

JAX

5 MONTHS LATER

"Jackson, where are we going?" Charlotte looks around from the passenger seat, anxious to know where I'm taking her since I told her it was another stop in my top ten favorite places in LA.

"Hanging in there, baby?" Squeezing her hand, I keep an eye on her in my peripheral vision as I navigate the hell that is traffic in my new hometown.

"Yes," she huffs. "What if I have to go to the bathroom soon?"

I laugh. "Gorgeous, have I let you down yet?"

After getting back from Austin, I'd found a house not too far away from Meredith and her parents. Charlotte loved the house but still hesitated to move in with me. Her protests had led to kisses that resulted in her naked and pliant body underneath mine in bed at the condo I'd been staying in.

Pumping into her from behind, I'd played her body like a practiced instrument, grinning like a lunatic when my whispered pleas to move in with me had been agreed to with a contented sigh.

The first few months had been spent getting the new house set up, and about a month ago, I started our tour of my top ten favorite places in LA. So far, they had consisted of the old zoo because I could picture what it would have looked like in its heyday, the first bar I'd played at after I signed my contract, and Fern Dell in Griffith Park because it reminded me of an enchanted forest.

From there, we'd revisited the hotel where we first said, 'I love you,' and the sound stage where I'd found her again. I'd also worked with Meredith to turn her backyard into an oasis one night since the pool where we'd had our swim together was another on the list of places.

"This isn't going to be like last week, right?"

Last week's hike to the Hollywood sign with a nearly-eight-months pregnant woman hadn't been my best idea.

Groaning, I respond, "No, baby, I learned my lesson. I'm sorry I tried that."

She'd made it just fine to the sign, but had had to go to the bathroom and, unfortunately, it's not like there were bathrooms along the trail.

"I know." She sighs. "Sorry I'm so grumpy."

Lifting our joined hands, I brush a kiss to her wrist. "You're not grumpy. You're beautiful."

She scoffs, rubbing a hand along the tank top stretched around her stomach. "I'm a cow."

"Shhh. You're talking about the woman I love." I tap our hands against her leg. "This isn't like the Hollywood sign hike. Think more our walk around Griffith Observatory."

"What number is this?" Charlotte leans against the head rest, looking at me. I sneak a kiss when we stop at a red light.

"Ten."

"Ten? But wait…" Her voice trails off as she ticks off our stops on her fingers. "I'm only counting seven."

"Did we really need to make a special trip to the condo?"

Her eyebrows furrow in confusion. "The condo?"

"One of my favorite places." I take another turn, getting closer to our destination.

"Why?" She wrinkles her nose. Fuck, I can't take how adorable she is.

"It's where I finally started to win you back."

"Jackson." Her voice is soft. "God. What am I supposed to say to that?"

"Love you, baby."

"I love you too." Her smile lights up the car, her hand relaxing against her stomach. "So that's eight. What about nine?"

"Our house."

"Really?"

I nod. "It's our home. Where we're going to bring Peanut home in just a few weeks."

"I can't believe it's finally time," she sighs and shifts in her seat to find a more comfortable position.

"You are a rock star. You know that, right?" I'm awestruck by everything she's done since moving to California with me. Even though she's not dancing right now, she's helping Garrett and Meric screen dancers and already has several requests to dance in additional videos after Peanut is born.

"I'm not doing anything."

"You don't give yourself enough credit," I complain.

She gasps, a hand fluttering on her stomach. "Peanut must think so too. I'm getting kicked."

"I can't believe Jessie hasn't conned the doctors into telling her what we're having." I grin. She had not been happy when we'd decided to be surprised.

Charlotte giggles. "I know. We'll make it up to her."

"She and Mama still coming out in a month?"

She nods. "Yeah. They figured then they can get baby snuggles but after we've had time to get to know Peanut and settle into our routine." She looks around the parking lot. "El Matador Beach?"

"Welcome to my number one favorite spot in all of LA. Well, actually it's that way." I point toward the cove where I finally won her back. "Feel up for a small walk with me?"

Charlotte sniffs, her eyes filling with happy tears—I hope—but nods. "O-okay."

We move slower on our walk this time, Charlotte gripping my hand when the surf plays with her equilibrium like before, but so much worse. Reaching the cove, I help her sit before sinking into the soft sand beside her.

"Hey there, gorgeous." Reaching over, my lips press a chaste kiss to hers.

"Hey." She smiles, alternately looking at me and the view in front of us. "It's so pretty here."

"It is." I don't take my eyes off her, the view in front of me better than the one in front of her. Nerves jump in my stomach, but taking a deep breath, I continue. "You're so beautiful. More so every day."

Reaching out, my hand rests against hers laying on her stomach. "Jackson."

She groans and I shush her. "You are beautiful. Every day, you get more beautiful than the day before. A feat I didn't think was possible when I first discovered an angel dancing on earth almost a year ago." I swallow, dipping one hand into the pocket of my jeans, remembering how badly I'd wanted to touch her when I'd first seen her. "Every day, I fall a little more in love with you. You and Peanut here, you are my universe. My driving force. My light. I promised you, all those months ago right here, that you owned me. Now...now, gorgeous, I'm asking you if I can make you mine. Forever." I shift to my knees in front of her and hold out a halo cut engagement ring that glitters in the sunlight. "Charlotte, will you marry me?"

The roar of the ocean is muffled in the eternity I wait for her to answer.

"Yes." She nods, tears of joy shining like crystals in the light as they slip down her cheeks. "Yes, Jackson, I'll marry you."

Moving, I close the gap between us. "I love you," I whisper before my lips take hers.

I break the kiss to focus on sliding the sparkling diamond on her finger with shaky hands.

"I love you too."

My lips slide against hers again and I rub my hand over her belly, connecting the three of us together in this moment.

♪♪♪♪♪♪

"Hello, City of Angels! How we doin' tonight?" My voice booms through the amphitheater later that night and the crowd explodes into screams.

My eyes constantly flit back and forth between the massive crowd in front of me and my beautiful *fiancée* who is laughing at my antics while she stands backstage with Meredith. Laughing with them, my voice echoes through the sound system.

"I'm so excited to be sharing this stage tonight with my fellow artists and even more excited that this is a hometown show for me and I get to have my girl here. Before I share some new music with you, I thought I'd give you some news." The crowd screams louder, and I wave my arms, encouraging them to quiet down. "No, baby watch is still on. But there is something else. Gorgeous?"

Charlotte glances at me, a blush brightening her cheeks as she hears my words. Turning, I hold out a hand. She hesitates before Meredith gently nudges her in my direction. Stepping toward me, she smooths her hands over her distended stomach, a cute maternity dress making her look beautiful.

Over the last five months, Charlotte and I have come to an understanding about publicity. It's not something we seek, but not something we shy away from either. We've given joint interviews and even used social media to tease fans about #BabyBryantWatch.

Leaning down, I kiss her flushed cheek. She had no idea I had planned on bringing her out on stage like this. She hides her face against my shoulder, her warm cheek resting on my chest.

"She's a little shy, aren't you, baby?" I say into the mic. Rubbing a hand along her stomach, I feel Peanut flutter against her side, translating to my palm. "You want to tell them, or should I?"

She nudges me and I laugh, wrapping my arm around her as I face the crowd.

"So, y'all, today. Well, today, I had something really important I needed to ask this beautiful woman by my side. Didn't I, gorgeous?"

She nods, her fingers wrapped around mine.

"So y'all, this beauty next to me is Charlotte Walker. Charlotte, meet them. Y'all meet my fiancée—" I don't get further before the crowd cheers, and both of us smile at the volume as they respond to our news.

Warm cognac eyes, the gaze that holds my heart, meet mine just before I lower my head, sealing our lips in a kiss that drowns out the rest of the world around us. When I finally remember where I am, I pull back, grinning, while the crowd continues to scream. I walk Charlotte back to Meredith, who is jumping up and down like a kangaroo and clamoring to see Charlotte's ring.

With a wink at Charlotte, I turn and head back to the crowd, ready to give them a show they'll never forget.

EPILOGUE

CHARLIE

"Ugh. Why am I nervous? It's not like it's me up for an award," I grumble, zipping into the beautiful forest green gown that Derek found for me this year.

Given that my body still isn't what it was pre-pregnancy—and I doubt it ever will be again—the man is a fashion genius. The gown is sleeveless with an embroidered lace overlay that makes me feel, once more, like a princess, extra weight and all.

Jackson steps into the bathroom with me, his eyes heating as they cling to mine in the mirror. His lips brush my shoulder. "It's okay, gorgeous. This year is our do-over. I get your nerves. I promise tonight is going to be amazing, whoever wins."

Jackson's latest album has gone multi-platinum since its release and he's up for two awards tonight.

"I'm sorry. You should be the one who's nervous, and instead I'm distracting—"

Jackson cuts off my apology with a kiss that immediately

makes me wish we weren't going out. Why waste a child-free evening with a red-carpet debut?

"No more apologies." He growls against my lips. "We need to go."

I look around the bathroom for my phone. "Is it time to go already?"

"If we don't leave, gorgeous," Jackson says, his eyes sparking a familiar emerald fire that starts heat simmering low in my belly, "we won't be leaving this room tonight."

"Promises, promises." Reaching up, I press my lips to his before ducking under his hold, heading for my shoes in the bedroom of our hotel suite. "You look amazing by the way."

"You stole my line." The smirk is obvious in his voice and I glance back where he leans against the doorjamb, eyes moving up and down my body.

Laughing, I walk closer to him to step into the tall heels needed for this gown, using his arm to balance. "Holy cow."

"Are those too tall?" He looks concerned and, reaching up, I rub the furrow between his brows.

"They're tall," I admit. "But I can handle them."

The car is already downstairs when we get there, the partition up as we lean against the back seat.

"I don't know that I like this dress," Jackson grumbles, pouting.

"What? Why?" Looking down, I try to see what's not to like about it.

"You can't curl your legs up like you normally do." I laugh and offer my lips as a consolation prize. Jackson's kisses help me forget my nerves, his tongue dipping into my mouth over and over again. Moaning in delight, I thank the universe for privacy partitions as Jackson's fingers discover the wet heat under my dress.

"No panties?" His fingers slide through my slick folds.

"Lines," I pant, trying to regulate my breathing. Even if I were wearing them, it wouldn't be the first time he's shredded a pair. "Jackson, we can't."

I say the words, but my body calls me a liar, my hips grinding onto his hand as his finger circles my clit.

"Oh, yes, we fucking can." Jackson nips at the column of my throat, circling his fingers again before they dip inside me. I cry out, clutching his forearm as my body rides his hand to my release. Biting my lip as the pleasure overwhelms me, I'm just recovering as the limo pulls into the line of cars waiting their turn. He sucks his fingers into his mouth, groaning, licking the taste of me off them.

I shake my head with a smile. "You're crazy."

Winking at me, he grins. "Crazy for you, gorgeous."

My cheeks are still flushed when we exit the limo moments later, but nothing else is out of place. Cameras blind us in a sea of white as he leans over, kissing my cheek. When I step back to let him walk the carpet first, his fingers tighten around mine, pulling me next to him. "Together."

I nod. "Okay."

"And we'll continue our conversation from the limo later," he growls against my ear, making my core throb again. Shivering, I continue to walk the carpet with him, lust driving away the nerves.

♪♪♪♪♪♪

"And the winner for album of the year is..." Jackson squeezes my fingers, the clench like a death grip, as we wait for the presenters to name the winner for album of the year. He already won male artist of the year earlier tonight.

"Jax Bryant!" the two presenters announce in unison.

I rise as Jackson pulls me to my feet, kissing me soundly

before making his way on-stage. Sinking slowly back into my seat, I'm so proud of him as I watch him accept the award and make his way to the microphone.

"Wow." He laughs and I can't help but grin as he grabs the back of his neck. "I didn't expect to be back up here tonight. My fellow nominees all deserve to be up here." He pauses as the crowd claps. "To everyone I've already recognized tonight, thank you, thank you, thank you, and thank you again. We did this together and I couldn't be prouder to be a part of our team. To Nick, I'll call you out separately, brother. Without you kicking my rear, I wouldn't be where I am today. In more ways than one."

He swallows, his bright green eyes capturing mine, a half-smile carving a dimple into his cheek.

"Hey there, gorgeous." He winks. "To my beautiful wife, Charlotte. You're the reason I am who I am. You're my muse, my heart, and my home. Thank you for loving me. Thank you for giving me the most perfect, most beautiful baby girl. McKenna Rose, be good for Aunt Meredith and keep Nick out of the ice cream. My girls, I love you both so much."

Blowing me a kiss, he waves as he exits backstage. Within minutes, he reappears back at my side.

"Congratu—"

I don't even get the word out before Jackson interrupts me with a kiss that starts innocently enough before morphing into a heated tangle of tongues. Breaking apart, both of us breathing heavily, he leans his forehead against mine. "I love you."

I never tire of hearing those words. Or that accent. "I love you too."

"Let's go home." His soft lips brush the tip of my nose and I sigh happily.

"Home." I agree. It's music to my ears.

The End

Thank you so much for reading!

Before you go! Are you curious to know what happens when Jax and Charlie travel to Austin to meet Jax's family for the first time? Turn the page to find out!

A VISIT TO AUSTIN

BONUS SCENE

CHARLIE

"Are you sure you're okay? Need me to turn down the A/C?" Jackson fumbles with the knob in the rental and glances at me when he stops at a light.

He's been like this since we left LA this morning on a private flight to Austin. Concerned. Hovering. *Smothering.*

"Jackson, I already told you, I feel fine," I try to reassure him. But his nerves definitely have the better of him. "Dr. Ward even told us that flying wouldn't be a problem."

Maybe the mention that my OB cleared me to fly will help.

"Plus, it's not like we were flying commercial. I laid down on the couch the whole way here," I remind him. We had talked about commercial flights but after being mobbed at DIA when we flew into and out of Denver to visit my parents, that was no longer an option.

"You weren't feeling all that great earlier." Another stoplight allows him to look at me longer—an examination of sorts—and my face heats under his scrutiny.

I shake my head. "No. That landing was bumpier than my stomach liked."

"I didn't like you that shade of green, gorgeous." His hand reaches out and squeezes mine before resting on my thigh. "Maybe we should have delayed this trip."

I bite back my smile. "Until when? Peanut is going to be here in just a few months."

"Maybe my family should have come to LA then," he argues, turning into a neighborhood filled with brick houses surrounded by big yards and shady trees.

"I thought you said your dad didn't like to travel?"

"He doesn't but—"

"I'm glad we're here. I want to see where you grew up." I smile at him despite the nerves that bounce in my stomach. Not from the flight but from meeting Jackson's family. I do want to see where Jackson grew up, but another part of me wonders what his parents will think of me. He and I have been together—again—for nearly four months. But I'm still pregnant and Jackson and I aren't even engaged.

"It's nothing special," he says, pulling me from my questions.

"Let me be the judge of that."

The driveway he turns into sits in front of a two story house, the brick faded gray and brown like it's been here for ages. A giant tree casts shade over the front yard and I can almost picture a tire swing swaying from the thick branches. There's a basketball hoop beside the driveway and the grass is a lush green. Flower boxes under the window show a few flowers that pop bright pinks and purples against the neutral backdrop of the house. It's charming. Idyllic.

"This is your house?" I turn to Jackson who smiles and nods.

"They're here!"

The loud screech causes him to wince and he doesn't get to say anything else. With a shake of his head, he opens his door and I do the same. A screen door slams as an echo to the sound.

"Sorry about this," he says with an apologetic look.

"About what?"

A tall, willowy brunette barrels around the corner of the garage and interrupts whatever he was going to say.

"Squee! You're here! You're here! Finally. Oh, you're so pretty." Jessie's mouth moves quickly but she stops just shy of me. The Jessie I've heard on the phone with Jackson is nothing compared to the spitfire, full of energy, in-person version who rounded the corner with more energy than a shaken up soda.

"Jesus, Jess, breathe." Jackson walks around the car, yanking his sister to him in a bear hug before releasing her to tuck me next to his side. "Charlotte, this goof is my baby sister, Jessica, Jessie to most. Jessie, this is Charlotte."

"I know who she is, dumb dumb. I don't need the introduction." She shoves at his shoulder and elbows him out of the way.

Her arms wrap around me and some of the nerves that have fluttered in my stomach for the thirty-minute drive from the airport to Jackson's parents' house fade. To be honest, the nerves had been a constant companion since he insisted we fly to both Colorado and Texas to share our news and meet each other's families. I sigh in relief as the never-ending nausea evaporates.

"I love your hair," she says when she finally releases me. "It's so pretty. I wish mine were more red, but Mama says not now and—"

"Jackson Matthew."

Jackson's hand finds mine and squeezes as another female voice interrupts whatever Jessie was going to say.

"It's okay." His whisper is quick, followed by a brief brush of his lips against my temple as the nerves come back full force. Swallowing, I press a hand to my stomach with a prayer that now is not the time that I decide to get sick.

Jackson's mom looks like a shorter version of Jessie. When she wipes her hands on her pants—something I've seen Jackson do hundreds of times when he's nervous—I smile.

"Hey, Mama." Jackson beams and his dimples bracket both sides of his mouth.

A laugh bubbles up at his innocent, contrite expression and I sink my teeth into my lower lip to hold it in.

His mom shakes her head. "Don't try that on me, boy. That look stopped working on me when you broke my vacuum when you were seven." She swats at his arm before she stops in front of me. "You must be Charlotte."

While Jessie's eyes are a dark brown, their mom's eyes remind me of Jackson's—the green so vivid they seem to glow. Dark brown hair curls around her face and I can tell that both Jessie and Jackson look a lot like her.

The smile she gives me is warm and easy to return. "Yes, ma'am. It's nice to meet you, Mrs. Bryant."

She scoffs and yanks me into a hug. "I'm a hugger, but I'm sure you're used to that with this barnacle you came with." This time I don't stop the giggle that erupts as Jackson huffs next to me. "But not Mrs. Bryant, sweetie. Please call me Danielle or Dani."

She releases me and pulls Jackson into a quick hug before she shoos us all inside the house. "Let's get out of this heat, y'all."

As we walk inside, she falls into step beside me.

"You can call me Charlie if you want," I offer.

Walking into the kitchen, the smells of barbecue sauce mingle with fresh lemon and make my mouth water.

"Charlotte is such a pretty name though."

I think I hear Jackson mutter behind me that it's his name for me, but when I glance at him, he's the picture of innocence.

"Jessie, get your brother and Charlotte some tea." Dani nods at the fridge. With a huff, the younger Bryant moves to the fridge before she pours four tall glasses of cold tea.

"Charlie." This time his voice is louder. His mom stares at him with her eyebrow raised until he ducks his head and his finger traces along the counter.

"Mm-hm." She takes a sip of tea then turns her attention back to me. "So Charlie, is it?"

"When we first met, I asked her if she was named for Charlie Daniels," Jackson says with a smile at the memory. My own lips quirk when I remember his question and that I had no idea who he was talking about.

She laughs. "Leave it up to you."

"I didn't even know who he was talking about." I admit, wrinkling my nose. He's played me a few songs since so at least I know who he meant *now*.

Jessie rolls her eyes at her brother. "You're such a dork."

Grabbing an ice cube out of his glass, he flicks it at her and she shrieks and dodges it.

"Jessica Elaine. Jackson Matthew. Enough. You're gonna scare this poor girl."

Dani and I both laugh when the two stick their tongues out at each other—something I'm sure they've done before. Another mom-look from Dani and the two compose themselves enough to be given kitchen tasks. Jackson is told to clean and chop vegetables for a salad and Jessie is tasked with starting the baked potatoes.

"Where's Dad?" Jackson asks as he stands at the sink.

"He got a call from work. Oh, here he is." If I thought Jackson looked like his mom, he and his dad could be brothers. They're the same height and both share the same dimples, but whereas Jackson's eyes are green, his dad's are brown like Jessie's.

"Sorry about that. I missed the welcome." His dad steps to Jackson first and embraces him before the two turn to me.

"Dad, this is Charlie." It sounds weird to have Jackson call me by my nickname, but I guess he didn't want to have to correct his dad too since he seems to be pretty possessive of using my full name. "Charlie, this is my dad, Tim."

"Nice to meet you," I say with a smile.

"You too, Charlie." He returns my smile and my handshake and seems more reserved than the rest of his family.

"You. Good." Dani hands Tim an empty plate. "The brisket should be done. Could you go grab it from the smoker please?"

Tim nods and, with a kiss on Dani's cheek, goes outside.

"What's my job?" I ask.

"You." She points at me with a smile. "Just sit there and tell me about yourself."

These questions always make me feel awkward, and my words stumble at first. Dani asks thoughtful questions about my stories of Colorado, of living in New York on my own, and my injury and rehabilitation. By the time dinner is ready, we've moved to stories about Jackson and my sides ache from laughing at memories that either make him blush or grimace. He laughs too, so I don't think he minds too much despite all his grumbles.

While Jessie, Dani, and Jackson all talk and share different stories, Tim doesn't say much, but listens intently to the other three and laughs along with us. He seems content to sit back and let the rest of his family carry on the conversation, but I can see the pride he feels for his family in the few stories he contributes and in the way he jokes with Jackson. The Texas night is warm and the sounds of dogs barking and the occasional lawnmower drift on the light breeze.

The food is delicious and I practically lick my plate clean.

"Feeling okay, baby?" Jackson leans closer to whisper in my ear while his warm hand rubs my thigh through my shorts. He knows meals are hit or miss with me, and his concerned gaze shifts between me and my plate before a smile quirks his lips.

I nod. "I'm good."

"I can see that," he responds.

"Lord, I had the worst morning sickness with Jessie. I thought I was never going to find a food that didn't make me want to throw up," Dani says as she catches our conversation. "How I knew I was having a girl."

Jackson's face blanches. He's terrified of having a girl even if he won't say it out loud. I bite back the grin that threatens with his predictable reaction.

"Oh, Mama, that's not even true. Look at Princess Kate. She had two boys," Jessie reasons with her mom. Her phone—which has been by her side almost non-stop—has been relegated to the house while we eat.

"And a girl." Dani smirks, winning the argument.

"We're not sure what we're having yet." I say quietly. Jackson's fingers link with mine to rest on my leg.

"When do you guys find that out?" Jessie's gaze shifts between Jackson and me.

"We're... well, we want it to be a surprise," I explain and Jackson nods next to me.

"What?" She looks crestfallen.

Jackson shrugs. "It's fun not knowing."

"I'm just—I'm so excited. A grandbaby." Dani's eyes sparkle in the light from the setting sun. "I don't want to be 'grandma' though. That's too old."

"You have plenty of time to figure that out, Mama." Jackson smiles at his mom who sniffs before her hands move to wipe at her eyes.

"How far along are you, honey?"

"Around twenty weeks or so, I guess. That's what my OB says," I tell her.

Jackson's fingers tighten around mine. Lately we've been talking about relocating out of LA—it feels too big to think about raising Peanut there. Jackson's argument is that LA is a good location for both of us with his record label based in LA. Granted I have a job in the city too as a consultant for Meric and Garrett since I'm not currently dancing, and am trying to convince Jackson that Boulder or Austin would be a better fit.

"Let's just hope the baby isn't as big as Jax was as a baby. Ten pounds." His mom shudders.

"Ten?" My stomach nosedives as I stare at my still mostly flat stomach.

She nods. "It looked like I had a basketball shoved under my shirt."

"Mama." Jackson sighs.

"It did. I was tiny like Charlie before I got pregnant with you. Maybe a little bigger."

Saliva pools in my mouth and I grab my tea and take a sip before I draw a deep breath through my nose. I've read stories about petite women and what happens when they have bigger babies. Jackson told me to stop sharing them with him after the first few. His fingers rub against my leg in a soothing pattern. But I'm not sure if he's trying to soothe me or himself. I think the last one I sent him—complete with pictures—may have scarred him for life.

"What are you going to name the baby?" Jessie's question distracts me from images of monster-sized babies and basketballs that hide under my shirt.

"Peanut," Jackson replies and sends a wink in my direction.

"Ugh, you're such a dork." She clearly has a favorite insult for him. "That's not a name."

"That's what we call the baby now." He shrugs.

"We haven't really talked about names," I answer.

Her face lights up. "I can help. I've been doing research. Tucker. Oliver. Ethan. Logan."

"Those are all boy names," Jackson teases.

"I have a longer list for girls. But my favorite name is Mia."

He shakes his head. "Jess—"

"I'll email you my list." She looks at me and I can't help but smile and nod.

"I'd like that."

Jessie nods and then gets distracted by her mom asking about the dress she found for her junior homecoming dance. Jackson is the typical overprotective big brother and doesn't like the idea of her going with the senior boy that has asked her to go. But the girls—me included—gang up on him to tell him that he doesn't get a say in that. The banter between the family is fun and something I love to watch.

I lean my head against Jackson's shoulder as he continues to spar with Jessie. They're close even though they're ten years apart. I want our baby to have a closer sibling so they can banter like this too someday.

♪♪♪♪♪

JAX

The weight of Charlotte's head is warm against my shoulder. I glance down and note the sleepy smile on her face as she watches Jessie and me with heavy eyes.

"We should get to bed," I whisper, and brush my lips across her forehead.

She nods. "Yeah. I guess."

Everyone else heads inside too, and I lead Charlotte to my childhood bedroom. The blue walls and plaid blanket on the double bed scream "boy room" but I watch as her attention darts to the different displays of music in my room. A hook on the wall holds my first guitar and pictures of artists on stage and a fan of concert tickets are tacked to my old cork board. Her lips move quietly as she reads through the different artists and I step behind and wrap my arms around her to graze my lips against the back of her neck. I smile at the shiver of her response.

"Hey," I murmur against her shoulder.

"Hi." Her lips quirk when I don't move away.

"Tired?"

She nods and a yawn overtakes her. "Yeah. Today was great though. Your family is wonderful."

I shrug. My family is bossy and nosy and loud, but they're mine. "They're okay."

She giggles at the mischief in my voice before she reaches up and pinches my hand.

"Be nice. They were way more relaxed than my parents," she reminds me.

I shudder at the memory of her dad. "You're telling me. Are you sure your dad didn't hire a hitman to take me out?"

To say that I had gotten the death glare from her dad when we told them we were pregnant would be an understatement. It made for a tense next day before her parents finally started to come around to the idea that Charlotte and I were having a baby.

She laughs again and shrugs. "I guess we won't know until it's too late."

I chuckle and tighten my arms around her. "Will you protect me?"

"Of course." She turns and wraps her arms around my neck, reaching up on tiptoes to brush a kiss against my lips. "Just like I'll protect you if Peanut ends up being a girl."

"Don't joke. That idea scares the shit out of me," I pout after returning her kiss.

"What? Why?" A frown creates a wrinkle between her eyebrows and I reach out to smooth it out.

"It's not so much the girl I worry about. But all those boys."

"That's a lot of years away," she teases me with a smile. I slide my lips over hers and my cock kicks in my shorts at the light moan that whispers from her throat.

"Next topic," I say as I wrench away from her lips. "What did you think of that house?"

A few days ago, the realtor had called me about a house that was going on the market. It was minutes from the beach and Meredith's parents' house. But while I thought it was perfect, Charlotte thought it was too big. She's agreed to move in with me

—thanks to my persuasive efforts—but didn't want anything flashy.

I want her with me. Yes, she's in LA, but she's still staying more at Meredith's than at the condo with me. I don't mind sharing her with Meredith, but I also hate to fall asleep without her next to me.

"Jackson," she sighs.

"It's perfect."

"It's big," she counters.

"It's close to Meredith." A look passes over her face. "What? What's that look for?"

"Are we sure about LA? We haven't really talked about the other options. Here, maybe?" Her hands gestures around us. "Well, not here, but you know what I mean."

I nod. "I do. LA is where Reverb is. Where Arabesque is," I argue. Arabesque is the name of the production company she consults for right now. "We can come here whenever we want. Go to Boulder whenever we want."

That last promise sticks in my throat because—well—her dad, but I'm sure eventually he'll warm up to me.

"Let me think about it?" She asks and looks up at me.

I drop a kiss to the tip of her nose. "Of course."

I'll wait forever for her answer if I have to. But it doesn't mean I want to. If this house isn't right for us, then we'll find something that is. I release her and she grabs her pajamas and her toothbrush before heading for the bathroom in the hall.

When she comes back, I'm propped against one of the pillows and tuning my old guitar.

"Ar—Aren't you going to put on a shirt?" My attention snaps to the way her tongue drags across her lip, the way her teeth sink into the soft flesh there.

I bite my cheek to hide the smirk that threatens. "No, why?"

The outline of her nipples are visible through the thin sleep tank she wears and my gaze dips there before moving back to her face in time to see her roll her eyes before she walks to the other side of the bed.

"Jackson, we're in your parents' house," she reminds me.

"It's hot," I complain, even though the air conditioner keeps the room cool.

"You're ridiculous." With a sigh, she lays down and turns to face me.

I smile and set the guitar next to the bed before I shift to face her.

"Getting that house means we get to do this every night," I say.

She sighs. "I'm thinking about it."

"Can I bribe you with anything?" My voice rasps into the quiet and I hear the quick intake of breath. Her pupils dilate as her chest rises and falls with her shallow breath.

"You're awful." She pushes at me and I snag her hand to bring it to my lips. I graze a kiss against her palm before shifting my attention to the pulse point that vibrates under my fingers on her wrist.

"You love me," I tell her confidently.

Her laugh turns into a moan when my lips move to trace her shoulder.

"Jackson—"

"Yes?" I lift my mouth where it hovers inches above her collarbone.

Her liquid eyes are at odds with her words. "We can't."

I scoff before I drag my tongue along her collarbone. Her fingers spear into my hair and her nails scrape my scalp.

My lips drop lower and I kiss the valley between her breasts through the thin cotton of her tank before I stop at her stomach.

I lift the cotton and my lips press against the bump that continues to grow.

"Hello, Peanut. You liked that house, right?" After a second I look back up to Charlotte's eyes. "Peanut says yes."

She giggles. "You're a nut."

"But you love me." My kisses drop lower and my hands move beneath the hem of her sleep shorts.

"I love you." Her agreement is a gasp as my fingers brush her through the silk of her panties.

I still don't think I've won the war on the house, but I have more important things to focus on right now. "Love you too, gorgeous."

PLAYLIST

Thank you for reading Written in the Beat. Both Jax and Charlie have a special—but unique—relationship with music. Their playlist, like Jax's Spotify, is an eclectic mix of so many types of music.

Up-beat country music like Thomas Rhett's "Craving You" mixes with mesmerizing songs like Bek and Bat for Lashes' "Let's Get Lost" and break-up songs like Illenium's "Gold (Stupid Love)" and OneRepublic's "Can't Stop."

Want to hear more? Head to Spotify and search for "Written in the Beat" playlist.

Happy Listening!

ACKNOWLEDGMENTS

Words don't feel like enough, but let me try.

First of all, thank you! Yes, you. For taking the chance on Written in the Beat. I hope you enjoyed reading Jax and Charlie's love story as much as I enjoyed writing it.

For my family—thank you for supporting me in this dream. Thank you for believing in me when I doubted and for picking up the belief that was missing without Nathan. I love you.

Claire and Alina—if I had an infinite amount of words and pages, I couldn't begin to thank you for the love, support, and shenanigans that make us us. Thank you for being my biggest cheerleaders, for answering questions, and for responding whenever I sent an SOS. While 2020 was a rough year, you two are the best things that came from it. Y'all are stuck with me whether you like it or not. <3

Editor Jess—Written in the Beat and Jax and Charlie have grown so much with your help. I could not have even attempted this without your guidance and patience with the endless amount of questions I had.

Beth—Thank you for being one of the first to read Jax and Charlie's story and for polishing it into what it is today. Thank you for cheerleading and telling me that you stayed up way too late reading their story. Best compliment EVER!

Kate Farlow—You are a graphics goddess! Thank you, thank you, thank you for bringing Jax and Charlie to life. Thank you for answering questions and for being another mentor as I start this journey.

Ladies of the RWR—Thank you for reading Jax and Charlie, for encouraging me to keep going, for being a shoulder to lean on and for every way you motivate me everyday just by being yourselves. RWR still remains one of my favorite places because of all of YOU.

To everyone who helped me create, mold, and polish Written in the Beat into what it is—thank you! This last year has been a journey and I couldn't have done it without you. XOXO

ALSO BY BREANNA LYNN

HEART BEATS SERIES

Written in the Beat

In The Beat of the Moment

Keeping the Beat

Want a sneak peek at Meredith's HEA?

Turn the page for Chapter 1 of *In The Beat of the Moment*.

IN THE BEAT OF THE MOMENT

CHAPTER 1

MEREDITH

With a sigh, I flip off the TV. The cameras had captured Jax and Charlie's fiery hot lip lock as the awards show ended and the credits rolled. Add in Jax's speech and Charlie's face as he spoke to her—there's a reason why they're currently what one magazine called *America's Favorite Love Story*. I can't help the way my stomach drops.

I *want* that. I want someone to feel the way about me that Jax feels about Charlie. But how? It's not for lack of trying, that's for sure. I've gone on a few dates in the last year and nothing. Zip. Zilch. I have zero prospects lined up. In fact, is it possible to claim less than zero? Can I claim negative prospects?

The warm weight in my arms shifts and draws my attention away from the path of depression that currently wanders through my lack of love life.

"That's okay, Mac. You're my favorite date anyway." Leaning down, I kiss her downy, dark hair and breathe in the sweet baby scent of lotion and powder. This smell is more addicting than the most potent drug. Little rosebud lips part, even breaths washing across my t-shirt where McKenna has been snoozing since right before her daddy won the award of the night. "Not everyone is as lucky as they are, baby."

"Did I miss it?"

The deep voice sets my teeth on edge.

Why, oh why, did Jax and Charlie issue an open invitation to Nick the Dick? On second thought, who uses that open invitation when their friends *aren't home?*

He lives to irritate me, and no level of man candy sexiness is worth the headache he creates whenever I have to deal with him.

His question is so stupid I don't bother to stop the visceral eye roll accompanying my response. "Well, maybe if you weren't so concerned with stuffing your face full of free food, you wouldn't have missed it."

He smirks, ladling more ice cream straight from the carton and into his face. The moan that rumbles from his chest is both exaggerated and obnoxious, and my teeth clench.

"What were you, raised in a barn?"

He shrugs, but amusement lights his eyes as he smiles around the spoon. "Close enough."

I stand and shift McKenna to my shoulder. She starts to stir, and I rock gently and rub my hand along her back.

"So? Did he? Win?"

I'm not his lackey. With perverse pleasure, I head toward McKenna's room, holding my breath as I pass him.

Dick he may be, but whatever cologne he wears magically makes me want to climb him like a damn tree. It's maddening. Why does such an asshole of a person need to smell so damn good? Too bad my traitorous body refuses to clue in to what my head keeps laying out. Even without a conscious inhale, hints of bergamot and sandalwood follow me up the stairs. Those subtle teases of scent create a skin-tingling, core-clenching, *unwelcome* response.

Get it together, girl. He's an enemy in Armani, a douche in Dior. He is not *attractive in the slightest.*

I concentrate on the baby snuggled in my arms and relax in a room that explodes in shades of pink. It's an oasis to escape the tantalizing cologne that still tickles my nose. The small lamp casts a warm glow on the frilly pink bumper and sheet against the stark white crib, both of which scream princess in training. I'd blame Charlie for all the pink, but since I watched Jax consider a pint-sized pink guitar right after McKenna was born, I know it's not just her. Only by persuading Jax to let McKenna pick her own guitar when she was old enough did I drag him out of the music store without spending a small fortune.

I lay her down, and cool air rushes in where her warm body was snuggled into mine. Her lips pucker and relax almost immediately. *Sweet baby.* I grab the monitor and take several steps toward the guest room, ready to leave Nick to his own devices.

But actually—no. I'm the one with a reason to be here. He doesn't get to make me feel uncomfortable. Descending the steps, I formulate my attack. First, I'll kick him out, then I'll curl up to watch a movie.

That plan goes out the window and I bite back the primal growl that threatens to escape when I get back to the living room to find him now kicked back on the couch watching a football game, shoes off like he's going to stay awhile. Is it too much to ask that he go bother someone else?

Remember your manners. I swear the voice of my conscience is actually Mom. And it's that voice that prevents me from telling him to go fuck himself.

"Don't you have a TV at home?" We aren't friends. Charlie and Jax are at the hotel, or at least on their way there. He doesn't need to be here.

"Not like this," he replies.

He might have a point. Jax has fitted out their family room with a massive TV—it's one of those projection ones that makes it perfect for movie night. Not some damn replay of the game from last season.

"They lose." Tossing the spoiler over my shoulder, I head for the kitchen.

"Who?"

"Whoever you want to win," I grumble. His laugh is raspy, like he hasn't used it in a while.

It's not sexy. Nope. Not at all.

"LA?"

"Yep."

"Well, good thing I want Kansas City to win." His laughter rings out again, and I count to ten with the hope of reining in my rapidly fraying temper.

Ice cream drips from the open container on the counter, with the spoon rising like a silver popsicle stick from the middle. Growling, I pick up the partially eaten container. The spoon hits the sink with a loud clatter, and I jerk on the faucet, rinsing ice cream down the drain.

I will not go dump this over Nick's head. I will not go dump—

"Everything okay in here?"

Surprised by his voice so close, I whirl and hold up the offending ice cream container. "Are you for real?"

"You dumped it?" He looks crestfallen, and I can't help the evil smirk that spreads across my face. "I wasn't done with it."

"Then why'd you leave it on the counter?"

"I was flipping on the game and coming back. By the way, I googled and saw Jax won," he gloats.

If he thinks I'm going to feel bad for not telling him, he needs to buy a damn clue. "Good for you. You can use Google."

The side of his mouth quirks up, drawing my attention to his lips. Are they as soft as they look?

Oh my god, Meredith, stop it.

Forcing my anger back to the forefront, the emotion that constantly simmers under the surface whenever he's around, I push out the unwelcome questions about how soft his lips are and if he's a good kisser.

"I wouldn't have had to if you'd just told me," he says.

"It's not my job to tell you shit." Crossing my arms, I level a glare his way. Instead of saying anything, he leans against the doorjamb and studies me like I'm an intriguing puzzle. "What?"

His undivided attention makes me self-conscious. Do I have spit-up on my shirt? Food in my hair? I run a hand through my curls but don't feel anything. Shrugging the shoulder of my shirt back up where it's fallen down, I toss the now empty container into the trash can and remind myself to tell Charlie she's out of ice cream *and* that it's not my fault.

"What what?" he asks.

He drives me insane. I turn back to the sink and load the spoon into the dishwasher.

"You don't like me, do you?"

The question catches me off guard. I've never made it a secret that I think he's a douche canoe, but I've never openly admitted it to anyone—especially Charlie or Jax. Taking my time with the dishwasher, I keep my face averted and secretly hope he'll go back to what he was doing. Or, even better, he'll finally go home. As much as I want to tell him *exactly* what I think of him, something tells me he'd take some sort of pleasure out of riling a response from me and making things more awkward than they are right now.

"Ignoring this question too?" His voice holds the hint of a challenge. One I'm trying really hard to ignore.

Standing back up, I stare at him. Curiosity is evident in the furrow of his brow, but he doesn't look away. Once again, the need to squirm under his intense gaze intensifies while heat licks along my skin.

"I'm not ignoring it." With a shrug, I head back to the family room and grab the remote before flopping on the other couch.

"You're not answering it either." His long legs eat up the

distance between us. With ease, he snags the remote, plopping down where he was when I first came downstairs.

"Hey!"

"Hey, nothing. I was watching the game."

"Ugh. Then go home. Charlie and Jax didn't ask you to babysit —thank fucking god—they asked me." Anger tightens my stomach and the rage that simmers there begs to be released. Why does he constantly push me like this? Why can't he just be a normal person and go away when it's clear he's not welcome?

"Hey, I'm a good babysitter."

My sarcastic laugh nearly chokes me. "Yeah, okay sure."

"I've watched McKenna before," he counters.

"When? When Jax was in the studio and Charlie had to pee. So what? A whole five minutes?"

"Yeah. It was fine."

I whistle and clap slowly. "Good for you. You watched a sleeping baby for five minutes for Charlie to go to the bathroom. You couldn't last an hour by yourself with her awake. Which is why they asked me." I lean forward and attempt to keep my temper in check when all I want to do is unleash it. "God, please go home so I can watch my movie in peace."

"What movie?" The half-smile that plays on his lips is another match to the fire. And yet it's like I can't help *but* react to him.

"Anything that will make you go home." He's trying to bait me. I need to ignore him, not react. It worked on kids in elementary school who used to tease me about my wild curls, so surely it will work on him. Right?

"Jax said I was welcome here anytime."

"He didn't mean that fucking literally." Flinging myself off the couch, I pace. "And he's not even here."

"I want us to be cool."

The change in his tone from defensive to persuasive freezes me mid-step, and I blink at him as I process what he's just said.

Did I hear him correctly?

"What?"

"Jax asked me to clear the air with you. He's tired of us bickering at each other like kids. He said it bugs Charlie." He runs a hand through his caramel brown hair before he stands and walks away from me. He's pacing too, striding toward the kitchen then spinning to face me again. "Clearing the air" with me wasn't his idea, so what's with that?

The idea was Jax's. Like Nick couldn't be bothered to be a decent human being. *He's a dick, remember?* If left up to him, he would continue to be his obnoxious self. Something snaps with that realization, and I'm done with holding back.

Done.

"Fuck you." My words start off quiet, some small part of me conscious of McKenna sleeping upstairs. "Fuck you and fuck your act. You may have Jax and Charlie snowed, but you don't fool me for a second. Get the fuck out!"

He blinks and confusion registers on his face. "My act? What act am I supposedly putting on?"

Like he doesn't know. I may not be as tall as he is, but squaring my shoulders and confronting him with facts makes me feel like a giant. "You're not a nice guy, you're not their friend. You're a fucking snake and I can see right through you."

Anger replaces his confusion. "What the fuck? A snake? Is that what you think?"

"It's what I know," I fire back.

"How the fuck would you know anything about me? It's not like you say more than two words to me. This is the most you've ever spoken to me in the years I've known you."

"I fucking heard you!" Frustration bubbles inside me, the truth punching out like a heavyweight champion. Red shrouds my vision.

He frowns, playing confused. "What the fuck are you talking about?"

"You said you didn't think McKenna was Jax's. You were on

your phone in the hallway." I point in the general direction like it matters.

The evil words I'd heard that day still slice me with pain. I'd been so happy that Jax and Charlie had made up, so happy that my two best friends had found love with each other, that I was going to be an auntie.

Until I'd listened to Nick the Dick talk shit about my best friend in her own fucking house.

I snatch his shoes from the floor and launch one and then the other. They hit barely to his right, thudding against the wall. He flinches but doesn't move. "I don't want you here. Jax and Charlie aren't here, and I don't want you around. I can't stand you. But you won't *leave*."

"You have no idea what you're talking about, little girl," he snaps back.

My vision tunnels and my ears buzz as fury boils to the surface.

Advancing on him, I shove at his chest, but he doesn't budge. "Little girl? Really, asshole?"

He looks contrite, but I don't believe it for a second. Then he steps deeper into my space, sucking away all the air in the room. My hands burn against the heat of his body, and I jerk them back. "I'm sorry, I didn't—"

"You're a horrible actor."

"I'm not acting." His voice is calm as he takes another step, and I back up in response. Bump into the wall.

It's suddenly very clear that I've bitten off more than I can chew. Warning bells clamor, adding to the cacophony of disbelief and anger, but I won't concede this. I *know* what I heard.

I give an unladylike snort. "Do you think I'm stupid? That you can say whatever you want—"

His lips against mine stop my tirade. I tense at that first touch, ready to push him away. Until. Until...my body turns traitor and melts into him. His lips *are* soft, pillowed expertly against mine as his fingers wrap around my upper arms to haul me closer to him. The smell of his cologne up close overwhelms all rational thought. His tongue runs the seam of my lips, pushing insistently until I open for him.

Fuck me. Nick the Dick can kiss.

He slants his mouth, and his scruff scrapes against my chin while his tongue drags against mine.

He tastes like chocolate and mint—*the ice cream*. His fingers grip my hips and align our lower bodies in a way that drags me deeper into the kiss's spell. White hot need claws through me at the feel of his thick erection pressed between us. My fingers slide up his chest, bumping along ridges of thick muscle I ache to feel against my skin.

I wrap my arms around his neck and grip his cool, silky hair. Then he shifts us, pressing me to the wall and grinding his pelvis against mine. Fireworks explode. There's no other way to describe the sensations that swamp me with his kiss. The moan that hums from me doesn't make it beyond his lips as his hand flexes against my leg. He lifts it and bends me to the angle where the heat of him transfers through the thin layer of my shorts.

"Oh god." Ripping my lips from his, I lean my head back against the wall, the need to breathe finally greater than the need to keep kissing him. Warm breath hits my neck, spreading delicious goose bumps, and I brace myself for another onslaught from his mouth and—nothing—what the hell? I lift my head.

He freezes, and his eyes open to reveal swirls of emotion that morph from lust to surprise as they widen. His hand drops from the leg I have wrapped around his and my foot crashes down without the warm pressure. As he steps back several feet, the distance he puts between us blows the cool air conditioning across my overheated skin.

I trace my swollen lips with one hand, the heat and wetness a reminder that I've just been thoroughly kissed by the man standing in front of me.

"Shit." His Adam's apple bobs with a swallow, and his hands weave through his short hair where my fingers clung just seconds ago. "I'm gonna go."

Turning, he trips over his shoes before grabbing them. He doesn't stop to put them on, doesn't turn around, and between one blink and the next, the door opens, and the dark night swallows him.

I blow out a breath, using the wall as a support for my shaky legs. What the hell was that? Why did he kiss me? Holy shit, he should have a job as a professional kisser. Is there such a thing? Shaking my head, I follow his path to the front door, twisting the deadbolt even as I steal a peek to see if he's still there.

Why am I disappointed he's not?

What's going through Nick's mind after that sizzling kiss? Want to find out? *In The Beat of the Moment* is available on Amazon and FREE in Kindle Unlimited!

ABOUT THE AUTHOR

Breanna Lynn lives in Colorado with her two sets of twins (affectionately referred to as the Twinx), their two dogs, and two kittens. A classy connoisseur of all things coffee, Breanna spends her time keeping the Twinx from taking over the world. When not coordinating chaos, Breanna can be found binge reading, listening to music, or watching rom-coms with a giant bowl of popcorn.

To stay up to date on the ramblings of her (often over-caffeinated) mind, Twinx Tasmania, or the latest news on her latest happily ever after, sign-up for her newsletter at breannalynnauthor.com/subscribe. Subscribers receive exclusive news, content, specials, and giveaways!

You can also stalk—er, follow—Breanna on a variety of social media, including her FB group Breanna's Book Baristas.